PRAISE

TOWARD A
SECRET SKY

"Full of intrigue, savvy world-building, and sizzling romantic tension, Maclean's enthralling storytelling will keep readers flipping pages—and wanting more."

—EMILY KING, author of *The Hundredth Queen*

"Five stars! This was the type of thrilling story I always dreamed of reading when I was younger (way before paranormal romance became popular)!"

—SHAILA PATEL, author of *Soulmated*,
winner of the 2015 Chanticleer
Book Reviews' Paranormal Awards

"Five stars! Mysterious, romantic, and totally fun! *Toward a Secret Sky* is the type of adventure I could lose myself in over and over again."

—STEPHANIE GARBER, author of *Caraval*

"I enjoyed this so much. It has just the right combination of magic, intrigue, and romance, and the beautiful Scottish backdrop and descriptions of various ancient sites just made it all the more appealing."

—HEATHER FAWCETT, author of
Even the Darkest Stars

"I would definitely recommend to anyone who liked *Angus, Thongs and Full-Frontal Snogging*, or even fans of the Princess Diaries. The book is fantastic overall!"

—Claire M. Andrews, author of
Olympus Rising

TOWARD A
SECRET SKY

HEATHER MACLEAN

BLINK

DEDICATION

To my childhood heroes: librarians.
Docents of the public domain
who regularly rescued me from my own small world
and sent me on countless adventures.

BLINK

Toward a Secret Sky
Copyright © 2017 by Heather Maclean

This title is also available as a Blink ebook.

Requests for information should be addressed to:
Blink, *3900 Sparks Drive SE, Grand Rapids, Michigan 49546*

ISBN 978-0-310-75474-9 (hardcover)

ISBN 978-0-310-75467-1 (international trade paper edition)

ISBN 978-0-310-75487-9 (softcover)

Any Internet addresses (websites, blogs, etc.) and telephone numbers in this book are offered as a resource. They are not intended in any way to be or imply an endorsement by the publisher, nor does the publisher vouch for the content of these sites and numbers for the life of this book.

This book is a work of fiction. Any character resemblances to persons living or dead are coincidental.

Cover design:Brand Navigation
Interior design: Denise Froehlich

Printed in the United States of America

18 19 20 21 22 23 24 /LSC/ 19 18 17 16 15 14 13 12 11 10 9 8 7 6 5 4 3 2 1

"This is love: to fly toward a
secret sky, to cause a hundred
veils to fall each moment. First
to let go of life. Finally, to take
a step without feet."

—Rumi

CHAPTER 1

I was okay until they started lowering my mom's casket into the ground.

Up to that point, the whole funeral had felt like an out-of-body experience. I walked around inside my own thick-walled aquarium. My motions were slow. My thoughts bogged down. I knew I was on display—everyone craning their necks to catch the slightest ripple of my movement. The obituary in the paper that morning hadn't helped:

Anna Hamilton, systems analyst for T.A., Inc., passed away in a freak accident on Tuesday night. She is preceded in death by her husband, Hugh, and is survived by her only daughter, Maren, age 17.

Freak. It might as well have been my middle name. And everyone knew it wasn't an "accident." I could hear the whispers of the people from her company at the funeral. I knew what they were saying; their too-loud whispers slithered through the air like a toxic smoke.

Isn't she the one who found the body? Poor thing.

What will she do now? She's a veritable orphan!

I heard they're shipping her off to his parents in Scotland. It's a shame she's never met them. It's a shame she never met him . . .

But I didn't care, because I was safe behind the glass. Nothing could get in and touch me, not even grief.

Nothing, that is, until the screaming started.

We were gathered around the jagged hole that meant

to swallow the most important thing in my life. My father died before I was born. Well, on the day I was born, and my mother was all I had. We'd been inseparable, and now we were going to be separated forever. I couldn't think that way, though, or I'd climb into the ground with her.

I was staring ahead, eyes unfocused, lost in the mournful symphony of the squeaking pulleys, when a sudden scream shattered everything. An unearthly, guttural wail unlike anything I'd ever heard before. For one horrifying moment, I believed it was actually coming from the grave; that it was my mom screaming.

Before I could think anything else, I was shoved forward. I fell, and tiny blades of grass bit at my face. Shadows darkened the ground as thunder roared. I'd grown up in Missouri, so I knew that early spring storms frequently rolled in with no warning. They didn't bother me; you just ducked and covered. It wasn't until I raised my head and saw the priest running for his car, his robe flapping wildly around his ankles, that I started to get scared.

By the time I got up, almost everyone was gone. All the handsome men from my mom's firm clad in their dark suits had disappeared—as if they'd been blown away.

Someone grabbed my arm to lead me away from the open grave waiting to digest my mom's shiny white coffin, but I dug my heels into the ground. I didn't want to go.

Who's going to protect her from the rain? I thought crazily. *The mud is going to ruin her pretty blue dress.* Not that I'd actually seen her in the dress. The manner in which she died demanded a closed casket. But I did pick the dress out of her closet.

The screaming and the thunder continued. Someone lifted me, tried to drag me away from my mother. I fought them and clawed at their back with my nails. I wanted to run back to the coffin, open it up, and lie down next to my mom. It seemed perfectly reasonable at the time. I didn't want her to be alone. I didn't want to be alone . . .

❀ ❀ ❀

I leaned against the cool glass and studied the scenery as the outdated, purple shuttle bus wound through the Scottish Highlands. The hills were broken up and sharp-looking. Prickly plants and crumbling rocks littered the ground. Huge pine trees rose to the sky like alien life-forms. And the mountains in the distance were topped with snow.

The van headed toward Aviemore, the tiny town where my dad had been born. The last time he'd been there, he hadn't yet married my mom. In fact, his parents didn't approve of the match and had refused to come to the wedding. They never spoke again, and when my mom had me, she must not have felt the need to reach out to people who hated her. People I was now going to live with.

That was twenty years ago, I reminded myself. Surely, they wouldn't hold a grudge against me, especially since, from the photographs I'd seen, I resembled my father . . .

My mother was totally beautiful—a former Miss Springfield—and I looked nothing like her. While she had olive skin and shiny black hair, I got my Scottish father's pale white coloring, light green eyes, and crazy, thick, curly blonde hair. The kind of hair that once made a hairdresser cry because the haircut came with a free blow-dry, and she hadn't counted on the whole process taking three hours. Of course, it wasn't California blonde or even all-the-same-color blonde. It was, someone once told me, "dishwater blonde." Just what my self-esteem needed: hair that reminded people of dirty water.

"Try 'n stay awake," the van driver offered, as we pulled up to a large stone house. "The trick to besting jet lag is to get into the new time as quickly as possible. Don't be taking a nap today, no matter what anyone says."

Before I knew it, I was standing alone on the gravel driveway between my two, large, soiled red suitcases.

It was hard to tell from the outside how many stories my grandparents' house was. The roof was impossibly steep, covered in zigzags where the shingles rose and fell at different heights. A single dormer window protruded out of the roof at the very top. I hoped it was an actual room and not just architectural decoration or a useless attic; someplace I could hide out.

Large, flat rocks covered the walls of my grandparents' house, so slick with the constant Scottish moisture that moss grew in the cracks. The house appeared old, but solid, like it could stand through any storm. I hoped I wasn't going to be the bad luck that brought it down.

Before I could survey the house any further, my grandparents burst out the front door. I had been dreading this moment for days, because old people make me really uncomfortable, especially old people I've never met, and especially old people that might possibly hate me. Would they be hunched over one of those walkers with tennis balls on the bottom? Still have all their teeth? Would they be cold to me? I braced myself just in case.

They answered my concerns about their sprightliness as they bounded across the slippery grass to greet me. And they seemed to like me well enough. They hugged and squeezed me, held me back at arm's length, admired me, squeezed me again, kissed me on each cheek, and clucked over me. But my grandfather took no time in proudly showing me his missing tooth.

"Murdo, stop it! You're scaring the girl," my grandmother scolded him.

"Och," he answered, with the thickest accent I'd ever heard. "I only wanted to show the wee thing that she oughtn't be alarmed at the space in my mouth, because I was getting my bridge back tomorrow!"

I smiled politely, but couldn't think of a single thing to say. Thankfully, my grandmother spoke. "How was your flight, dear?"

"Fine," I mumbled. I glanced around, desperate for some common ground, for something, anything to say. "Do you play a lot of golf?" I asked, nodding at a set of clubs on the porch.

"Do I play a lot of golf?" my grandfather boomed. "Does a bear crap in the woods?"

"Murdo!" my grandmother chided again. I couldn't help but chuckle just a little. These were definitely not the mean old people I'd expected to meet. They were actually kind of funny.

"Yes, I play as much golf as Mother Nature and my bum knee will allow," my grandfather continued. "As Liz here well knows, my fondest wish is that I die on the golf course. Club in my hand, right by the tee, what a way to—"

"MURDO!" my grandmother shouted. "Do shut up!"

"Oh, sorry, sorry," my grandfather apologized. "Me and my big mouth. I shouldn't be joking about death . . . with your mum and all."

I kept smiling, without teeth, but my eyes filled with tears. *Is this really my new life?*

I felt my grandmother's thin arm around my shoulders. "Come now, dear. I've got your room all prepared for you. You must be exhausted after such a long journey. What you need is a wee nap, and you'll be right as rain."

❀ ❀ ❀

I lay on the bed in my new room, determined not to fall asleep.

The small room was stuffed with ancient, mismatched furniture: a rolltop desk marred by varnish bubbles, a shabby, fabric-covered armchair, and a massive armoire for clothes. Faded pink floral wallpaper that oozed apart at the seams clung to the walls and even the vaulted ceiling.

I didn't care about the room's décor. Its location more than made up for anything. The rooftop window did belong to a real room—a single room at the very top of the house. And it was mine.

❀ ❀ ❀

I was kissing the hottest guy ever. He was so hot, even his hair was red. We were lounging in the long grass, kissing deeply, like it was our new way of breathing.

It was hot outside, and the kissing was making me even hotter. Everywhere he touched me, my skin burned. I'd never kissed anyone before, and certainly not like this.

The sun was blinding me, searing my eyes. Even when I squeezed them shut, I still saw and felt a deep, hot red.

When he started kissing my neck, I wanted to melt into him. I opened my eyes and discovered that he actually was melting. His body liquefied into a pool of blood that burned into my stomach. I started cramping, curled my body into a tight ball, and screamed.

My eyes shot open. Tiny pink flowers. Sloped ceiling. So moving to Scotland wasn't a dream.

Hopefully, I hadn't screamed out loud. I shook my head and tried to calm my racing heart.

I hadn't had a bad dream since the night before my mom died. I slid off the soft bed, not wanting to believe that my nightmares had followed me to Scotland. Maybe they weren't back for good. Maybe this was an isolated one—a hallucinatory effect of extreme emotional and physical exhaustion. At least no one had died in this one. Except maybe me . . .

I shook my head and reminded myself that my worst nightmare had already come true: I'd lost my mom. At this point, if I died kissing a hot guy, so be it.

CHAPTER 2

Fear of future nightmares didn't stop me from spending my entire first week in Scotland in bed. And, thankfully, neither did my grandparents. They were super sweet, but treated me like a guest, not a long-lost grandchild, which was fine with me. I wasn't up for a family reunion. I wasn't up for anything. I wasn't even up.

I missed my house, my old room, and more than anything, I missed my mom. When I crawled under the covers and closed my eyes, I was back in Missouri, back with her.

I only emerged to eat, and I was not excited by the food I found waiting for me. Breakfast, which I'd always assumed was a fairly safe meal for picky eaters, in Scotland consisted of insane things like clotted cream and black pudding. The first is exactly what it sounds like: chunky, spoiled, warm cream. The second is not to be believed, let alone eaten under any circumstance: congealed pig's blood deep-fried, sliced, and eaten with a knife and fork.

Even the "normal" food in Scotland wasn't normal. French fries, which were called "chips," looked like the fries back home, but instead of being crispy and yummy, they were soggy and not. Chips were called "crisps," which was a true description, but they didn't have any fun flavors like ranch or hickory barbeque. In fact, they didn't barbeque anything at all. They'd never heard of brownies or cornbread ("Why would you put corn in a bread?" my grandmother asked). They'd heard of peanut butter, but they didn't believe in eating it. They didn't put ice in their drinks ("Waste of money," my grandfather explained). And even though the can was identical, their Diet Coke tasted gross.

By the sixth day, after I'd eaten every crushed mint and fuzzy piece of gum in the bottom of my backpack, I couldn't ignore my rumbling stomach. I was miserable enough without the headache from my unintentional hunger strike. I needed to get out and find edible food.

When I came down the stairs and announced my desire to go to the grocery store, my grandparents greeted me with the same exaggerated politeness I'd gotten since I'd first arrived. My grandfather said he would be delighted to drive me, and my grandmother smiled widely from around her romance novel.

They were nothing but nice, but I had the feeling they would treat a beggar off the street the same way. The thought stirred something inside me. I wanted them to treat me differently than a stranger—bad, good, anything but this fake pleasant nothingness.

I'd been frozen in a state of numbness since my mom died, but I'd always been the opposite: very passionate about everything, bordering on histrionic, according to my mother (although, compared to a systems analyst, like my mom, anyone with a pulse could be considered overly dramatic). I realized I needed to feel something again.

I wasn't ready to dig into my own damaged life, but decided it would be interesting to pick at my grandparents'. I didn't know how, but I was going to break through their façade and find out what they were hiding behind their charming, gap-toothed grins.

❀ ❀ ❀

My grandfather took the opportunity of my first trip out of the house to give me a quick driving tour of Aviemore. Scotland felt a little like being in Wonderland; everything looked pretty much the same, but was ever so slightly different. The people spoke English, but I had trouble understanding them because they had such thick accents and used weird words for regular things, like *brollie* for "umbrella" and *bairn* for "baby." The cars not only drove on the wrong side of the road, the driver and the passenger seats were switched. And I discovered via an almost-accident that you had to pay money to unlock public restroom stalls, like a vending machine for pee.

When we arrived at Tesco, the town grocery store, I was surprised at how small it was. Six Scottish grocery stores could fit inside the Super Walmart near my old house.

My grandfather continued his tour guiding through the aisles, taking great delight in explaining every single item to me.

"Do you have Wheatabix in the US?" he asked, gesturing toward an unappetizing cereal that looked like dog food. I shook my head. "What about Frosties?" I smiled at the box of what we called Frosted Flakes, a welcome remembrance of home. I never thought I'd be so happy to see a cartoon tiger.

"Yep," I confirmed.

"We'll get some for you then," he said, lifting a small box into our cart. "Gran doesn't approve of the sugary cereals, but we'll make an exception." He winked at me, and my anger toward him dissipated a little. He was painfully nice. So nice, I got the feeling he'd give me the shirt off his back if I mistakenly admired it. Maybe it wasn't his fault he was holding me at arm's length. Maybe he didn't know how to act after suddenly inheriting a teenage girl. In any case, I decided to cut him some slack. I had the feeling my grandmother was the one who controlled everything anyway.

I was debating how best to approach her when my grandfather handed me a sample of steaming meatloaf in a small, crinkled wrapper. Absentmindedly, I tossed it in my mouth.

"So you enjoy haggis, do you?" my grandfather asked. I shrugged. It was spicier than I'd expected. "I'm surprised. Most foreigners haven't the stomach for it." He grinned extra-wide, as if he'd made a joke. I stared blankly, but something told me to stop chewing. He continued, "Because it *is* stomach, you see? Sheep stomach."

I spat the offending meat into my hand and tried not to gag while my grandfather chuckled.

Desperate to get the filmy taste out of my mouth, I left my grandfather in the meat section and headed for the bakery counter. This country might not know how to make regular food taste good, but surely they could still do dessert.

A girl my age was working behind the counter. She had shockingly red hair, was delightfully curvy, and had the roundest, happiest face I'd ever seen. She smiled when I walked up. I nodded awkwardly and asked her how the cookies were.

"Sorry, you mean the *biscuits*?" she said, in the Scottish singsongy way.

"No, the *cookies*." I pressed on the glass in front of the chocolate circles. I couldn't wait to taste them.

She smiled again. Her top lip was a perfect bow and gave her the unusual ability to smile with the corner of her lips turned downward. I'd seen an actress with the same smile in a movie once, but when I tried it at home in a mirror, I looked like I was frowning. Or demented. I loved the upside-down smile; it made your whole face light up.

"You're from America, aren't ya?" she asked.

"How'd you guess?" I asked, my ears slightly pained by my own boring, non-musical voice.

"The accent kind of gave you away," she answered. "Are you enjoying your stay at the Hamiltons'? It's a beautiful house, isn't—"

"How do you know where I'm staying?" I interrupted.

"It's a small town, Aviemore. Everyone's heard about the Hamilton girl from America living with her gran and granddad."

So much for starting over in Scotland, I thought grimly.

"What else do you know about me?" I asked, trying not to sound too accusatory.

"I know your mum just died, and that any day now your gran's going to force you to come out of that attic room and actually go to school," she said.

I raised my eyebrows at the news of my grandmother's academic intentions for me. It was already spring, so I'd assumed I wouldn't have to finish out the school year . . .

especially in Scotland. And I sincerely doubted she could force me to do anything.

"But that's it. Honest," she continued, still smiling. "I don't even know your first name."

"Maren," I stuttered. "It's Maren."

"Nice to meet you, Maren. I'm Joanne, but everyone calls me Jo. Oh, and I do know another thing about you," she said, handing me a cookie wrapped in a square of tissue paper. "You're going to love our biscuits."

I thanked her, and walked away, munching on the dry, chocolate chip-filled "biscuit." In the interest of actually finding friends in Scotland, I decided not to tell her that her cookies tasted like crap.

CHAPTER 3

On the drive back, I mentally perfected the first question I was going to ask my grandmother about our family. I was going for the kill: a direct accusation. I wanted to shake some emotion, and some information, out of her.

As we were putting away the groceries, I attacked.

"So," I said casually, "what exactly did you guys hate about my mom?" I stared at them, ready to catalog any sign of discomfort.

"Don't be silly," my grandmother said, scooping coffee grounds into the machine. "Your mother was a lovely woman."

"But you didn't want her to marry my dad," I challenged. "You objected to the whole thing."

My grandfather practically climbed into the refrigerator, so I had no chance of seeing his face, but my grandmother continued, nonchalant.

"Oh, rubbish." She sang, tapping the plastic spoon to free the last of the grounds. "Your father was a grown man. He did as he pleased since he was a teenager. We were happy if he was happy. We were happy he found love, happy he had you, and now, of course, we're happy to have you here."

I got flustered. She was making it seem like there was never a problem, like she and my grandfather had always been part of my life. I knew I hadn't imagined it, but now that I tried to think of the specifics, of anything my mom had said about my grandparents, I drew a blank.

"Maren," my grandmother continued, "an airmail package arrived while you were out. I left it in your room. I believe it must be a box of your mother's belongings."

I tried to process what she was saying. A box of my mom's stuff? What stuff? I'd already let the Salvation Army take most of my mom's clothes; they were hopelessly out-of-date anyway. And since she owed more on our house than it was worth, the bank repossessed all of our furniture and appliances, right down to the dented toaster. I couldn't imagine what was left.

"Um, okay," I sputtered. I pulled the candy bars and small crossword puzzle book I'd found at Tesco out of a bag, grabbed a bottle of fizzy orange soda, and went to face the unexpected package.

As I trudged up the stairs, I imagined thick glass forming around me, separating me from my emotions, shielding me again from the grief that threatened to strangle me. I wanted to feel something again, but not that.

The only way I'd been coping at all was by lying to myself, pretending that my mom wasn't really dead, that she was just on an extended business trip. She traveled a lot for her job, so I was used to not having her around for periods of time. This time, she would be gone for a few months, I told myself, so I needed to stay with my grandparents. Probably not the healthiest fantasy, but I didn't care.

A battered box sat in the middle of my room. It might as well have had teeth, because I knew opening it was going to hurt me.

I took a deep breath and sat down beside it. *What are the chances that there is anything good inside?* Considering my life, none. I steeled myself for the worst, slit the packing tape with my fingernail, and dove in, but all the box held was paper. Lots and lots of paper. Like someone had just emptied my mom's desk into a single box and mailed it to me. A neon green sticky note from our realtor confirmed exactly that.

"Thought you might want the stuff from your mom's office," it read. *Not really . . .*

I sifted through it: old utility bills, receipts for dry cleaning, crumpled, unused envelopes. I found a couple stamps, a handful of colored paperclips, some half-chewed pens. *Why bother mailing this crap 5,000 miles?*

I was ready to throw the box away, relieved that it didn't hold anything sentimental, when my hand hit something hard on the bottom. I pulled out a rectangular block of wood about the size of a large book. It was heavy and completely smooth, with no latches or hinges; just four interlocking Celtic heart designs carved into the top. I shook it and felt something moving inside. So it was hollow, which meant there had to be a way to open it.

I contemplated smashing it open, but that might ruin whatever it was holding. I ran my fingers over the edges, searching for a clue.

A clue. I smiled to myself. My mother loved clues. Every Easter, she couldn't just hide my basket, she had to send me on an elaborate hunt with clues that took hours to complete. They got harder every year, until I was getting clues in Morse code, and Japanese characters that needed to be read backward in a mirror.

My mom's job was to analyze computer programs, or

something, for a foreign company—the same company where she'd met my dad—but I always thought she should have been a history teacher. She had a passion for ancient forms of communication, especially coded messages. Every Sunday, after I made my famous milk chocolate chip pancakes, we'd race to solve all the puzzles in the newspaper: the crossword, the word jumble, the Sudoku, the cryptograms. I was able to beat her by the third grade, a fact that seemed to thrill her. She had tons of little puzzles lying around her office: magic rings, golf tee checkerboards, Rubik's Cubes. They weren't personal—she'd pick them up at airport gift shops or roadside restaurants—so I didn't save any. This particular box, though, with its engraved, endless hearts on the front, was prettier and bigger than most, and I didn't remember ever seeing it. *Why does it seem so familiar then?*

I had to get it open. I squeezed it, twisted it, tried to pry it open. Nothing. What could it possibly hold? Obviously, something my mother had wanted to keep secret, but why?

I traced the intricate hearts with my fingertip, and noticed one of the loops move slightly. I pushed on it again, and again it wiggled. I flattened my finger and put more pressure on the carving, twisting it to the right. The bottom of one of the hearts swung toward the middle of the box with a distinctive *click*.

I quickly rotated the bottom of the other hearts: *click, click, click!* As soon as I turned the last one, the box fell onto my lap, with a gaping hole where the carving had been. I scooped the box up, held my breath, and reached inside. Out came a necklace, a vellum envelope, and a journal bound with dark brown leather.

The necklace caught my eye first. On the end of a rustic silver chain hung a thick, sculpted flower charm: a white, dimpled blossom in the center of a red rose surrounded by shiny green leaves. The colorful petals reflected the light like stained glass. I didn't wear jewelry very often—I tended to lose it or break it—but the necklace reminded me of the dogwood tree outside my bedroom window back home. I slipped it over my head.

I picked up the envelope. It was sealed shut, and marked on the outside in my mom's small, precise handwriting: "Le Mont-Saint-Michel, Normandy, France." Obviously, it was French, but I had no idea what it meant since I'd opted for the Spanish route in school. I slid my finger along the edge to open it and left a streak of blood behind. *Typical*, I thought. *I can crack coded boxes, but I can't open a simple envelope without getting a giant paper cut.*

I removed a letter and thrust my now-throbbing finger into my mouth. In the top right corner, my mother had written the date: two days before her death. The rest of the page was blank. *What was my mother going to write? And if she didn't finish the letter, why seal it?* Her familiar handwriting coupled with the date so close to her death toppled my peace like dominoes. I quickly folded the letter and stuffed it back into the envelope.

The journal was the only discovery left. A ragged cord looped around a translucent blue bead on the soft leather cover held the book closed. As I opened it, tiny golden flakes fell from the page edges and left a glittery trail on my jeans. On the first page, my mother had drawn a calligraphic pair of letters: AD. Underneath, she'd spelled out

Arcēs Daemonium. Great, Latin. I sighed, completely regretting my foreign language laziness.

I turned the delicate pages and found blueprints and elaborate architectural plans sketched inside. My mom's detailed notes, addendums, and plenty of exclamation points cluttered the margins, but didn't make any sense to me. Was it for her job? It was possible, since I didn't really understand what she did.

I flipped through the book, past dozens of buildings, none of which I recognized, but again seemed somehow familiar. They were interspersed with a few odd drawings of body parts—a hand with extremely long fingernails, an angry face that seemed to growl through scribbles. I doodled in the corners of every notebook I'd ever owned, especially in school, and especially during the more boring classes, but these didn't seem like they were drawn out of boredom. They were creepy, almost ominous, and they made me uncomfortable.

The last two pages were stuck together. I slipped them apart with my forefinger, careful not to smear any of my blood on the book.

The final sticky corner gave way, and instead of more drawings, I found my name.

My Dearest Maren,

It breaks my heart to write this, because I know if you ever have to read it, that means I'm dead and, worse, you're in grave danger. I'm so sorry I couldn't protect you, my darling girl, but remember you are not alone. You will never be alone. All of heaven will be with you, watching you and guiding you. I can't tell you much more here in case this journal falls into the wrong hands, but know that the longer you possess it, the more danger you are in. Deliver it quickly. Be careful whom you trust. Things and people aren't always what they seem.

> All My Love,
> Mom

The letter from my mother shattered my carefully constructed walls. Tears that seemed to come up from my heart spilled down my cheeks as I tried to keep my sobbing as inaudible as possible. I couldn't stop a giant teardrop from escaping, though, and it fell onto the page, near the word *Love*. Without thinking, I brushed it away. The ink smeared, and I cried out, sick to have ruined something so precious, one of the last words from my mother.

My bedroom door rattled under a sharp knock, and I lurched, slamming my elbow against the corner of the armoire. "Maren?" my grandmother called out. "Are you all right?"

I slammed the journal shut and dropped it back into the box. I pushed the package under my bed and jumped up. I didn't want my grandmother to see me crying or try to comfort me. I didn't trust her yet, and according to my mother, I wasn't supposed to trust just anyone. Was her warning meant to apply to grandparents I'd only just met? Maybe.

"Just a minute," I called. I checked the mirror and wiped my cheeks with my sleeve, thankful I hadn't been wearing mascara.

I opened the door, a fake smile plastered on my face.

"Your grandfather wanted to show you my old golf clubs," my grandmother said, peeking over my shoulder to see if anything was amiss. "See if they'd suit you."

"Great," I replied, leaving the room to prove I was fine. I wasn't, of course. I didn't know if I'd ever be "fine" again. Especially not in Scotland. But I'd become great at pretending.

CHAPTER 4

Even though I knew it came from an animal, still the screaming sounded like a girl in terrible pain. I ran through the woods, branches scratching at my face, trying desperately to find her.

I saw movement in the brush to my left. I turned and pushed the scraggly bushes open like a curtain. She was there, lying on a carpet of pine needles and blood. The baby deer. An arrow was sticking straight out of an oozing wound on her neck.

As soon as I burst into the little clearing, I was greeted with complete silence.

I'd had the dream about the baby deer three times in the last week, and it was starting to wear me down. Every time, I arrived too late to save her, and woke up with a sick heart and even sicker stomach.

As if the recurring dream wasn't bad enough, I was haunted by a thought that would pop, unwanted, into my head during the day. *Find the fawn*, it echoed. I had to do something about it. Maybe if I could find the deer in real life and see that she was okay, the nightmares would stop. It sounded crazy, even to me, but I didn't know what else to do. I couldn't sit in my bedroom crying about my mother's desperate letter to me one more day, and I couldn't dream about someone or something dying one more night.

The forest across the lane from my grandparents' house looked like a good place to start. I was going to walk until

I found the familiar clearing or it turned dark—whichever came first. Since the sun stayed up until eleven p.m. in Scotland this time of year, I was hopeful.

Up close, the trees were phenomenal. They were some kind of evergreen, although nothing like Christmas tree pines. They twisted hundreds of feet up into the sky like giant strands of black licorice. They were crazy fairy-tale trees. I imagined if they wanted, they could yank their roots up out of the mud and walk away.

The forest floor was soft, covered in a dusting of pine needles and dewy, green moss. Everything shimmered like it was never completely dry. I found a small stream and followed it uphill.

As I rounded the top of a knoll, I spotted her: the tiny deer from my dreams. She was standing alone, pulling strands out of a patch of grass and eating them, quietly, daintily. It might have been my imagination, but a perfectly straight sunbeam seemed to shine directly on her.

I froze. I knew the tiniest crunch of a broken twig underfoot would send her bounding off, and I didn't want to lose her. It was silent, except for the gurgling of the brook and the whistle of a . . . *THWACK!*

I screamed like I had been shot, even though I saw the arrow lodged in the tree bark, still quivering from impact. The tree was a good twenty feet away from me—I was nowhere near in danger—but I'd never been shot at before. Before I could scream again or decide which direction to run, a thickly accented male voice bellowed, "Crivens!"

I couldn't see anyone. "You didn't have to holler like that!" the voice continued. "Now you've cost me my supper."

As if disengaging invisible powers, a young man emerged from the woods. I had been staring in that exact spot and didn't see him until he came crashing toward me. He wore a rough-looking kilt of green-and-brown plaid. The pattern clearly did a perfect job of camouflaging its wearer.

Even though I knew the boys back home would mercilessly call it a "skirt," there was nothing girlish about Scottish kilts, especially this one. Its ragged edges fell across his tanned knees in a way that was more masculine than any pair of jeans. His hands were as rough as his clothing, but he gave the overall impression that he could take care of . . . anything.

As he got closer, his eyes flared for just a second as if he recognized me, but then the look passed. I desperately wished I did know him.

"I'm sorry," I stammered, taken aback by how beautiful he was. I'd never thought that word, *beautiful*, about a boy, but it popped into my head instantly, and in this case, it definitely applied. He was the most breathtaking guy I had ever seen, and—*thank you, God!*—seemed to be about my age. His wavy, chestnut-colored hair fell over his forehead, but not enough to hide his dark blue eyes. He was tall and broad shouldered, but had a thin waist. He carried his bulging frame like he was wearing football shoulder pads, but I could see from where his white tunic shirt hung open at his chest that he was all bare skin and muscle.

"You should be," he answered. His accent was thicker than anyone else's I had heard in Scotland, but I had no trouble understanding him. In fact, the way he spoke, his particular cadence and rhythm, seemed to suck the breath out of me. He was literally making me dizzy.

I'd never gotten dizzy over a boy, and I certainly wasn't going to start with a baby deer killer. I had to pull myself together.

"Well, come to think of it, I'm *not* sorry," I said, hoping my voice didn't crack. "That's my deer you were trying to murder."

"Your deer?" He cocked his head. "Is that right?" One corner of his mouth rose in a half smirk, and I wasn't sure, but I think he winked at me.

"Yes, it is," I answered. "My deer. My baby deer. I came out here with the specific purpose to find her and make sure no one harmed her—like you were about to!"

He crossed over to the tree, and pulled the arrow out of the bark as easily as if it were attached by Velcro, not lodged three inches deep. Despite my best effort, I was impressed by his strength.

"Well, seeing as this is *my* forest, you're going to have to come back every day if you want to save that doe, because I intend to kill her." He looked so intently, directly into my eyes, that even though he said "kill her," I was sure I heard "kiss her" in my head. For one insane second, I didn't know if he was talking about me or the deer.

In the ultimate act of betrayal, my knees buckled, and I tumbled to the ground. I blinked, and he was instantly standing over me. His entire face blocked out the sun, so that when I looked up, he had a golden halo of light around him.

"Are you a'right?" he asked, looking at me with such earnest concern, it almost made me cry. His voice made me feel like no one in the world had ever cared for me so much. It was unnerving.

"I'm fine," I said, completely mortified. Before I could jump up on my own, he extended his hand to help me. Instinctively, I took it. Touching his hand as he pulled me up sent a small shockwave through my body—a warm electricity that didn't fade away even when he let go. I brushed the leaves off the back of my jeans.

"That's good," he answered. "Because I've no time to rescue a damsel in distress."

"I'm not a damsel in distress," I argued, slightly irritated at the label. "I just tripped on something."

He took a few steps back, shouldering his giant bow. "Are you sure? 'Cause from where I'm standing, it kind of looks like you fainted." His teasing mixed with his gorgeousness tormented me.

"I didn't faint," I said, probably too quickly. "I've never fainted in my life. I don't faint."

"If you say so," he said. He turned as if he was going to walk away. My heart sank. I had to stop him.

"I'm Maren," I blurted out. It worked. He looked back over his shoulder with a dazzling smile.

"Nice to meet you, Maren," he answered. "I'm Gavin."

When he said my name, I got the same glorious drop in the pit of my stomach as I did when I drove too fast over a small hill. I searched my brain for something else to say to keep him around a little longer.

"Do you live around here?" I asked lamely. I was

desperate for him not to leave. I didn't know why, but there was something about him. Something that pulled me to him. Something I wasn't ready to let go of.

"Aye," he answered.

"Where?" I pressed, realizing a specific answer would mean nothing to me since I didn't know the local area, but not caring as long as he kept talking in his amazing accent.

"Across the way," he answered. He leaned against a tree, folded his arms across his chest, and waited. It was maddening, his short answers and long silence. I studied my shoes. He'd effectively killed my attempt at a conversation. I couldn't think of anything else to say that wasn't completely idiotic.

"Is that it?" He raised his eyebrows, and his brilliant blue eyes danced a bit. He was enjoying my frustration.

"Is what it?"

"Are you done interrogating me?"

A new heat—anger—washed over me. I was furious he was having an effect on me that I couldn't control. And now he was making fun of me for it. "I'm not interrogating you," I shot back. "I was just making polite conversation."

"Asking where a perfect stranger lives is polite conversation?"

"It's . . . I'm new here, and I just wondered . . . I thought maybe you were a neighbor or something," I stuttered.

"Are you sure there's nothing else you want to know?" he asked. "My height? My hobbies? What I ate for breakfast?" He smiled, and I swore I saw him wink again. My ears prickled.

"No, I'm good." I tried in vain to sound casual.

"Well, you best be getting home then," he said. "It's not safe out here after dark." Almost as if he willed it, the sun went behind a cloud, and mist seemed to roll in from nowhere.

"Why?" I asked.

A piercing cry echoed through the forest, as if a bird had been struck down from the sky midflight. It reminded me of the inhuman scream at my mother's funeral. A cold wind blew around inside of me. I stroked my arms to dissipate it.

Gavin stiffened and raised his head, like an animal sensing a predator . . . or a predator catching a whiff of his prey.

"I have to go," he said, ignoring my question. "Can you find your way out?"

"Yes," I said. The woods did suddenly look a hundred times creepier, but I was pretty sure I could get home. And after hearing that sound, I wanted to.

He didn't look so convinced. His face was tense, as if he was torn about something. "Are you sure?"

"Yeah. It's no problem. I never get lost," I lied.

"Like you never faint?" His entire face lit up when he teased me. It was mesmerizing. I blushed. He took a step toward me and leaned in so close, I could feel his warm breath on my lips. "Promise me you'll go straight home?"

I nodded ever so slightly, afraid the tiniest movement would break the spell and he would move away from me.

"You have to say it, or I can't leave," he breathed.

A sweet warmth flooded my entire body. I fought the

completely irrational urge to throw my arms around his neck and rest my head on his chest.

"I promise," I gulped.

"Thank you, love." He grinned like he had just won a prize.

My heart leapt at the tiny, affectionate nickname. Anything that came out of his mouth, however short, sounded like poetry.

Love. I was looking at this strange—although incredibly handsome—boy and thinking about *love*. How was that even possible? I had never been in love before. I'd never even been in deep *like*. But my heart was jumping around inside my chest and sending my brain definite love signals. Is this what people meant by "love at first sight"? I'd never believed in that, but I'd also never met anyone like Gavin . . .

Get a grip, I chastised myself. *This isn't love. I'm just attracted to him—a pure, physical, completely understandable attraction. Why wouldn't I be? His eyes, his lips, his chest . . .*

I shook my head. What was going on with me? I never had thoughts like this. He had me completely transfixed.

"Go on then," he said, breaking me out of my reverie. He wasn't going to leave until he was sure I was safely on my way.

"Okay." I smiled weakly, and started walking back the way I'd come.

"Faster," he commanded.

Dutifully, I picked up the pace a bit. After a hundred feet, I looked back. He was still standing there, watching me go. I had always been uncomfortable when people were looking at me, especially boys. But for some reason, I felt wonderful knowing Gavin was watching me. It gave me a thrill and made me feel safe.

As I turned away and headed toward my grandparents' house, I prayed he wasn't just a dream.

CHAPTER 5

The next afternoon, I was sitting at the kitchen table trying to figure out how *not* to eat the "chip butty" fries-and-butter sandwich my grandmother had made me for lunch. No one spoke. My grandparents read their books as they ate, while I mentally filled in the daily paper's crossword puzzle. There was no point in getting a pen; it was too easy.

A rap on the screen door broke the silence.

"Oh, Maren dear, I forgot to tell you, you're getting a visitor today," my grandmother said.

I barely had time to check my face for crumbs and stand up before Jo walked into the kitchen.

"Hi!" she chirped. "We met at Tesco, remember? I'm Jo Dougall. I live down the road, and your grandmother thought I could help you get settled at Kingussie." I stared at her blankly. "The high school . . .?"

"Oh, hi," I answered. I held out my hand, and she used it to pull me into a big hug. I was surprised when she kissed me on the cheek. British greetings were so . . . friendly.

"You already met? I knew you'd make friends quickly, Maren," my grandmother said, proving she didn't know me at all. "Why don't you take Jo upstairs and pick out an outfit for tomorrow?"

Tomorrow? So Jo was right; my grandmother was going to send me back to school.

"Of course, Mrs. Hamilton," Jo said, still holding my arm.

Jo talked nonstop from the kitchen all the way up to my room. And she talked fast—really fast.

"I'm so excited you've come!" Jo said, flopping onto my bed. "We hardly ever get anyone new at Kingussie. And certainly no one as foreign as you!"

"Um, thanks," I said.

"Oh, don't take it the wrong way," she gasped. "Foreign is amazing. Foreign is so *not* Scotland. Foreign is bigger, better, and far, far away!" She fell back against the pillows, as if she had exhausted herself.

She didn't stay down long, however, springing off the bed in an acrobatically unbelievable way. She was rather exhausting to watch, since, along with talking a mile a minute, she seemed in perpetual motion. She would be talking, and then, midsentence, fall away into a backbend, throw her legs over her head, and pop up again in front of you without missing a syllable. I wondered if her bones were elastic.

"So what kind of classes do you take here?" I asked.

"The usual," she said. "Science, maths, modern languages . . ."

"Modern?" I interrupted. "As opposed to ancient?"

"Yeah." She nodded. "I'm sure they won't make you take Gaelic right away, but if you need help, I'm great at it."

"Gaelic? Seriously?" I asked. She nodded again. "What else?"

"Um . . . Music, Writing, and Rural Skills. I think that's it."

"Rural Skills?" I asked.

"Oh, it's great fun. We put on our Wellies and raincoats and learn how to build stone walls and repair fences . . ."

"Now you're just making fun of me," I said. "There is no way fence building is an actual school subject here."

"No, it is, I swear." Jo peered at me with big eyes that said she wouldn't dream of making fun of anyone, let alone me.

"What are Wellies?" I asked.

"Tall boots for walking in the rain. Wellington boots."

As if on cue, it started to pour outside.

"Yeah, I can see needing those," I said.

❁ ❁ ❁

Jo and I talked for two hours. Well, mostly she talked and I listened. We discovered we had more than a gravel street and the same grade in common: we were both missing parents.

When she was seven, Jo's dad ran off with her babysitter and left a tsunami of scandal behind. Her family was left with no money, so her older brothers went to work on the oil rigs in the North Sea, Jo got an afterschool position at Tesco as soon as she was old enough, and her mom took the only job she was qualified for: a cocktail waitress in a touristy restaurant. The locals saw the Highland maiden costume she had to wear as less than appropriate for a woman "her age."

I thought I was a loner, and kind of a loser living with my grandparents, but Jo was apparently an actual outcast.

"After my dad ditched, my friends weren't allowed

to come to my house anymore. I guess their parents figured we were a bad influence or something. It's rubbish, is what it is, but I don't really care. The girls I used to hang out with are all jerks now, anyway." She beamed as if she'd just told me she was named prom queen.

"Don't take offense," I said, "but why are you so *happy*?"

She shrugged. "I don't know. I was just wired this way, I guess."

I wished I was wired that way, for happiness. Instead, I seemed to have been born cursed. No parents, no friends, and no sleep. And since I'd found my mom's letter to me, no peace. I jumped at every little thing: every branch that scraped the roof, every creak in the steps. I was waiting for someone or something to attack me for having the journal, but I didn't know who, what, where, or why. I didn't even know if the warning was serious or some kind of sick joke. My mom didn't have that kind of humor, and she definitely didn't joke about death—probably because of my dad—but none of it made sense. No one was ever after her or us. Why would they be?

"So, do you have a boyfriend?" Jo interrupted my thoughts.

"Nope. Are there any cute guys at Kingussie?" I asked, hoping she might say something about Gavin. My heartbeat quickened as I realized seeing him every day would be more than enough reason to go back to school.

"Cute to me, or to everyone else?" She smiled.

"Both," I answered.

"Well, there's Stuart . . ." A slight blush spread across her cheeks.

"Is he your boyfriend?"

She sighed. "I wish. We've been friends since third grade, but that's it."

"What's he like?" I pressed.

"He's really tall, not too skinny, he has dark red hair, and I don't know . . . he's just . . . he's just great." She fiddled with a small ring on her hand. "He's not really popular, but since he's so tall, the other guys leave him alone. I guess you can't really bully a guy who's so much taller than you, right?"

"Who would bully him?" I asked, praying she didn't suddenly mention Gavin.

"Anders and his crew. They pretty much rule the place."

"What about Gavin?" I asked, unable to keep it in one more second. I couldn't get him out of my head. I'd been trying to figure out how to find him again, and the best I'd come up with was camping out in the woods and hoping not to get shot by him.

"You mean the First Year in the wheelchair?"

"A First Year, like a freshman?" I asked. "I don't think he's that young. And he wasn't in a wheelchair when I met him." The details of my forest encounter came spilling out.

"There's only one Gavin at Kingussie," she said wistfully, "and he's certainly not the guy you met."

"Maybe he already graduated," I offered.

"Could be," she said. "Gavin's a pretty common name here, and Kingussie's the only high school for eight towns. I'm sure I'd recognize him if I saw him."

Jo continued to tell me about the other things I

wouldn't find at Kingussie: no big football games (unless you counted the soccer matches they called "football" in Britain, which I didn't), no cheerleading, no Homecoming, or Prom. They did have a year-end "KAY-lee" (spelled *cèiligh* for some insane reason) that she described as a "cool square dance" where everyone wore their kilts, but how a square dance could possibly be cool was beyond me. And I learned that even though Kingussie High was a public school, everyone had to wear a uniform.

I hated the idea at first, until I realized it would probably be a lot easier to blend in if I wasn't immediately judged for my Midwest fashions.

It turned out the wrong clothes were the least of my problems at school. I apparently had the wrong everything else.

CHAPTER 6

I stopped outside my new high school and studied it for a minute, even though Jo was pulling my arm and practically dancing to get inside.

"Come on!" she said. "We'll be late!"

"I know, I know," I answered. "I just want a good look at it before I go in to the slaughter."

I am not exaggerating at all when I say Kingussie could have been a prison. Or an old, abandoned factory. If it weren't for the "Kingussie High School" wooden sign mounted outside in a weird little wishing well, you could never tell the difference. Unlike American high schools, there was no welcoming front entrance—no covered walkway or grassy area or steps or anything—just two dull, crimson metal doors on the front of the flat, gray-brick building.

As we passed through the doors, I noticed plastic flowerpots hanging from a hook on either side of the door, but instead of bringing cheer or comfort, they only served to scare me more. The plants inside were prickly and dead, and as they swung in the wind, the chains creaked as if saying, "Run away. Run away."

There were less than three hundred fifty students in the whole school, so of course, everyone knew everyone. As I walked down the hall with Jo, I felt the stares as keenly as if I was an alien from another planet. Sure, I was new, but in my uniform, what made me stand out so much that people were looking me up and down and whispering?

I didn't have to wait long for the answer.

As Jo helped me open my locker, three girls walked up to us. The one in the middle grabbed my hand and held it in both of hers.

"Jo," she cooed. "Who is this lovely creature? Introduce us!"

"This is Maren," Jo answered. "Maren, this is Elsie." I could tell by Jo's flat tone that Elsie was not her favorite person. I'd have to remember to cheer her up later by letting her know "Elsie" was mainly a name for cows in America.

"Lovely to meet you," Elsie said, smiling entirely too widely.

"Hi," I replied, consciously trying to keep my answer as short as possible to hide my "foreign" accent.

Elsie suddenly let go of my hand, which I wasn't expecting, and my arm fell clumsily against my leg. It was the perfect gesture, though, to accompany Elsie's line of sight, since she was now looking at my shoes.

"Nice shoes. Good tights. Well done, Jo. You got her properly outfitted," Elsie said. I was actually wearing Jo's tights and an extra pair of her shoes, and mentally thanked her for saving me from a foot mocking.

Elsie continued her inspection, opened her mouth to say something, and then changed her mind. Instead, she reached for my neck with both of her hands. Instinctively, I jerked back, and bashed my head against the lockers.

"Sorry to startle you, Dewdrop," Elsie said. "I was only

trying to fix your tie. While Jo might insist upon wearing hers like a *nob*, we want you to be posh." As she talked, she undid the perfectly looped, thin, orange-and-black-striped tie around my neck and retied it with a big, sloppy, loose knot. I was glad my mother's necklace was hidden under my blouse, tucked away from scrutiny. "There," she sighed. "Much better." Her own tie was fashioned the same way, so at least she wasn't setting me up to be made fun of . . . at least I thought so. "So, what's with your hair?" she asked.

"What do you mean?" I replied, realizing I was twisting a lock of it in my fingers. Thankfully, I no longer chewed on my hair when I was nervous, like I did until junior high.

"It's pretty," Elsie said. "But it's just so . . . big. And so . . . styled. Why do you do it like that?"

Styled? Who knew crazy and naturally curly was a style? I stepped away from the lockers, scanned the crowd, and realized all the girls had the same hairdo: straight, or wavy at best, mostly short, and cut very sensibly.

"Um, my hair's just always been like this," I answered.

"No way," Elsie replied, still sounding nice despite her actual words. "No one has hair like that, except on the television. That's it, isn't it? All the magazines say you Americans get your hair cut like the celebs. Is it true?"

"No. I mean, I guess I know people who get their hair cut like a celebrity they like. But I don't."

"Oh, rubbish, you all do," she continued. "You've got movie star hair! Nobody walks around with movie star hair for no reason." She addressed her posse. "I've heard they splash out a fortune in the salons over there."

"They splash out on more than just their hair," a male voice breathed into the back of my neck.

"What are you getting on about, Anders?" Elsie said with not a small amount of jealousy.

I swung around to find the infamous Anders, popular but mean according to Jo, standing far too close to me. He had light blue eyes, bleached-blond hair, and was apparently spoken for. Yet he kept speaking to me.

"So, are they?" he asked. He smirked with the confidence of someone who knew he was handsome. I hated guys like that. Especially when it was true. Anders was pretty gorgeous.

"Are they what?" I asked, wanting to take a step away from him, but standing my ground because everyone was watching.

He either didn't notice my discomfort or didn't care, because he leaned in, his lips brushing against my cheek when he spoke. I had never been so near to a boy's mouth, and I got goose bumps all over my body.

"Real," he exhaled. "Are they *real*?"

I held my breath. "Wh-what?" I managed to stutter.

"Your *diddies*," he whispered.

"My what?"

Suddenly, Anders was shoved from the side, away from me.

"Leave her alone, you *nugget*!" A tall, thin guy was now standing between us. Stuart.

Anders made as innocent a face as he could muster. "I was only askin'," he said. "It's a perfectly natural question. I mean, look at them, they're huge!"

I realized that Anders had been talking about—well, talking *to*—my breasts, and my entire face got so hot, I worried it might catch fire.

"You're so rude," Stuart continued. Stuart was a good seven inches taller than Anders, and Anders took a step back. "Don't you know how to talk to a lady? I thought you were a baron or something."

"Lord," Anders spat out. "I'm a lord. And I would definitely know how to talk to a lady . . . if I saw one. But all I see here are girls. Wee girls, although some of 'em are a bit bigger than—"

Stuart gave Anders another shove, causing him to swallow the end of his sentence. Anders stumbled, recovered, and then started down the hall. After a couple of steps, he stopped, turned around completely composed, smiled, and said, "Come now," and held out his arm. To my amazement, Elsie grabbed it. She and the other girls left with him.

"You're *mental*!" Jo slapped playfully at Stuart. She turned to me. "'Mental' means 'tough,' by the way."

Good to know, I thought. *Although the American meaning would work just as well for these Scottish boys.*

"If he's such a jerk, why do girls like him?" I asked.

"Because he's rich," Stuart answered. "Most girls would love to be his girlfriend, because they know if he married them someday, they'd pretty much be royalty."

"Who cares about being rich?" I asked. "I mean, I wish I had tons of money, but I would never marry a creep for his."

"You have no idea how rich Anders Campbell is," Jo

said. "He's not sports-car-and-mansion rich, he's castle-and-landed-title rich. Not that I'm into that, either," she added, shooting a worried look at Stuart. "I'm just saying . . ."

"What does that mean, 'landed-title rich'?" I asked.

"His family is one of the most powerful in the Highlands," Stuart explained. "Up until just a few years ago, we all paid taxes to them."

"Lies!" I said.

"No, it's the truth," Jo answered.

Jo and Stuart walked me to the office so I could officially check in. The hallway incident had delayed us, so they had to leave me if they were going to make it to their homeroom before the first bell rang.

I got my schedule, but no map. "So I start in Room 312?" I asked the woman behind the desk. She wiggled her chins, then turned away to answer the phone.

I left the office, but as soon as I was out of sight of the doorway, I sagged against the wall. I didn't want to be the new kid, didn't want to be the foreign orphan everyone stared at all day. I fought a violent urge to run away.

"Are you lost?" A guy I hadn't seen before was striding confidently toward me. He was slender, had reddish-brown hair, and was attractive, but almost in a feminine way. There was something very familiar about him. He reminded me of the British movie stars who are always getting the girl on film, but probably didn't in real life.

"Aye," I answered, mimicking the Scottish affirmation I'd been hearing since I arrived, and immediately regretting it because of how lame it sounded coming from my mouth. "I mean, yes. I'm lost. Sort of hopelessly."

"You're Maren Hamilton, aren't you?" he asked.

"The one and only," I mumbled.

He smiled. "Well, I'm Graham Campbell, and it's a pleasure to meet you."

"Campbell?" Without meaning to, I spit the word out as if it were poison. "Like Anders Campbell?"

Graham smiled even wider. "I take it that you've already met my cousin. And if history serves, you are probably owed an apology for whatever he said to you. Please accept mine."

I couldn't help but smile back. Graham was like the gentlemen in Jane Austen novels: sweet and chivalrous. He didn't look like he could throw a punch, or survive one for that matter, but he oozed charm without even trying. I bet mothers loved him.

"Is it true what they say about your family?" I asked, unable to resist questioning someone with royal blood. As a little girl who grew up playing princess, I had to admit, I was kind of fascinated by the whole thing. "Are you really all powerful and stuff, and had people pay taxes to you?"

"Yes, it's true," he answered. "Why?"

"It's just crazy, that's all." I shrugged. "We don't have that kind of thing in America. It's like something out of the Middle Ages. Do you have serfs too?" The rude comment slipped out before I could stop it.

Thankfully, Graham didn't show the slightest sign of annoyance. "Not so much anymore." He grinned. "You have to remember, yours is basically an infant country," he said, somehow without making it sound like an insult. *It must be the accent*, I decided. *Makes everything sound so much more civilized.* "America has been around for, what, three hundred years? Britain has been populated for over three thousand. Change comes really slowly here. But change is good, right? I can tell you're going to mix things up. You've got a fire in your belly." He cocked his head toward me.

For the second time that morning, a warm flush fell over my body. I drew my notebooks tighter against my stomach, recalling my first nightmare in Scotland, when kissing a hot guy with red hair made my guts spill with blood.

If only you knew.

CHAPTER 7

A few days later, Jo and I were hanging out in downtown Aviemore, if it could even be called that. The main drag was only six blocks long and ended at the Tesco. There wasn't even a stoplight.

My grandparents had insisted I stop moping around the house, and to be honest, it was nice to do something besides sit and worry, imagining a million different insane scenarios about my mother's death and the cursed journal she sent me.

It was an unusually warm day for Scotland—a whopping 70 degrees—and we were celebrating the sun with ice cream. As much as I wanted a hard scoop of caramel mocha fudge, the only choice in town was vanilla soft serve. The clerk stuck a long piece of waxy, crumbly chocolate in it before she handed me the cone. Jo said that made it "a 99" but couldn't explain why, since it cost more than 99 pence and it was definitely more than 99 calories.

"Your grandparents don't have a dog, do they?" she asked, swirling her chocolate bar through her ice cream.

"No. Why?"

"I heard there's something weird going around. People's dogs are dying. Like, a lot of them. Stuart's did just last night."

"Oh my gosh, that's terrible," I answered. "Is it like a disease?"

"Sort of. I guess the dogs are going crazy and freaking out and strangling themselves on their collars and stuff."

"Is it rabies?"

She shrugged. "Dunno. I just heard that if you have a dog, you're supposed to keep it inside."

"Scary."

"I know," she agreed.

We sat on a splintered wooden bench and broke off tiny pieces of cone for the round, gray birds at our feet. We watched the small cars whiz by—the three-wheeled ones genuinely freaked me out. And we took turns embracing and then pretending to lick the giant plastic ice cream cone outside the sweet shop. I was taking Jo's picture with my phone when I saw him.

Gavin.

Even though he was wearing a white oxford shirt with jeans and not a kilt, he still somehow looked like he was from another time. There was something otherworldly about him.

"Jo, look! It's him!" I whispered, cocking my head across the street. "Gavin. The guy I met in the woods."

"He *is* hot!" she murmured appreciatively.

"Don't look!" I scolded.

"You just told me to!"

"Well, stop now," I said. He disappeared into the small, bright blue post office. "So, did you recognize him?" I asked. "Did he go to Kingussie?"

"Nope," she said. "I know everyone, and I certainly wouldn't forget a face like his."

"What do you think he's doing here?" I asked.

"Visiting? Enjoying the scenery? Tons of tourists pass through here, especially when the weather gets warmer. We even have a seasonal bum, Bertie. Crazy-looking bald guy with a big beard, but totally harmless. Comes up for the summer every year. Sleeps in the woods."

"Creepy!" I said, wondering if that was the danger in the forest Gavin had warned me about. "But Gavin said he lived nearby."

"Maybe he just moved here." She shrugged. "It's rare, but people do that, you know." She raised her eyebrows to mean me.

"But why was he hunting with a bow and arrow? Don't you think that's weird?" I persisted. I hadn't been able to stop thinking about Gavin for more than five minutes since we'd met, and it was driving me crazy. I caught myself actually fantasizing about him, about what it would be like to hold his hand, what it would be like to kiss him . . . ridiculous thoughts only ridiculous girls had. I'd never been that girl. How could this guy I just met have such an effect on me?

"Not really," she replied in between licks. "A lot of people hunt that way in the Highlands. It's sort of old school, I guess. Man, you're obsessed with this guy."

"I am not!" I protested.

"Really? Prove it. Go buy me a stamp."

"What?"

"If you're really not into him, then go into the post office and buy a stamp. What's the problem?" She grinned mischievously.

"There is no problem," I answered. "I just don't need a stamp."

"Sure you do," she said. "Everyone needs stamps." She gave me a tiny push toward the street. It was all I needed, since I was dying for an excuse to go in and see him. Just once. To prove to myself he wasn't really that handsome or worth dreaming about. I handed my cone to Jo, and crossed the street armed only with my stamp excuse.

Inside, the post office was dark. I was temporarily blinded, having gone so quickly from the sunshine to the cool interior. My vision cleared a second too late, and I ran straight into Gavin.

"I'm sorry," I gushed.

"It's okay," he mumbled. His face was blank, like he didn't recognize me, but he was still hyperventilatingly gorgeous.

Why did I feel such a connection to him? Maybe it was because we were both outsiders; were both new to a town where everyone had a shared history that dated back to their birth.

"Hi, it's me . . . Maren," I stuttered. "We met the other day?"

"Yes, I remember," he said coolly. He looked at me, waiting. I couldn't read anything in his sapphire-colored eyes, but it didn't stop me from wanting to melt into them.

"So, I got home safely," I said.

"I know."

I perked up. "How?" *Had he followed me home, secretly watching me?*

"You're standing in front of me," he said, slowly, as if I might not understand at normal speed. "Blocking the door," he added.

"Oh, sorry." I slid out of the way. He nodded, and started to walk past me. I couldn't let him leave so soon. "I'll see you around?" I called after him.

"Hopefully not," he muttered.

The words hit me like tiny daggers. "What?"

He stopped, realizing I'd heard him. His shoulders sagged, then he took a deep breath and spun around. "It's nothing personal," he said roughly. "You just need to stay away from me."

"I'm not a stalker," I found myself spitting back. "I can stay away from you just fine."

"Good," he answered. "Then do it." Even when he was angry, his face was almost too lovely to look at. It radiated with an intensity and energy that took my breath away.

I was heartbroken our conversation was going so horribly wrong. In my fantasies, he was always wonderful to me. What an idiot I was, thinking a guy like Gavin would like me for even a second. I had to let him know I didn't like him either.

"Done. I'm not into the whole bad boy thing anyway," I lied.

He raised an eyebrow. "You think I'm a 'bad boy'?" The idea seemed to amuse him.

"I don't know." I shrugged, not wanting to inflate his ego any more. "You're certainly not very nice."

He leaned toward me, and his expression was softer. "I'm sorry you think that," he said quietly. "I'm a good guy, I really am. I just have a bad . . . job. Well, it's not bad. It's more . . . dangerous. And the danger sort of rules out the ability to have a girlfriend." He looked at me as if he might actually consider me girlfriend material. I got a little light-headed.

"Who said anything about a girlfriend?" I whispered.

He moved in so close, I thought for a thrilling moment he was going to kiss me. "Please," he whispered back. "Forget you ever met me."

I blinked and he was gone, the door slamming behind him. I peered out the hazy, rectangular windows and spotted Jo. She made a face and shrugged.

Forget I ever met him. Short of getting a lobotomy, I had exactly zero chance of succeeding at that.

CHAPTER 8

The old man had a sweet face, like Santa Claus, with his red cheeks and bushy white beard. His clothes were ragged, though, and dirty. So was his face.

He smiled at me. It was a sad smile. I felt sorry for him. He knew, like I did, that he was going to die.

I heard the dogs before I saw them. Barking fiercely. Madly. They seemed to come out of nowhere, jumping on the old man, tearing first at his clothes, and then at his flesh. He reached out his hand to me, but there was nothing I could do. He slumped to the ground, and the dogs covered him completely, their mouths now dripping with red foam.

I couldn't go back to sleep after my latest nightmare. The baby deer had become a helpless old man, and I was worn out watching him die every night.

I'd curled myself on the window seat in my room, watching the dawn break, a blanket of crocheted roses wrapped around my legs. Outside a cold, wet wind blew, soaking everything in sight. It was technically raining, but the drops were so small, you couldn't see them. It was more like a constant mist. *Smirr*, my grandfather called it. A fitting name.

I cradled a warm cup of tea against my chest. My mother had introduced me to tea when I was young. It was one of the ways she tried to incorporate my dad's

Scottish heritage into our American lives. My grandmother couldn't understand why I didn't want milk or sugar in my tea, how I could stand it "black," but it's how I'd been drinking it forever. Milk and sugar were for cereal. I didn't want anything to get in the way of the pure, earthy liquid.

The leather journal from the box of my mom's stuff sat on my lap. I'd been flipping through the pages, examining the drawings, trying to make sense of them. It was comforting to look at her sketches and little notes to herself; it made me feel connected to her. I still had no idea what *Arcēs Daemonium* meant, although I had an odd feeling that I should know.

Although the window was closed, a breeze blew past and ruffled the pages of the journal, sending the vellum envelope I had tucked inside it fluttering to the floor. I set my teacup next to me, and picked it up. I opened and unfolded the letter to examine it again. The date was definitely written in her handwriting, but the rest of the page was empty. *Why would my mom seal a blank page inside an envelope addressed to some place in France? Was that where I was supposed to deliver the journal? Or was it part of what she was warning me about?*

All I had were questions, and the white paper wasn't giving me any answers. I balanced the page on top of my teacup and returned to the journal.

I had figured out that the hundreds of pages of floor plans, room layouts, and what looked like secret passages all belonged to just three buildings—none of which I recognized despite a strong sense of déjà vu every time I looked at them. One was so large and ornate, I imagined it was the summer home of a royal family. Another resembled a library built around the turn of the century. The last was a fairly simple, perfectly square castle with a turret at each corner, although I noticed three of the towers were square and one was round. The buildings could be in any European country; maybe they weren't even still standing.

Why was my mother so interested in these buildings? She wasn't an architect—at least as far as I knew—she was a systems analyst. What systems was she analyzing? The buildings she'd been drawing would be lucky to have electricity, let alone high-tech anything.

Frustrated, I reached for my tea.

The empty page setting on top of my cup was no longer blank. In the middle, a perfect circle had appeared, cluttered with my mother's frantic writing:

tercepted comm
Dangerous experiments a
animals first, then hum

I picked it up, and the writing disappeared, leaving the page blank once again. I blinked. *Had I really seen words?* I laid the paper back over the steaming mouth of my teacup, and the message reappeared. Invisible ink!

Suddenly, memories from my youth came rushing back. A doodle pad with a big, green plastic pen. I was crying because it had run out. My mom, with her love of encryption, had gotten me a kiddie spy kit with an invisible ink pen. She wiped my tears away, and told me that the pen itself wasn't that special, it was the process. She showed me how regular household things could also "write" on paper invisibly: lemon juice, baking soda, even spit. Whatever you wrote would darken when it was heated, making it magically show up.

The heat from my tea must have activated whatever was covering the blank letter. I had to find a way to heat the entire piece of paper.

I tiptoed downstairs to the kitchen. The house was still quiet. I turned a sticky, round knob on the oven. As I waited impatiently for it to warm up, I contemplated what I had already read. Dangerous experiments involving animals? *I thought Mom worked on computers . . . What else didn't I know about her?*

The oven beeped, and I carefully laid the paper on the middle rack. I switched on the oven light and stared through the smeared glass door. I needed enough heat to reveal the message, but not enough to set the paper on fire.

Slowly, words started to form. I waited as long as I could, until the outer edges of the paper began turning brown, then I lifted it out. I could now read the entire letter. It was signed by my mom, and addressed to something called the "High Council":

To: High Council
Re: Project 666

The intercepted communications have been cracked. Dangerous experiments are set to start this week—on local animals first, then humans. They are rolling out the program in small, rural towns, beginning alphabetically. We must get additional soldiers on the ground in these locations immediately, or there will be great loss of life.

Anna Hamilton, Agent

#ROM1221

Soldiers? Great loss of life? Anna Hamilton, agent? Who exactly was my mom? Did she work for the CIA or something? Was she a spy? And more importantly, how did I not know any of this? How could she not tell me?

According to the date on the letter, the "dangerous experiments" had already started, at least on animals. What had Jo said about a dog? Stuart's dog had died, and so had a bunch of others. No, I was being insane. That was just a coincidence. Besides, my mother was based out of Missouri. What in the world would she have to do with Aviemore, Scotland?

Although Aviemore did start with an *A*, I realized with a chill—the top of the alphabet. It was definitely a small town and definitely rural. My mom did work for an international company, and the envelope had been addressed to some place in France . . .

I ran back upstairs to get a pen and write the message down before it disappeared. The drawings and the letter were connected, and I was going to find out how. I had to. I sensed my life depended on it.

❀ ❀ ❀

Two hours later, I was driving my grandparents' tiny car along the narrow, deserted road that led to Speybridge, the next town over, twenty miles away. Proof that Aviemore was one of the most remote towns on Earth: no one had an Internet connection in their house, and any Wi-Fi was blocked by the mountains. You could get online at the high school, but it was Saturday, and Kingussie was closed. I told my grandparents I had a project to work on and headed to the nearest public library to translate the Latin phrases in my mom's journal so I could start to figure out how it all fit together.

Even though the car was a stick shift and completely backward, driving it with my left hand wasn't as hard as I assumed it would be. And I loved the freedom of revving around the bends of barely paved roads.

It was still misting, but more clouds had rolled in, making it darker now than it had been at dawn. I was well past any signs of civilization, zipping by the thick, dark forest. The car, like everything in Scotland, didn't have air conditioning, and I couldn't get the defroster to work correctly, so I drove with the windows halfway down to keep the windshield from steaming up. The cool air stung my cheeks.

I was driving up a fairly steep hill when an old man bolted across the road, right in front of my car. I screamed and slammed on the brakes, pulling my foot off the clutch at the same time. The car screeched to a stop, sputtered, and stalled. I missed hitting him by less than an inch.

The bald, bushy-bearded man leaned on the hood for just a second, his eyes wide with fear. Bertie! I screamed again, and he ran to the other side of the road and crashed through the underbrush, stumbling then disappearing into the trees.

Dream or no dream, I was not going to stick around in the middle of nowhere to see where he was going. My heart thumped in my chest as I fumbled with the pedals, trying to restart the car. Since I was on an incline, every time I tried to get the gas and clutch pedal just right, I got it all wrong and started rolling backward. After three tries, I stopped, afraid I would flood the engine. I sat behind the wheel, shaking, when I saw more movement out of the corner of my eye. A stream of animals—deer, foxes, rabbits—darted across the road, flanking my car on all sides as they ran the same direction Bertie had gone. *What were they all running from? A forest fire?*

A soupy fog rolled out of the woods, and my windshield started to steam up. I furiously rubbed at it with my fist, trying to swallow my fear. A high-pitched screeching echoed overhead—a beyond-the-grave scream that gave me instant goose bumps. Panicked, I rolled up the windows.

A sickening, cracking sound rippled through the air, followed by a gigantic thud that made the entire car shake. I looked at the sky, my Midwest instincts searching for a tornado. The thick, gray clouds were unmoving. A creaking moan and the sound of splintering wood made me look to the left as a giant pine tree crashed down from the forest and onto the road, landing not two feet from the front of my car. My head almost hit the ceiling of the car as it jumped.

I was so terrified, I lost my ability to scream. My mind was racing. I couldn't think clearly. I didn't want to get out of the car, but I didn't want to die in it, either. The thought of running into the forest seemed like the kind of bad idea the heroine in a horror movie gets . . . right before she's killed. I fiddled with the door handle, unsure of what to do.

As the moisture started clouding the windshield again, I saw another person dart across the road. He was young, muscular, and dressed in a kilt. It was Gavin! He didn't stop or even glance in my direction, but leapt over the small bushes on the opposite side like he was jumping hurdles on a racetrack. Another ghastly scream echoed through the valley like the call of a giant, prehistoric bird. My blood ran cold.

I jumped out of the car. Following Gavin was my safest bet.

The foliage had been flattened by the recent stampede, so it was easy to find their trail. I tore through the woods, wet ferns smacking against my jeans, my shoes skidding on the damp earth. My ears strained in anticipation of another ungodly wail, or a warning that another tree was going to fall.

Suddenly, I saw him. Gavin was standing near a fallen log fifty feet ahead. I slipped to a halt.

"Gavin!"

At the sound of my voice, four pig-like animals with slippery, crimson backs darted out of the bushes near him and galloped away, squealing. He searched for the reason and spotted me. Even in the forest, his beauty was overwhelming. He seemed to be almost glowing. It took me a second to stop staring at his face and the bulge of muscles in his chest to notice his hands were dripping with blood. At his feet was a motionless lump of torn clothing.

Bertie.

My stomach lurched. My nightmare had come true again, and I hadn't been able to stop it. Another person had died, I'd known it was going to happen, and instead of telling someone, I did nothing.

A second wave of shock brought me to my knees. Not only was Bertie dead, Gavin had killed him. Like he'd tried to kill the baby deer. Like he'd killed how many others?

How could I have ever liked a murderer? No wonder he told me to stay away from him. I fought back the urge to throw up. It couldn't be. Gavin couldn't be. He had been cold the other day, but a killer?

"Get out of here!" Gavin yelled. The ferocity of his command forced me to stand up, to pay attention. "Now!" he snarled. "Get out of here, Maren! Run back to your car and go!"

I didn't even think about it. I turned and ran. Tears streamed down my cheeks as I tore open the car door and flung myself inside. I let the car coast down the hill in reverse until I could swing it around, then I engaged the clutch correctly, gunned the engine, and sped away as fast as I could.

❁ ❁ ❁

I was still shaking when I drove back up to my grand-parents' house. No one was home; my grandparents must have been out on one of their morning walks. For the first time, I actually wished they were around. I didn't want to be alone.

I bounded up the stairs to my room, slammed and

locked the door behind me, and jumped into bed. I pulled the covers up under my chin and tried to calm down. I was home. I was safe. It was over. I couldn't have seen what I thought I'd seen.

I had to talk to someone.

I reached for my phone and called Jo.

"Hello?" she mumbled.

"Hi, it's me," I said.

"What are you doing up so early on a Saturday?" she yawned. "It's not even nine."

"I've been up for a while," I answered. "I had this terrible nightmare . . ."

That seemed to wake her up. "Ooooh, tell me about it! I love scary stories!"

"It's not funny, Jo—this is serious. I think I saw that bum you were talking about get killed."

"In your dream?"

"Yes, in my dream, and in real life!"

"Are you kidding?" she asked.

"No, I saw him. In the forest. Gavin killed him."

"Are you asleep right now?" she asked. "Did you dream-and-dial?"

"No, I'm not asleep. I told you, I've been up since before dawn. I took my grandparents' car to go to Grantown Library, but the car died on a hill, and that's when I saw it."

"Saw what, exactly?"

"Bertie. He ran across the road, I almost hit him, then all these animals were chasing him . . ."

"Rabid dogs?" she breathed.

"No, deer and rabbits and stuff."

"Oh." She sounded disappointed.

"Then Gavin ran across the road, and a tree fell and almost smashed the car, and I couldn't get it started, so I ran into the woods after them."

"A tree fell on your car?" Her voice was laced with worry.

"No, next to the car," I assured her.

"Are you okay?"

"Yes, I'm fine. I mean, as fine as I could be after running into the woods and seeing Gavin covered in blood . . ."

"Hang on, slow down," Jo soothed. "One thing at a time. Take a breath. Where were you when this all happened?"

"On the road to Speybridge."

"The A95?"

"No, I missed my turn. I was on the, what is it, the B970?"

"How long had you been driving?"

"I don't know," I answered. "About thirty minutes, maybe."

"And you've been up all night?"

"Pretty much," I said. I was beginning to see where she was going.

"Are you sure you didn't fall asleep at the wheel?" Jo asked.

"No. At least, I don't think so."

"Most people don't think they did. They just close their eyes for a second, and *bam!*"

"But I didn't crash," I protested. "There was a tree in the road."

"I'm sure there was," Jo said. "It happens all the time when the wind gets going. But as for the other stuff . . . I don't know . . . It sounds like you had a rough night."

"You think I just imagined it all?"

"Honestly? Yeah," she answered, yawning.

I sunk back into the bed. She was right. It didn't make any sense. I must have imagined it. As the tension started to drain out of me, my body got heavy with sleepiness.

"Maren? Are you still there?"

"Yes," I said. My eyelids weighed a hundred pounds each. I struggled to keep them open. "I'm here."

"Do you want me to come over?"

"No, I'm good. I think I'm going to go back to sleep." I glanced out the window. The brightness burned my eyes. They wanted to be closed. "Now that it's light out, I shouldn't have any more bad dreams, right?"

"Right," Jo cooed. "You won't have any more. Get some rest, and call me later."

As I drifted off to sleep I tried not to think about the strange road-trip dream: the giant tree almost crushing me in the car, the bum and his scraggly beard, the blood shimmering as it pooled under his body. As soon as the images popped into my head, I shoved them out. But the one thing I couldn't get out of my mind, the picture that hovered behind my eyelids as I drifted off to sleep, was the same as the first day I'd met him: Gavin.

Whether he was smiling or scowling, flirting with me or angry, innocent or guilty, it didn't matter. I was completely and utterly smitten.

CHAPTER 9

After a three-hour nap blissfully free of nightmares, I found myself back in the car again, running an errand for my grandmother. It was well after lunch, and the sky had cleared. Everything—the trees, the grass, the pavement—was still wet and sparkled in the sunshine. The rain had washed a layer of gray off the world and left behind extra-bright, super-saturated colors.

The happy, almost cartoony feel of the landscape convinced me I'd dreamed most of my morning excursion—at least the scary forest bits. I *had* taken the car out and returned it safely. My grandfather reported there *was* a fallen tree blocking the road to Speybridge. I was glad I wasn't completely crazy. And that I couldn't attempt another trip to the library even if I'd wanted to. But delivering muffins to a church down the street for their bake sale—that, I could handle.

I swung left onto the unmarked road just past the barn with the red, rusted roof my grandfather had described. A small stone church that looked at least five hundred years old emerged from the shore of a glistening blue lake ringed by heather-covered mountains. Sunlight illuminated the steeple and the large, stained glass rose window beneath it, making it seem like I'd just driven into a postcard. A cracked, green wooden sign on the gravel driveway spelled out "St. Mary & St. Finnan" in gold lettering. I wondered which Mary the church was named for, although I'd never heard of St. Finnan.

A statue was perched in an alcove high up on the smooth front face of the church. I thought it might be Finnan, but as I got closer, I saw the sculpture had angel wings and a sword, and a serpent coiled around his feet. Much more dramatic and creepy than churches back home, I decided. I liked it, though. I found it hard to get inspired in rooms that looked like a modern-day coffee shop with plush theater seats. This building—with its textured turrets and gables, ornamented cornices, and a different stone cross atop every peak—stirred me up inside and made me feel like anything was possible.

I walked around the church, wondering if the doors would be unlocked. I'd learned in history class—or maybe it was a Disney movie—that churches in Europe didn't even have locks on their doors. They were always open to provide a safe place where the oppressed could find shelter—from bad weather, bad people, bad governments. Anyone could run in, say the word "sanctuary," and be given refuge in the church for as long as they needed. I couldn't think of a single building in America that didn't have locks.

I yanked on the heavy, arched wooden door. As it gave way, I noted that the doorframe was smooth and completely without a lock, or even a latch. So it was true. Just for good measure, I whispered "sanctuary" under my breath as I crossed the threshold.

A middle-aged man wearing brown monks' robes was just leaving the rectangular foyer.

"Hello?" I called out to his back.

He spun around. "I'll be right with you. Please have a seat in the church. I'm just wrapping up my previous appointment." Before I could say I didn't need an appointment, that I was only dropping off muffins, he was gone. I stood in the empty room for a minute, contemplating just dropping the basket and taking off. But then how would my grandmother get credit for her baking? I could leave a note, I thought, but decided that would only leave written evidence that my grandmother had a rude delivery girl. I sighed and headed for the double doors.

Inside, the nave was as still as a graveyard—empty, dark, and a little cold. I shivered, and shrank deeper into my jacket. The walls were lined with the same natural stones inside as out. The floor was covered in unstained wooden planks. I couldn't help but count the dark, circular knots as I stepped on them.

About three rows from the front, I slid sideways into a buffed wooden pew and sat down.

"Hey!" a voice under my butt shouted. I jumped up a split second after I felt someone's shoe in my bottom.

A girl my age sat up next to me. "Watch it!" she said, a little late.

"Sorry," I answered. "Were you . . . lying down?"

"Yes, I was," she replied, pulling tiny speakers from her ears. "I guess you couldn't have seen me when you entered then, eh?" She gave me a half smile.

I was glad, since I had no desire to get in a fight inside a church. "Do you, um, usually lay down here?" I smiled back.

She shrugged. "I do lie on the pews whenever I can, rather than sit on them. Gives you a much better view, I think. But I've never been here before. I'm only visiting. What about you? I'm guessing you're not a regular parishioner, since you don't have a Scottish accent either." Her accent was slightly higher pitched, although it was definitely still British.

"No, I'm from America," I said. "I'm just visiting too . . . Well, I guess I do live here now, but I've never been in here before. I was just delivering these for my grandmother." I held up the basket.

She jumped to her feet and thrust out her hand.

"I'm Hunter," she said, pumping my hand up and down while rattling off her personal information as quickly as all the other British girls I'd met. I wondered what made them all talk so fast. "I'm from Brixton, it's near London, or I was from Brixton anyway, before my parents passed. Now I'm in Westminster, at the Catholic Children's Society. Only for three hundred forty-two more days, though, since I turned seventeen last month."

"Both your parents are dead too?" I didn't mean to blurt it out, but I'd never met another orphan. I kind of thought they only existed in Dickens novels and my own unlucky life.

"Aye, they died in a car crash three years ago."

"I'm so sorry," I stuttered.

"No worries. Not your fault," she answered, pushing her champagne-colored bangs out of her eyes. They fell right back.

"I'm Maren," I said. "My mom just died recently. That's

why I'm in Scotland now . . ." I faltered, not wanting to talk about my mom, fearing if I picked at that scab, I might lose it. I had to change the subject. "So, how long are you here?"

"Just today," she answered. "The Mother Superior had to come speak with the pastor about some new adoption laws that just passed Parliament."

"So, you work at a children's society?" I asked.

"No, I live there. It's an orphanage. Although we all know no one's going to adopt me now. That's why I'm count-ing down until I'm eighteen. Then I get my pass, get some tin money, and off I go." The look in Hunter's eyes was weary, as if she'd seen too much. But it couldn't hide her prettiness.

"Where will you go?" I asked.

"I don't know yet. Maybe the Abbey."

"You want to be a nun?" I asked. Somehow, Hunter didn't strike me as the no-talking type.

"No," she explained. "Not an abbey like a convent. *The* Abbey, like where our parents worked."

The hairs on the back of my neck stood up. "What do you mean, *our* parents?" I asked.

"Oh, sorry, I just assumed you knew . . . because of your necklace . . ." She motioned at my throat.

"What about my necklace?" I asked. I immediately put my hand over the dangling flower and rubbed the petals under my thumb.

She crinkled her forehead. "Where'd you get it?" she asked suspiciously.

"It was my mom's. I found it in a box of her stuff."

Hunter looked relieved. "That's what I figured. My mom had one too. See?" She opened her sweater a bit at the neck to reveal she was wearing the exact same necklace. "It's the Tudor rose, the symbol of the Abbey. Girls get the necklace; guys get cufflinks. They used to get tattoos, but that's too hard to hide if you're captured." She sat down matter-of-factly, as if she'd just told me her favorite ice cream flavor, and picked at a piece of fuzz on her skirt.

"Captured?" I said. "What are you talking about? My parents didn't work for a place called the Abbey. The necklace is just a coincidence."

Hunter stared at me, suddenly very serious. "There's no such thing as coincidence," she said. "And there's only one way to get these necklaces, and that's by working at the Abbey."

I wasn't convinced. "What's so special about them?" I asked. "How do you know my mom didn't buy it on the Internet?"

"The rose is an ancient symbol of secrecy, and I know because they don't sell it on the Internet," she answered. "They don't sell it anywhere. You have to earn it."

"By doing what? What's the Abbey?"

"You really don't know?" Hunter seemed worried for me. "Where do you think your mom worked?"

"She worked for a foreign company called T.A., Inc." I answered, confidently. More confidently than I felt since discovering her journal.

"T.A. . . . The Abbey . . ." Hunter rolled her hands as she said the words, as if she might somehow fan understanding into my brain.

I shook my head. "Coinci . . ." I stopped myself. "She was a systems analyst."

"So was my mom," Hunter answered. "What about your dad?"

"He died before I was born—well, the day I was born, actually. I never met him."

"But where did he meet your mom?" she countered.

I knew the answer, but for some reason, I didn't want to tell her. It fit too easily into her insane story. "They met at work," I said slowly. "They both worked at the same company . . ."

"Mine too," she answered. "That's pretty typical, since they spend so much time away on missions together; although the Abbey strongly discourages couples from having kids. Clearly, that doesn't always work out." She motioned at both of us.

"Missions?" I said. "Are you serious? So what is the Abbey, exactly? Like the CIA?"

"Sort of," she answered. "Except it's not political or tied to a certain country." She looked around nervously, like she wasn't supposed to be telling me if I didn't already know. She lowered her voice. "It's a secret organization that helps fight evil forces around the world."

"Like terrorists?" I asked.

"Yeah." She shrugged. I could tell this wasn't the entire truth.

"I'm pretty sure my mom wasn't involved in anything like that," I said, although at this point, I wasn't. I wasn't sure about anything that had to do with my mom anymore.

"Really?" She raised her eyebrows at me. "You didn't find anything in her belongings that was unusual? Or encrypted?"

"Nope," I lied. I hoped she couldn't read the truth on my face.

"Well, if you find anything weird, be careful," she said. "You don't want Abbey information falling into the wrong hands. And they'll come after you if they think you have anything. Remember, there's no such thing as an accident."

Who was this crazy girl practically quoting my mother's warning message to me? And she didn't believe in coincidence *or* accidents? Of course there were accidents. My mom . . . Hunter's parents . . .

"But I thought you said your parents died in a car accident?" I prodded.

"No, I didn't. I said car *crash*. It wasn't an accident."

A bolt of heat shot through my chest. My father had died in a car crash while driving my mom to the hospital when she was in labor with me. The other driver came out of nowhere, plowed into them, and then disappeared. We never made it to the hospital: my dad was pronounced dead at the scene, and my mom delivered me by the side of the road. I didn't like hearing that car crashes weren't accidents—that they were somehow preordained . . . or planned.

A side door opened with a scrape, and I jumped. A priest and a nun walked in.

"Hunter," the nun called. "We need to check in at the Priory for the night."

"A priory, like full of monks?" I whispered as Hunter stood up. I suddenly did not want her to go. Crazy or not, I felt comfortable with her, like she had more in common with me than anyone I'd ever met.

"No, the Priory Hotel," she answered. "It's great. Nice, comfy beds." She told them she was coming, and then turned back to me. "Remember, churches and temples are always safe. Any house of God. They can't follow you in."

To my dismay, she started walking away. I stood up. "Who? Who can't follow you in?"

"Demons," she hissed.

I got a chill down my back. I didn't believe in werewolves or vampires, but demons were another story entirely. The idea of evil personified wasn't too hard to swallow, especially if you ever watched the evening news.

"Demons? Like evil spirits?" I asked.

"No, like hairy beasts with claws and wings. They only look like that right before a kill, though. The rest of the time, they look like humans. Well, super good-looking guys, actually." She looked over her shoulder. The priest and nun were heading back out the door.

"Why do they look like normal guys?"

"Not normal—hot, gorgeous guys," she corrected me. "It's how they gain trust, recruit humans to help them, and move around undetected. Listen, you probably don't have anything to worry about. It's not like they're everywhere. They tend to stay in big cities where their crimes blend in. I have to go. Here." She pulled a pen and scrap of paper out of her purse and scribbled on them. "It's my number. Call me anytime and I can tell you more. Especially if you find something from your mom."

Then she turned and dashed out the door to catch her ride.

❀ ❀ ❀

As soon as Hunter left, the church filled with such an emptiness, it made my ears buzz. I still had to deliver the muffin basket, so I turned sideways and swung my feet up onto the bench so I could see more of the church while I waited. As I scanned the outline of benches, I was startled to see I wasn't alone. A boy about thirteen years old with messy, dark blond curls was sitting in the very last row.

"Hello?" I called out.

He stared straight ahead as if he didn't see me. It was actually hard to see him. He was covered in a light mist that seemed to emanate from his skin. As I squinted to get a better look, he disappeared, slowly fading away in his seat. I rubbed my eyes. He was gone. *Great, another hallucination. At least this one wasn't being murdered by wild dogs in front of me.*

I slunk down to lay across the pew like Hunter had, hoping the new position would shield my obviously overwrought brain from any more imaginary sightings. It felt weird at first, and then strangely comfortable.

I stared straight up at the wooden ceiling and tried not to think about demons, but it was impossible. My mind whirled with images of hairy beasts, my mom fighting them, her "accident" . . . I shook my head. I couldn't go there. Not yet. It was still too raw.

I have never been able to shut my brain off, especially when it's in overdrive, and I was miserable at meditating, but I had to do something. I could feel pent-up emotions—grief, fear, rage—straining to be let out of the box I had locked them in. I remembered reading once that a simple form of meditation was studying an object in front of you. I gazed at the heavy iron and glass lamp hanging directly over my head. I followed the curves with my eyes, tried to stay focused on the rippled panes, but instead found myself wondering if it would kill me instantly if it fell, or if I would survive.

What is wrong with me? I'm trying to clear my head, and all I can think about is my brains splattered on the pew? I must be seriously damaged.

I closed my eyes, took a deep breath, and decided to try again. I opened my eyes and stared upward. Suddenly, the lamp started swaying. I jolted upright like I'd been electrocuted. The priest was standing in front of me.

My heart was pounding, but I quickly determined that the lantern wasn't falling, that the wind probably blew in when the priest opened the door, and that it wasn't a sin to lie down on a pew.

"Sorry to startle you," the priest said. *Why did people keep saying that to me?* I thought. *And why am I so easily startled?*

"No, no, it's . . . I . . ." I had no idea what to say.

"It's fine. We encourage people to use St. Mary and St. Finnan however they like," he said. "I see you're practicing Hunter's 'holy nap.'"

"I wasn't trying to sleep!" I protested.

He smiled. "Och, I know, Maren. I was only joking with you. I'm not sure if you're used to our humor in Scotland yet, but it's a wee bit dry. Quite unlike our weather."

"You know who I am?" I asked.

"Hunter told me your name was Maren, and from your American accent and your lack of a tourist's camera, I can only surmise that you are Maren Hamilton," he answered.

"Small town," I said.

"Quite," he answered. "But that's exactly the way we like it. In any case, I'm very pleased you've come."

"I'm not here for services or anything," I explained. "I'm just dropping off muffins from my grandmother." I handed him the basket.

"That's wonderful. Please thank her for me. And you're welcome here anytime, for Mass or not. We're happy to offer sanctuary to anyone seeking peace."

Sanctuary. How weird that he used that word.

"Can I ask you a Latin question?" I said. I might not be able to get to the library, but maybe the priest could translate the title of my mother's journal. Hunter's warnings were freaking me out.

"Of course." He nodded.

"What does 'Arcēs Daemonium' mean?"

"Well, *arx* is a stronghold or a fortress. And *daemonium* means demon," he said. "So it would be 'demon strongholds.' Why?"

Demons. My stomach dropped.

"Do you believe in demons?" I asked back. "Are they real?"

"I'm afraid so."

I expected that answer from a priest, so I decided to push him a bit. "Have you ever seen one?"

Before he could answer, the peal of church bells echoed

against the walls. He seemed relieved, and wasted no time in making his exit.

"Would you look at that? Late again! It was a pleasure meeting you, young Maren, and I do hope you'll forgive me, but I have to run."

And he practically did.

I was left with the sudden revelation that I had not only seen a demon . . . I had a crush on one.

CHAPTER 10

I pulled into the driveway as my grandfather emerged from the small storage shed in the backyard, carrying a weathered cardboard box. He stopped and waited for me to join him.

"Knickknacks for your gran," he explained. "She said it was safe to bring them out again."

"Safe?"

He carefully ignored my question, set the box down, and removed a bronze, scalloped picture frame from it. It was a photo of a young boy with a pointed collar and shaggy haircut. I'd never seen the boy before, but I recognized him all the same. *It was the boy I saw sitting in the church!*

"He's a little younger than you here, but I'd say you definitely take after him!" my grandfather enthused.

"Who?" I gulped, wanting my grandfather to confirm it.

"Your father, of course," he answered.

My chest seized up. How could I possibly have seen my dad—or his ghost, or whatever that was—when I didn't even know what he looked like at that age? I was almost used to the frightening, futuristic nightmares, but now I could somehow see into the past too? In broad daylight? *What was wrong with me?* I wondered if I was going crazy, or if maybe these were all signs of an early brain tumor or something . . .

My grandfather noticed my shock. "You've never seen a picture of your father at this age, have you?" I shook my head. "Well, it's about time they went back up on the walls," he declared.

"Why?" I sputtered.

"I suppose because we never sent any to your mother," he said, answering only why I'd never seen a photo of my dad before and not why they were locked in a storage shed.

"So you did have a problem with my mom," I challenged. My grandfather glanced away. I rested my hand on his wrist and softened my voice. "Please," I said. "I need to know the truth."

He looked over his shoulder at the house, as if seeking permission. "Yes," he finally sighed. "Your gran . . . I mean *we* were not happy they married."

"Why not?"

"It was very unfair of us, I suppose, but we were afraid . . ." He trailed off. "She recruited him, you know. We didn't want him working for that place, and I guess we blamed her for convincing him. All those secrets, the danger . . ." He clucked his tongue.

I hadn't wanted to believe Hunter about the Abbey, but my mother's demon journal and now my grandfather's admission suggested she was right. *Why was I the only one who thought they just worked for a benign computer company?* I was about to ask how much more he knew when I felt his hand over mine.

"It's not time yet, Maren," he said. "Your grandmother can't cope with it all just yet. We'll talk more soon, I promise, but give her time. These photos are a big step."

I nodded, and he let go of me.

❀ ❀ ❀

Back inside, I couldn't wait to pore over my mother's journals again. I was bounding upstairs when my grandmother stopped me.

"Maren?" she called out from the living room. "Is that you?"

I hesitated on the fifth step. "Yes," I tried not to sound exasperated. And failed.

"You've got a guest."

I turned and shuffled down toward the front room, knowing that Jo or anyone my age would be in the kitchen, and dreading the old person I knew would be sitting in there. Probably a friend of my grandma's, excited to meet me. I didn't feel like playing show-and-tell in front of a stranger for the next hour. I would say hi like a good girl, then beg off to do homework or something.

When I entered the sitting room, I felt as if I'd walked into a brick wall. Gavin was sitting on the couch, grinning at me like we were best friends.

It was almost funny, his muscular body on the peach-colored couch, his rough hands holding a dainty cup of tea. He was wearing his hunting kilt again, and if it was possible, he was even more gorgeous. His eyes danced at my obvious surprise; his smile filled the whole room with light. My grandmother was taken with him as well.

"Look, dear, it's Gavin," she gushed. "Your Gaelic tutor from Kingussie. Isn't it kind of him to stop by on a Saturday?"

I raised my eyebrows at him. *Tutor, huh?*

My grandmother stood up. "I'll leave you two alone."

I couldn't wait to grill him, but not anywhere in the house, where my grandparents could hear us.

"We're actually going to go outside," I stated, carefully not asking permission. "I really need to learn the names of . . . the trees and stuff."

Gavin stood up, locked eyes with me. "I was just going to suggest that," he agreed.

"Alrighty, then." My grandmother shooed us out the front door. "Have a nice time." She was as giddy as if she'd played matchmaker. I marveled that Gavin even had an effect on old ladies.

We scuffed along the loose gravel driveway, clouds of dirt hovering about our ankles. As soon as we were out of earshot, Gavin spun around, his face completely changed. It was sour and dark.

"I hope you're happy now," he scowled. "You got your wish. I'm stuck with you."

I was as offended as I could be at his beautiful face. *Why was it so hard to be mad at him?* Good looks shouldn't get him off the hook for being rude and nasty. Why did I like him? It couldn't just be because he was hot. There was something more. Something magnetic that drew me to him, told me that I was supposed to be with him, that my life wouldn't be the same without him.

I was starting to wish it would wear off.

"Me? This is my house. You're stalking me now, not the other way around," I reminded him.

"I was serious when I told you at the post office to

85

stay away from me, but you couldn't do it, could you?" he practically snarled.

"What? You mean this morning? That was a total coincide . . ." I trailed off, remembering Hunter's view about coincidences. And I had convinced myself while talking to Jo that I'd only dreamed being in the woods.

"Yes, this morning," he confirmed. "What were you doing out there?"

So I hadn't imagined it. It was real! "I was just . . . on my way . . . to the library," I stuttered.

"There's no library in the forest," he said sarcastically. He turned and stomped across the lane. Like an idiot, I followed.

"A tree fell near my car, and I didn't know what to do," I explained. "And you ran past, and I thought . . ."

"You thought what? That I'd rescue you? That's not my job." His eyes were cold, taunting.

A hot wave of anger flushed through my body. Attraction or not, no one was going to talk to me like that. I was done trying to be nice to him. "Yeah, I know, apparently your job is killing innocent people," I spat out.

"What?" He had the nerve to look offended.

"I saw you," I said. "You killed that old guy in the woods. Bertie."

"You think I killed him?" he asked incredulously.

"Um, yeah. The blood sort of gave you away."

"That wasn't Bertie's blood," he said. He looked hurt, and I almost felt sorry for him. But how do you feel sorry for a killer? "I was protecting him," he continued.

"I thought you didn't protect people," I countered.

"I protect people who are being attacked," he explained. "I don't protect daft teenage girls who wander into places they shouldn't."

"Really, I'm daft? Then you're a . . . *gobermouch*!" I shouted at him, pleased I'd remembered an Old English insult I'd learned from watching the History Channel with Mom. Swearing wasn't really my thing, but my blood was boiling. I wished I had the nerve to slap him.

He jerked a little, as if I had actually struck him. "I'm sorry if it seems I'm insulting you," he exhaled, "but I don't know how else to explain it. Your interference got me taken off my mission and put on Guardian patrol. I'm frustrated because I'm a Warrior, not a babysitter."

"Oh, I know what you are." I was seething inside. "You're lucky I don't turn you in to the police."

He raised one side of his lips in amusement. "The police couldn't touch me."

I wanted to wipe the smug smile off his face. "Of course not." I raised my palms in surrender. "I forgot: you're a big, bad demon. No one can touch you. Except you seem aggravated enough by a dumb teenage girl who's not scared of you one bit, by the way."

He looked stunned. "What did you call me?"

"It's all right, I know what you are, but I don't care. For some insane reason, I keep trying to be friends with you anyway. Even though it appears you'd rather slit my throat than talk to me."

He stopped walking, and grabbed me by the arm to stop me as well. His touch was electrifying. "You think I'm a demon?" he asked.

"I don't think, I *know*." I loved having his fingers on me, but I shrugged his hand off and took a step back in defiance.

He started laughing. Not a little chuckle, but a deep-down belly laugh. It sounded like music, but it aggravated me all the same.

"What's so funny?" I demanded.

"Oh that's rich, that's really rich. You think I'm a demon," he chuckled.

"You prefer 'cold-blooded murderer'?"

He wiped his eyes. "I'm no murderer, Maren," he said. "I'm not even allowed to kill humans. And I'm certainly not a demon."

He stopped talking and stared into my eyes like he was trying to penetrate them, to see more deeply inside of me. His blue eyes were like calm water. I wanted to swim in them. I couldn't help myself, but I still wished that he would lean in and kiss me. I more than wished; I prayed for it. His face was sweet again and he looked happy, like he'd figured something out.

When he finally spoke, his voice made my knees weak. "Maren," he said softly, "I *kill* demons. The blood on my hands was demon blood. They attacked Bertie, and I was too late to save him. You saw the demons running away like the pigs that they are, but more importantly, they saw you. That's why I have to guard you now. Until their group leaves the area."

I was confused. I was so sure he was a demon. *If he isn't a demon, what is he?*

"I'm sort of the opposite of a demon, Maren," he said, answering my thoughts. "I'm an angel."

I blinked. Special forces, secret police, even mobster I was prepared for. But an angel?

"You are not," I said.

He looked at me again with a sweet sincerity that seemed almost heavenly. "You don't believe in angels, then?"

"No, I . . . I do. I believe in angels," I said. "But they're just . . ."

"They're just what?" He smiled gently.

"They're all good and perfect and passive," I said. "They're calm and nurturing, and they don't fight!"

"Really?" He raised his eyebrows. "Tell me more."

"Angels are little, and they help you sleep," I said stupidly.

"I think you're talking about fairies, and those *are* fictional." His bemusement was palpable. I wanted to melt into the ground in embarrassment. "You've never seen angels depicted in paintings or on cathedral walls or anything?" The statue of the angel on the side of the church flashed in my mind. "Young men with flaming swords?" he continued. "We figure pretty heavily in the Bible."

He was right, of course. Angels in the Bible were always smiting demons and bringing wrath to the wicked. My heart heaved with guilt. While my mom and I didn't go to church regularly, the Bible was required reading every Sunday morning in our house . . . at least until she died. Babbling about baby angels made it sound like I only got my religion from greeting cards.

"We're not perfect," he said. "We're flawed and we struggle, just like humans. The only difference is we're immortal, and we were created for one purpose: to counteract evil."

Could it be true? Was it even possible? He certainly looked human, although he was insanely handsome. His smooth voice and amazing accent made me want to believe anything he said. He could tell me he was half pumpkin and I'd buy it. I didn't like that he had such sway over me. I didn't want to be gullible just because he was gorgeous. Especially since, as hard as I tried not to, I was falling for him.

I had to know who he really was.

"Prove it," I demanded.

"Prove what?"

"Prove that you're an angel. Fly or something," I said.

He motioned at my grandparents' house. My grandmother was high-fiving the windowpane like a fruitcake. Horrifying.

"I can't exactly just take off in front of her," he explained.

"Likely story," I answered.

"I can take you home with me," he suggested. "Will that work? Will you believe me then? A fighting party went out today that I was supposed to be a part of." He scanned the sky. "I would like to know how they made out."

I had no idea if his "home" would prove anything, but I was dying to see where he lived. If he had a normal house with a normal mom, maybe she could explain his lunacy. Remind him to take his medication . . .

"Sure," I agreed. "Where is it?"

"My clan is here in Scotland," he said.

Angels live in clans? Interesting.

"Why do you live on earth and not in heaven?" I asked.

"Angels were sent to earth to help battle the forces of darkness," he explained, "but as the human race grew, so did their need for protection. So we could be where we were needed more quickly, we set up camp around the world."

"So where is it? This clan of yours?"

"My village is in a valley a few miles from here. In a different dimension, of course, that humans can't see."

"Of course." I nodded. His story was getting more bizarre by the second, but I wanted to see where it was going.

"How do we get there?" I asked.

"We walk."

"Walk? You can *walk* into another dimension?" *How convenient.* He wouldn't be able to prove anything when we *walked* right up to his regular house. Except that he was crazy, and I wasn't. I couldn't believe in the space of an hour I'd gone from liking someone who'd shifted from a murderer to a demon to an angel or possible mental patient. A super-hot mental patient, but still . . .

"Aye," he answered. "As long as you're walking with me. Come on. You'll see."

He spun on his heel, and headed into the woods. I held my hand up and squinted at the house. My grandmother was still in the window. I motioned after Gavin, and she nodded. Gavin seemed to have charmed her out of any parental fears about me hiking into the woods with a strange boy. Cool.

As I followed, I wondered why I wasn't afraid of him. I had seen him that morning, covered in blood. I had no proof he wasn't a killer—*aren't serial killers usually good-looking?*—I had no proof of anything. Yet I was blindly following him into the forest. I hoped my intuition wasn't on the fritz, but somehow in my heart, it felt right. I felt safe with him. Safer than I had ever felt in my entire life.

He was walking much faster than I was, and I had to admit, looked incredibly handsome in his open white shirt and rugged kilt. Walking behind him was no chore. The muscles in his calves flexed with each step.

As I sprinted to catch up, I noticed the handle of a small weapon peeking out from the top of his right boot. *Score one for serial killer . . .*

"You've got a knife?" I asked.

"Och, you've really been looking me up and down today, then," he said. My face caught fire.

"No," I stammered. I hoped he couldn't tell what I'd been thinking. I cleared my throat and tried to recover. "I would just like to know if my 'guardian' is armed and dangerous. Clearly, you're armed."

He stopped so suddenly, I almost ran into him. He swung around and leaned toward me. "And I'm most definitely dangerous," he whispered.

In a flash, he was holding the dagger beside his face. Considering that his face was inches from mine, I was glad to see the blade was covered by a black sheath.

A giant smile broke over his face. If I had freckles, I'm sure they would have melted off my cheeks.

"It's called a *sgian dubh*," he said, pronouncing it "SKEE-in dew."

I couldn't resist. "Can I hold it?"

"Sure." He pressed it into my hand. "Just don't take the blade out."

"Why not?" I turned it over, my stomach fluttering with excitement. It was about twelve inches long from the silver-embossed tip to the amber-colored stone set in the handle.

"Because if the *sgian dubh* is drawn," he answered, "it must taste blood before it can be resheathed. And I would hate to have to use some of yours."

"You're kidding!" I said, handing it back to him, sincerely hoping he was. He restored it to his boot as quickly as he had drawn it. "You would never hurt me . . . right?"

"Of course not," he said. "I would only give your finger the tiniest prick. Wouldn't hurt at all." He winked, then turned and continued walking. "Where'd you get your necklace?" he called out over his shoulder.

"You've really been looking me up and down today, then," I answered. When he chuckled in response, I felt like the luckiest girl in the world. "It was my mom's."

"She worked for the Abbey?" he asked.

My ears pricked up at the mention of the secret agency. "How do you know about the Abbey?" I asked.

"Who do you think helps the humans fight demons?" he asked. "The Abbey was created as a human and angel consortium. Humans can get a lot of places we angels can't, and vice versa. So, your mom worked there?"

"Yeah, and my dad, apparently," I said.

"That explains the attraction," he mumbled.

"The what?" *Does he mean "attraction," like between my parents, or like he is attracted to me?* I could barely contain my excitement at the possibility. I wanted him to confirm, to clarify, to at least say it again. No luck.

"I said, it's no wonder you can't keep your nose in your own business," he replied. "It's in your genes to want to get involved. Good for your folks. It's a great organization."

"Do you work for the Abbey?" I asked, thrilled to be on a little adventure with him, even if it was only to his house.

"I wish. It's only for the most elite Warriors . . ." He trailed off, and I decided to stop talking for a bit. Better not to remind him that babysitting me was keeping him from pursuing his supernatural military career.

We walked for what seemed like a couple of hours, but it was hard to tell which direction we were going. I wondered if Gavin had purposefully walked us in circles to mess me up. I had to give up trying to figure out where we were and trust that Gavin would bring me back. Hopefully alive.

We emerged from the forest onto the edge of a cliff. A sweeping, green valley rippled with sloping hills, all falling away from the tree-topped mountains spread out before us. Thin waterfalls shot out of the rock face and fed fast-moving streams that twisted down to the bottom.

"There." Gavin pointed into the valley.

"Your home is down there?" I asked, rather doubtfully. I couldn't see the bottom. It was completely obscured by fog.

Gavin nodded, still gazing into the distance. "Aye, my village."

"How do we get there?" I asked. "This hill is, like, straight down and covered in rocks."

While the valley seemed green from our vantage at the top, at my feet I saw the sides were actually made of small, flat rocks with bits of emerald-colored scraggly plants somehow growing out from under them.

"It's not rocks," Gavin said. "It's—"

"*Scree*," I interrupted. "The slippery shale that lines the glens is called scree." I instantly regretted how geeky I sounded. *Why couldn't I stop things in my brain before they came out of my mouth?*

"I see you've read your Scottish geography books." He said, seemingly not put off by my being a huge know-it-all. Only I hadn't read any geography books, and I'd never heard of scree before it popped into my head. Weird.

"Why is it called scree?" I asked, trying to redeem myself by proving I didn't have all the answers. "Because of the noise you make when you fall down it?"

"It's from the Old English word for 'slip,' actually," he answered.

"You don't say," I replied, peering anxiously over the side at what could be my imminent death, or at least a lot of ugly scabs.

"You can snow ski, right?"

"Kind of," I answered. Skiing down a big hill into powdered snow was one thing. Hitting rocks that would hurt like heck, if not rip the skin right off me, was another.

"Perfect, because we're going to slide down it rather

quickly, like skiing. All you have to do is stay upright." He reached out his hand. "Are ya ready?"

I probably grabbed his hand a little too eagerly, and as I did, a delicious shock reverberated through my entire body. "R-r-ready," I answered in my best Scottish accent, slightly rolling my *r*. He smiled at my pathetic effort.

"The trick is to just keep going," Gavin said, "and stay a little ahead of the slide."

The first step was beyond scary, because the ground seemed to slip away from under my shoe, but I figured out that as long as I picked up my feet every once in a while to control my balance, and stopped whenever I could, it was actually not too bad. And once I made it halfway down without wiping out, it got fun. The thrill seemed to echo down from the pit of my stomach in a tingly, happy way.

Gavin began showing off, scree-ing backward, and doing little circles around me. "Come on," he laughed. "Give it a good go. Show me what you've got."

He didn't know I'd grown up ice skating on the knobby frozen ponds near my house. If I wanted to, I could deliver a wicked hockey stop. And I wanted to.

I waited until he was in front of me, then dug in for an abrupt, angled skid that sent a shower of rocks spraying over him. He opened his mouth in surprise, and when the deluge stopped, he grinned and spat a pebble out in a tiny arc. I laughed so hard, I thought my sides might split. I couldn't remember the last time I'd actually laughed like that.

"Will ya look at that?" he marveled. "She's happy. Deep down, honest-to-goodness happy to her bones."

I continued to laugh, grateful for the joy that seemed to spread to every part of my body. Joy that wasn't tainted with even the slightest bit of sadness or guilt. *Finally!* I gulped it down greedily.

We continued our rollicking descent until we were enveloped in the cool, speckled fog. The scree ended abruptly, and we hopped onto a grassy path, stumbling for a few steps, and holding on to each other for balance.

"That was amazing!" I breathed.

"Ach, no," Gavin answered. "'Amazing' is just round the bend."

CHAPTER II

Standing in the fog was like standing on another planet. The damp gray engulfed us on all sides, blocking out the sun, giving everything a muted glow. White clouds, perfectly compact and cottony, rolled around our feet and floated past our knees like lost sheep.

As we walked, I lost all sense of direction. I could see we were following a faint path through the grass, but the landscape more than an arm's length away was obscured. The fog also seemed to mute all the sounds of the world. The eerie silence kick-started my serial killer sensor. *Why am I stupidly following a stranger into the mist in the middle of nowhere? If he turned on me, they'd probably never even find my body . . .*

Just as my brain started to peak with panic, his beautiful accent wafted through the air.

"Nearly there," he said, and a warm peace settled over me once again.

A gigantic, flat, sharp-edged column of rock twice as high as me appeared on the side of the path like an ancient signpost. It was shaped like a rounded headstone, with a bit notched out near the top left. The dark, wet stone was speckled with bright orange lichen that curled around an elaborate engraving of a cross.

"Right," he said, "we're about to cross over."

I peered down the path and saw nothing different from where we were standing.

"This is your village?" I asked.

"No, this is just the entrance," he answered. "You won't see anything until we cross over, which you can do thanks to your necklace, and the fact that you're with me."

I was not convinced. "How does this work again?"

He sighed, as if exasperated to have to explain himself to such an idiot. "There are dozens of different dimensions in the universe," he began. "Humans can only experience four: your three-dimensional idea of the world and time. You can enter another dimension with me, but your wee brain—ahem, I mean your *human* brain—wouldn't be able to handle it."

I clenched my teeth as my wee brain exploded with a million insulting comebacks.

"Your Abbey necklace has a touch of angel essence embedded in it that acts sort of like a translator," he continued, "so you can perceive the experience. Make sense?"

Nope.

"Yep," I said.

"I'll just be needing your hand so I can transfer my energy to you, and we're off," he said. He extended his palm to me and waited for my permission.

I slipped my hand into his. Fireworks exploded under my skin. I was ready to pretend I could see his imaginary village just for the thrill of holding his hand, when the necklace suddenly got heavier. And hot.

"What is that?" I asked, grabbing at the pendant with my free hand.

"Nothing to worry about," he assured me. "Just the

necklace working. The sensations will calm down once your body acclimates."

In a few steps, my neck cooled, and the tingling feeling subsided.

I smelled the village before I could see it: wood smoke and something delicious being cooked over an open flame. A few more steps, and the fog miraculously dissipated, revealing a low, stone wall and the straw-topped roofs of small buildings. Men's voices and the sound of children laughing drifted over them.

We turned a corner and found a woman standing in the middle of the path, blocking our way. She had been waiting for us.

Gavin unceremoniously dropped my hand, and galloped up and gave her a big hug. With his arm still around her, he introduced us.

"Maren, meet Rielly."

Rielly was in her late forties or early fifties; I couldn't tell. Her face had the wrinkles of someone who lived and worked outdoors, but there wasn't any gray in the brown hair twisted into an elaborate knot at the nape of her neck. She wore a long skirt made of the same plaid as Gavin's kilt, with an oatmeal-colored blouse, and more plaid wrapped over her shoulder.

I held out my hand. "Nice to meet you."

She took my hand in both of hers, and held it up to her heart. "Och, she's a bonnie lass, ain't she? More beautiful 'an a sunset! You were right, Gav." He blushed. *He told other people about me?* And apparently told them I was pretty? I could have fainted at the revelation.

"You're only missing one thing," Rielly continued. She lifted a thick ring of flowers and ivy gathered together like a fairy crown, and placed it on my head. "Now you're a proper maid! On to the festival!" She started toward the village, and we fell in step beside her.

"There's a festival?" I asked.

"Aye." Gavin smiled. "It's kind of a regular thing around here."

As we walked through the village, it seemed as if we had walked back in time. Every building was crafted entirely of stone, with open rectangles for windows and thatched, grass roofs. Gavin said they were *crofts*, small Highland houses. He explained that unlike demons, angels preferred to live as simply as possible.

My mother would love this, I thought. *She was such a history buff. Although maybe with her secret job, she'd already seen things like this . . .*

The whole village exuded an undeniable peacefulness. I hadn't been there five minutes, and already I felt a heavy contentment. Even though I didn't see any halos or wings, the people we passed were literally glowing with happiness.

Everyone in the village appeared human and was dressed in rustic kilts like Gavin and Rielly. They looked like men, women, and children of all ages, even little babies gnawing on their fists, but there was something ethereal about them, something I couldn't quite put my finger on.

"Is everyone here an angel?" I whispered to Gavin.

"Almost everyone," he whispered back.

An enormous tree trunk stripped of its branches and

bark rose from the center square. It was decorated with long, twisted, blooming vines. Dozens of colored ribbons fluttered in the breeze from the top of the pole, and what looked like little girls danced with them, weaving in and out around each other. I was relieved to see that they had exquisite flower garlands in their hair too. I didn't mind wearing it as long as I wasn't the only one. A group of musicians began playing homemade instruments: skin-covered drums, wooden reed pipes, and handheld harps. The music was so cheerful, I found myself bouncing the tiniest bit as I walked.

Any doubts I had that Gavin was really an angel were disappearing quickly, especially when we met a positively cherubic little girl with a cereal bowl face, light blonde curls, and perfect pink lips. She was unpacking a picnic onto a large woolen cloth. Rielly and Gavin sat down, so I did the same. The blanket held a feast: loaves of bread, cheeses, berries, and even a little crock of butter.

"Angels eat regular food?" I was shocked.

"Of course," the girl replied. She was busy buttering what looked like a scone. "We eat and drink and dance and belch just like you humans do, at least when we're on earth . . ."

"Cassidy!" Rielly scolded.

"Sorry," Cassidy mumbled through a mouthful of pastry, "but it's true!"

"True or not, the Chief wouldn't think very much of your manners," Rielly said.

"The *Chief*?" I asked.

"Aye, the clan chieftain, Hector," Rielly answered.

"He's the most senior angel, sort of like the father of this outpost."

"Father, bother, aunties, panties . . ." Cassidy sang.

I glanced at Gavin and found he was staring at me. Intensely. I stared back. His gaze was so penetrating, I felt vulnerable, but somehow strengthened. I couldn't hear Cassidy anymore, couldn't hear the band. All I could hear was my own thumping heartbeat.

"Right, young lady!" Rielly stood up, and helped Cassidy to her feet. "That's enough out of you. Let's go find you a drink. That mouth could use a fresh rinsing."

The interruption caused Gavin and me to break our gaze. When Rielly and Cassidy were gone, he spoke to the ground. "I apologize for staring at you. I just didn't expect to . . ." He stopped, looked back up, and I felt the same piercing gaze again. "You're not the first girl I've had to play Guardian to." His voice slithered into my ears like a hypnotizing tongue. "I've done this a dozen times, and nothing like this has ever happened to me. I have to keep reminding myself you're only a human."

"I'm not sure I'm following you," I said, my entire body warming up the more he talked, "except that last part sort of sounded like an insult."

He shrugged and looked away. I was not going to let him start brooding. There were too many things I wanted to know about him, and when he was paying attention to me, it was like basking in a warm ray of sunshine. I didn't want the feeling to go away. Ever.

"So, there are other angel villages like this one?" I asked.

"Aye," he said, avoiding my gaze.

"Where?" I pressed.

"There are angel clans spread out around the world: Italy, Russia, Japan, New Zealand . . ." He trailed off, as if he were too bored to continue. I was determined to break him down.

"How long have you been in Scotland?" I asked.

"A long time, but I was just stationed to Aviemore a month ago," he said. He ran his fingertips across blades of grass near his knee.

"How old are you?" I asked.

"Two hundred eighty-three."

"Be serious," I chided.

"I am. Dead serious," he answered, glancing back at me with a look that said he was.

"But you don't look that old. You look like you're my age."

"I've chosen to look this age because it helps with my job," he answered.

"Your job? You mean, rescuing all those damsels in distress?" I said lightly, trying not to reveal how jealous I was at the thought of him spending time with other girls. Even if he was just protecting them.

"No," he said, irritated. "I told you my job is to be a Warrior, not a babysitter." He examined the sky, possibly searching for the returning party. It was obvious he wanted to be anywhere else but next to me. *But why would he talk about me to Rielly?* I was sick of his mixed messages. Why did he like me one minute and detest me the next?

"Right, right," I sulked. "You hate being stuck with me. I get it. Go. Find a sword or something."

A strange look—regret, maybe?—crossed his face. "No, I can't leave you alone," he said.

"I'm sure I'll be fine. We're in a village full of angels, right? What could possibly happen?"

"It's rude," he protested.

"Since when do you care about being rude?"

"I do care," he said, his face reddening. "I'm just not very good at sitting still. Please don't take my restlessness as a sign I don't want to be with you. That's what you're doing, isn't it?"

I bit back a smile, amazed that he'd pinpointed exactly how I was feeling.

"I'm sorry." He lowered his voice to a tender level. "I've been terrible to you. Can you forgive me?" He flashed me a grin that about broke my heart in two.

"Maybe," I said, tucking my legs up under me, hoping he didn't notice I was moving just to distract myself from his perfect lips. "What are you going to do to make it up to me?" I said in what I hoped was a flirty way.

"How about a tour?"

"That could work," I said. Before I could even uncross my legs, he was on his feet, reaching down to help me up. I let him, and thought I might really faint for the pleasure of touching his hand again. Miraculously, once I was standing, he didn't let me go.

"Great!" he said, tugging gently on my hand as he entwined his fingers in mine. "This way."

I looked around nervously to see if anyone was

watching us. *Was he allowed to hold my hand? Would we get in trouble?* Maybe it was just an angel's way of communicating with a friend, although I desperately hoped it meant more to him.

We walked around the village, but I could barely focus on anything. My entire being was concentrated on the four square inches of my skin touching his. I couldn't believe how electric it felt, like our entire bodies were plugged into one another through our hands.

We strode past a small garden, through an overgrown thicket bursting with thistles, and into the woods. We walked for a bit through the forest, and then he suddenly stopped and turned toward me.

"Close your eyes," he said.

"Um, no thanks," I answered.

"Come on," he begged. "Please."

"Why?"

"Just trust me," he said. "You're going to love this."

I looked around. There was nothing but trees as far as I could see. "All right, but don't walk me into anything."

"I promise," he said. "I won't walk you *into* anything."

His emphasis concerned me. "Or through anything," I added.

"No problem. Not into or through. Got it."

I closed my eyes and let him lead me, although I shortened the distance between us to keep from stumbling. Instead of holding his hand, I wrapped my arms around his left one, hugging it close to my chest.

Without sight, my other senses roared to life. The scent of him—woodsy and masculine—filled my nose.

The sound of his breath coming quicker now—*or was that my imagination?*—filled my ears. The movement of his muscles beneath my palms—hard and yet somehow still soft—thrilled me.

The spongey ground beneath my feet hardened in one step, and he instantly swooped out of my grasp and repositioned himself. He was now standing behind me, pressed close, his hands over my eyes. I put my own hands up to his in protest.

"What gives?" I asked.

"Can't have you peeking," he said. "Not when we're so close."

Even though I still couldn't see a thing, I could sense a change in the atmosphere. There was more wind. It made me a little dizzy. I heard the sound of water. A waterfall, I decided. He wanted to show me a secret forest waterfall.

We continued walking for a few paces when, midstep, my right foot still in the air, he tightened his grip on me. "That's enough," he said. "You can open your eyes."

In one swift movement, he let go of my face and moved his hands to my shoulders and squeezed them, almost too tightly. I wondered why he needed to hold me so tight. The wind was stronger now and lapped at my cheeks. I opened my eyes.

I was standing on the very edge of a cliff, staring straight down into the churning water far below. I was leaning forward at an impossible angle, with nothing but air under my body.

I screamed and almost squirmed out of Gavin's grip. My right foot scrambled to settle on hard ground, sending a small cascade of rocks hundreds, if not thousands of feet straight down. *Was this a murder-suicide mission? Did he mean to kill me?*

"It's a'right," he said in his crazy-sexy accent. "I've got you."

Still panicked, I looked down to make sure I was touching some part of the cliff when I saw that his boots, on either side of my feet, were halfway over the edge. But he *was* standing on it. Barely. He was somehow suspending us both with a supernatural strength.

"Relax, Maren," Gavin said in a voice that made it very hard to do anything else. "Enjoy the view."

I took a deep breath and forced myself to lift my eyes from the jagged, jet-black rocks flecked with florescent green that leered up from the swirling water. The sea spread out before me on all three sides. A million shades of blue shone through the water and the sky, making it hard to tell which was which. I felt like I was in the clouds and part of the earth.

"Beautiful, isn't it?" he said. "I just had to show you. Let you feel it the way I can."

Seeing the world from this perspective was both dizzying and wonderful. There was nothing around us. Just open, empty space. Just me and him.

"It's great," I sputtered. "Super fun. But can we reel it back in?"

"Sure," he answered. I felt him flex his shoulder muscles as he straightened up, tipping us away from the edge. He took a step backward, and I practically threw myself off him. My heart was beating so fast that I was shaking, but I realized with amazement that I liked the feeling. It was a good shaking. A thrilling shaking.

I crumpled to the ground, grateful for the warm rock beneath me. "That was not funny, dangling me over the edge like that," I breathed, although I couldn't hide my joy completely.

"Och, it kind of was," he answered, sitting down next to me.

Secure now that I was safe on solid ground, I surveyed my surroundings. The forest behind us ended abruptly, but the cliff continued, a wide-open space floored with large, flat boulders. The smooth rock surface seemed to rise slightly and disappear into the sky.

I scanned the endless horizon. The blues in the sky were beginning to dissolve into dark purple. Small islands seemed to float in the clouds and bob in the ocean at the same time. I felt like the beautiful vista was secretly painted just for us. Sharing the spectacular view with Gavin made me feel special, like I was chosen just for him, and this was "our" place.

"What do you think? Pretty amazing, right?" Gavin asked.

I nodded, still trying to calm down. Being so close to him made it hard. Our bodies were now touching from shoulder to thigh. "It's breathtaking," I said. "But how are we so high? We were just in a valley and didn't really go up a very big hill."

"Scotland's funny like that," he replied. "So you like it?" He was eager for my approval. A good sign that he didn't despise me.

I closed my eyes as the wind swirled past my face. A warm peace burst inside and then settled over me. "I love it. It's like being on top of the world."

He smiled. "I come here whenever I need to think." He paused. "I don't know why, but I wanted you to see it."

"It feels like we're the only two people on earth up here," I marveled.

"Maybe we are."

I turned and found he was admiring me, not the scenery. I stared back, trying to memorize the different shades and shapes of blue in his eyes. After a few minutes, he finally spoke. "Your eyes. They're such a strange color."

"You mean *green*?" I said, not daring to look away.

"No, 'green' is entirely too small a word to describe them."

We sat still, looking at each other. I didn't want to break the silence and hoped he would continue. He did.

"There's a place not unlike this on the northeast coast, called Whaligoe. The sea cliffs drop straight down, but if you know where to look, there are steps carved in the rock—three hundred sixty-five of them—that you can take to the water's edge. Most of the sea around Scotland is dark blue, but down there, at the very bottom of Whaligoe's cove, the water is the most amazing emerald color. It's hard to describe, and I've never seen it anywhere else. Until today. Your eyes are the color of that water."

I was speechless. It was the best compliment I'd ever gotten. He moved his head toward me, and I held my breath. He was about to kiss me. I closed my eyes and waited, but he must have changed his mind, because I felt a small breeze as he pulled away. I opened my eyes and saw that he was lying on his back. I was horrified that I'd misread the signals so badly, but only for a moment, because he put his hand on my shoulder and pulled me down next to him.

"Look at that." He pointed to the clouds above as he kept his arm wrapped around me. I rested my head against his shoulder and decided I might like this even better than making out. Well, maybe not, since I'd never actually made out with a guy, and I was absolutely bursting to kiss him. But it was divine being nestled against him. We watched the clouds roll overhead. They were so low, I thought we might reach out and touch them.

He stroked the hair at my temple, and I fell just a little bit deeper in love with him. I didn't want to move—ever—but I did want to know more about him, this amazing creature under my cheek.

"Tell me about your life," I said. "About your most exciting mission."

"Can't," he said. "It's top secret."

"What about the biggest battle you've ever been in?"

"Nope. Classified."

"Seriously? I won't tell anyone."

"You think you won't, but if you were being tortured, you might think again," he said as he continued casually playing with my hair.

"Tortured? Who's going to torture me? A demon?"

"Can't say. Too dangerous," he replied, adding, "I told you it's not a good idea to know me. For the terrible conversation alone."

"There must be something you can say," I protested. I ran my fingers over his chest, exploring every dip and bulge. I drew a little heart and wondered if he could tell.

"Mmmm," he said, pretending to think about it. "I'm not sure. There are a lot of rules against it."

"There are angel *rules*?" I asked, desperately hoping they had nothing to do with dating a human. "Tell me one."

"I've already told you one: we're not allowed to kill humans."

"Not even bad ones? Not even murderers?" I asked.

"Nope, none."

"What about demons? Can they *not* kill humans too?" I asked.

"No, they can. They have their own set of rules, I'm afraid."

"Are you allowed to kill demons?"

"Of course," he said. "That's sort of the whole point." I wondered how many he had killed. I had a feeling it was a lot.

"Can humans kill demons?"

"Not without supernatural help." He gave my shoulder a squeeze.

"That doesn't seem fair," I mused. "They can kill us, but we can't kill them."

"I haven't found much about evil that's fair," he answered.

"What happens when you kill a demon?" I pressed.

"I really shouldn't be telling you any of this," he reminded me.

"You're helping protect me," I offered. "Knowledge is

power." I cringed inside. I sounded like a cheesy public service advertisement.

"Mmmm," he answered, closing his eyes. I propped up on my elbow to get a better look at him. I hadn't been this close to him while he was still and not watching me back, so I was able to study his features. They were perfectly made, as if chiseled by a great sculptor, which I supposed was true. I wondered if he had been made for me. My soul whispered that he was.

His skin was smooth and radiant. He certainly didn't look like he was more than eighteen or nineteen years old. I wondered if he really was two hundred eighty-three. What would it be like to live so long? How many wars had he seen? How many presidents and leaders and inventions? Did time go more slowly for him since it was endless?

"What's it like being immortal?" I asked.

"What's it like being mortal?" he responded. "I don't have anything to compare it to. I only know what I know."

"But to know you're never going to die? That must be nice."

"Immortals can die," he said, without opening his eyes.

"What?" I was startled. "I thought 'immortal' meant you couldn't die."

"No, it means we can live forever. 'Can' being the operative word. Just like we can kill demons, we can be killed by them."

"What happens when an angel dies?" I asked.

"Same as a human. We go back to heaven."

"And demons?"

He opened one eye and looked at me sideways. "I think you know where they end up."

I laid my head back down on his shoulder. I didn't feel like talking about death or demons any longer. *Way to kill the mood,* I reprimanded myself. "What's another angel rule?" I asked, trying to make my voice lighter.

"The one that applies most readily to you is that a human can only visit an angel village during the day. You have to be gone before nightfall. In fact," he said, shifting his weight and gently removing my head from my shoulder. "We'd better get back."

I sat up reluctantly. I wasn't anywhere near ready to leave. I wanted to stay, to bask in the warmth of his body. I wanted so badly to kiss him. Everything had seemed to be headed in that direction, but now the interlude was over. I wondered if I had messed up my big opportunity with all my questions. *Why hadn't I kept my big, stupid mouth shut?*

He helped me to my feet, and I was relieved to find he kept hold of my hand. At least he still liked me, or was being angel-friendly with me, or whatever.

He led me back into the forest.

"Why do I have to leave by nightfall?" I asked as we crunched along the forest floor. "That seems like a stupid rule."

"I suppose because if it weren't a rule, humans would want to live with angels every time they found themselves in a scrape."

"I guess that makes sense," I conceded. *Although I'd certainly volunteer.*

"Humans are only allowed to stay in angel villages if a

demon legion has locked onto them," he continued, "and there's no other way to keep them safe."

"Has it ever happened here, in this village?"

"Aye. Just once. A girl got mauled by a demon and her Guardian angel found her just after the attack. Since her injuries were supernatural, he brought her back to heal."

"The demons didn't chase them in?" I asked.

"This is sacred ground. Demons aren't allowed here."

"What happened to her?"

"Our healers were able to save her, but she couldn't leave, because the demons were tracking her. Every time she tried, she was hunted down again. She lives here permanently now."

"She's still here?" I asked. I couldn't believe it.

"Of course," he answered. "The village adopted her. You've already met her."

My mind snapped to attention. "Rielly?" I asked.

"Aye," Rielly answered. "The one and only." I looked up and saw she was standing in front of us, waiting for us again. Gavin spotted her too and immediately let go of my hand.

"You're a human girl?" I marveled.

Rielly nodded. "I am—or at least, I was. I don't suppose I'd be called 'girl' now by many."

"Where are you from? How long have you been here?" I had so many questions.

"I'm from Inverness, and I've been here twenty-five years, I think. It's hard to tell when those around you never age," she said, motioning at Gavin.

"Are you the only human here?"

"Why don't you come and help me with some of the

daily chores?" Rielly asked. "That way you can ask me all the questions you want, and we won't bore poor Gavin here to pieces. Gavin, the hunting party has come back. Go listen in on their report."

Gavin looked at me. I had barely nodded for him to go before he was halfway through the yard. *Wow, he wasted no time in getting away from me,* I thought sourly. Just then, he turned back and gave me a crooked smile. Our eyes locked, and my heart jumped.

Rielly and I crossed to the western side of the village and approached a croft. It was much more open than the others I'd seen so far: only three sides were walled, the roof slanted away from the front, and inside, the space was filled with high tables, pottery of all shapes and sizes, and food.

"So, angels don't just eat at festivals then?" I asked, looking at the crocks of ground wheat and root vegetables.

"Yes, they eat, they drink, they dance, and all the rest of it as wee Cassidy explained." Rielly began organizing bowls and crudely carved spoons. "When they are on earth, angels are like humans in almost every way, except they have supernatural powers, and they can't be killed by mortals."

"Well, why don't the angels just kill all the demons and be done with it?" I asked. "Rid the earth of them. Isn't that what they're supposed to do?"

"It's not quite that simple," Rielly replied, taking a wooden pitcher from a shelf, and pouring what looked like milk into a knee-high, narrow cylinder that sat nearby on the dirt floor. "There are a lot more demons than you might think. When Lucifer was cast out of heaven, he took a third of the angels with him."

"A third?" I said. "How? How did he convince them?"

"Evil is contagious," she answered simply. I had never really thought about it that way, but it did make sense.

She continued, "Since demons are fallen angels, they are physically weaker than angels, so demons avoid open conflict with good because they know they will lose. Even a young lad like Gavin would slice a demon in two soon as look at him. Demons would rather mess with humans."

I felt a ripple of pride for Gavin, hearing him praised by someone else.

Rielly stopped talking, and looked at me strangely for a minute. Then she shook her head as if to deflect an annoying insect. "Here," she said, directing me to sit on a small stool next to the bucket of milk. She covered it with a donut-shaped wooden disk and shoved a stick in the hole. She motioned for me to move the stick up and down, which I did.

"Is Gavin really two hundred eighty-three?" I asked. "How is that possible? I thought Gavin said angels didn't age."

"They don't, not really," Rielly replied. "They're created, but as baby angels, sent to live with other angels to learn the ropes." *I was right!* I thought, remembering Gavin mocking my belief about baby angels. *Well, sort of . . .*

"That's why you see the younger angels around here. They're all apprenticing, as it were. Once they reach a certain level of maturity, they get their assignment—Guardian, Warrior, Governor, Record Keeper, Messenger—and choose the human age appearance that best suits their job."

"What about Archangel?" I asked, trying to prove I had a least some knowledge of heavenly hosts.

"Archangel isn't an assignment," Rielly replied, "it's a promotion."

I wondered if it was Gavin's goal, to be an Archangel, and why he was so devastated at being demoted. Because of me.

After what seemed like hours of pounding the wooden stick, Rielly lifted the lid of the bucket and showed me the results: a light-yellowish cream.

"Butter?" I asked, crinkling my nose involuntarily at the not-so-fresh smell.

"Very good," she answered.

She lifted the bucket with one hand, and deftly emptied the gooey butter into a larger wooden barrel. She poured wax over the top of the spread, and then used a rock to pound the tight-fitting lid in place. She wrapped the barrel in rope both horizontally and vertically, flipping the two-foot-high tub as if it weighed nothing, even though it had to be over fifty pounds. When she was finished looping and tying the rope, I saw she had woven two even handles, one on each side. She slipped a long, thick stick through the loops.

"Grab on," she commanded.

I stepped forward and lifted my end of the stick, as she did the same. The barrel was crazy heavy.

"Where are we taking it?" I asked.

"To the bog," she answered.

CHAPTER 12

By the time we finally stopped walking, my arms were shaking with exhaustion. As we set the barrel down, I began vigorously rubbing above my elbows.

"Do you do this every day?" I asked Rielly.

"Aye, and usually by myself," she answered. "You'd be surprised how strong you are when you have to be."

"So this is the bog," I said, looking around. I'd learned about the famous Scottish bogs in my Rural Studies class at Kingussie, but actually seeing one up close, I wasn't impressed. Our teacher told us they were like swamps that could suck you down like quicksand, but all I saw in front of us was wet grass and mud.

"'Tis," Rielly said. "The bog itself is technically outside of the village boundaries, but it's the nearest one, and we need it."

"What do we do now?"

"We bury it."

"By the bog?" I asked.

"*In* the bog."

"Why?" I asked.

"Keeps the butter nice and cold. Preserves it for, well, for forever, if I fancied a guess."

I realized that they didn't exactly have refrigerators in the village, or electricity. I also noticed we didn't have anything to dig with.

"How are we going to bury it?" I asked. "I'm assuming,

as humans, we can't walk over there, and besides, we don't have a shovel."

"No need." Rielly smiled. She untied the rope we had used to carry the barrel and fastened it once around the barrel's middle. She laid the end of the loose rope on the ground at her feet, lifted the barrel over her head like a comic strip character, and heaved it into the bog. It fell with a resounding *thunk* about three feet away, stuck in the mud, but definitely quite above ground.

"Um, that's it?" I said, trying to hide how her super strength scared the crap out of me. "It just sits there?"

"Watch," Rielly replied, picking up the rope's end. Suddenly, the bog hissed. A large bubble of mud at the base of the barrel popped. Other bubbles formed, grew, and then exploded with a sloppy sigh. Each bubble's demise seemed to suck the barrel down into the mud. In just a few minutes, the barrel was half gone, and sinking noisily.

"How deep is the bog?" I asked.

"Several miles, I would expect," she answered. "No one really knows. Deep enough to suffocate a man. Or hide a body." I glanced at her to see if she was kidding, but she looked serious enough. "But the butter isn't heavy enough to go down too far."

She was right. When the barrel had disappeared, there was still a good bit of rope left at Rielly's feet. The last bubbles burped over the butter's muddy grave. The bog was still again. You would never know there was anything buried right in front of us, and even if you saw the rope, you might not think anything of it. I wondered what or who else was in that bog.

Once Rielly was certain the rope had stopped moving, she tied a large knot in the end and laid it back on the ground. She gathered stones and arranged them in a pyramid around the rope knot. I assumed this was to help with future butter reconnaissance.

I found I was extremely comfortable with Rielly. Even though she was older than me, she was a human wrapped up in this supernatural situation, which gave us more in common than anyone else since I'd met Hunter. I felt like we had bonded, and we were becoming closer every minute.

So I was surprised when she turned and said in a strange, almost accusatory voice, "You can't fall for him, you know. He's not like us. He's a different race."

A jolt jogged down my spine. I knew she was talking about Gavin, but it was mortifying to be called out so bluntly.

"I'm not falling for him," I protested.

"Well, he's falling for you," she replied. "I see the way he looks at you. His judgment is clouded. It can't happen."

"Why not?" I said, a little defensively.

"Angels are sworn to protect humans. To do that, they must stay objective. Enhanced emotions can compromise the safety of the very people they were created to save. Loving you could kill him, get you killed, or worse." *There is something worse?*

"How?" I said. "He's immortal, and I'm just a human. You said so yourself: humans can't kill angels. Even demons are pretty bad at it."

"You're forgetting that angels, like humans, have free will. If he wanted to, he could choose to abandon his powers. Stop being an immortal."

"Why would he do that?" I asked.

"For love. The same reason most of us do stupid things," she snorted. "If an angel falls in love with a human, the only way they can be together is for the angel to give up everything and become human. The result is the opposite of happiness—it's heartbreak."

"How do you know?"

"Because it happened to me," she answered.

I clamped my teeth together to keep another question from slipping out, hoping that if I was silent for a change, Rielly would just keep talking.

"When I came here, I was your age," she said. "Once I recovered from my injuries, I was so grateful that Colin—he was my Guardian—had saved me. But after a month, I got so lonely. I missed my family. I missed my mum. I even missed arguing with her, if you can believe it."

I could, actually, since I missed every single thing about my mom. But I'd already lost mine. I wasn't sure I'd be entirely unhappy to live among angels forever . . .

"Colin was so sweet to me," Rielly continued, "making sure I had everything I needed. Keeping me company. Making me laugh. He was so handsome, and his laugh . . ." She trailed off, and I realized she was talking about Colin in the past tense.

"So what happened?" I asked, unable to contain myself any longer.

"We fell in love," she answered. "We broke all the

rules, and fell hopelessly in love. He gave up his angelhood and became a human, so the Chief gave us permission to marry." She stopped talking again, and I could tell she was remembering a very special day. I tried not to picture Gavin dressed and waiting for me as my groom, but it was hard.

"Then what?" I asked, more to interrupt my own thoughts than hers.

"He had a hard time adjusting to being a human, to being so powerless. After a thousand years of fighting demons, just hunting rabbits in the hills wasn't enough for him. He didn't have his powers, but he still had the pull. He watched as his clan mates went out on missions, and he felt helpless. Angels aren't used to feeling helpless like humans. We're well aware of our fragility, but for him, it was new, and terribly hurtful.

"One day, he just snapped. He couldn't take it anymore, so he joined a war party even though he was only a human." She stopped, and when she spoke again, her voice was quieter, remorseful. "He was killed, of course."

"I'm so sorry," I whispered.

"I was too. I blamed myself, and believed my heart would never heal. But God gave me a son, my Caedon, and I realized my job was to raise him to be a credit to his father, not weep for myself. And we'll be together again in heaven someday. That I know."

I wished I felt that same calm and acceptance about my mom's passing. I wondered how long it took Rielly to find her peace.

I opened my mouth to ask another question, but before

I could manage a syllable, a familiar voice came screaming toward us.

"Riiiiiiiiellyyyy!" It was Cassidy. She ran up to us, her tiny face tense with the importance and urgency of her message. "You must come quick! They just got back, but there was an injury . . ."

Before Cassidy could explain anything else, Rielly was running back toward the village.

"Maren, look after Cassie," she called to me over her shoulder. "She'll lead you back."

I stood motionless for a moment, watching Rielly disappear. Then, I felt a small, cool hand in mine. Poor Cassidy looked terrified.

I squatted down on my knees. "What happened, sweetie?"

"One of the party came back awfully bloody. I don't think he can even talk," she said.

"But why did you call for Rielly?" I asked.

"Because," she answered, her bottom lip quivering, "the bloody one is Caedon."

❀ ❀ ❀

As I walked through the village, hand in hand with young Cassidy, I could immediately feel how the mood had changed. The flowers and garlands that were draped over everything blew mournfully in the wind, lonely reminders that there had once been a happy festival, but it was now over.

I looked around and saw that the few angels not in

the "Healing Hut" with the injured Caedon were either on their way to it or rushing away from it to fetch something.

Only the younger angels remained, still skipping about the grassy village center, swishing bloom-covered sticks like magic wands or swords. If any of them beside Cassidy knew about the accident, they didn't show it. They giggled, chased each other, and rolled around in the dirt as if it were still the happiest day of their lives.

That's because it is, I realized. When you're little, every day is a happy day. Everything is easier. You don't even know how to worry. I wondered at what age stress and fear and self-doubt started to creep in. It was certainly well before seventeen . . .

Cassidy let go of my hand and ran off to join the fun. I sat on the grass and watched until a little angel with chestnut curls, who looked about four years old, wandered up to me. She held out a fistful of tiny daisies.

"Hi," I said. "What's your name?"

"Here," she said. When I took the flowers, she sat down next to me.

Without even thinking about it, I began to make a daisy chain: tying the stems into a circle, slipping a new flower through the loop, tightening it, and starting again. In no time, I'd made a pretty necklace. I put it over the little angel's head, and her face lit with delight.

I was happy to feel useful, even if it only meant making flower chains; and soon I had sticky, green fingers and a group of tiny admirers. Before long, we were all covered in necklaces, bracelets, rings, crowns, and even blooming anklets.

From where the little angels and I sat, there wasn't a trouble in the world. *If only that was true,* I thought.

I have no idea how long I played with the angels, but I could have continued for hours more. I sent a message to Rielly asking if I could do anything, and heard back that my entertaining the little ones was an enormous help, and to stay put. I was prepared to do just that until forever, but the way Gavin came sprinting across the grass with his forehead twisted in knots told me otherwise.

"Maren!" he called. "We've got to get you home!"

"Why?" I asked. "What's wrong?" I noticed the sky was a little darker, and my imagination instantly got the best of me. "Are the demons coming here?" I asked, my voice cracking a little.

I was determined to appear brave to Gavin, but my eyes double-crossed me and started to fill with tears. He was beside me now, and placed a hand gently on my cheek. He looked into my eyes and lowered his voice.

"I'm sorry, I've given you a fright. Some Guardian I am! First I forget about you, now I've made you cry." He clucked sympathetically. "I told you, this is sacred ground. Demons aren't allowed here. But we've got to get you home. The sun's almost down, and your grandparents will be worried sick."

His strength and calm comforted me. I couldn't believe I'd practically burst into tears. I must have been more affected by the stress of the day than I thought. And *I* was perfectly safe. I guiltily remembered not everyone was.

"Caedon, is he going to be okay?" I asked.

"Yes," he assured me. "And I'll tell you all about it

on the trip. But I'm afraid there's no longer any time for walking. We're going to have to fly."

"You mean, like, fly with wings?" I said, wiping at my eyes. "But you don't have any."

"Of course I do," he said, pretending to be hurt. "How can you even say that to me? It's . . . it's crushing!" We were flirting or *something* again. And I loved it. It made the blood race extra hot through my veins.

"Are they invisible? Can't be seen by the human eye?" I teased.

"You can see them," he answered. "You just *haven't* seen them yet. It's a rare treat, you know, getting to see an angel's wings. Not many humans do."

"Let's have it, then," I said. "Let's see these big, fancy wings of yours."

If our playful banter hadn't made me forget my fear, the sight of Gavin removing his shirt did. In one fluid move, he pulled his tunic over his head and stood before me bare chested. As I stared at his muscle-covered body, he started to shrug his shoulders, and I noticed he was clenching his jaw a little. I heard a rustling sound, and then two giant wings exploded out of his back. When he flexed them out to their full width, a small pocket of wind rushed past me, like warm breath on my face. I was dumbstruck.

"Well?" he said, turning a bit from side to side, like a boy showing off his moves in gym class. Each wing was at least five feet across, and covered in rows of glistening white feathers. The feathers were small and tightly packed near the arched curve at the top, and then gradually grew bigger until they were each longer than a foot. I squinted to see if they were actually laced with sparkles, or just so shiny they reflected even the tiniest bit of light. I couldn't tell, but I could easily see that he was seriously stunning from every single angle.

He held out his white tunic. "Wrap this around your shoulders. It can get cold up there." I did as he suggested, shivering not at the anticipated drop in temperature but at the realization that the cloth that had just caressed his body now hugged mine. His shirt was soft, and still warm from his body heat.

"All right," he commanded, walking closer to me. "Let's be having you."

To my simultaneous delight and horror, Gavin swooped my feet out from under me and cradled me against his spectacular chest. I wrapped my arms around his neck, as he pressed me against his bare skin. It was the closest I'd ever been to a guy, the most I'd ever touched or been held by someone since I was a child, and my body sang in response. He was warm, soft, and strong—a heavenly combination. I felt like I was at home in his arms.

"Hold on," he whispered. He began to run. Feeling his muscular body working under me was exhilarating. As he ran, the rhythm was smooth, not at all jerky or awkward. Like our bodies were meant to fit together.

I was expecting him to float or at least flap upward, but we took off like a jet plane, him gaining speed until a swift jump sent us soaring at an angle. In seconds, we were cruising over the treetops.

When he moved his wings, it was slowly but powerfully,

and I could feel his chest muscles flexing with the effort. I peeked over his shoulder and looked at them. His wings sounded like a heartbeat every time they opened. The rhythm was soothing. I pressed my head back against his chest. I heard his actual heartbeat and found that it matched the beating of his wings.

After a few blissful minutes, I looked down and recognized the landscape as the area near my grandparents' house.

"We're almost back, and you promised you'd tell me how Caedon got hurt," I said quietly, hoping my question wouldn't upset him.

"Killing a demon," he answered simply. Too simply. If that was all that had happened, there would have been more celebration in the village.

"I thought it was really hard for humans to kill demons," I said. "So that's good, right? I mean, one less demon . . ."

"Aye, but there's also one less girl."

"What do you mean?" I asked, alarmed.

"The party was chasing the demons that killed Bertie, but a girl got in the way. I told you this was a dangerous business."

"What do you mean, a girl 'got in the way'?" I asked.

"One of the demons grabbed some girl who was out hiking and started flying away with her. The girl wasn't about to let the demon have her, so she jumped."

"*What?*" I said, arching my back and causing Gavin to readjust his grip on me. "She jumped and she fell and she *died*?" I could hear the panic in my own voice.

"Sometimes it happens, Maren," he said, holding me

tighter. "But I promise, it will never happen to you. Never to you."

I closed my eyes and tried not to picture a girl my age falling to her death, jumping on purpose to escape the claws of a demon. I wondered if I could ever be that brave.

My body jerked and my eyes shot open, like when you dream you've fallen and the impact wakes you up. My heart was racing.

I was lying on my own bed.

What happened? How was I back in my bedroom? Where was Gavin? I had been flying with him just a second ago, talking to him about demons and the girl . . .

The entire thing must have been a dream. An elaborate, detailed, heartbreaking dream from the troubled mind of a teenager living a nightmare.

I did a quick mental check: I was in my new attic bedroom in Scotland, my own mother was still dead, and I was having crazy hallucinations about gorgeous angels saving me. Yep, I was officially in hell.

Then I saw a garland of fresh flowers with ribbons sitting on the seat of the armchair. The same garland I had been wearing in Gavin's village.

So maybe this was just purgatory.

CHAPTER 13

"What's wrong, Maren?" Jo asked.

We were sitting in the science lab at school, getting ready for our first field trip. I had hoped for a trip to a theater or an old castle, but instead we were getting a muddy hike through the moors. I wanted to tell her about my strange trip to the angel village the day before, but I still wasn't convinced it had really happened.

"Nothing, I'm just not sleeping well," I assured her.

"Oh," she said, bending down to fasten the clips on her Wellington boots. "That makes sense. You do look tired."

"I agree, Jo," Elsie said, shimmying onto a stool next to us. "Maren does look knackered. Like your boots."

"What's wrong with my boots?" Jo asked, struggling to close the rusty buckle on her cracked, dull brown boots. Most of the girls were wearing shiny, knee-high, slip-on Wellies with bright, designer colors and patterns. I felt guilty about my new black-and-beige plaid-covered ones, but I didn't have older brothers to hand me down stuff like Jo, and I wasn't going to tape garbage bags over my tennis shoes like my grandfather had suggested.

"Everything," Elsie answered.

"What's wrong with your boyfriend?" I asked Elsie, smiling innocently but knowing I'd hit a nerve, because as much as she wanted him to be, Anders wasn't anyone's boyfriend.

"What?" she practically spat at me.

Stuart joined in, as I noticed he always did to defend Jo. "Yeah, where's Anders? Is he sick or something?"

"Anders and I are not exclusive, not that it's any of your business," Elsie fumed. "And he's at a funeral with Graham. They had a death in the family this weekend."

"Oh, it's not that girl from Culloden Academy, is it?" Jo asked.

"What girl?" I said.

"Some girl died hiking yesterday," Stuart answered. "They found her body at the bottom of the cliffs. She must have fallen."

A wave of nausea rolled over me as I remembered Gavin telling me about the girl who jumped to her death to escape a demon. That decided it—my trip to his village must have been a dream, because that's how my nightmares worked: I dreamed that someone died, and they did. My gran must have put the flower crown in my room, and I saw it before I fell asleep, and it ended up in my dream too. A part of me was relieved, but a bigger part was disappointed.

"No," Elsie answered. "It was their uncle or something who died."

Mr. Drackle, our Rural Studies teacher, poked his head into the room and shouted, "All right, people, let's queue up. The motor coach is leaving!"

❀ ❀ ❀

After a thirty-minute ride, we disembarked in a lush, green, but very soggy valley. Mr. Drackle had given us brown paper bags and checklists of things we had to do or find. A lot of people groaned, and I heard a few comments about how scavenger hunts were lame, but I thought it sounded like fun—more fun than sitting in a classroom with a textbook, anyway.

We had to find thistle, blaeberry, bedstraw, and butterwort (thankfully, we had pictures of them, or I'd fail hopelessly), a piece of granite, and a sandstone pebble. We needed to identify one animal print, and do a pencil rubbing of at least three different textured surfaces. Extra credit would be given for sketches of anything bearing historical importance.

I was behind in every one of my classes and desperate for extra credit, so Jo and I started out for a small stone building first. Elsie, Stuart, and a couple of other boys seemed to have the same idea.

Once we arrived at the roofless structure, everyone started climbing it, shifting rocks and causing damage to the already crumbling walls. Jo did a cartwheel off a corner.

"What is everyone doing?" I asked her when she landed.

She shrugged. "Just faffin' about."

"But won't you get in trouble? Aren't these, like, national treasures?"

"They're just old crofts," Jo replied. "They're everywhere. No one cares much about tiny stone huts."

I was amazed. In America, you couldn't even breathe near a historical anything, and our stuff was only a couple hundred years old at the most.

We followed a faintly worn path through the valley,

which rose and fell along hills studded with prickly plants and purple thistle. I looked up at the bright, cloudless sky and almost ran right into Stuart. He'd stopped to make a pencil rubbing on a flat stone that was, almost impossibly, taller than him. As the lead danced across the paper, it traced a shape I recognized.

"What is that?" I stammered as he removed his paper, revealing the Celtic cross-engraved signpost I'd seen with Gavin. Or thought I'd seen, anyway.

"That, ladies and gentlemen, is perhaps one of the most famous remaining Pictish stones," Mr. Drackle said, almost wheezing with excitement. "Left behind by the Pict tribe, believed to have been named such by the Romans for their elaborate blue, full-body tattoos. You'll all know this towering specimen is called the Maiden Stone, but does anyone know why?" He wisely didn't stop to wait for an answer. "Legend has it that a young maiden bet her hand in marriage that she could bake a bannock—"

"A plate of scones," Jo whispered in translation for me.

"—faster than a handsome stranger could build a road to the top of a local mountain. He won, of course, because he was the Devil disguised. She ran away, praying, and God turned her to stone for her safety. That missing piece is where the Devil grabbed her shoulder as she fled."

The fact that my teacher had a demonic story about the familiar stone confirmed it for me, along with the fact that there was no sign of a village: I had dreamed the entire thing. As I walked past the stone, my head started pounding, and I wondered if déjà vu was supposed to hurt so badly.

The farther I got from the cursed artifact, the quicker the pain subsided. While the class spread out all over the valley, our group followed Elsie toward a marshy bit to seek out the flower specimens.

We were still about thirty yards away from the murky, standing water, when suddenly my boot sank in invisible mud. It was like stepping off a small ledge; one minute I was walking on seemingly normal ground, and the next, the ground gave way. I looked down and saw that my entire left foot had disappeared in the earth, which had greedily closed in around my boot at the ankle. It was so weird; the right foot was standing on a piece of ground that looked exactly like the spot where my left foot was now submerged.

While I stared at the mystery that was my buried foot, the mud must have congealed or turned super sticky, because when I tried to lift my foot out, it wouldn't budge.

I couldn't believe my foot was really stuck. In a heroic act of idiocy, I tried to pretend it wasn't and just walk forward, and almost ripped my leg off. I caught my balance just before I fell and did any serious damage.

"Hey, Stuart!" I yelled.

He turned and saw me standing unevenly, one foot set deeper than the other.

"Och, you've found the bog then!" he hollered. He whistled for the others, and then walked back to me.

"This isn't the bog," I said, pointing ahead to where the ground actually was all muddy and wet. "That is. This is just dry ground."

"Then where, might I ask, is your left foot?"

"I must have stepped in a little hole or something," I replied.

He stopped in front of me and smiled. "Then step out," he said, crossing his arms across his chest.

"I tried," I answered. "I can't. My boot's stuck."

"That's because you've stepped in the bog," he said. "Here, put your hands on my shoulders. Let's get you out of the boot, and then we'll get the boot out of the bog. They'll never come out together."

I did as he said and eased my foot out of my boot, then hopped one-legged over to Jo. Stuart bent down, twisted my Wellie, and then with both hands yanked it upward. There was a loud sucking sound as the ground resisted, but he was able to free my shoe from its underground prison. He placed it on solid ground next to me with a small flourish. The bottom half of the boot was covered with a light tan mud that dried the second it hit the air. I stepped back into it and thanked him.

"My pleasure," he said, bowing exaggeratedly.

Elsie came stomping up. "What's the hold up?" she demanded.

"Maren just met the bog," Stuart said.

"Don't you know to watch where you step out here?" she said, disgusted, before stomping off. I couldn't believe a girl who looked like Scottish Barbie was advising me on hiking.

"I know the bogs are deep," I said, "but I thought that was the bog over there."

"The bog is everywhere," Stuart said.

As we all continued our walk toward the obviously *wet*

bog, I tested each step with my toe before I committed to it. This slowed me down a lot, but Stuart hung back with me.

A bank of mist started to roll in, blocking the sun and giving the whole area a spooky feel.

"This is so weird," I said to Stuart. "Does the mist always just come in like this, out of nowhere?"

"Yeah, especially over the bog," he intoned. "The bog is no joke. People have used it for centuries to hide their dirty deeds."

"What do you mean?"

"Like their dead bodies. Dump one in the bog, and no one will ever be able to find it."

"You're making that up," I said.

"No, I swear, there's no bottom to the bog," Stuart said, "and the police can't skim it or anything, so the bodies stay sunk forever. Well, not forever. Every couple of years, it'll spit a body back up for no reason and everyone will go *doo-lally*."

"This is total fiction," I said.

"It's true," he protested. "*National Geographic*'s done tons of documentaries about bog bodies, because the chemicals in the peat preserve 'em like mummies."

I did remember an article about mummified bodies, when scientists discovered some ancient dude in the ice in Greenland. *Maybe he isn't pulling my leg.*

Satisfied he had my attention, he continued. "A few years ago, a body popped out of the bog that they decided had been in there forty years. So the police started looking through all the missing persons reports from back then. They found that this local lady had disappeared, without a trace, and they went and visited her husband. They told this old man they'd found her body, and he went crazy, thinking she had come back to seek her revenge. He confessed to everything—that he had killed her and thrown her body in the bog."

"That's awesome," I said. "She got him back."

"It's even better than that," he said, "because after he was in jail, the forensics guys figured out the body was actually four hundred years old, not forty. He confessed for no reason."

"No way," I said.

"'Tis true," he answered. "You can ask anyone. The bog is to be feared. Beware the bog."

"Beware the bog?" I said.

"Aye, beware the bog."

❁ ❁ ❁

"What are we looking for, again?" Elsie asked, clearly sick of wading through the wet grass and mud. We'd been wandering the moors for two hours, and still hadn't found half of the things on our lists. Most of the class was scattered around the bog's edge now, including Mr. Drackle.

"What are you missing?" he asked Elsie.

"I can't find the blaeberry," she whined.

"Ah, the noble blaeberry," he said. "Also called blackhearts in the nineteenth century. Has anyone read Thomas Hardy's *The Return of the Native*?"

Elsie rolled her eyes and turned away. No one else answered, but as teachers are fond of doing, he continued talking anyway.

"Smashing book," he continued. "Features black-hearts, of course."

I wanted to walk away, but everyone else beat me to it, and I found myself stuck standing in front of Mr. Drackle alone. I smiled and tried to listen politely.

"Did you know, Maren, that blaeberries are believed to improve night vision?"

I shook my head. "In World War II, the Royal Air Force pilots were required to eat a half pint of blaeberry jam every two days in preparation for night missions."

Jo appeared at my elbow. "Sorry, Mr. Drackle, but I need to steal Maren. We've partnered up, and I think I've found our phyllite rock."

"Well done. You know phyllite is commonly found at the base of cliffs, while slate makes up the scree on the sides . . ."

I kept smiling as Jo dragged me backward. Mr. Drackle didn't stop talking even while he strode in the opposite direction to find new listeners.

"Thanks," I said. "I couldn't get away."

"I noticed." She flashed her famous upside-down grin.

"Did you really find phyllite?" I said.

"No, but we'd better. I need an A to keep up my average."

I got a strange whirring feeling in my brain, and I stopped walking.

"What is it?" Jo asked.

"I just had this crazy sensation . . . like I've been here before."

"Like in a dream?" she asked.

"I guess so," I said, trying to sort myself back into the present.

Maybe I had the weird feeling because Mr. Drackle had said "scree," and I was standing by a bog like I had with Rielly in my dream. If it was a dream. *Why do I have to have such detailed dreams?* I was sure a normal girl could easily tell when she was dreaming and when she wasn't.

Jo continued her search while I scanned the valley. I wasn't paying attention to where I was walking, and I tripped over a small pile of rubble.

Jo turned back at the noise.

"Sorry," I said. "I just ran into some rocks."

"Are they the kind we need?"

"Oh, good question. Let me check."

She came over, and together we uprooted the plants around the little mound so we could see it better. Once the brush was cleared, it looked like the rocks were set on top of each other to purposefully make a pyramid. I froze. *Is it possible?*

I started throwing the rocks, digging to get to the bottom.

"Hey!" Jo said. "You're tossing rocks before you're even looking at them."

I stood up. My dismantling had revealed a large knot of rope.

"What is that?" Jo said. She grabbed the knot and tugged. The rope popped out of the dirt and led away from us, leaving a small trench behind. We could now see that it ran all the way into the wet bog and disappeared.

"Hey, Stuart!" Jo called. "Come here!"

Before I knew it, the entire class had gathered around us. Mr. Drackle was directing as the strongest boys heaved on the rope, trying to drag whatever it held out of the bog. I knew exactly what they'd find.

"It's a barrel!" Stuart said, when it was finally dragged to dry ground and could be inspected. "What do you think is in it?"

People started throwing out guesses. "Gold," someone said. "Mud." "Body parts."

"Butter." The word popped out of my mouth before I could stop it. Everyone stared at me.

"Butter?" Elsie said. "What the—"

"Ah, yes!" Mr. Drackle interrupted. "Bog butter! She's right. It could very well be. In ancient times, the Highlanders used to store their butter in the bogs, an early form of refrigeration. We might have a true historical discovery here, class! No one touch it. I'm going to call the news station." He pulled out his cell phone. "Fantastic find, Ms. Hamilton."

It had actually happened. I had been with Gavin to his village. I had been to the bog with Rielly. Images of curly-haired angels and bloody demons and a dead girl flooded into my head. I couldn't deal with talking to the media.

"It wasn't me," I blurted out. "Jo found it."

"Splendid!" he said. "I'm sure they'll want to interview her!"

He put his finger in his ear, as if his own excitement was causing him to lose his hearing, and walked away chattering into his phone.

"Why'd you say I found it when it was you?" Jo whispered to me.

"I just want you to get your good grade," I said. "I don't care."

She gave me a tight hug. "You're a crackin' good friend! You really are!"

I knew "crackin" was a synonym for "super," but all I could think about when I heard the word was the girl from Culloden falling to her death.

I didn't know yet that there were worse things than cracking your head open. Much worse.

CHAPTER 14

When I got home from school, I burst into my room, anxious to find the flower garland I'd left on the armchair. I nearly dropped my books in surprise. Gavin was sitting on my bed.

"Crap, you scared me!" I said, my entire body warming at the sight of him again. He glowed with gorgeousness.

I conjured every ounce of restraint I had to stop from jumping onto his lap. He was real. Our trip, his village, the secret place at the top of the world, flying back home . . . it had all happened. He was live, in the flesh, sitting on my crocheted bedspread, waiting for me.

"Wait, how did you get in here?" I tried to sound casual to cover my elation.

"You left the window open." His tone was serious. I wondered if he was going to chide me for neglecting my safety.

"Did you see my grandparents?" I asked, to remind him I didn't live alone. I also wasn't sure if they would care I had a boy in my room, but I didn't want them to tell me I couldn't, either.

"They're not here," he said. "But don't worry. I can't stay long. I only came to say good-bye." For the first time, I noticed he wasn't smiling.

"Good-bye?"

He must have seen my face fall, because his own darkened with pain. He waved his hand, as if trying to physically change the mood in the room. "It's good news, really. The Warrior party successfully chased the demons out of the area. There's no more threat to Aviemore, or to you." He attempted a half smile. "You're rid of me."

Doubt cast a shadow over me. Our first reunion after an entirely magical day was supposed to be passionate, or at the very least more familiar. I knew I hadn't imagined the trip, but was I completely delirious imagining he liked me?

"Don't you mean you're rid of *me*?" I challenged, trying to stir up some emotion in him. "No more babysitting, right?"

"I was relieved of Guardian duty, yes." He chose his words carefully. "Restored to Warrior Patrol. I'm still assigned to Aviemore, just not to you in particular."

Still assigned to Aviemore. Hope beat in my chest like a drunken butterfly. Rid of my guardianship, we could be together more openly. No rules. No bitterness that he was in an inferior position. It was great news.

Relieved, I crossed the room and stood in front of him. I couldn't help myself; I reached out to touch him. "We can see each other more easily now, right?"

He gently circled his hand over my outstretched wrist and held it still. "You seeing me while I was working is what placed you in danger in the first place. So that doesn't happen again, you won't be seeing me again. Ever." He moved my hand to the side, stood up, and broke contact with me.

My heart dropped to the floor. "Why? You said the demons were gone."

"Those demons are gone, but there's still something

going on in the area that I have to . . . I really can't talk about it."

His passivity infuriated me. "Right." I threw my hands in the air. "Or I'll be tortured."

"It's not a game." His face flared with intensity. "This is serious, Maren! I'm serious! Don't joke about things like torture. If you saw . . . This is exactly why I can't get close to you . . ."

"It's too late, isn't it?" I interrupted. "You're already close to me. Too close, and it's freaking you out. That's why you're doing this." I held my breath and waited to see how he would react. His face drained of all color. He sunk back onto my bed and buried his head in his hands.

"I can't," he whispered at the floor.

"Can't what?" I crawled onto the bed next to him and brushed at imaginary lint on his shoulder just to touch him. The air crackled with tension.

"I can't be with you," he moaned. "I want to. Believe me . . . The temptation is crushing . . ." He lifted his eyes and locked me in a sultry stare.

"I want it too," I whispered. "Being with you is just so . . . easy. I can't explain why it feels right, but it does. You know it does."

"But it's wrong." His gaze was penetrating and intimate. "I can't do this to you."

I swallowed hard and blinked to keep some semblance of control. "Do what to me? Break my heart? Because you're kind of already doing that."

A heavy grief colored his voice. "I can't change who

I am, Maren. I'm an angel, and I'm a Warrior. I have a dangerous job."

"I know your job is dangerous." I wiggled a loose stitch on the bedspread, kept my own voice even and calm. "You've told me. I don't care. I can handle it."

"*I* can't handle it!" He slammed his hand on the mattress. "Loving you would make you a target to every demon I ever go after. They'll hunt you down and kill you, and I can't put you in that kind of danger!" He thumped to his feet. "I'm sorry, Maren. I'm sorry it has to be this way. But it's done. It's over. You need to stay away from me, and I from you. For good." He leapt for the open window, climbed on the ledge, and disappeared.

I couldn't move, couldn't follow him, couldn't even watch him leave. Confusion ricocheted from my head to my heart and back again. *Did he just tell me he loved me and then broke up with me in the same breath?*

I threw myself down on the bed, prepared to cry my eyes out, when I spotted a white bundle on the floor near the headboard. I stretched out my arm, hooked it with my finger, and brought it close. It was Gavin's shirt. The shirt I'd wrapped around me when he'd flown me back. I lifted it to my cheek. I could smell Gavin in the fibers. And, somehow, the tunic was still warm.

I scrunched it into a ball, clutched it to my heart, and let my tears wash over it. *What had I done in a past life to deserve so much heartbreak in this one?*

I fumbled at my neck for the Tudor rose necklace from my mom and rubbed its cool glass petals to soothe myself. Instead, self-pity tried to swallow me whole. I finally found a guy I liked who actually liked me back, and somehow I'd messed it up. How? Could I ever fix it? And why did it have to hurt so badly?

I never talked to my mom about boys, because there had never been any worth mentioning. Now there was one, I was desperate to talk to her, and she was gone. *So was he,* I reminded myself.

My phone buzzed in my pocket. I wiped my face with the back of my hand and pulled it out. I hit the side button and found a text from Jo:

OUR BOG BUTTER IS GOING TO THE EDINBURGH MUSEUM!!
HOW COOL IS THAT? IM AT TV STATION. TALK LATER

Sweet Jo, she was always so darn perky. How did she manage it when she had a crappy life too? I thought about calling her, but I didn't want to interrupt her with my sob story. And I wasn't sure her eternal optimism was going to help anyway. I needed to talk to someone a little more dark and twisted.

I dialed Hunter.

"Hey, I was just thinking about you!" she said.

"Really?" I sniffed. "Why?"

"Wait, are you crying?"

I sniffed again. "No, I mean . . . not anymore."

"Aw, is it your mom?" she asked.

"Kind of, but not totally."

"A guy?"

"Good guess."

"It's always a guy, isn't it? What did he do? Want me to come knock him out for you?"

I smiled into the phone. Calling Hunter was definitely a good idea. I told her about meeting Gavin in the woods, him showing up at my house, and my trip to his village.

She was impressed, and started babbling on, probably to distract me from the painful parts. "Oh, you're so lucky! I've never met an angel. I know my parents worked with them. I can't wait to work for the Abbey myself. Finally get out of here . . ."

"Where is the Abbey?" I interrupted. I rolled over and slid my mom's journal out from under my bed.

"France."

I slipped the decoded letter from between the pages and ran my fingers over the smooth outside of the envelope. "Le Mont-Saint-Michel in Normandy?"

"Why are you asking me if you already know?"

"I don't. I found an envelope my mom had addressed there right before she died."

"So you found something?" Her voice went up an octave; from excitement or fear, I couldn't tell.

"Yeah," I admitted. I described the heart box, the journal, and the letter.

"How did you know it was written in invisible ink?" she asked. "Did you decode it?"

"Yes," I said, remembering the cup of tea. "Sort of on accident."

"There are no accidents," she reminded me. "It's amazing you could do that, you know. Not everyone can cryptanalyze. You must have inherited that from your parents. The Abbey's going to want you for sure!"

"Maybe I don't want them," I replied. "And I think you were right."

"Of course I was," she said. "About what?"

"My mom." I sucked in my breath and closed my eyes. "I don't think it was an accident that she died. I think she was killed . . . by demons. I think a demon dropped her." *Like the hiker from Culloden.* "My mom was found in the middle of an open field, dead from impact injuries, but there was nothing around for her to have fallen from. The coroner said she fell from about eighty feet up, too low for an airplane or a hot air balloon or something along those lines. It made no sense. She was crushed into the ground with no reasonable explanation."

I decided not to tell her about my premonitory dreams and how I could have stopped my mom from leaving the house that day, how I should have but didn't because I was holding a grudge from the night before. I couldn't even remember what our fight had been about—something small and stupid, no doubt—but I was a bad enough daughter that I let her leave without warning her. The truth was, the Abbey would want nothing to do with me.

"Why do you think they did it?" Hunter shook me out of my miserable musing. "Because of the journal?"

"Maybe. She named it 'Demon Strongholds,' and it has a bunch of drawings of three different buildings."

"If you have maps into demons' strongholds, you'd better be careful. They will not take losing those lightly. Obviously, if they killed your mum for them. Do you know where the buildings are?"

"No. I don't recognize any of them."

"Take pictures with your phone and send them to me. Maybe I'd know them." I knew Hunter was anxious to prove herself to the Abbey, and I was happy to help her get in. Let her dreams come true, even if mine couldn't.

"What about the letter?" she continued. "What did it say?"

I read it to her.

"'Soldiers' definitely means Warrior angels," Hunter said. "Like Gavin. No wonder he just showed up in your area. He's probably scouting for this program. You live in Aviemore, right? With an *A*? Has anything weird been going on in your area?"

"Just some crazy dogs or something. Nothing serious."

"Well, you'd better keep an eye out, because it's likely to get serious soon. And don't tell anyone anything about this," she warned. "Not your grandparents, not your friends . . ."

"Why not?" I thought about Jo. I'd already told her about meeting Gavin, and I was planning on showing her my mom's stuff. I would feel terrible keeping such a big secret from her.

"For their own protection," Hunter said with no small amount of gravity. "Trust me, the less they have to do with demons, the better."

She was probably right, although the minute I started having bad dreams starring Jo, all bets were off. I wasn't going to make the same mistake I'd made with my mom.

"Except Gavin," she added. "You should tell him about the journal if you see him again."

"I'm sure I won't," I sighed. "He's gone, and he can't stand to be around me."

"I wish I had a hot angel who couldn't stand to be near me, so much so that he took me home with him," Hunter teased.

"Yeah, well, now he hates me."

"I highly doubt that," she said. "Angels don't hate anyone. You probably just have him so mixed up, he doesn't know what to do with himself—because he's definitely not supposed to love you, either. So he threw a big, bad tantrum and stormed off. He'll show up again, especially if something happens in your town." She crunched into the phone, as if she was eating popcorn as we talked. "Who knew angels were so much like kindergarten boys?"

Gavin was nothing like a kindergarten boy, I thought to myself, recalling his muscular chest, the way his hair fell over his dark blue eyes, his gorgeous lips. He was nothing like a boy at all. He was nothing like anyone I'd ever met.

In spite of myself, I hoped something bad would happen so I could meet him again.

❀ ❀ ❀

The next week, something bad did happen. Bertie's mauled body was discovered in the woods.

The official cause of death was reported as "attacked by wild animals," but I knew better. The "wild animals" were demons, but like Gavin said, they seemed to have moved out of the area.

The animal madness, however, hadn't. It migrated from dogs to bigger animals, like horses and cows. Farmers were told to kill even prized animals that showed any signs of sickness to stop the spread of the unknown disease, but so far, it hadn't seemed to work. A woman died after being kicked in the head while milking her family cow. A man was thrown from his horse when it apparently went berserk. More people turned up dead in Aviemore that week than had in the past four years.

The local government was investigating, but all they could really advise was to keep your pets inside, and avoid walking by yourself. Word was they were afraid the large deer in the area might gore someone.

True to his word, I didn't see Gavin. I thought about him all the time, though. So much, I had trouble concentrating on just about anything else. I scanned the woods for a glimpse of him. Imagined I saw him on the street. I was always wrong.

I figured he was out doing what he loved best: fighting demons. I fantasized about him tearing up the bad guys, his muscles bulging, his eyes blazing. I found myself sketching my own pictures of him in the margins of my notebooks. And every night before I went to sleep, I replayed the best day of my life—the day I visited his village. I recalled every moment in painstaking detail: holding his hand, lying against his chest on the warm rocks, what it felt like being held in his arms. I relived every caress, memorized every smoldering look, remembered every word he said to me in his amazing accent.

I added a million new scenes in my mind. All of them ended with us in a passionate embrace. I imagined that when we were lying on the boulder, he reached over and rolled me onto his body, my hair grazing his cheeks as we kissed. I dreamed that as we were walking through the woods, he suddenly pushed me up against a tree trunk and stole a kiss, a kiss I was shocked to receive but more than happy to return.

I reflected on how much my life had changed since I was little—not even as little as the tiny angels in Gavin's village, but just in the past few years. When I was twelve, I had crushes on boys, but most of them were on the posters in my room. I never expected I would have such strong romantic feelings about someone I actually knew.

I had only met Gavin a few times, and I did hardly know him, but I ached without him. He took a piece of me with him when he left.

CHAPTER 15

I was swimming in a pool. A giant waterfall cascaded into it,
making the surface of the water pulse and filling the air with
a soft roar. There was something entrancing about the water, the
way it rippled against my body.

There was a boy in the pool with me. He swam past, and I felt
the heat of his wake. I couldn't see his face, but I knew it was handsome. His muscles glistened as he stood up and waded over to me. He
smiled, and I laughed. He leaned forward to kiss me, but I bent my
head to avert his lips, stared at the turquoise water. A few bubbles
appeared, floating up from the bottom. The water got warmer. More
and more bubbles rose until the whole pool was boiling.

I wanted to get out, but he was holding my shoulders, hugging me to him. As the water churned furiously around us, he
tried to kiss me again, and again I turned away. This time, when
I looked down, the water was dark red. It was hot now—too hot.
It made me dizzy. I closed my eyes to stop the spinning. I felt the
water rise around me, only it wasn't the water moving. It was
me. I was sinking.

Even though I'd lived with my grandparents for more
than a month, I'd never been inside their bedroom before.
I needed a pencil sharpener, and my grandfather had sent
me in to fetch it. He'd promised that a small silver one
was in a drawer of the antique "dental cabinet," but I was
having no luck finding it.

I was lucky to have found the cabinet at all. I was expecting a white, mirrored compartment on the wall, like in a bathroom, but the dental cabinet turned out to be a huge mahogany dresser with more than two dozen tiny drawers, each with a shiny glass knob. I ran my hands over the smooth, faceted drawer pulls. The little girl in me wished that they were real diamonds.

The thin drawers were stuffed with random objects: pens, coins, matchbooks, a crystal frog, cocktail stirrers shaped like little sabers, corks from long-drunk bottles of wine. I was about to give up when two sparkling discs rolled out from the back of a dark drawer. I picked them up. They were cufflinks embossed with the Tudor rose—exactly like my mom's necklace. I rolled them between my fingers, staring at the colorful petals.

"What are you doing?" my grandmother called from behind me. I dropped the cufflinks and pushed the drawer shut.

"Nothing," I said, swinging around to face her. "I mean, looking for a pencil sharpener . . ."

"And did you find one?" she mused. I shook my head. "Well, what did you find?" I didn't move. She waggled her fingers. "Come on, out with it. I know you've found something."

Obediently, I retrieved the cufflinks and deposited them into her open palm. "Whose are they?" I breathed, afraid I was somehow in trouble.

"They belonged to your father," she said. "I'd almost forgotten about them. Your mum mailed them to us after he died. Said they were a gift from his work . . ." She closed her hand around the cufflinks.

"Where, exactly, did my dad work?" I asked. I didn't want to bring up any of Hunter's crazy suggestions about the Abbey, but I was dying to know more.

"Where do *you* think he worked?" my grandmother replied.

I sucked in my breath and decided to dive in. "For an international spy agency?"

She bit on her top lip for a few seconds before she answered. "As far as we know, yes."

"You don't know for sure?" I pressed.

She shook her head. "It was all very top secret. Once he joined, we heard from him less and less. Then we got a phone call . . ." Her eyes glazed over a bit.

I didn't want her to stop talking. I needed to know what my grandparents knew about my parents' secret lives. "A phone call?" I repeated. I sat down on a beat-up leather armchair to show I wasn't going anywhere. She lowered herself onto the edge of the ottoman.

"Yes. In the middle of the night, your father called. He was quite upset. He said he wouldn't be able to contact us ever again, and that we should remove all record of him from our lives, even the photographs on the walls, for our protection. Something about being tracked by evil forces . . ." She studied me for a reaction, but I held my face still even though I was panicking inside. *Maybe Gavin hasn't been exaggerating about putting me in danger . . .*

"And?" I swallowed.

"Well, of course we didn't do any of that—at least not at first. But two days later, we got news that he had been killed in a terrible accident, and that your mother had gone into hiding with you."

"So you didn't know where we were?" I was shocked. All those years, I'd just assumed my grandparents wanted nothing to do with us.

"No, and it broke our hearts." She sighed and blinked back tears. "I always felt we should have tried harder to find you and your mum, but we didn't know where to start. We didn't even know the name of the agency they worked for, or where it was."

Seeing her pain, my heart melted for her, for me, for our whole family torn apart by the mysterious Abbey.

My grandmother patted me on the knee and stood up. "What's done is done. The important thing is that we have you here with us today."

She smiled at me like she really might love me. I hoped it was true. I needed someone to love me. Everyone else I loved had died or disappeared.

❁ ❁ ❁

Later that afternoon, I was sitting in my favorite spot, my window seat, trying to finish my homework. Like most of the area, I was stuck at home, imprisoned by the weather. I'd learned that rain didn't stop Scottish people from most anything, even golf, but when you added a cold wind, they preferred to stay indoors. A teeth-chattering gale had chased all the clouds out of the valley, but somehow added even more darkness to what was otherwise the middle of the day.

Out of the corner of my eye, I watched a long, black, impossibly shiny car pull up to our house. A man in a black suit climbed out of the back carrying a silver tray, and promptly disappeared onto the porch. The doorbell pinged.

"Maren!" my grandmother called from downstairs.

"Yeah?"

"Come here, please. You've got a visitor."

The only person I knew who drove around—or was driven around—in a limousine was Anders Campbell, but he and Graham hadn't been at school since their family funeral. I'd heard they went directly to the Bahamas on an annual family trip. *Lifestyles of the rich and famous. Must be nice.*

My grandmother stood by the open front door. Outside—as if he was too good to come into our common house—stood the man with the tray. As I approached, he held it out to me.

"Miss Maren Hamilton, I presume." He possessed a snootier-sounding accent than I normally heard in Scotland.

"Yes."

"This is for you." The tray was as shiny as the car outside, and it held a thick envelope with my name elaborately scrawled across it in black ink. I picked it up.

"Thank you," I said. He bowed, clicked his heels together, spun, and returned to his car without a word.

"I'll leave you to it," my gran said, eyeing the envelope as if she really didn't want to leave. "I've got to get ready for my ladies' golf club luncheon."

"Okay," I agreed, turning away from her in case it was somehow a message from Gavin. She closed the front door, and walked down the hall without a word.

I flipped the envelope over and found it sealed by a big clump of wax stamped with a cursive *C*. I slid my finger under it, careful not to get a paper cut, and gently pried up the seal. Inside was an invitation to a gala celebrating the eighteenth birthday of one Anders Campbell.

I hadn't gotten through reading the first page when the phone rang. "It's Jo," my grandfather called from the kitchen. I went in and took the receiver from his outstretched hand.

"Did you get it?" Jo breathed into the phone. I imagined she was just coming out of a back handspring or something. She certainly sounded excited.

"Get what?" I stalled.

"The invite! To Anders' party!"

"Who?"

"I know you've gotten it, because I saw the limo drive toward your house after it left mine. Isn't it exciting? Anders' parents throw him an epic birthday party every year. When he was eight, they had the Guards Polo Club come and play a tournament just for him. When he was twelve, it was an appearance from David Beckham. Last year, I heard they had Guy Ritchie, Madonna's ex-husband, give a special screening of his latest film before it hit the theaters!"

"What do you mean, 'you heard'?" I said. "Weren't you there?"

"Of course not. I've never been invited."

"But you're invited now?"

"Yes, same as you. Probably because of you, actually. We know Anders has a big crush on you, and he probably figures inviting me will convince you to go."

I cupped my hand around my mouth and leaned into the wall in case Jo's voice traveled out of the receiver. "First of all, we don't know Anders likes me. All evidence points to the contrary, in fact. He's a total jerk to me. And secondly, doesn't he know you can't convince me to do anything?"

"Come on, Maren, it'll be fun!"

"Fun? What's fun about spending an evening with an egomaniac?"

"Lots—if the egomaniac showers you with attention in front of Elsie and her crowd at his lavish mansion party," she sang. "Wouldn't it feel just a little amazing to have a handsome, wealthy . . ."

"Don't forget obnoxious," I said.

She ignored me. ". . . aristocratic lord wooing you?"

"Did you really just use the word *woo*?"

"It's just one night," she persisted. "You need to get out and have some fun! All you've been doing lately is staying home and moping." She was right. I'd been miserable since Gavin left. I doubted he was sitting around crying about me. Maybe it would be good to flirt a little, mix things up. Gavin might even sense it and be overcome with a fit of cosmic jealousy. The idea perked me up a bit.

"All right," I conceded. "I'll go."

"Just like that? Don't you have to ask your grandparents first?"

"Oh yeah, good point." I glanced over at my grandfather, who was at the kitchen table pretending to read the newspaper. He cleared his throat loudly and shook the pages for effect. "I'll ask and call you back."

"Tell them it's desperately important to your social standing at school."

"Since when do you care about that?" I asked.

"I don't, but adults eat that stuff up. And I *have* to go, Maren, but I can't go alone! This is my only shot! The gardens, the ballrooms . . . I've heard they even have a solid gold toilet. I'm going to pee on that toilet."

"Fantastic visual," I said. "Thanks for that."

"You're welcome," she giggled. The funny thing was, I knew she wasn't joking. Peeing on the Campbells' gold toilet would be the highlight of her year. "Ring me back soon as you know," she concluded.

Immediately after I hung up, my grandfather abandoned his paper pretense. "So, what's this I hear about a party?"

"It's nothing." I shrugged. "Just a birthday party for a guy in my class."

"And what fine gentleman is requesting your company?" he said, eyes twinkling.

"He *is* a gentleman, actually, by title or something. But I'm not sure he's fine. His name is Anders Campbell."

"Campbell?" my grandfather practically spat on the table. "Good-for-nothing clan, the Campbells. Their name means 'crooked mouth,' you know. Can't trust 'em."

"All of them?" I said sarcastically. "Every single Campbell is untrustworthy?"

"Aye. It's in their blood. Just ask a MacDonald."

"The MacDonalds hate the Campbells?" I smiled, since in America those two names suggested french fries didn't like soup.

"Oh, Murdo," my grandmother scolded, returning from her bedroom. She was wearing a bright blue sweater with a sparkly, brown brooch pinned to her shoulder. "Don't tell her such things!"

"But 'tis true, Liz!" he protested. He turned back to me. "The Campbells broke the Highland code of hospitality."

"What's that?" I asked.

"In Scotland, if someone asks you for lodging, even if they're your worst enemy, you're obliged to give it to them, to lay aside any grievances and promise no harm will come to them while they're under your roof."

"Don't listen to him, Maren," my grandmother said. "He's talking about the 1600s. The Massacre of Glencoe. Really, Murdo!"

"There was a massacre?" Mention of an ancient mass murder piqued my morbid curiosity.

"Aye," my grandfather answered, excited that he had my attention. "In 1692, a group of the Campbell clan asked for shelter from the MacDonalds. They were graciously accepted, of course, even had dinner with the clan chief. Late that same night, the Campbells murdered their unarmed hosts in their beds!"

"Murdo!" my grandmother chided again. "Why are you telling her all this?"

"She brought it up!" he protested. "She's been invited to a party for Alistair Campbell's son, she has."

My grandmother blanched. "Oh, well, those Campbells *are* bad. Your grandfather's right. Best stay away from their lot."

Just stay away, I thought. *Just stay away from the most popular kid in a class of only eighty-two students? Easier said than done.*

I convinced my grandparents to let me go.

CHAPTER 16

I spent the afternoon of Anders' party at Jo's house, getting ready. I'd never been to a gala before—I'd never even been to a formal dance or a church social—and apparently I had a lot to learn. When I showed up at the Dougalls' door, they immediately took pity on me.

"Oh, Maren, dear, it's . . . You're looking lovely," Mrs. Dougall said, trying but failing to hide a smirk behind the back of her hand.

Jo was blunter. "Great dress, but what happened to your face?"

"What do you mean?" I asked. I didn't usually wear a lot of makeup—just concealer and blush and sometimes mascara—but I thought I'd given myself smoky eyes rather well. Especially for my first time.

"I mean, you look like Cleopatra meets Catwoman meets a stripper," she said.

"Jo!" her mom scolded, playfully slapping her shoulder. The simple loving gesture made me ache for my own mom. "It's not that bad, honestly!"

They took me inside, sat me down at the small vanity in the bathroom, and proceeded to scrub my face clean to start over.

"Whatever made you think to put eyeliner on the rim *inside* your eyelashes?" Jo marveled. "Doesn't it burn?"

"Well, yeah," I admitted, gritting my teeth against the rough washing. "But I figured it was supposed to. Like how no one tells you how much high heels really hurt or how scratchy a bra strap is."

"Did your mum never teach you how to apply makeup, love?" Mrs. Dougall clucked.

I shook my head. *My mom was too busy fighting the forces of darkness,* I thought bitterly. Before I could even start to feel sorry for myself, though, my brain conjured up an image of Gavin. I missed him with a pain inside that echoed how much I missed my mom. Maybe even more. I guessed this was what love was all about. When you reached a certain age, you stopped needing your parents and started needing a soul mate to love and to love you. I wondered if Gavin was my soul mate. Why else would I be so obsessed with him after so little time together? I would have given anything to see him again. If I could gaze into his eyes just one more time . . .

"Hey, dreamer," Jo said. "Open your eyes."

My reflection in the mirror startled me. Mrs. Dougall had worked a small miracle. My eyes were somehow brightened, and framed by dewy black lashes I didn't know I had. My skin was glowing and a little sparkly. My blonde hair was suddenly shiny, and half swept up in a neat chignon with loose curls dancing on my shoulders.

"You clean up pretty good, Hamilton." Jo grinned.

I smiled back, and noticed I had sticky lips. "Lip gloss?" I smacked. "Really?"

"Absolutely." Mrs. Dougall pressed her hands against my arms. "Makes your lips extra kissable. The boys won't be able to resist the pair of you!"

"Mummy!" Jo giggled.

There was only one boy I wished couldn't resist me, and smile as I might, I was fairly sure I wasn't going to see him.

❀ ❀ ❀

I'd never been in the back of a British limousine. I'd only ever been in the back of an American one, and that was when I was five and the flower girl in my next-door neighbor's wedding. I'd had too much soda and candy—everyone kept bribing me to shut up or stand still—and their plan backfired quite horrifically when I threw up all over the bride's dress. I was hoping this ride would end better.

"How is it that Anders can have a big party on a Friday night when he didn't even go to school today, and hasn't even been for more than two weeks?" I asked Jo, who was perched next to me on the slippery leather seat. I still couldn't believe they'd sent a car to pick us up. "Everyone knows he's been back from the Bahamas for days. You can just skip school in Scotland?"

"The Campbells can do anything they want," Jo replied, staring out the tinted window. "They practically own the whole county."

"Is it true what they say about the Campbells?" I asked. "About them murdering innocent people in their beds?"

She turned back and grinned wickedly. "Where'd you hear that?"

"My grandfather. So, is it true? For all their wealth and fanciness, do people secretly hate the Campbells?"

"Not everyone. Elsie and her pack would change their

name to Campbell in a heartbeat. But, yeah, a lot of the Highlanders don't like the Campbells. There's a famous hotel in Glencoe, near where the massacre took place, called Clachaig Inn. They have a sign that says, 'No Campbells.'"

"Shut up!" I said.

"No, 'tis true. I've seen it."

"That's awesome," I said.

As the car pulled into the sweeping, circular drive, I got my first peek at Campbell Hall. "Hall" really didn't describe it. Neither did "mansion." It was a palace crowned with two giant turrets, glittering lead-paned windows, numerous carved stone balconies, and a four-story entrance more ornate than the front door of a cathedral. There was something eerily familiar about it that made the hairs on my arms stand on end, but I couldn't place what it was.

"Why is it black?" I asked Jo, noting the eerie color of the stones on the front façade.

"Soot," Jo answered. "They made their money mining coal on their property. I guess everything comes with a price, even the biggest private residence in Europe."

A giant, glistening fountain, big enough to swim laps in, stood in front of the house, circled by a line of chauffeured cars like ours.

From the car to the foyer, we were greeted by five different people ("Servants," Jo whispered in my ear). A uniformed man opened our car door and helped us step out; another man opened the huge, carved front doors and welcomed us; two stiff-lipped women, one for each of us, took our coats; and a man wearing bright white gloves escorted us down the hall to the grand ballroom.

The walls were set with stone columns and lined with tapestries and huge paintings of scowling men, all wearing the same dark-green-and-blue tartan. Our heels clicked on the marble floor, and I grabbed Jo's arm tightly, terrified I might slip and break something. Jo was spinning around, taking it all in, and literally shaking with excitement.

"Are you all right?" I asked. "Do you have a fever or something?"

"This is exactly how I imagined it. Only a little better," she whispered. "I can't believe I'm here. Me. A Dougall, in Campbell Hall!"

Our guide pulled open a six-paneled door, and we were blasted in the face with a song. *"It's getting hot in here! So take off all your clothes!"*

I had expected a string quartet and crumpets, but it seemed even Scottish lords had MTV-style birthday parties. The room was dark but bouncing with strobe lights, a huge disco ball, a DJ booth, and more than two hundred revelers.

Jo was apparently expecting exactly this, since she grabbed my arm and dragged me inside, shaking her body to the pulsing beat. Thankfully, she was too shy to actually join the mob, so we skipped past the throbbing mass on the dance floor and headed directly for the back wall. It was lined with long banquet tables covered in food. Turns out there were crumpets after all . . . and sushi, sausages, shrimp, mini meat pies, and even iced "biscuits" that had "Happy Birthday Anders" printed on them.

Just as I picked up a cookie, Elsie and her friends spotted me. *Game on.*

"Love your dress, Dewdrop," Elsie said. "It really flatters your bits." She motioned at her breasts, and I realized she was making fun of mine.

"Yours too," I replied, happy that I had practiced for this very insult since my first humiliating day at Kingussie. "Better to hide the *bee stings*, yeah?"

I hardly got to enjoy her shock at my Scottish comeback highlighting her own lack of "bits," because her friend jumped in.

"Let's go get some britneys," she said, steering a speechless Elsie away from us.

"That was pure dead brilliant!" Jo exclaimed.

"It was, wasn't it?" I said. "Thanks for teaching me the *bee stings* slang, but what's a *britney*?"

"A beer," she replied. I stared at her, not comprehending at all. She expounded: "Britney Spears . . . beers . . .?"

"Because it rhymes?"

"Yeah, that's it," Jo confirmed. "Like 'baked bean' refers to the queen, and 'brown bread' means 'dead.'"

"I don't even want to know how those last two are related," I said, biting down on what turned out to be a surprisingly good cookie.

Jo and I soon figured out that there was more on tap than just britneys. A full bar in the corner of the room was staffed by three very busy bartenders, all handing out free liquor as fast as kids could grab it.

Jo handed me a crystal tumbler with clear liquid and a lime hanging on the rim for dear life.

"Vodka?" I guessed.

"No, club soda," she answered. "My mum has a portable breathalyzer at home. She'd literally kill me if we drank."

"Wow," I said. "That's kind of harsh."

"My dad was an alcoholic." She shrugged. "I guess she's just afraid it runs in the genes."

"I'm sure you'll be fine," I assured her. "You're nothing like your dad." I realized how lame that must sound, since I didn't know her dad at all.

"Yeah, well, I don't want to make things more difficult for my mum. She has enough to worry about. But once I go to university, all bets are off! Cheers!" She clinked her glass against mine. I smiled and took a drink. I was surprised to see a sparkly lip print on my glass. I wasn't used to wearing anything on my lips, and the remnant grossed me out. I smudged it away with my thumb.

Judging by the number of people chugging beers and cradling their own champagne bottles, Jo and I were the only ones attempting to stay sober. We learned that aside from the staff, there wasn't an adult anywhere in the building. Anders' parents were in Tenerife, an island off the coast of Spain, at their vacation villa. Jo said they were hardly ever home. I wondered if that was why he was such a jerk.

By the time a cake the size of a small car was rolled into the middle of the room, and a half-naked woman jumped out and started making out with the birthday boy, I was ready for a break. Jo and I found double doors that led outside to a stone balcony, and we happily snuck away.

The balcony was bigger than the first floor of my

grandparents' house. Topiary trees twinkled under tiny, perfectly spaced lights, and industrial patio heaters hummed softly.

Jo and I walked to the stone railing.

"Wow," I exhaled.

While the front of the building had seemed massive enough, I now saw that it was only a third of the entire structure. Two more wings, each covered with double French doors and smaller, private balconies, stood impressively on either side. The giant courtyard below seemed to spread for acres—from a manicured landscape out into the forest.

Rows and rows of tall, precisely trimmed hedges lined the garden. Hundreds of rose bushes hugged the hedge bottoms. I marveled at the luscious fruit trees, their branches heavy with the weight of snowball-sized blossoms, and the carved marble benches, their seats held high by miniature gargoyles. In the middle, a fountain corralled life-sized granite horses swimming among arcs of shooting water. A flagstone path wound around the entire garden, set at precise 90-degree angles. Glowing lanterns hung from the trees and small footlights hidden along the base of the stones bathed it all in a soft, shadowy light.

"Why are the bushes all cut with square edges?" I wondered.

"It's a labyrinth," Jo replied. "A hedge maze."

"No way!"

"Yeah, you can't tell from up here, but I'm guessing those bushes are taller than both of us."

"Actually," a new voice added, "they're exactly ten

TOWARD A SECRET SKY

feet high." It was Graham. "The yew trees took fifty years to grow that tall, and the gardeners are required to keep them trimmed within a half inch."

I smiled at Graham. He was wearing a turtleneck and blazer, and I couldn't help thinking how nice he looked. Not handsome like Gavin, but he was the kind of guy you could take home to meet your family—polite, soft-spoken, and well-mannered. I thought about Anders licking icing off the cake girl's cheek, and wondered how he managed to miss all the good breeding of his cousin. Graham would never do something so gross in front of a room full of people.

"Are you enjoying the party?" Graham asked.

"It's fantastic," Jo offered. "You have a beautiful house."

"You live here too?" I asked.

"Guilty." He seemed a little embarrassed about it. "My parents' estate is in Edinburgh, but I've been living with my aunt and uncle since primary school."

"Why?" I blurted out.

"My parents work for the embassy, and are overseas most of the year. They didn't want me raised by nannies. Apparently, nannies hired by my aunt and uncle were a more palatable idea." He smiled, but something sad flickered in his eyes.

Jo's phone started buzzing. She excused herself, and stepped away to read the incoming text.

"Aren't you lonely?" I asked Graham.

"Who could be lonely in one hundred twenty-six rooms?" he said, sarcastically.

"Are there really that many?"

172

"At last count. Ten ballrooms, thirteen dining rooms, four kitchens, seven libraries . . ." He stopped. "I sound more like a tour guide than a tenant, don't I?"

"No, it's interesting," I said. I ran my palms along the cool, concrete banister. "Tell me more about the maze. I've never seen one before. Unless you count ones cut into cornfields at Halloween."

"Well, let's see, there are more than sixteen thousand trees. The theme is—"

"Theme? It has a theme?"

"Yes, labyrinths have a history of twisted entertainment, if you will," he explained. "They represent how the path of life is hard to navigate, but that you mustn't give up until you reach salvation."

"You mean, 'get out,'" I said.

"Precisely. But walking through bushes can get boring after a while, so most labyrinths have a theme, usually a humorous one, with little secrets and surprises along the way."

"What's the theme of this one?"

He pointed to the start of the maze, where two large statues loomed on opposite sides of the path: a beautiful woman and a man with wings. "Cupid and Psyche," he said. "The angel of love, and the beautiful human girl he fell in love with."

A wave of hot energy burst from the base of my scalp and seeped down my back. "I've never . . . never heard of them," I stammered, trying not to think of Gavin . . . and failing.

"They're from a Latin fairy tale called . . ."

"*The Golden Ass*," I finished.

He ran his hand across his forehead, up into his auburn hair. "I'm impressed. I thought you'd never heard of them."

"I haven't." I blushed. "I have no idea where that came from. It just popped into my head." I looked down, embarrassed to have interrupted him with my random trivia brain.

He continued, "The labyrinth symbolizes their journey. Psyche must visit the Underworld to earn Cupid's love."

Is that all it takes? I thought sourly. I considered the choices, and decided visiting hell to get Gavin back was much preferable to being loved and left behind. I was bouncing between self-pity and bitterness when Jo reappeared, worry creasing her face.

"What's wrong?" I asked.

"I got a text that my grandmother had a stroke," she said. "I have to go."

My throat caught at the word *grandmother*. It took me a second to register that Jo meant hers, not mine. I realized I must care about my grandparents more than I thought, since I couldn't bear the idea of something happening to either of them.

"How awful," Graham said. "We can have a car take you directly to the hospital."

"I don't want to be a bother," Jo said.

"Of course not. Come, I'll arrange everything."

"I'm coming," I said.

"No, stay and enjoy the party," Jo replied.

"But . . ." I faltered, "I only came for you." I widened my

eyes at her to signal I couldn't say more in front of Graham without insulting his family, but I wanted to scream, *Don't leave me here with the rich freaks!* Unfortunately, Jo missed my silent message entirely.

"Don't be silly," she said. "You'll have a great time. And you don't want to sit in a tiny visitor's room for the next five hours, trust me."

"But . . ." I was stuck. How could I argue that I would like anything better than to stay at the party when one of the hosts was right in front of me?

"You should definitely stay," Graham confirmed. He turned to Jo. "I promise I'll take good care of her."

They left, and I was standing alone. I gazed back over the garden. The moon slid out from behind a patch of clouds and bathed the statues of Cupid and Psyche in an eerie light. I heard a strange, high-pitched scream in the distance. Even though it wasn't cold at all, I shivered. As beautiful as it was, something about Campbell Hall wasn't right.

❀ ❀ ❀

While I was content to stand at the balcony's edge until the party was over, Anders found me and had other plans.

"It's our very own American princess!" he said, sucking on a cigarette and blowing smoke above his head.

"I prefer 'queen,'" I replied. "And you know smoking kills." Even though he acted like a pig, there was no denying Anders was attractive. Aggravatingly so.

"Eventually, everything does," he said with a smirk, taking another drag.

"Well, it's disgusting, anyway," I retorted.

"You've never had a ciggy, then, have you?"

"No. I told you, it's gross."

"I've been smoking since I was eleven," he said. "I should probably stop, but I've never found a good enough reason."

"Not even for a girl?"

"Psssh." He shrugged. "Never happen. Most of the Scottish girls I've kissed don't seem to mind."

"Ugh, I would never kiss someone who smoked." I turned back to the garden as if I couldn't be bothered to continue our conversation, but inside, I was reeling. Talking about kissing with a gorgeous guy, even if he was smoking, was titillating.

"Wouldn't you?" he asked. "If I gave them up right now, just for you, would you kiss me?"

"Your mouth is already completely ruined for the night," I said. We were definitely flirting now, and I was sincerely enjoying the rush of power it gave me.

"What about tomorrow?" he asked.

"I'm busy," I said.

"So you wouldn't kiss me, even after I gave up smoking for you and everything? I'm crushed." He took a few exaggerated steps backward, clutching his heart.

"'Fraid not."

"How about a dance, then?" he asked, putting his cigarette out by squishing it on the stone railing just an inch from my hand. "Look, my last one. You've convinced me. I'm through forever. The least you could do is dance with me."

Like all the guys in Scotland, his accent made him a million times more gorgeous. He bent his head and gave me an impish smile, making him really hard to refuse. What could possibly be the harm of a little dancing?

CHAPTER 17

Anders was actually fun to dance with, and I was relieved he gave me space instead of trying to grind up against me. The DJ played a couple of my favorite songs, and despite my best efforts, I was having a good time.

The room was stifling, though, and Anders was kind enough to get me a drink. I went with him, to make sure I was only getting soda. I lied and told him I was trying to pace myself.

"Smart girl," he said, clicking his finger and thumb like a gun at me. I was sure he had no problem holding his liquor, but he didn't order anything for himself.

Before I'd had two sips, Elsie stomped over and dragged Anders away.

Thankfully, Stuart appeared out of the crowd and asked me to dance. I didn't want to be stuck alone again, and another great song came on, so I agreed.

Three, or maybe four, songs later, I started to get dizzy.

"Are you okay?" Stuart asked.

"I'm just overheated," I said. "I think I'm going to find the ladies' room."

"Do you need me to walk you?"

The thought of being escorted to the bathroom was horrifying. "No, I'm fine. Just point me in the right direction."

"Go back out the doors you came in, turn right, go down the hall until you see a staircase. Go down a flight of stairs, and you'll find it on the left."

"Got it," I said. "Right, right, down, left."

I bobbed through the crowd and emerged into the wood-paneled hallway. I walked down to the right, but found three sets of stairs—two going down and one going up. A girl with a shiny silver dress and disheveled hair emerged from the middle staircase.

"It's down there," she said.

"Thanks," I answered.

On the next level down, I finally found a powder room, but it was to the right, not the left. The bathroom was as ornate as the rest of the house, but sadly did not contain the famous golden toilet. I smiled as I thought of Jo and her pee promise. The walls were covered in a dark red velvet paper. The fixtures were jet-black, glistening with little crystals in them. I twisted the sparkly black handles over the sink and splashed cold water on my face, careful to avoid my eye makeup.

As I did, I noticed the sprawling mural painted across the entire ceiling. *Only a rich person would hire an artist to paint the ceiling of their bathroom.* The scene was mostly dark red, like the walls, and I realized it was a painting of hell. Little angels were falling from the sky like baby birds, landing in the flames below. *How very twisted.*

The entire room started to throb along with my head. Maybe it was the painted fire, or maybe it was the walls, but I got crazy hot again. Being in the room felt like being inside a big, red mouth.

I fumbled with the door handle, successfully unlocked it, and practically fell into the hall. I walked back toward the staircase, but found it was no longer there. I must have taken a wrong turn. There were so many passages and closed doors, I was afraid of opening the wrong door and finding who-knows-what or, worse yet, people I *did* know doing who-knows-who. I kept walking, but never found another stairwell or another person. My ears started ringing, and I was afraid I might throw up. *Not on the fancy carpet*, I prayed.

I turned another corner and found a larger door with a round, golden bar horizontally across it. I pushed on the bar, and was relieved to taste the cool night air. I was on a patio at the ground level. I spotted the giant stone party balcony above to my right, but I had no idea how to get there, and no desire to go back inside. I plopped down on a stone bench near a fragrant flowering tree.

I pulled my phone from my pocket to text Jo. As I was typing the message, a shadow crossed over the screen. I lifted my eyes.

"Hello, Bombshell." It was Anders. I expected him to be passed out, sloppy drunk, or making out with Elsie or some other girl by then, but he stood in front of me perfectly composed, perfectly sober, and still perfectly handsome.

I smiled and found my eyelids felt heavy, like they were dropping all the way down to the corners of my mouth. I shook my head and tried to perk up.

"Hi," I said.

"I see you've found our garden."

"Yes," I replied. "By accident. I'm lost."

"No, you're not," he said, settling down beside me. "You're with me, and I most definitely know where we are. I grew up here, remember?"

"Oh, that's right," I said. "Isn't it your birthday or something?"

"That's what they tell me. Did you bring me a gift?"

I was mortified for a moment, because I hadn't. "I thought the invitation said 'no gifts.'"

"That's the polite thing to write, of course, but you could have brought me something anyway." He smiled. Why did he look so darn gorgeous? Maybe it was the moonlight. Maybe I was drunk and didn't know it. Could you get drunk without drinking alcohol?

"I am your gift," I heard myself saying. "Aren't I what you wished for?" Now I was giggling.

"More than I could ever wish for," Anders said, lowering his voice and sounding even sexier than usual. He stood up, and held out his hand to me. "And now I have a gift for you."

I took his hand and let him pull me up. It seemed like I was weighed down with concrete somehow, but he managed to get me upright anyway.

"What is it?" I asked, giggling again.

"A private tour," he answered, leading me away from the bench. "To hell and back."

"What do you mean?" I said. My legs felt wobbly, and I wondered if the stones we were walking on were set unevenly on purpose so damsels in distress would have an opportunity to fall into their hero's arms. *Was I finally a damsel in distress?* I decided yes to the damsel, no to the distress. And to heck with Gavin. He'd left, and I needed to move on. There were plenty of other accents in the sea.

"You're a very special girl, Maren," Anders said. "I knew it from the moment I set eyes on you."

I realized we were still holding hands as we walked. His hands were warm and soft. We were walking toward the hedge maze, and then into it. *I wanted to explore you, hedge maze,* I thought, *from the moment I set eyes on you.*

I spied a white ghost to my left and jumped. It was the statue of Cupid. I laughed uncontrollably. Now that I was closer, I could see his wings. *Rather small,* I thought, remembering Gavin's impressive span. Anders pulled me farther into the maze, and I followed.

The air was heavy with the smell of night blossoms, and every time I stumbled against Anders, I inhaled his cologne. I wanted to bathe in it.

I don't remember the entire maze walk, but I know it was full of surprises I found quite hilarious. We approached an adorable statue of a naked nymph. As I walked closer, he suddenly became animated and peed on me with a little fountain of water from his private parts. I realize now that motion simulators must have been hidden throughout the maze, but at the time, I couldn't figure it out. I think I stepped back and forth in front of the peeing statue four times before Anders finally dragged me away.

"You've gotten yourself all wet," he said playfully.

I laughed hysterically in response. "He peed on me!"

Anders took off his sport coat and set it across my shoulders. He took my hand again, and hurried me along the path more quickly.

"We're almost there," Anders said.

"Almost where?"

I heard the gurgle of running water. It got louder the deeper we went. A shrill scream pierced the shadowy silence. I practically jumped into Anders' arms, wrapping myself around him as if I'd been frightened to death.

"What was that?" I whispered.

"Just the peacocks, darling," he whispered back. Even his breath smelled delicious. How was that possible, when he'd been smoking cigarettes? I started to think about what it *would* be like to kiss him.

We emerged from the maze and found ourselves in front of a small temple with a round dome on top. The rushing water sound was coming from the building itself, and I saw there were jets of water shooting out from at least ten different spots on the front side alone. Amazingly, water even gushed from the top of the dome, sliding down the entire structure, making it glisten. Statues of half-robed women playing with the water decorated the building: they reclined against the temple sides, holding buckets; squatted at the base with elaborate catch basins on their heads; lazed across the top edge, clutching their water jugs like a lover. It was the most elaborate fountain I'd ever seen.

"Welcome to the cascade house," Anders said.

I was speechless. I had literally lost the ability to speak. I was sure I didn't look at all attractive with my mouth hanging open, but I couldn't seem to close it. The water was mesmerizing. I wanted to lie down next to the women on top and go to sleep.

"Come on," Anders said, tugging on my hand. I just stared at him. "Inside," he offered. I still couldn't answer, but allowed him to lead me past streaming waterfalls into the darkness of the open archway.

Inside, the cascade house was damp, cool, and extremely dark. Water thundered overhead and added to the fog of tiredness that threatened to envelop me. I spotted a long, low concrete bench and wanted desperately to sit on it. Thankfully, Anders understood and led me to it. I sat down, but jumped back to my feet instantly.

"It's so cold on my bottom," I heard myself say in between giggles.

"You won't be cold for long, I promise," Anders reassured me. He gently removed his jacket from my shoulders and laid it across the bench for me to sit on. He patted it, and I sat back down. *Much better.*

The benches were extra wide, almost like stone beds. They reminded me of altars. I thought about Romeo and Juliet, and decided she would have stabbed herself on just such a bench.

Thoughts rushed through my head like the water above me. How odd that I was with a lord, inside a fountain in Scotland after dark. Maybe I should be afraid. Why wasn't I? Why should I be? Anders was big and strong and handsome.

I imagined being a lady and strolling through gardens like this anytime I wanted. I was starting to see why Elsie would want to marry Anders. It wasn't a bad life.

I felt my eyes closing, and every time they did, it felt so good, like I'd just taken a little nap. I repeatedly opened and closed them, blinking a little longer each time. Anders mumbled something into my neck, but I couldn't hear what; I could only feel the warmth and vibration. I did hear myself moan.

Anders put his hand into my hair, and it felt divine. I heard a scratching noise, and couldn't figure out what it was. A small breeze blew on my back. My dress fell off my shoulders, and I couldn't figure out why. Anders was tugging at the sleeves near my elbows, but I couldn't straighten them out to help him. I wasn't sure what he was doing, but I couldn't stop him either. Everything was so hypnotizing.

I felt another gust of wind, and Anders was ripped out of my embrace. I heard yelling, but it sounded like it was at the end of a tunnel. Another person was with us in the cascade house. Another guy. He was dancing with Anders, or wrestling with him or something. Anders went to sleep on the floor, and the new person came over to me. He pulled my dress sleeves back up to my shoulders. I heard him refastening what I now realized was my zipper. He gathered me up in his arms.

"Let's get you out of here," he said. "Anders won't bother you again."

I looked into his face and knew I was safe. I settled my head against his chest. "Thank you, Graham," I whispered before I let my eyelids finally fall closed.

CHAPTER 18

"Maren! Maren!"

I opened my eyes. They felt swollen and heavy. I blinked and tried to figure out where I was.

"Yeah?" I croaked. My cheek pressed against something cold and hard. I was sitting on the ground, leaning heavily against the side of a stone bench. A carved gargoyle screamed silently at me, his forked tongue frozen in midair. I tried to move away from it, tried to get up, but found I couldn't move my body. I saw walls of bushes in all directions and realized I was still in the maze.

"Maren! Listen to me," Graham said.

I felt like I was at the bottom of a swimming pool. My vision was wavy and my ears were clogged. I heard distorted laughter and the sound of people talking somewhere nearby.

Graham lowered his voice to a whisper. "This is for your own good, but please stay quiet." He was crouched next to me, waving something thin and shiny. He plunged it into my arm. The impact burned, but I was paralyzed to stop it. When he yanked it back out, I saw it was a syringe. I couldn't believe it. He was trying to kill me! And after he just saved me from Anders?

I heard him counting: "Thirteen . . . fourteen . . . fifteen . . . sixteen . . ."

Didn't the nurses on television always count backward when they wanted someone to black out after a shot? Why was he counting at all? Why did he do this to me? Why couldn't I stop him? I attempted to scream, but nothing came out.

"Fifty-six . . . fifty-seven . . . fifty-eight . . ."

My entire body convulsed as if I'd been hit by lightning. In a single instant, I was able to sit upright, feel everything, and speak.

"WHAT THE WHAT?" I shouted.

"You're welcome," Graham replied, yanking me to my feet. I felt like I'd been beaten with a bag of bricks, but at least I could think clearly again. Perfectly clearly.

"What's going on?" I rubbed the needle mark on my arm. "What did you just do to me?"

"Link arms with me, smile as if everything is fine, keep walking, and I'll tell you."

The chattering voices were getting louder. Other people from the party had discovered the maze and were exploring it. I reluctantly grabbed Graham's elbow and let him lead me down the path. We turned a corner and saw the group: three boys and two girls I didn't recognize. "Hey, Graham!" they said.

He nodded brusquely at them—as if I was his girlfriend and they shouldn't interrupt us, I thought—and steered me past them. As soon as they were out of sight, I jerked away from him.

"Explain," I demanded, pointing to the now-purple hole in my elbow. "What did you poison me with?"

"I didn't poison you. I un-poisoned you, actually."

"You shot 'un-poison' into me?" I wasn't buying it.

"I injected you with flumazenil. Now, let's keep walking."

I wanted answers, but I also didn't want to be lost in the maze anymore, and Graham knew the way out.

"What's that? A flu shot?" I asked, as we started back along the path.

"No, it's to counteract the Rohypnol," he replied. I stared at him blankly. "The date rape drug . . ." he explained.

I froze. "The what?"

"The date rape drug. Someone must have slipped it into your drink."

"But I wasn't drinking! I didn't have any alcohol. I only had soda."

"It doesn't matter. A tiny pinch of Rohypnol will work in anything, even water. It's colorless, tasteless, and odorless, so you'd have no way of knowing."

"How did *you* know, then?" I asked.

"I didn't. I was only guessing. When I saw you on the patio with Anders, I knew you were either extremely drunk or had been drugged. In either case, I wanted to make sure you were safe, so I followed you. When I got to the cascade house, I intervened because you were obviously not coherent, and I didn't want you doing anything you'd regret."

He started walking again, and I followed, grateful for the sudden motion. Graham stumbling upon Anders removing my dress was mortifying. I looked down at the path.

"Thank you," I said.

"No need to thank me," he replied. "I'm appalled that my cousin would try and take advantage of someone . . . especially you." Now he sounded embarrassed.

"So explain the needle thing to me again."

"Rohypnol is very similar to alcohol, in that it takes away a person's inhibitions, but also immobilizes them. It can kill you quite easily, you know."

"Um, no, I didn't."

"Well, you do now, I'm afraid. The effects of it usually last about six hours, but of course, that would put you in no fit state to return to your grandparents' house. And I did promise Jo I'd return you safely. Seeing as how I couldn't wait for the drug to wear off, I had to give you the flumazenil."

"And it works, just like that?" I said.

"Within a minute," he confirmed. "It instantly reverses the effects."

"What if I wasn't drugged? What if I was just drunk?" I asked.

"It still would have perked you up, just not as quickly."

I couldn't believe it. I had actually been drugged. With the date rape drug. I wondered why Graham had the remedy on hand, and decided I didn't want to know.

❁ ❁ ❁

True to his word, Graham made sure I got home safely. He accompanied me in one of the chauffeured limos, although I insisted he not walk me to the door. I couldn't handle an awkward front porch good-bye.

When I slipped into the house, I found my grandfather sitting up, waiting for me.

A sweet sadness flushed over me. I didn't know if I was just feeling extra sorry for myself, but my eyes started to water. I'd never had a dad to wait up for me. But here was my grandfather—his dad—filling in.

"Hello, there," he said, clicking the remote to silence the TV. "How'd it go?"

"Great," I said, blinking away the tears and casually folding my arms to hide the puncture mark in my elbow. "Really fun."

He crossed the room and stopped in front of me. He cradled my chin in his hand and gazed at me with a mix of love and longing. He seemed to want to say something, but couldn't find the words. I wished I knew him better.

"Thank you for waiting up for me," I offered.

"It was my pleasure," he said with a nod.

He moved toward the stairs, and I followed like a little kid who didn't want to be left alone. I wondered if I should tell him what had happened, but decided against it. It was far too humiliating to talk about with anyone, let alone my estranged grandfather. I wasn't even sure if I could tell Jo or Hunter. Maybe in a few days, I decided, when the whole experience wasn't so fresh in my mind and raw in my heart. Even though I knew I hadn't done anything wrong, I felt stupid and exposed. Why, *why* did I follow Anders into the maze in the first place?

At the first landing, my grandfather and I parted ways. I continued up the stairs to my attic room and shut the door firmly behind me. I surveyed the room. Everything was exactly how I'd left it: my bed was sloppily made, the top of my mom's journal peeked out from the side cushion of the armchair, and the floral garland from Gavin's village hung from the scuffed metal knob on the wardrobe.

I'm safe, I reminded myself. And I would never go near Anders Campbell again.

Still, I couldn't get Campbell Hall out of my mind. And for reasons besides Anders attacking me . . . There was something about the actual building. Something eerily familiar.

I shuffled over to the wardrobe to get my pajamas, and carefully opened the doors so as not to destroy the delicate, intertwined flowers on the hanging garland. I thought about Gavin, and how things might have been different had he been with me at Campbell Hall. He would have protected me. But Gavin was probably halfway across the country, taking care of more important things.

I started feeling sorry for myself. I was alone and abused. And I didn't want to be either.

When I swung the doors closed, I watched the ribbons bounce softly against the dark wood. They were curled and massed together, and, I noticed, sort of knotted.

I stooped to untangle them, but stopped short. *No, it couldn't be.* I took a step back and bent my head sideways. Was I losing my mind? The ribbons looked as if they had been purposefully gathered and tied into small knots in just such a way. Yes, there was a definite pattern.

In lowercase script, the ribbons clearly spelled out *roof*.

Someone had been in my bedroom. I walked across the room until I was in front of the window. My bedroom light made it pitch-black outside, turning the normally transparent glass into a mirror. I was surprised to see I still looked pretty even though my hair was tousled.

My stomach was swirling, but I was sick of being scared.

I took a deep breath and turned the cold, metal handle in the middle of the window that allowed it to open like a double door. I shoved the windows out, but jerked back inside at the same time in case someone or something sprung at me. Nothing happened.

I gathered my courage, leaned against the windowsill, and peered into the darkness. There, sitting on the roof, not five feet away, was Gavin.

Seeing him—his handsome profile, the way his muscular arms wrapped around his bent knees—filled me with such a mixture of relief and elation, I let out a small cry of delight that sounded embarrassingly like a kitten.

He put his finger to his lips and extended his hand to me. I kicked off my heels, climbed up on the window seat, took his hand, and stepped out gingerly. Unlike the sandpaper shingles in Missouri, the roofs in Scotland were smooth slate: slippery enough in a dry climate. But somehow, holding on to Gavin's hand made my bare feet stick to the roof. Once again, no matter what the circumstance— even on the tippy top of a very slanted, extremely slick roof high above the ground—I felt safe because I was with Gavin.

He was back. And I was so ecstatic, I wanted to dive into his arms. Until I remembered how he'd left. The agony of missing him and the hurt of not hearing from him diluted my happiness. I sat down next to Gavin hard, and in a huff.

"What are you doing here?" I blurted out, completely bypassing any type of greeting.

"I was in the area," he answered, his voice as smooth

and amazing as ever. "And I just wanted to check on you, make sure you were okay." I noticed his face was creased with worry.

"You're a little late," I taunted.

"What do you mean? Did something happen at Campbell Hall?" He looked far more upset than an angel should.

"How did you know I was there?" My ears began to burn at the mention of Anders' house.

"I can hear your heartbeat." His voice was soft and intimate. "It's a tracking thing. Angels and demons can remember a particular heartbeat and use it to always find someone." He leaned a little closer to me, and I got a lot hotter. "I memorized yours," he whispered.

"But everyone's heartbeat sounds the same," I said.

He shook his head. "The rhythm of every heart is unique, like fingerprints." One side of my mouth twisted up in disbelief. "It's true, I promise."

The revelation made me feel a little naked in front of him. *If he could hear my heartbeat, what other private details could he sense?*

"Did something happen at Campbell Hall?" he repeated. I noticed he was clenching his fists. I picked at a loose stone, not wanting to answer him out loud. I didn't want to tell him about Anders and the almost-crime. Once again, I knew I shouldn't be, but I was embarrassed, embarrassed to have even thought for one second about kissing Anders. But since Graham saved me, in the end nothing actually happened.

I changed the subject. "Why didn't you just come

to the party if you knew I was there, and you were so concerned?"

"I can't go in there," he answered.

"Why not?"

"It's a demon seat." He shrugged as if it were the expected answer.

"A *what*?" The hairs on the back of my neck prickled at the mention of demons.

"Like my clan's village is sacred ground and the demons are forbidden from it, so are angels blocked from entering a demon lair," he said.

I realized with a jolt why Campbell Hall had seemed familiar to me: it was one of the buildings in my mother's journal. Huge, blackened columns with a two-story staircase flanking the front door; how had I not recognized it when we first pulled up in the limo?

More pieces fell into place. Campbell Hall was in my mom's book, the book she called "Demon Strongholds." Gavin had called Campbell Hall a demon lair. Which meant demons lived there. Which meant *Anders was a demon!*

A tidal wave of panic crashed over me. I had been with a demon. I had been poisoned and almost taken advantage of by an actual demon. A handsome, blond beast. And I'd walked right into his trap. *Or more like skipped into,* I thought sourly. From his butler-delivered invitation to my pampering session with Jo and her mom, I'd been excited to be his prey. I'd wrapped myself up in sparkly eye makeup and a fancy hairdo like a freaking present.

I was such a fool. I should have paid more attention. Or maybe I should have been warned. How was I supposed to know some book from my mom would lead to this kind of danger? She could have at least told me a little bit about what she did, her secret life, and how it would all come back to haunt me one day. And Gavin! He'd known about Campbell Hall too.

"How could you not tell me there's a demon fortress nearby?" My anger bordered on hysteria. "That I go to school with a demon? That's not information you thought I needed? You said the demons had left the area."

"It's completely forbidden," he said, his face a mash of confusion and anguish. "If we told humans where demons were all the time, there would be complete chaos. I'm breaking all the rules telling you this much. But only one demon lives there, and he's not all that dangerous."

"Oh, really," I shot back. "Some demons aren't dangerous?" *Tell that to Anders and his girl poison*, I thought.

"It's not that they're not dangerous, they just aren't *jinn*. Their primary objective isn't to kill."

"Jinn? What are you talking about?" I interrupted. "There's more than one kind of demon?"

"Yes," he answered. "There are three. Each has a singular purpose. One steals, one kills, and one destroys. The demons that kill are called jinn; that's what I hunt, the kind that killed that homeless guy in the woods. They roam the world in packs, killing regularly to fill their bloodlust. But they never settle in one place, because they know they'd get caught and wiped out."

"What kind of demon lives at Campbell Hall?" I asked, carefully avoiding saying Anders' name out loud.

"*Incubus*," he answered. "They're thieves."

"What do they steal?" I asked, relaxing just a bit. Maybe I wasn't in as much danger as I'd imagined.

"Mostly virginity," he said.

"*What*?" I screeched, visions of the fountain house flooding back into my brain. Gavin shot me a look, and I calmed myself down. "I mean . . . I don't get it."

"The incubus are pleasure seekers," he said, still eyeing me anxiously. "They drug and then seduce girls. They're really the lowlifes of the demon world. No one respects them. They don't really have any power."

"Oh," I said, trying to sort out how I managed to be one of those girls.

"I know how clever you are, though," Gavin continued. "I knew you wouldn't be fooled by their charm."

"I wasn't," I lied, grateful that he saw me as smart, and thankful that he hadn't seen me idiotically flirting with Anders. "What about the third type, the demons that destroy?"

A dark cloud passed over his beautiful face. "I can't talk about them. To even say their name can be deadly." He didn't look like he was kidding.

The conversation lulled, and I began working out everything in my head. Anders was a demon, but a *relatively* harmless one. I would just stay away from him and from Campbell Hall at all costs and, without revealing too much, made sure Jo did the same.

As I sat in silence next to Gavin, I knew I should be mad at him, but I found I couldn't be. We weren't touching, but a sizzling energy pulsed between us. The delicious excitement made it difficult to breathe. It enveloped my entire being, soaked through my skin.

He stood up abruptly. "I have to go. I have . . . other duties." He held out his hand to help me up. When I took it, my hand tingled as if I was touching a low-voltage electrical current. He didn't let go until I was safely back inside my room.

I leaned out the window. I didn't want him to leave.

"Thanks," I said. "For stopping by and checking on me."

"It's no problem." He shrugged as if it was just another part of his job. But something in his eyes told me it wasn't. "I . . . Well, goodnight."

He ran and jumped off the roof, falling for a few feet until his wings suddenly burst out of his back. He flew away as gracefully as a bird, without any noise, but I imagined his wings beating to the same rhythm as my heart. *My heart. The heartbeat he'd memorized.*

I realized that he hadn't taken off his shirt; that his wings seemed to come out through his clothing. I guessed angel clothing wasn't like human clothing. Why had he taken off his shirt in front of me in the village, then, if he didn't have to?

Show-off. I smiled to myself. *Gorgeous, gorgeous show-off.*

CHAPTER 19

*H*unter was being chased through dark alleys and cobble-stone streets. Shadows swam along the walls, pushing ahead of her, blocking her way. She tripped and slammed into the ground, opening a large gash in her knee. She sat still, hugging her wound to her chest, knowing she was doomed.

It began to rain. She looked up, hoping the rain would soothe her throbbing wound, make the shadows disappear. A drop of liquid fell into her eye, causing her to blink. It burned, and she rubbed it furiously, trying to stop the pain. When she opened it, everything was blurry, but she could see the dark splotches on her arms and legs.

It was raining blood.

I slept like the dead for eleven hours straight. When I finally did emerge from sleep, it was sudden, as if I had been thrown from the back of a moving car. My eyes flew open, and I instantly remembered my nightmare had been about Hunter. She hadn't died—yet—but I couldn't bear it if anything bad happened to her. I reached for my phone.

"Hi," she answered on the first ring.

"Are you okay?" I blurted.

"Yeah. Why wouldn't I be?"

"I had a nightmare about you."

"Was I hot?" she asked.

"What?"

"In your dream. Did I look hot? No point dying if I didn't look good." She cackled at her own vanity. She was a sick puppy. I kind of loved that about her.

"It's not funny," I chided. "And what makes you think you were dying in my dream?"

"Why else would you call me?" she answered. *Good point.*

"Well, you didn't die, but every time I've dreamed like this, the person did," I explained.

She was unmoved. "So what happened to me?"

"You fell and skinned your knee."

"Ouch. I can see why you'd be concerned."

"I'm serious, Hunter! My dreams are serious."

"I'm sure they are." I heard a distinct exhale.

"Are you smoking?" I challenged.

She cleared her throat. "No . . . no, of course not." I could tell she was lying. "Why, was I smoking in your dream too?"

"Yeah, smoking hot," I assured her. It was useless. I wasn't going to scare her out of . . . what? Not running down an alley? I was glad I'd called, and she was fine. I decided to change the subject. "Guess who visited me last night?"

"Your angel boyfriend?"

"He's not my boyfriend," I protested.

"So it was him. What's his name, Gavin? You should be worried about yourself." She blew into the phone again. "I checked into it. Messing around with an angel is no joke."

"You checked with who?"

"Just watch yourself," she repeated.

"Maren!" my grandmother called up the stairs. "Can't sleep the entire day away."

"I have to go," I said. "Call you later."

We said good-bye, and I tried Jo's number. I wanted to make sure everything was okay with her gran. Straight to voice mail. I hung up and fired off a quick text instead.

As soon as I hit *send*, the events of the previous night at Campbell Hall rushed my still-foggy brain. I tried not to give in to them. *Happy thought. Surely, I could find a happy thought. Gavin.* A warm peace flooded over me. I held my hand up and remembered him holding it again. I could almost feel the pressure of his strong fingers. I had zero desire to move.

I rolled over and blinked at the clock. It was almost noon, definitely time to drag myself out of bed. And, thankfully, it was Saturday; two days before I had to worry about seeing anyone at school. How was I ever going to face Anders . . . or Graham? Maybe I could just take classes on the Internet, or convince my grandparents to homeschool me.

As soon as I sat up, I regretted it. My head felt like it was full of rocks, and my stomach was sour. I didn't know if it was from stress or poison. Probably both.

I shuffled to the bathroom and surveyed the damage. I looked tired and pale, but that was pretty much my standard appearance. My hair still had a few shiny curls molded into it, and there was a trace of sparkle on my neck. I dabbed concealer under my eyes, and over the bruise on my elbow, brushed some blush on my cheeks to at least pretend I wasn't a zombie, and headed downstairs.

While I fixed myself some tea and toast, I listened dutifully to my grandfather's new joke. It had something to do with Irish men on a plane. I willed the toaster to work faster while I waited for what I knew would be a terrible punchline about poop. British jokes were always about poop.

"That's nothing, you should see the mess in the back of mine!" my grandfather exploded. My grandmother just rolled her eyes. "Do you get it, Maren?" he asked me.

I got it. But it wasn't remotely funny. I smiled and nodded, stuck a triangle of toast in my mouth so I couldn't possibly talk to them, and took my breakfast back upstairs.

Once back in my room, I lugged the giant armchair around so that I could sit in it with my feet up on the window seat, and snuggled down under the rose blanket with my mom's journal. Now that I knew one of the buildings was Campbell Hall, I wanted to look more closely at those pages to see if I could learn anything else.

I flipped to the first page that showed the sprawling country mansion. Definitely Campbell Hall. I couldn't believe I hadn't recognized it right away. It was exactly the same in the drawing as in person—from the balconies under the front windows to the huge columns by the entrance. I traced the outline of the sketch with my fingertip. How crazy that my mom had drawn the very building I'd just been inside.

After a while, my legs started falling asleep, so I decided to tuck them under me. As I shifted my weight, the leather-bound book fell to the floor. When I reached down and scooped it up, a thin, pink ribbon about ten inches long, with a silvery pattern printed on it, fluttered free. When I picked it up, I saw that the decoration was actually a vertical row of tiny letters. *Probably a bookmark with a lame inspirational quote.*

GAITRMNITQMLJCSUKDMANAENDEO-
AIC•SLERWSVOYOXTPTTOFMGFA•

I tried to read it, but it made no sense. It didn't spell out a single legible word except END, which didn't inspire any confidence in me. Why would my mother have a ribbon in her journal with a random string of letters on it?

Once I looked closer, I realized the letters weren't printed, but handwritten in her dainty, swooshy script; all capital letters, with two dots—one about two-thirds of the way down, and one at the end. If my mother took the time to write it, it wasn't random. It had to mean something.

I found a pen and paper in the desk, and copied the letters. I looked at what I wrote upside down, sideways, and then held up to a mirror. I tried rearranging the letters, grouping them into words, using every third one . . . nothing.

It was possible that there was a key somewhere else, where the letters were randomly assigned to others, such as all *W*s equaling *A*s, but my mother wasn't a fan of such simple cryptograms. They were either too easy to work out, hence their popularity in newspaper puzzle sections, or they were too hard because they required spiriting two different messages to the same person separately but quickly.

I tried again. I wrote the letters in boxes, in crosses,

and even circles. I tried reading the letters backward, and then backward in twos and threes. Still nothing.

I was shocked my scribbling didn't amount to anything. I was great at puzzles. Why couldn't I solve this one? Frustrated, I tossed the pen aside. It skipped off the desk and landed in a nearby tin trashcan with a satisfying thunk. *Exactly,* I thought. *Garbage. The pen is precisely where it belongs.*

Being free of the pen suddenly freed my mind. Maybe that was my problem. Maybe I wasn't supposed to be using a pen at all.

Most of the historical secret messages my mother studied came from ancient wars. When scrambled communications were received on the battlefield, they were read immediately. Soldiers didn't get to sit down and ponder the possibilities with a piece of paper. They usually had a custom contraption or tool to arrange the letters automatically for them.

I fell back into the squishy armchair, twisting the slippery ribbon nervously, sliding it between my fingers. *Was my mother in a war?* Considering what I knew about the Abbey and my recent encounter with demons, it seemed likely.

I glanced down at the ribbon, now looped across my fingers three times. Three of the letters lined up to make a word: MET. Nothing else around it could be read, and "met" wasn't enough to go on, but it reminded me of how strips of letters were decoded: they were wrapped around something.

What was I supposed to wrap it around? I moved the ribbon around my fingers a couple different ways until I was satisfied that was not the answer. I tried my wrist. Nope. I had a flash of a soldier with a gold helmet holding a thick bar. That was it! On one of the many rainy Sunday evenings we spent snuggled up with popcorn and the History Channel, my mom and I had watched a documentary about how the Greek army used codes printed on long strips of leather. The recipients had a dowel—sometimes wooden, sometimes metal-covered—crafted with the specific diameter needed to make the letters line up correctly. What was it called? Something like "scale" or "style." The word popped into my head: *scytale*.

My heart started racing like it always did right before I solved a puzzle. Now, I just had to actually solve it.

I needed a cylinder. I was fairly certain modern spies—*like my mom?*—didn't walk around with decoder cylinders. No, they would use something easily found wherever they were. *Cylinder. Cylinder.* What kind of cylinder would anyone have access to? I thought about a drinking glass, but it would have to have the exact same diameter for the writer as for the receiver, and glasses, even those in hotels, came in all shapes and sizes. Whoever sent the message had to have the same cylinder at their disposal.

Disposal. My grandfather's poop joke barged into my mind. Disgusting. I closed my eyes. Thinking about crap was not going to help me . . . or was it? I jumped up and ran into the bathroom.

I found it perched on top of the small, tin trashcan: the cylinder that every house in Scotland—every house in the Western world—had dozens of at all times. It had the same dimensions in every country, and had been the same for the last fifty years or more.

An empty toilet paper tube.

I went back to my room and shut the door behind me. I held the ribbon against the tube and wound. It only circled three times, but the letters lined up next to each other perfectly. The letters spelled out:

GET

ANT

IDO

TEF

ROM

MAG

NIF

ICA

T••

I didn't even have to write them down. Reading them in order and stopping where each word ended, the message was revealed:

GET ANTIDOTE FROM MAGNIFICAT

I took a minute to let it all sink in. A secret message from my mom stared at me from a slip of ribbon. And I had decoded it! I was proud of myself, for a second, until I realized I had no idea what it meant. Antidote for what? And from where? A place called *Magnificat*? Yet another Latin word I couldn't begin to translate.

The window next to me rattled. I saw a large man on the roof, inches away. I was so startled, I threw the toilet paper tube over my shoulder.

When I realized who it was, my heart lifted like a kite in the wind. But I didn't want to let him know how thrilled I was to see him again so soon. I opened the window latch.

"Gavin! You scared me to death!"

He beamed. "You look alive."

"Barely." I self-consciously smoothed my hair behind my ear. Thank goodness I had put on a little makeup, but I was sure I still looked terrible. "You're going to have to start using the front door," I said, nervously glancing over my shoulder to make sure my bedroom door was still closed. "At least in the daytime."

"Sorry," he said. "It's an emergency." He searched my face with his beautiful blue eyes.

"What?"

"Have you talked to Jo?" he asked.

"No. I texted her, but she hasn't answered back yet. She must still be at the hospital with her grandmother."

"She's at the hospital," he confirmed, "but not with her grandmother. She's been admitted."

"What? Why? What's wrong with her?"

"The same thing that's wrong with about thirty of the kids from the party at Campbell Hall last night," he answered. "They're all sick."

"Sick? How sick? Like food poisoning?"

"Really sick. And I think it's more like *outright* poisoning."

"But Jo left the party right away," I said. It made no sense. I'd been poisoned, and I was fine. She wasn't even at Campbell Hall for an hour.

"I'm headed over there now to find out more. I thought you might like to come," he answered.

"Yeah, of course. Um, meet me downstairs," I said. "I'll see if I can borrow my grandparents' car."

"No need," he said. "I've got one."

"What?" I was surprised. I'd never seen him drive. I kind of assumed he couldn't. "Angels have cars?"

"We can get one when it's needed."

"And you know how to drive?" I raised my eyebrows.

"Yes," he answered, smirking at my question. "Have to be able to get around same as you, and I can't fly in front of people—well, *most* people."

"So you *drove* over to my grandparents' house?" I continued. He nodded, and his eyes sparkled. "Then why did you fly up to my window?"

"I didn't," he said. "Too dangerous. Couldn't have anyone see my wings, could I? I climbed up the drainpipe."

He was definitely showing off, I concluded. A good sign that he really liked me. I wasn't going to give him the satisfaction of knowing how strong and romantic I thought he was, though.

"Well, you'd better climb back down quickly"—I shrugged—"because I'm leaving to go see Jo, with or without you." I slammed the window on his surprised look, and turned my back so he couldn't see me smile.

CHAPTER 20

There was nothing to smile about once we got to the hospital.

The Kingussie Sanatorium was a two-story building made entirely of brown stones, and looked like it might crumble at any moment. Inside, the hallways were long and dark, and surprisingly dirty. And not with the kind of dirt you could just clean up, but with grime that looked like it had become part of the walls centuries earlier. Cracked florescent lights, which had probably been added to the ancient structure with the advent of electricity, flickered ominously. Even though it was daylight outside, inside, it might as well have been midnight.

I was relieved to get out of the creepy hallway and into Jo's room, but only until I saw her. She was lying still, her skin sallow and her cheeks sunken in like she hadn't eaten in weeks. Long, bloody scabs bisected her face. I wasn't prepared for her to look so bad so quickly. And I definitely wasn't prepared to see that she was tied down to the bed with wide restraints.

"She kept trying to scratch out her eyes," her mother explained to us tearfully from the corner. "They finally had to sedate her. She was going wild. All the kids are."

"How did it happen?" I asked.

"I was hoping you could tell me, Maren," Mrs. Dougall said through sniffs. "Weren't you with her? Why aren't you sick?"

I wondered if I had gotten more than the date rape drug at Anders' party. Maybe Graham's antidote had saved me from two horrible fates.

"I was, but she left pretty early to go see her grandmother," I said.

"What are you talking about?" Mrs. Dougall's face twisted with confusion. I wondered if lack of sleep and worrying about Jo had made her a little loopy.

"She got a text that her grandmother had a stroke," I reminded her. "She came to the hospital to see her?"

"Her gran is fine," Mrs. Dougall said slowly. "We didn't text her. We found her this morning, lying on the front lawn. When we woke her up, she attacked us. The ambulance workers had to chase her out of a tree."

I didn't know what to say; I couldn't explain it. *Had I imagined Jo getting the text? Was that part of my drug hallucination?*

"Where's her phone?" I asked, wanting to prove myself not crazy as much as I wanted to help any investigation find out who had set up Jo.

"We don't know," Mrs. Dougall replied. "It's missing."

And not by coincidence, I thought grimly.

Twenty-eight other partygoers were in the hospital with the same symptoms. There were originally twenty-nine, but one boy struggled against the staff so fiercely, he bit his tongue in half and drowned in his own blood. Since then, all the patients had been strapped down and sedated.

Gavin excused himself and left me with Mrs. Dougall.

"I'm so sorry," I said, my eyes suddenly swimming in tears. "I didn't mean to abandon her. I thought . . ."

"Of course you didn't, dear," she said, crossing the room and wrapping me in her arms. "It's not your fault. The police will find out what happened, don't worry."

But it was hard not to worry, and even harder not to blame myself. If only I hadn't let her go. If only I had insisted on going with her . . .

I sat down next to Jo's bed. I wanted to comfort her, but I didn't know how. Her face was a mess. I reached down to squeeze her hand, to let her know I was there. Her skin was ice cold.

I kept Mrs. Dougall company, tried to keep the mood light and my outlook optimistic, but it was hard with Jo lying next to us, looking like she was knocking at death's door. And my good-friend guilt didn't make it any easier. I didn't know if I felt worse that Jo was hospitalized or that I wasn't.

Stuart arrived to visit Jo, looking healthy but worried. I was glad he was unharmed, but at the same time, I couldn't help but wonder why. How was he spared? And what happened to him after I left for the bathroom? I never came back, but he never seemed to go looking for me, either. What did he think happened to me? Where had he been?

He wasn't my guardian, of course. I shouldn't have expected him to be, or think less of him because he wasn't. Why couldn't he have saved Jo, though, like Graham had saved me?

Gavin reappeared in the doorway.

"I promised your gran I'd get you back before dinner," he apologized.

I stood up, probably too quickly. I was ashamed at how

badly I wanted to leave, to be out of the world's most depressing hospital.

"Say hello to Mr. and Mrs. Hamilton for me," Mrs. Dougall said as we hugged good-bye. "I promise I'll call you if we hear anything.

The cool outside air helped clear the dank and dust out of my head. As we walked across the parking lot to Gavin's car, he told me what he'd learned.

"The early toxicology reports are totally clean. Nothing is showing up in the bloodstream of the kids. No drugs, no poison, no substances of any kind," he said.

"How did you see the toxicology reports?" I asked.

He tossed me a smile that made my heart leap. "Charm will get you far in this world."

"I know," I answered. "But how did *you* get to see them?"

He stopped walking. "You don't think I'm charming?" he asked. He looked crestfallen, but I couldn't tell if he was serious or just playing with me.

"I'm sure you could be," I said. "I just haven't seen it yet."

"I guess you haven't been around me enough, then," he said with a smile.

Is it possible to be around him enough? I thought. My stomach was full of tiny champagne bubbles.

He opened the car door for me, just as he had in my grandparents' driveway. It made me feel grown-up and special and almost like we were on a date.

"The High Council knew something might happen in this area; that's why I was assigned here," he said as he drove me home. "But they didn't know what. I guess we do now."

The High Council. My mom's letter had been addressed to the High Council. I guess they received reports from agents around the world. I kept quiet, hoping he would keep talking. He did.

"It looks like a faction of jinn demons are testing a new kind of killing, a chemical warfare that poisons the population."

"Killing?" I thought of Jo. "Will everyone who's infected die?"

He nodded. "Unless we get an antidote out here quickly, I'm afraid so."

Antidote. The scrambled ribbon message from my mom's journal flashed in my brain. *Get antidote from Magnificat.*

"What's Magnificat?" I blurted out.

"How do you know that name?"

"I read it in some of my mom's stuff," I said. "What is it?"

"It's a place. Well, more than one place, actually. Magnificat is a safe haven for humans working with angels. There's one hidden in every major city."

"Where's the nearest Magnificat to us?" I asked.

"London. Why?"

"I think my mom was working on this project when she died," I said quietly. I didn't know if he would be upset I hadn't told him earlier, but for Jo's sake, I felt like I had to tell him now. "She left behind some details . . ."

"Go on." His face darkened.

"I found an encrypted note that spells out, 'Get antidote

from Magnificat.'" I got excited, realizing we could save Jo and the others—Gavin and me, working together. "She must have meant an antidote for this poisoning program!"

"Hold on a minute," he said. "Have you shown this stuff to anyone else?"

"No," I lied. No need to incriminate Hunter just yet.

"What you found is very sensitive, very dangerous information, Maren. You need to be careful."

"I know," I said. "But—"

"But nothing," he interrupted. "I need to go report in with my village. I'll tell them what you told me, and see what they think is best. In the meantime, I want you to stay home. Don't go anywhere."

"Where would I go?" I huffed. I wasn't used to being bossed around, especially by someone who looked my age. I knew he was technically older than me, but still . . .

I sulked until we pulled up to my grandparents' house. He parked by the mailbox, and when he turned to me, his expression was unexpectedly soft. He leaned over, crossing the middle of the car and stopping just inches from my face. "If you don't mind," he whispered, his voice drawing me even closer, "I'd like to sit outside your window tonight."

I would have been less shocked if he said he wanted to make out with me. "Why?" I asked, holding my breath, hoping he *would* try to kiss me.

He pulled away. "I just . . . I just want to make sure you're safe . . . until we figure out what's going on."

I raised my eyebrows at him.

"What?" He feigned innocence.

"You're serious," I answered. "You, Mr. I'm-Not-a-Babysitter, are volunteering to be my personal night watchman? What's the catch?"

"There is no catch." He tried to look all business, but his eyes said he wasn't thinking about business at all. There was a hot energy coming off him again—and it was pointed at me. He stammered, "It's just . . . Well, you do have the information from your mum. Someone should at least protect *that*."

I pretended to be hurt. "What about me?"

"I thought you didn't need protecting," he said.

"I don't," I replied. After breaking my heart and leaving me without warning, he wasn't getting an all-access roof pass without working for it.

"Please," he sighed. I was glad I was able to shake him up a little, since he seemed to have no problem messing with my emotions. "For once, can you just try to not be so difficult . . ."

"*That's* your idea of convincing me to let you sit outside my window all night? Some sweet-talker."

He closed his eyes for a moment, and when he opened them, they seemed bluer than ever before. "Maren," he pleaded softly, "I would really like to make sure you're safe tonight. Please." He slid his strong hand over mine. The heat between us was so intense, my heart threatened to jump out of my chest. It was all I could do to sit still.

"All right," I exhaled. I didn't dare move my hand. I didn't dare move anything. I wanted so badly for him to kiss me, but he just sat there, staring at me. I couldn't take my eyes off his beautiful lips. I wanted to dive into them.

I'd never wanted to do anything as badly as I wanted to kiss him. But there was no way I was going to make the first move.

Please, I silently willed him, *just move your head the tiniest bit toward me. I'll meet you in the middle. I want to kiss you. I want you to want me too!*

His gaze bore into me, but he sat completely motionless. I couldn't take it anymore. I had to break the tension before my body turned traitor and I made a fool of myself.

I slipped my hand from under his and swiveled to unlock the car door, turning away from the passion that threatened to suffocate me. I wasn't going to give in that easily. Not if he wasn't going to say something first.

"You can sit up there if you want." I shrugged. "But don't go peeking in my room or anything."

"I wouldn't dream of it," he said with a sly grin.

Damn!

❀ ❀ ❀

I couldn't sleep. The wind screamed around my attic room—an otherworldly wailing that spoke of demons and my mother's death. Loose shingles rattled against each other with a concrete scraping that made my skin crawl. I imagined a corpse trying to climb out of its coffin. The gale tormented me, not just because I was scared, but because I knew Gavin was right outside, keeping watch on the roof.

Thoughts of him consumed me. *Can he be blown off? Is it too chilly? Do angels even get cold?* I remembered the warmth of his chest and doubted it.

To calm myself, I rubbed my hands over my new pajamas; I'd been wearing his shirt to bed every night since he'd left it. The fabric still held his scent: a delicious, heady smell like the first spring breeze of the season. I closed my eyes and tried to remember the wind as a gentle thing, not the invisible, deadly force that beat outside.

Something banged overhead and then thumped away like a lopsided coconut. *What is going on out there? Did something happen? What if Anders came back for me?* I bolted upright.

Gavin was standing at the end of my bed. He put a finger to his lips, silencing the yelp that revved in my throat.

"What are you doing in here?" I croaked.

"Making sure you're all right," he whispered. "Your heart was beating a bit wildly there." I was embarrassed, remembering he could hear it.

"It's the wind," I confessed. "Kind of sounds like screaming. I'm not a fan."

"Och, the wind can't hurt you."

"Says the guy who can fly," I answered. "It's not the wind as much as the things it carries: large tree trunks, flying cows, demons . . ."

He shook his head. "We'll be having none of those tonight."

"Can you maybe make the wind stop, then?" I hoped.

"Sorry, I don't control the weather." He smiled, not helping my heart rate one bit.

"What can you control?" I demanded.

"Apparently, not my wardrobe," he mused. "That's my shirt you're wearing!"

I gathered the collar in one hand. "No, it's not."

"Aye, it is. You pinched it!" His playful familiarity made my bones turn to liquid. I sunk into the mattress a bit.

"If by 'pinched' you mean 'stole,' no, I didn't," I protested. "You left it here."

"So we're agreed, it is mine."

I shrugged in response. I couldn't believe he was in my room, in the dark. I was glad I had locked my bedroom door. No adult, no matter how laid back, would let a hot guy inside a girl's room in the middle of the night. The idea of breaking everyone's rules started my blood flowing again.

"Now, young lady," Gavin interrupted my fantasy. "You've got to get some sleep."

I found his old-fashioned terms terribly romantic. I didn't want him to leave. "I can't," I assured him. "I've tried."

A shutter slammed against the side of the house, and I jumped. Between the storm outside and Gavin inside, I was wound up.

"Shhhh, it's all right," he soothed. "The way that heart of yours is pounding, I can see why you're having trouble falling asleep." He took a few steps closer to the bed. "Is there anything I can do?" The things that came to my mind were a far cry from sleeping . . . "Did your mum have a special trick?" he asked.

"My mom?" I faltered.

"To help you fall back asleep," he explained. The mention of my mom was as good as a cold shower. Guilt, loneliness, and grief bullied all other emotions away.

Did Mom do something to help me sleep? If she did, why can't I remember it? Am I that terrible of a daughter, or was she just too involved in her work?

"She wasn't really touchy-feely." I blinked back tears.

"Well, when I was a wee angel first on earth, and none too happy about it, one of the elder female angels used to stroke my hair to help calm me down," he replied. "Worked every time. I could . . ." He motioned to me. "No funny business, of course. This is strictly professional."

I couldn't suppress a giggle.

"What?" His eyes widened in defense.

"When you first told me you were an angel, and I said angels helped people sleep, you were all offended, and now, you're actually . . ." I smiled in spite of myself.

"I don't have to." He raised his hands.

"No, please," I said. "I . . . want you to."

He sat next to me, resting his back against the worn headboard. Instinctively, I laid my head on his shoulder. He cradled me into his arm. With his free hand, he caressed my temple with short, soft strokes. My body molded into his like we were two halves always meant to make a whole: my knee tucked against his thigh, my arm draped across his stomach, my cheek resting in the swell of his chest. Heaven.

I willed myself to stay awake so I wouldn't miss a minute of the divine closeness, but the warmth of his body, the rhythm of his heart, and the tender massaging hypnotized me. Serenity engulfed me and I slipped into the deepest, sweetest sleep of my short life.

CHAPTER 21

An angry buzzing rang in my ears. I opened my eyes and found I was alone in my bed. The first rays of the dawn were peeking from beneath my curtains, and the whole house was still. It was Sunday morning, but barely. I rolled over at the noise on my nightstand. My phone was vibrating its way to a seizure.

I picked it up and tried to focus on the screen to see what time it was and who in the world would call me so early. I prayed the call had nothing to do with Jo.

5:30 AM
HUNTER

She must be up with the nuns for disciplinary breakfast duty. Knowing Hunter, it wouldn't be the first time . . .

Before I could even say hello, Hunter started whispering frantically, "Maren! Is that you? You've got to help me. I'm in so much trouble!"

The desperation in her voice kicked me awake. "What's wrong?"

"Everything!" she said. "Oh, Maren! He was such a nice guy, he was only trying to help me, and they killed him. They killed him! Then they came after me"—she started to sob—"and I ran to the first place I could find . . ."

"Hunter, Hunter . . ." I tried to sound soothing while my body prickled with fear. She was freaking me out.

220

Hunter was anything but a crybaby. "You're talking too fast. I can't understand you. Who's 'they'?"

"The guard, the demons, and then these shadows. Everyone! They're all after me!" Her crying escalated in passion but quieted in volume, as if she'd put her hand over her own mouth.

"Where are you?" I asked.

"In the church. It was down the street. They couldn't follow me in."

Sanctuary. She had been chased by darkness, just like in my dream. I crept to the window and cracked it open. Gavin was sitting on the ledge of the roof, about ten feet away. I motioned for him to come back inside.

"Slow down," I said. "First, are you safe?" Gavin settled next to me on the window seat. I tilted the phone so he could hear too.

"I think so; as long as I stay inside, anyway. But you've got to help me, Maren! I've no one else to call!"

"Of course," I answered, unsure of exactly what I could do. "But what happened? Start at the beginning. And calm down. You're fine. You're going to be fine."

She took a deep breath and tried to stop crying. She managed, mostly, but little wheezy hiccups still snuck into each sentence.

"I knew I shouldn't have gone—*hh-huh-hh*," she said, "but I wanted so badly to prove I was good enough for the Abbey—*hh-huh-hh*—and they must have seen me looking at the drawings, because—*hh-huh-hh* . . ."

"What drawings?" I interrupted.

"The ones from your mom's—*hh-huh-hh*—book," she exhaled.

Gavin's look reminded me I'd sworn I hadn't shown anyone. I scrunched up my face into a contrite expression and mouthed the word *Sorry*. I'd have to tell him about Hunter and why I'd sent her the secret pictures; how she was an Abbey orphan too, and that I'd wanted to help her land her dream job.

"I recognized one of the buildings, so I decided to go check it out," she continued. "The square castle with the turrets. It's the Tower—*hh-huh-hh*—of London."

Even though I didn't know what it looked like, I did know what the Tower of London *was*: the infamous fortress where prisoners like Henry VIII's wives were kept before they were beheaded.

I instantly regretted not telling Hunter I'd been to one of the demon strongholds myself and had barely gotten out alive. I thought about Jo in her hospital bed, her body wracked with poison. Why didn't I warn Hunter when I'd had the chance? My stomach turned sour. It was all my fault. I brought this evil to Britain with me, thanks to my mom's journal, and now two of my friends were in danger of dying at the hands of demons. I had to do something.

"Maren? Are you there?" Hunter asked, jolting me out of my thoughts.

"Yes, Tower of London. So what happened?"

Hunter took a deep breath. "This terribly ugly guard started bothering me, pushing me on the shoulder, and telling me I was in trouble. He tried to take my phone away, and this nice bloke—this tourist, I think—he came to my defense. He was really lovely, Maren, not as hand-some as you said Gavin is, but very good—"

"Okay, I get it. Then what?" I interrupted, now morti-fied that Gavin was listening in. I leaned away from him a bit, but he followed, moving closer to me. I was pretty sure I saw him smile out of the corner of my eye.

"Then this other guard came—he must have been a superior or something. He was amazingly good look-ing too, but he got into a fight with the tourist, and then he . . ." She started crying again.

"He what, Hunter? It's okay. It's not your fault." *It's my fault.*

"Th-th-they started swinging at each other," she gasped, "an-and the new guard punched th-the guy in the face, and his n-n-neck snapped." She was back to sobbing.

"Noooo!" I breathed.

"Yes, I swear. He killed the guy. In one blow. And then it was absolute chaos. The guy's friends all ran off, the guards tried to grab me, and I just ran. It was horrible. It was like a call went out to every demon in the country, and they came after me. They were like shadows, pushing and tripping me. I fell and bashed my knee." *Just like in my dream.* "I even lost my necklace, Maren," Hunter wailed, "the one from my mum. But I just kept running. I must have run a mile when I saw the church dome all lit up. They chased me all the way. I barely made it in."

"How are you still there?" I asked. "It's five thirty in the morning. Did they give you permission to stay overnight?"

"No, I hid until all the visitors left, and I've been hid-ing ever since. I could live in this place for a year and no one would find me," she said. "Crap! My phone's about to die. It took me forever to find a signal in here . . . You have to come get me! I can't even step outside—they're out there waiting for me. I can hear them!"

"No, of course, of course, I'll leave right away," I said. Gavin was vigorously shaking his head in the negative direction, but I ignored him.

"Thank you." Hunter sounded like she wanted to start crying again, but discovered she was too tired. "I knew I could count on you."

"Wait!" I said before I lost her to the empty battery. "Where are you?"

"St. Paul's," she answered. "Hurry!"

The line clicked and went dead.

I turned to Gavin, panicked. "St. Paul's? That's all we've got to go on? St. Paul's? There must be a million St. Paul's churches!"

"Actually," Gavin answered, "when it comes to London, there's only one."

❀ ❀ ❀

St. Paul's, it turns out, is the largest cathedral in London. I should have recognized the name, because it's where Princess Diana married Prince Charles. My mom wasn't sentimental about things, except when it came to Princess Diana. My mom told me that when Diana died, she called in sick to work and lay on the couch in front of the live television coverage, crying for two straight days. When I was born, she gave me the middle name Diana in tribute to the real-life princess who had to navigate a not-so-fairy-tale world.

Now Hunter was hiding there. Five minutes after she hung up, I got a single text from her. She must have tried to send it out before she called, but it had been delayed. It was ominously short, just five words: "STUCK IN ST PAULS. PLEASE HELP!" I was glad I had gotten to speak to her, because the message alone would have freaked me out, but it did underscore the urgency. I had to get to her quickly.

"How long is a plane ride down to London?" I asked Gavin, already moving around my room and throwing things into a small backpack.

"With heightened security at the airports, the train is faster," he answered. "Only four hours from Glasgow to London. But for you, it's zero."

"What do you mean, 'zero'? Are we going to drive there or something?"

"No, I mean there's zero chance that you're going," he answered. "Why would you?"

I stopped packing and studied his face to see if he was joking, but he looked pretty serious. Which made me pretty furious.

"Why wouldn't I?" I said.

"It's too dangerous," he answered.

"Well, I don't care." The words tumbled out of my mouth. "She's my friend, and she's in trouble, and it's all my fault, and she doesn't have anyone else."

"Well, I *do* care, Maren," he answered. "And it's not happening." I loved when Gavin said my name in his thick accent. My heart melted like summer snow. Until he ruined it with the whole telling me what to do part.

"'Not happening'?" I said. "You're not the boss of me.

It *is* happening." *Did I really just say, "You're not the boss of me"?* Now *I* was acting like the kindergartener who teased the boy she liked. *Ridiculous.* He made me act like this. He made me crazy.

"What exactly is your plan?" he asked, far too smugly. "You're going to race down to London, go to St. Paul's, and then what?"

"We'll find Magnificat," I said. "I'll turn in my mom's stuff, get the antidote, and we'll all be safe."

"How are you two going to leave the church when there are demons outside who've surely recorded Hunter's heartbeat?"

"I don't know." I threw up my hands, anger rushing through me. "I honestly have no freaking idea about anything!" I hissed, wanting to holler but not wanting to wake up my grandparents any further. To my extreme frustration and embarrassment, my eyes brimmed with tears. But there was no holding them back. There was no holding anything back. "Is that what you want to hear? *I don't know!* All I know is I lost my mom—who apparently kept her entire life a secret from me—and I'm alone in the middle of nowhere. My only two friends in the whole world are either on their deathbed or trapped in a church. All because of me. And I have to try to do something about it. I don't know what, I don't know how, but I have to try." Tears rolled down my face, but I didn't care.

Gavin, however, did. He inhaled sharply, like he didn't know what to do with my burst of emotion. "I'm sorry," he said gently, placing a hand on my shoulder. "I didn't mean to make you upset. I just . . . I just don't want to see anything bad happen to you. I'll take care of it. I was waiting for you to wake up to tell you that I was going to go to Magnificat anyway."

"What you mean?" I asked, wiping at my cheeks. My fury dissipated like clouds in the sun. Gavin somehow had the ability to make me instantly happy no matter what the circumstance.

"The village decided I should go to Magnificat to see if there's an antidote," he replied.

"So they believe my mom's encryption?"

He nodded. "We knew something was being planned. Now we know what."

"Why you?" I asked. "Why are you going?"

"Because it's my assignment. This is my town, my time," he said, pride illuminating his eyes.

"Well, I'm coming with you," I said.

"No, you're not," he answered.

I wasn't going to get mad again. I had to stay focused. I turned away and continued filling my backpack. I got my mother's journal, carefully wrapped it in a scarf, and zipped it inside.

"What are you doing?" he asked.

"Packing," I said simply.

"Why?"

"You've got your duty, and I've got mine. You're going to London. Great. I'm going to get Hunter. Maybe I'll see you there, maybe I won't."

"You're serious?" he said. "You're going to go?"

"I'm sorry, but I have to. I started this by sending Hunter pictures from my mom's book. I've got to go finish it."

❀ ❀ ❀

Gavin sat sullenly in the overstuffed chair while I finished getting my things together. Short of locking me in a closet, which I was pretty sure was against his "angel rules," he knew he couldn't stop me. And I guessed that since I was going and he was going, he would just go with me. But he wasn't going to be happy about it.

I peppered him with questions, hoping he would forget to be in a bad mood. "Who's going to watch over Aviemore while you're gone? Are they going to send another angel?"

"Aye," he mumbled.

"Just one?"

"One's not enough?" he asked, arching one eyebrow in an incredibly sexy way.

"I'm sure it is, I mean, *you* are . . ." I stammered, trying to regain my composure. "But why does each town only get one angel? It seems like there should be more."

"For bigger towns, there is," he said with a shrug. "But there are a lot of areas to cover all at once. We're spread pretty thin."

"Are you going straight to Magnificat, or to St. Paul's first?" I asked, trying to sound casual.

"I suppose I'm following you to St. Paul's," he sighed.

I stopped packing and perched on the arm of the chair. "I know you're this huge Warrior and I'm upsetting your mission, but there's no reason we can't work together." I flashed my sweetest smile. "Isn't that what they do at the Abbey? Angels and humans work together?"

"We don't work for the Abbey," he reminded me. "I'm

not supposed to be interacting with humans at all, let alone sitting in their bedrooms watching them pack."

For balance, I rested my right hand on my knee. With his forefinger, he began tracing the outline of it. It tingled so deliciously, my entire being focused on his one finger lightly brushing against my skin. Every nerve ending tickled, and I could feel laughter all the way down to my toes. It was an unexplained but glorious electricity. I could hardly bear it.

Suddenly, he stopped, as if he only just noticed what he was doing; as if he'd lost control of himself and didn't mean to. He opened his mouth to say something, then closed it, changing his mind. He yanked his hand away from mine, and stood up quickly, almost knocking me off the chair's arm as he did.

"All right, let's go," he said, abruptly.

So much for this love story.

❁ ❁ ❁

There was no way I could tell my grandparents I was taking off on an emergency trip to London in order to help a teenage orphan they'd never met battle demons. But I couldn't just disappear, either. I needed a good cover story.

By the time the sun rose and they woke up, I had it ready. I was headed to London with the after-school choir, I told them. That with all the worry of Jo being in the hospital, I'd completely forgotten to tell them about the London competition. I had my phone, I assured them, Gavin the trustworthy tutor was waiting to drive me to the train station, and I had to run.

I don't think they bought it, but they didn't stop me from going. They exchanged a few glances I thought might qualify as worried, but my grandmother set her lips into a thin line, nodded her permission, and I was out the door.

I felt terrible about being so dishonest with them, but what else could I do? I knew lying was a sin, a commandment even. But it wasn't going to hell after I died that worried me. It was going there beforehand.

CHAPTER 22

My first breaths in England's capital were heavy with anticipation. The platform at London's Victoria Station where we disembarked was outdoors, but covered by an arch of twisted steel and glass windows that whispered of a thousand good-byes.

My awe was short-lived, though, as we needed to catch the quickest subway to St. Paul's. Following the round, red "Underground" signs that promised to deliver us to the "Tube" meant traversing through endless, dingy passages that reeked of an unhappy mixture of urine and ash. The tunnels were ancient, but not in a charming, historical way—more a depressing, bomb shelter way. The dismal off-white walls lacked any luster at all; in fact, they seemed to absorb what little florescent light there was.

Just when I thought our dank, claustrophobic wandering couldn't get any worse, we turned a corner and discovered a filthy bum with matted hair on his head and his face hunched on the ground next to an empty coffee cup.

Gavin must not have liked the look of him either, because he stopped, told me to wait where I was, and walked over to the guy. After crouching down and talking for a few moments, Gavin dropped a couple of what he called "quid"—the funniest word for dollars I'd ever heard—into the battered container, grabbed my hand, and ushered me back out of the tunnel, back the way we'd come.

"The Tube isn't safe," Gavin said. "We need to catch a taxi."

"What did that man tell you?" I asked, as I hurried to keep up with Gavin's long strides.

"That demons regularly ride the rails looking for innocent young girls heading into London," he answered.

"What does a homeless man know about demons? And how did you know *he* wasn't a demon?"

"I can see demons and angels as clearly as if they were wearing signs on their foreheads," he stated with a shrug.

"They don't just blend in with the rest of us?"

"Happily, not to me, or I'd have a heck of a time protecting you. They look like humans, but with breath. I can see their breath."

"Like it's a cold day?"

"Precisely."

"And that guy wasn't a demon?" I persisted.

"No; actually, he was an angel."

I jerked to a stop, yanking his fingers as I did. "That disgusting homeless man was an *angel*?"

"Aye. Lots of the homeless are angels. Since most people walk right past and ignore them, it's the perfect way for us to protect the public while hidden in plain sight."

Gavin held the battered metal-and-glass door that led to the street open for me. Once we were through, he tightened his grip on my hand. "Come on," he said. "Let's queue up for a taxi."

The line was long, and full of strange people jostling for room. I was bumped more than once. Every push made me nervous, since I had my mother's secret journal in my backpack—the journal she possibly was killed for. It wasn't heavy, but it weighed me down with a thousand pounds of guilt. I had to get to Hunter and then to Jo before it was too late.

❀ ❀ ❀

Our driver, a rough-looking, very crabby older woman with sagging cheeks and a snarl etched on her face, was named Flora, which struck me as funny since that was the name of one of the nice, grandmotherly fairies in Disney's cartoon *Sleeping Beauty*.

I was restless during the thirty-minute trip, anxious to get to St. Paul's, and worried both about Jo dying in the hospital before I could find her a cure and Hunter being stuck in a church surrounded by demons. The acid bubbling in my stomach from skipping breakfast didn't help.

I was still wearing my backpack—I'd refused to take it off and let the driver put it in the trunk. It bulged behind my back, adding to my discomfort. The only good thing about being crammed into the back of the small black car was being crammed next to Gavin. His muscular body barely fit in the cab, forcing our legs to rest against one other. As always, he smelled amazing; this time like a combination of musk and fresh grass. I tried not to be obvious that I was inhaling it, loving it, but it was hard.

As we approached Ludgate Hill, the massive dome of St. Paul's finally appeared, floating above everything like a giant, ethereal slice of architectural heaven. Hunter's humongous hiding place. I'd read in a guidebook on the train that at 365 feet tall, St. Paul's was the tallest building in London until 1962. Except for St. Peter's Basilica in Rome, there is no bigger church dome on the planet.

We were still a couple of miles away, but as we got closer, I strained in my seat to get a better look. London streets, I discovered, tended to run in large circles rather than neat squares, and as such, we got to see the cathedral from all sides. From one direction, it looked like a massive train station, very long and solemn. From another, it reminded me of the United States Capitol building in Washington, D.C. And at what I guessed to be the main front entrance, it looked like a giant church with bell towers, clock towers, and Roman columns littered with statues.

We were only a few blocks from the cathedral when a loud thud echoed across the roof of the cab.

"Must 'ave hit a bird," Flora grunted, flexing her stubby fingers. "Or a squirrel."

"But it sounded like it was above us," I said.

"Maybe it bounced off the grill or fell out of a tree," Gavin suggested.

Flora growled, "Better not 'ave damaged my car."

We sat in silence at a traffic light, probably all thinking about the poor, most likely blind, creature, when we heard honking. The driver of the car to our right made a terrible face, and then hit the gas as the light turned green, cutting us off and speeding away.

"Piss off!" Flora shouted to his tailpipe. "Honking doesn't give you permission to drive like a beast!"

A car to our left honked as well. The driver was contorting his face and pointing at the roof of our cab before he too sped off.

"What's he on about?" Flora asked.

"Maybe there's still some of the bird or squirrel on the roof . . ." I said, hoping I was wrong.

"Crikey," she answered. "Wouldn't that just be a fine how-you-do?"

Her radio crackled: "Lady Cab number 121 . . . do . . . read?"

"This is LC 121," Flora answered.

As we pulled up to another red light on the quiet neighborhood street, a sickening scraping reverberated above our heads—the sound of metal on metal. I couldn't imagine a squirrel was trying to hold on with his little paws as we drove along, but since there were no low-hanging branches around, I couldn't figure what else would make such a noise. I tilted my head to try and see the top of the car. All I saw was a curve of shiny black paint.

"I'm . . . Livery . . . to your left. Do . . . see me?" the male voice on Flora's radio asked. We all looked over and saw a cab next to us, its driver holding his handset to his mouth. His eyes bulged from their sockets.

"Aye," Flora answered.

"You . . . something . . . roof," the radio reported. The scratching and static both got louder.

"What's that?" Flora hollered into the mic. She held up her radio, pointed to it and shrugged, then motioned for the other driver to roll down his window.

He rolled his eyes, shook his head wildly, and gunned his engine through the still-red light.

"Noo . . . ooo . . . ," the radio crackled again.

"I'll be a monkey's uncle," Flora said. "Everyone's gone daft today!"

Gavin squeezed my hand and signaled for me to slide closer. "Climb over me," he whispered.

"What?"

A tapping on the glass near my face made me turn back toward my window. A hand with wrinkled, reptilian skin and sharp claws was inching down from the roof.

I opened my mouth to scream, but Gavin planted his lips over mine. I was so shocked, I forgot how to breathe, let alone scream. He let go of my hand, and buried his hand in my hair, holding my head to keep our silent lips locked. He climbed over me, and I slid into his seat. We were still kissing as he slowly started to roll down the window. The demon hand slid in the car, Gavin kicked my door open with his foot, and abruptly pulled his face away from mine.

"*Run!*" he yelled.

I froze just long enough to see him grab the demon's hand with both of his and yank. I hurled myself out of the car and ran. The cathedral was still several blocks away, peeking out from between the buildings. I glanced back. I couldn't see Gavin, but a large, scaly creature flipped off the car toward Gavin's side. The air was pierced by the familiar high-pitch screaming from my dreams, and the sound of glass shattering. I ran faster.

I pushed myself through the alley, emerged into the plaza in front of St. Paul's, and bolted up the stairs toward the massive wooden doors. A breeze caught my hair just as I approached the entrance, followed by a violent tug on my backpack. I slipped down two shallow stone steps as the supernatural scream rang out again. This time, it was right in my ear.

I was still standing, so I twisted to get a better look at what had caught me. A thin sheet of crimson skin, criss-crossed with veins, obscured my view and beat at my face. Just as my brain registered what it was, a searing pain exploded across my back around the edges of the pack. The demon had a hold of me, and was dragging me back-ward, away from the church. I couldn't let them have my mother's journal, but I was no match for this nightmare creature. I wondered exactly how strong the straps on my backpack were. Would they break, or would I be lifted off the ground until I fell to my death too?

A stronger gust of wind knocked me to the ground. I was free, the backpack still securely attached. I picked myself up, threw my body up the stairs, and crashed through the doors screaming "Sanctuary!" just to be safe.

The cold air of the lobby hit me in the face like a slap. A small woman with large, round glasses and gray hair pulled into an entirely too-tight bun sat in the ticket booth, staring at me with mouth open. I smoothed my hair, ignored the blood trickling down my knee under my jeans, and walked toward her as if lunging through the door was the way all Americans entered famous cathedrals.

"How many?" she asked.

"Two, please," Gavin answered. He was standing at my elbow, perfectly composed. He winked at me and stepped forward to take our tickets.

"Enjoy your visit to St. Paul's," the volunteer said in a monotone voice that suggested we might not.

My heart was thumping wildly in my chest, and my body started to quiver involuntarily. To steady me, Gavin rested a strong hand on my shoulder, which kept me upright, but didn't stop my thoughts from tumbling over one another like pebbles in a toddler's pocket. Demons were real. Demons were here. I'd seen them with my own two eyes, or at least parts of them. And those parts were horrifying. Hulking and vicious, all scales and membranes and blood. While I had seen the beasts in the forest, they were running away from me, not trying to slice my guts open. And awful as he was, Anders didn't have wings and claws . . . that I knew of, anyway.

And there were at least two of them. How many more? How strong were they? Not so strong that Gavin hadn't been able to protect me, but what if he wasn't around? I had barely made it inside, and now, I realized with a shiver, I was as stuck as Hunter.

CHAPTER 23

My body was still trying to ward off tiny tremors of shock as Gavin led me through the lobby and into the cathedral. We slipped into a short pew at the back that butted up against one of the church's soaring carved columns and sat down. I leaned my cheek against the cool stone pillar and tried to calm myself down. Having a nervous breakdown wasn't going to help rescue Hunter or get an antidote to Jo. I needed to get a grip as quickly as possible so we could get moving again.

I tried not to think about the demons outside, although their screaming still rang in my ears. I searched my brain for something safe, something calm. I glanced at Gavin. Everything about him looked peaceful. How was that even possible? He'd just battled a demon, maybe two, and he looked fine. He looked better than fine; he looked wonderful. His hair, his cheeks, his lips . . . his lips! The kiss in the cab. I could still feel it on my lips. Why had he done it?

Obviously, he had kissed me to protect me, to keep me from screaming, to buy us extra time. But wouldn't his hand over my mouth have worked just as well? It might not be a polite way to silence someone, but I was also pretty sure making out with human girls was not part of his job description. He had chosen to kiss me. I had to say something before I burst.

"So, what was that all about back there . . . in the cab?" I asked.

239

"You mean the demons?" He was staring straight ahead, eyes fixed on the front of the church. "Not to worry, I took care of them."

"No, I mean the kiss."

He whipped his head around to face me, his eyes flashing, as if he couldn't believe I'd actually said the words out loud. A parade of emotions marched across his face: surprise, confusion, adoration, guilt. I clung desperately to the fleeting look of adoration, but as quickly as it came, it was gone. "Nothing. That was nothing," he said.

I wasn't giving up. "No, it was *something*."

"Please respect the sanctity of St. Paul's Cathedral by not speaking loudly," a man with a formal-sounding English accent said. I looked around, but didn't see anyone. "The use of photographic or video recording devices of any kind is strictly forbidden." Gavin pointed at a small speaker embedded in the wall as the recorded message began to replay in French.

Then he shot me a new look, a look I remembered seeing during our encounter in the post office: it was commanding and cold. "Not here," he whispered between clenched teeth. "Not now." He stood up and walked down the main aisle.

It was my turn for a flood of confusion, sadness, self-pity, and heartbreak. Now that he finally had given in, did he regret it? Was I a terrible kisser? Did I repulse him? If so, he was a great actor, because he'd kissed me more than was necessary. It wasn't a simple peck. It was a deep, probing, passionate kiss. Maybe he was scared to admit to himself what had happened, what might happen next . . .

I followed Gavin, but was determined not to look at him. I looked up instead, and I was instantly overwhelmed. Although I'd watched a grainy recording of Princess Diana's 1982 wedding, it didn't do justice to St. Paul's Cathedral in person. The enormity of the open space felt like being inside a carved-out mountain so intricately decorated, it was hard to take in; every surface burst with engravings, paintings, and mosaics. Soaring marble arches decorated with cherubs nestled in sculpted leaves flanked the long aisle to the altar. Tiered golden chandeliers hung in the center of each archway, while thirty-foot black-iron candelabras rose protectively from the floor near each supporting column. While everything above the floor was gilded and magnificent, creamy white and shining gold, the floor itself, a stark black-and-white checkerboard pattern, threw me. It underscored the uncomfortable feeling that I was a pawn in a cosmic, deadly game of chess, which I supposed I was.

As gigantic as the cathedral was, it was equally as quiet. Even though visitors streamed in and out, they were all silent. Perhaps they took the audio instructions to heart, or perhaps, like me, the tremendousness of their surroundings left them dumbstruck.

The cathedral was cross-shaped, and we were at the bottom. We started up the longest aisle, the nave, scanning the seats for Hunter. At the intersection of the cross where the left and right transepts began, the ceiling opened up even more as we found ourselves standing under the cavernous Great Dome. Hunter was nowhere to be found.

"Let's go check out the quire," Gavin whispered, his

lips brushing my ear. I shivered even though I wasn't cold. *Is he warming up to me again?*

He took my hand and guided me around the pulpit and into the choir area behind it. On either side, the quire was lined with tiered wooden benches that faced each other. It reminded me more of an elaborate jury box than a place where young boys would sing. Gavin did a quick check to make sure Hunter wasn't lounging on any of the cozy pews.

"Any idea where she might be?" he asked. I thought I saw something in his eyes, like he wanted to tell me something but couldn't.

"Her phone died before she could say," I replied. "I had no idea this place was so big."

We visited the High Altar and the American Memorial Chapel in the Apse, and then circled the outer aisles of the church, peeking into dozens of small chapels and prayer rooms. I was especially interested in the Chapel of St. Michael, the archangel, and St. George, the Christian soldier who slayed a dragon, considering who I was with and what had happened on our way in. There was no sign of Hunter. As we looped back around the cathedral, having walked over a mile in the process, worry gnawed at me.

"What if she's not here?" I asked Gavin.

"Nonsense," he answered, his accent adding extra syllables to the word so it sounded like a song. "Where else would she be? We know from recent experience that there are demons outside quite on guard. She'd not have gotten far."

"Exactly," I said. "What if she didn't think we'd come,

went outside, and got . . . killed?" I could hardly say the word. I was afraid admitting the possibility might somehow jinx Hunter—and Jo.

"Not likely," he said. "First, we're not late. We've come when we said we would. Second, she knows better than to go outside. She'd not give up that easily. And third, if they had gotten her, I don't believe the demons would be still prowling around, waiting."

"I guess," I agreed. "What do we do now?"

"I'm going to go back to the front door and grab a map," he answered. "Stay here. I'll be right back."

As he walked away, I turned my attention to the alcove next to me. Unlike the others lined with white marble, this one was dominated by a towering doorframe painted shiny black. The double doors were guarded on either side by life-size alabaster angel statues, one holding a dark, bronze sword, the other a thin black horn. While most of the inscriptions in the cathedral were in Latin, the gold lettering etched into the lintel at the top were in English: "Through the gate of death we pass to our joyful resurrection." I rubbed the backs of my arms. Thankfully, the doors were knob-less and sealed shut, but the statues' expressions were anything but joyful. Their vacant eyes stared at the floor like all was lost.

I turned away and leaned against the curved wall to wait for Gavin, forcing my own face into an expression of confidence. I didn't want to look lost.

"Are you lost?" I accepted my failure as a kind-looking elderly man with a black-and-white mustache and twinkling blue eyes appeared next to me. A large flashlight dangled from the belt of his security guard uniform. His name badge read "Alfred."

"No, I'm not," I said, embarrassed for no reason. "I am looking for someone though. A teenage girl by herself? Blonde hair, bangs?"

He squinted his eyes, as if trying to remember. I wondered how long that would take, and wished I'd never asked. Finally, he spoke. "You might try the library upstairs," he answered slowly, jerking his thumb over his shoulder.

"There's an upstairs? And a library in here?" I asked.

"Of course," the guard said with a chuckle. "And a downstairs too. We've got a museum, a movie theater, a shop, even a crypt with a café."

You can eat with dead bodies? Creepy.

Alfred continued. "The library's upstairs, east wing. I believe there's a young girl who's been sitting there for the better part of today."

"Thank you so much," I gushed, relieved that while he had tripled our search area, he'd also given us our first real lead.

He touched the tip of his hat, nodded, and walked away. When Gavin returned, I practically shouted the update.

With the map, we found the stairs to the library in no time. They were perfectly circular and rather dizzying. Gavin took the stairs two at a time; I tried my best not to fall on my face. Gavin's hurry was frightening me. I wondered if he knew something I didn't, something about what was going on back in Aviemore.

As soon as we passed through the doorway into the library, I spotted her. Hunter was sitting at a long wooden table, a book open in front of her. She was resting her head on her hand, and her eyes were shut. *A holy nap, no doubt.*

We hurried to the table and slid into chairs next to her. She immediately sensed the intrusion to her space, and her eyes shot open. When she saw me, she nearly knocked me off my seat with a sideways hug.

"Maren!" she cried, and was promptly greeted by several much louder "shhhs!" from a group of old ladies in colorful hats sitting on the opposite side.

Hunter dropped her head and voice. "Oh, Maren! You're here! You've come for me! Thank you, thank you!" She wrapped herself around me like a love-starved snake and squeezed.

I patted her on the back, but wriggled out of her grip at the same time, uncomfortable from the display of gratitude. *How am I going to tell her that the only thing we managed to do was barely make it into the cathedral and become as trapped as she was?*

I leaned forward so Hunter and Gavin could shake hands and exchange introductions.

"Did you have any trouble getting in?" she asked. Worry spread across her face like a fast-moving fog.

"Only if you count being attacked by demons." I tried to sound braver than I felt. "Don't worry," I added. "Gavin took care of them."

"But there will be more," Gavin added, ominously.

"What are we going to do?" Hunter's eyes were wide and shiny.

"We're going to take you to Magnificat with us," I said. "It's a safe haven. For humans working with the Abbey."

She perked right up, clearly eager to leave her pew-filled prison, especially for the mysterious Abbey. "Well, let's go, then!"

"It's not that easy," Gavin answered. "First, we have to locate it. The entrance to Magnificat changes, and I don't know where it currently is in London."

"How do we find it?" Hunter asked.

"It's well marked. You should be able to see it for miles," he assured us. "We've just got to get outside and take a look."

"What do you mean, 'outside'?" Hunter asked.

"What do you mean, 'marked'?" I said. "By what?"

"By a giant spider," he replied, smiling as Hunter and I both instinctively recoiled.

CHAPTER 24

After climbing an astounding 528 steep steps through dark, windowless, circular passages and tunnels so narrow, I doubted Santa Claus could make it, we reached the top of the Great Dome. Or as near to the top as they let visitors. Our destination, the Golden Gallery, an external lookout that wound around the highest tower above the dome, would give us panoramic views of London.

Hardly any tourists made the climb all the way to the top. Most stopped halfway, at the Stone Gallery, so we were alone. We huddled just inside the open doorway, the wind howling in our ears, waiting for instructions from Gavin.

"Remember, keep your back to the wall at all times, and you'll be safe," he said.

"You mean, like, safe from a demon swooping by and plucking us off this crazy-high perch?" Hunter asked. Her cheeks were a little pale. It was odd to see her flustered. She was always so tough and in control. I wondered if she had a fear of heights.

"They can't touch a single part of the cathedral," he assured us, "nor can they touch you if you're touching it."

"And we're looking for a giant *spider*?" I asked.

"Aye, a giant spider sculpture. It's usually perched on a rooftop or next to a building's entrance. It's black, and it's thirty feet tall. So between the three of us, we should be able to spot it, no problem."

As Gavin had explained on our way up, at the turn of the last century, several prominent art patrons who supported angels had commissioned giant spider sculptures to be placed in key international cities, marking the entrance to Magnificat to help ensure that the safe haven could be more easily found. The spiders were installed in Bilbao, Spain; Seoul, Korea; Tokyo, Japan; Ottawa, Canada; and London. There was an additional army of traveling sculptures that moved around the world as they were needed, from St. Petersburg to Havana, Paris, Washington, D.C., and even Kansas City, Missouri. *My home state.*

The giant spiders were created by a French sculptor, Louise Bourgeois, and named *Maman*—"Mother" in her native tongue.

"Am I the only one who finds this vaguely disturbing?" Hunter continued. "Aren't spiders more of a demon thing? Why would angels want to use them?"

"Well . . ." Gavin started. "In many cultures, they are signs of good luck. They decorate their Christmas trees with spider webs in Germany."

"Yeah, I'm not buying it," Hunter replied.

"The spider was really nice in *Charlotte's Web*," I said, trying to help Gavin out. It didn't work.

"Never heard of it," she answered.

"You've been to Scotland," Gavin said, trying a new angle. "I know you've heard the story of Robert the Bruce and the spider."

She perked up a little, obviously remembering. "My mum used to tell me that story when I was little."

"Who's Robert Bruce?" I asked.

"Robert the Bruce was a great Scottish warrior," Gavin answered. "One day, he was sitting in a cave in the Highlands, depressed about recent defeats, when he saw a spider try to spin her web in the mouth of the cave. Every time she tried to make a connection between the roof and the wall, she failed. But she never gave up. She just kept trying until she got it. Supposedly, Robert was inspired by the spider and decided to press on. He won several big victories, and was crowned King of Scotland soon after."

"So the spider is supposed to remind us not to give up?" I looked at Gavin.

"Yes, you're to stay strong, both of you," Gavin concluded. "No matter what."

"No Matter What" seemed like an ominous destination. One I didn't want to visit.

❀ ❀ ❀

The Golden Gallery wasn't golden and was hardly a gallery. Instead of a sightseeing promenade, we stepped out, single file, onto a crumbling stone ledge less than two tennis shoes wide, ringed with a rusted guardrail that reached just above my waist. The wind repeatedly whipped my hair into my eyes, and made the protective fence in front of me wobble. I didn't feel very protected.

As Gavin and Hunter circled around out of sight, I pressed my back firmly against the wall and gazed out between the two front towers of St. Paul's—one had a clock in it and the other one just had a big hole where a clock should be. Across the horizon, construction cranes lifted their heads like mechanical giraffes. A massive Ferris wheel pushed its enclosed bullet-shaped buckets on an infinite ride. And a big, brown river I assumed was the River Thames slithered lazily past to my left. I wondered why they pronounced it "Tems," like "stems," in Britain, instead of how the word looked. I counted four bridges crossing it; the nearest one, all shiny gray steel, seemed like the newest.

I shuffled my feet a bit to get a better look at the closest bridge. It began at St. Paul's and swooped across the river to a large building that resembled a factory due to its bland, brown façade, lack of windows, and huge smokestack-like square tower. The bridge itself was narrow. As I squinted, I saw that it was covered with people, not cars.

Why would so many people want to walk from the cathedral to a factory that they would build a whole bridge for it? Then I saw it: an enormous, black, spindly spider statue. *Maman!* It was perched right next to the factory, rising up from the grass, facing me, practically staring me down. Dozens of people gathered around its legs, taking pictures and pointing. Surprisingly, especially considering my distaste for modern art, I didn't find *Maman* to be ugly or scary or particularly villainous. Instead, she was elegant and otherworldly, like she had just crawled out of a fairy tale.

"I found it!" I yelled. "The spider. I found it!"

Gavin called out from my left, and Hunter from my right, when I heard an all-too-familiar screeching overhead. A sudden breeze hit my face, and I closed my eyes, half expecting to be torn off the ledge by demon claws. Instead, Gavin grabbed my hand.

"It's okay," he soothed, as I physically flinched. "You're fine. We're fine. There's Hunter. See, everyone's accounted for." His voice was calm, but his eyes darted around the sky. There were two of us girls, who knows how many demons, and only one of him.

"Where is it?" he asked.

I pointed. "Over there. By that factory."

"That's not a factory," Hunter said. "It's the Tate Modern. The museum of modern art."

It made perfect sense. Where else could you put a giant spider in plain sight? I had thought about the zoo, but as I looked at the towering, black arachnid, I realized it would probably scare the pants off small children. Yes, the modern art museum was perfect. But perfectly far away.

"So that's it? That's the entrance to Magnificat?" I asked. "At the Tate?"

"It would seem so," Gavin said. He was studying something intently, but it wasn't the spider.

"What?" I asked.

"The bridge," he said. Unlike the other heavier, squared-off bridges along the river, the bridge to the Tate was all swoopy and loopy, like a treetop bridge supported by giant concrete *Ys*.

"That's the Wobbly Bridge," Hunter declared.

"The what?" I asked.

"Well, technically it's the Millennium Bridge, since it opened in the year 2000, but it swayed so much when people first walked on it, they had to close it for two years. So we all call it the Wobbly Bridge," she explained.

I leaned toward Gavin. "The quickest way to the Tate is over that bridge, isn't it? And it's an open-air pedestrian bridge. We'll never make it across," I concluded.

"I'm not sure," he answered. "But I know how to find out." He ushered us back inside and down the stairs.

❀ ❀ ❀

We stopped at the last observation deck before the floor: the Whispering Gallery. This balcony was inside the dome, but still close to one hundred feet up. It held a ring of seats behind a safety rail so you could sit and ponder the art on the inside of the Great Dome without getting dizzy and falling to your death. Gavin led us both to a seat.

"Why is this called 'The Whispering Gallery'?" I whispered.

"Because if you face the wall and whisper, someone clear across on the other side can hear you," Hunter answered. "At least that's what the guidebook I read today said."

"Get out your iPhone, please, Hunter," Gavin interrupted.

"How'd you know I have an iPhone?" she asked, eyes wide.

"Because I read 'sent from my iPhone' on the bottom of your text last night," he answered.

She took it from her pocket and handed it to him, no longer impressed. "It's out of battery."

"I know, but we can fix that," he said. He flipped the phone over and pried off the back cover. He proceeded to remove all sorts of electronic plates, and I could sense Hunter's fear that he was permanently wrecking her phone. He found the battery and slid it out of the case.

"Hands out, palms up," he said to Hunter. He then

placed the remains of her phone into her hands, clutched the battery in his, and stood up. "I'll be right back."

Her face registered total dismay. I shrugged. I had no idea what he was doing. We watched as he walked back toward the door, where two young guys had just entered. He nodded a greeting and spoke to them. One of the guys handed him something and he took it, ducked back into the stairwell, and disappeared.

Less than five minutes later, Gavin reappeared. He tossed a small object back to the guy, nodded in thanks, and came toward us. He took the back piece of Hunter's phone from her hand, popped the battery back in, reassembled all the layers, and snapped it shut. He turned it over, hit the power button, and it miraculously blinked to life with a full charge.

"How did you do that?" Hunter asked, her voice tinged with genuine amazement.

"Let's just say you can do a lot of things with a pack of cigarettes and a lighter," he said, flipping rapidly through colorful screens, "including charging dead batteries and blowing your face off. Thankfully, I only managed the first one."

He held out the phone to Hunter. "I'm going to need you to put this down your shirt."

"Um, what?" She leaned away from him a bit.

"I need you to stick this on your chest. We're going to record your heartbeat."

"Why?" she asked.

"Humans have a distinct heartbeat that demons and angels can hear," he explained. "It's harder to hear in some places, like large crowds. I want to see if the demons outside can hear your heartbeat if you're crossing the Millennium Bridge."

"So you're going to send me across like a guinea pig, and you want my heartbeat recorded as a souvenir?"

"No, I'm going to send someone else across the bridge as a guinea pig, with your heartbeat in their pocket. I downloaded an app that uses the microphone to record your heartbeat. We'll record it, and then set your phone to replay it very quietly. I'll slip it in the pocket of those guys over there, and we'll go back up and watch what happens."

"How do you know they're going to the Tate?" Hunter asked.

"They told me," he said. "Now hurry up. I don't want to keep them waiting." He tapped the phone a few times to set it up, then handed it to Hunter. She held it under her shirt, over her heart, and we waited silently. When Gavin nodded, she pulled the phone out. He clicked the screen a few more times. He held it up, and we could see an animated heart pulsing. "Can you hear it?"

We both shook our heads. It must not have recorded correctly.

"Perfect," he said. "It's working, but I've got the volume low enough that humans can't hear it. Now to darken the screen, and done." He stood up and headed off after the guys who had just left the Whispering Gallery. When he returned, he motioned for us to follow him up the stairs.

Back on the windy Golden Gallery, we slid along the outside wall to the left, together this time, positioning ourselves in front of the Millennium Bridge.

"There they are!" Gavin said. He pointed to the young men as they walked across the St. Paul's courtyard and approached the bridge. So far, so good. They were pushing each other on the shoulders and goofing around. One of them lit a cigarette, and offered to do the same for his friend. They entered the bridge, both of them now smoking and chatting away.

We watched as they crossed, unharmed.

"I guess we're clear, right?" Hunter spoke too soon. A giant birdlike creature streaked across the sky and dove down toward the bridge. It grabbed one of the guys in its claws, let out a high-pitched scream, and then disappeared in the clouds. It happened so quickly and was such a blur, no one else saw it except for me, Gavin, and Hunter. The guy's friend didn't even know what had happened. He ran to the edge of the bridge and called down to the water, as if his friend might have been blown off.

I glanced at Hunter, who was three shades of pale and had her mouth hanging open. My own heart was pounding against my chest. I turned to Gavin.

"That guy . . . he's . . . he's gone. The demons . . . Did you see that?" I stuttered. The poor guy. I couldn't believe it. Gavin just stared straight ahead. "I . . . I thought you weren't supposed to kill humans?" I finally spit out.

"He's not dead . . . yet," Gavin answered. "And besides, he should know better than to smoke."

"Wh—" I started to protest, but he kept talking before I could get a full word out.

"I'm joking, I'm joking!" he added quickly, still not looking away from the bridge. "I'll be right back. Don't move!" He climbed onto the railing, stood straight up, and jumped. He plummeted down out of sight.

"Ga-a-a-av-i-i-i-i-n!" I shrieked, lunging forward. I hit the rail just in time to see him gliding away over the edge of the roof, wings outstretched. A second later, he shot upward in a burst of speed and was gone, leaving only the faintest trail of cloudy wisps behind him. I looked out over the Millennium Bridge, breathless, waiting. I felt Hunter at my side.

"Holy crap!" she whispered.

BOOM!

The noise was so loud, and so unexpected, we both nearly jumped out of our skin.

"What was that?" I grabbed Hunter's arm. It sounded like thunder, but the only clouds in the sky were lazy, low-lying white ones.

BOOM! BOOM!

We saw a flash in the sky to the right of the bridge, like the afterglow of a fireworks finale.

"Look!" Hunter pointed. "I can see them! They're fighting!"

Far above, what appeared like two birds—one light and one dark—dove in and out of the clouds. But Hunter and I knew better. They circled and swooped around, occasionally diving directly at each other. Whenever they made contact, an audible crack tore through the air, followed by a burst of light. I hoped Gavin was winning, imagined him punching the demon with otherworldly strength.

The next impact was the loudest, and my heart leapt. Maybe the fight was over. The two shapes parted, but while the dark one rose, the light one was falling with alarming speed toward the ground. *Gavin!*

The darker shape suddenly swung around and sped in our direction. I slammed back against the outside of the dome, pulling Hunter with me. I wished the doorway back inside was closer, but I didn't want to risk running toward it in case I could somehow be lifted off and carried away—maybe when I was airborne off the protective cathedral for just the slightest second in between steps . . .

"It's coming straight at us!" Hunter screamed.

The demon hurtled toward us in a streak of dark smoke, like a heat-seeking missile, at a terrible speed. *Maybe the demon isn't going to try and take us,* I thought. *Maybe he's going to smash into us at a million miles an hour and kill us that way.*

I closed my eyes and braced for impact. The high-pitched screaming soon filled my ears. I spread myself as flat against the stone wall as I could, wishing I could liquefy and slip into the cracks toward safety.

A whoosh of air fluttered past my cheeks, and then . . . nothing.

I opened my eyes a tiny bit and saw that the demon was hovering an inch from my face. He wasn't technically touching me, but he was as close as he could possibly be.

In total shock, I opened my eyes all the way, and found myself staring straight into his. His eyes were dark, almost black, but long lashes curled around them, making them unexpectedly beautiful. He had a handsome human face with sandy, reddish hair. He grinned at me—wickedly, and yet somehow flirtatiously. The smile of a confident guy who could get anything he wanted and liked what he saw. He inhaled deeply, sucking in the scent of me, like a lion getting his first taste of an upcoming dinner via the wind. The rest of his body looked human as well, except for the tail flicking between his legs, his large bat-like wings—thin, tissue-y, and covered in veins—and his scaly red claws. He was wearing all black, from the pants to the shirt over his muscular torso, and I wondered if his entire body was covered in scales.

I heard a soft groan and saw that the cigarette guy was slung over the demon's right elbow like an unstuffed teddy bear. The demon looked down and, as if remembering the boy was only a useless decoy, opened his arm. The guy fell stomach-first onto the railing and lay suspended there, unconscious, his feet dangling toward the roof.

The demon swung back to me with a blast of hot wind. I could taste his breath in my mouth. He licked the corner of his lip with the forked tip of his tongue, slowly, disgustingly. I clenched my lips closed, trying not to vomit.

I saw the demon's head contorting to the side before I saw why. Even though it happened at light speed, almost too fast to see, for me it played out in slow motion: Gavin's foot flying in from the left, smashing into the demon's face, knocking the demon a hundred feet away; Gavin following with fists and kicks and airborne fighting maneuvers that looked more like a graceful acrobatic dance than a deadly attack. But it was a deadly attack, for after Gavin landed a ferocious punch on the demon's neck, the creature's wings stopped flapping, and it fell straight down like a rock.

As soon as the demon's body hit the cathedral's roof, it

began sizzling, bubbling, and then melting until it disappeared, leaving nothing but a black smudge in its place. I noted all the other black marks on the cathedral's surface, marks I'd thought were signs of pollution and time, and wondered if they were also demon residue.

I couldn't stop my body from shaking. Even my teeth chattered as I physically reacted to the supernatural carnage. Gavin appeared and hovered in front of me, his gorgeous white feather wings a welcome, calming sight. He cupped my face in his hands and looked deeply into my eyes.

"It's okay, I've got you," he said. "I promise you will come to no harm as long as I have breath. Do you believe me, Maren?" I nodded. He smiled. "You have to say it."

"I . . . I believe you," I stuttered.

"Good." He drew his fingertips from my cheeks, picked the cigarette guy off the rail, and threw him over his shoulder. "I've got to get this chap back to his friend, but I'll be back in a flash, okay?"

I nodded again, and he shot off toward the bridge. I turned to Hunter. "Are you all right?" I asked.

She didn't answer. Instead, she hit the ground.

CHAPTER 25

Hunter had passed out. Miraculously, she didn't hit her head on the way down.

In less than five seconds, Gavin was back, his wings tucked in before his foot touched the ledge. He checked Hunter's pulse, made sure she was breathing, and then lifted her up into his powerful arms. I followed as he carried her back inside like a baby.

I was a little jealous to watch him carry another girl, but I took solace in the fact that it wasn't *my* heartbeat that had caused the entire attack. It wasn't Hunter's fault, of course, but I could see how she got overwhelmed.

By the time we stepped back down on the cathedral floor, Hunter was awake. Gavin set her down on a nearby chair.

"Oh my gosh, oh my gosh, oh my gosh," was all she could say. She rocked back and forth a bit, changing her chant. "I can't do it. I can't do it."

"Of course you can, Hunter," Gavin said. "You'll be fine. You're strong."

"No, I'm not," she said, looking at him with big, tear-filled eyes. "I'm not. I pretend to be, but really I'm not."

He knelt down and took her hand. "I know you're scared, Hunter, but we're going to get you out of here." I wondered why I wasn't freaking out as well, especially considering what I'd just come face-to-face with. Somehow, Gavin made everything seem all right.

"Let's go get you something to drink," he continued. "I think we all need a little break right now." He led us to the steps that curled down to the crypt and the café.

❀ ❀ ❀

The café was much nicer than I expected—a small, upscale bistro with warm, terracotta tiles on the floor and cheery white paint on the walls. The arched ceilings were filled with tiny spotlights that made you forget you were actually underground.

As the three of us ate, we talked about our next steps. I told Hunter about the sickness in Aviemore, about Jo and the other kids being hospitalized, and how we had to hurry to get the antidote from Magnificat.

Gavin still thought the safest way to Magnificat was the quickest way, which meant going in a straight line instead of meandering around the city in a cab or a subway. We'd been warned about the subway, and we'd already found out how the cab thing would go.

"I get that crossing the Thames is the fastest way," Hunter was saying, now back to her regular color and energy level after some nourishment. "But we can't get over that pedestrian bridge. It's impossible."

"We can't go over the Thames, true," Gavin said, "but I bet we can go under it."

Since the city had been inhabited for over a thousand years and because it sat on a bed of clay, London was one of the most tunneled cities in the world. Hundreds of tunnels wound under London, as well as carved-out shelters, war rooms, military fortresses, and escape routes from all sorts of places—including, of course, Buckingham Palace. Most of the underground tunnels were completely secret and unknown to the public. Gavin was convinced there had to be a tunnel from St. Paul's going directly across the Thames, directly to Magnificat. We just had to find it.

"If there is a tunnel from St. Paul's, it would have to start down here, below ground, in the crypt," I said.

"The crypt is huge, though," Gavin mused. "It's as big as the entire footprint of the cathedral. We can't just walk around looking for loose stones or secret panels in a place this vast. It would take weeks."

"We have to narrow it down, then," I said. "Whose tombs are down here? That might give us a clue."

"There are over two hundred tombs," Hunter answered. "Admiral Nelson, the Duke of Wellington, Florence Nightingale . . ." Gavin and I stared at her. "I've been in here for twenty-four hours," she reminded us. "I've read the guidebook fifty times."

"Is there one that might lead us out of here?" I asked.

"I'm not sure. There's the Sullivan guy from Gilbert and Sullivan. There's a memorial to Winston Churchill, but he's not really buried here. There's the architect Sir Christopher Wren," she rattled off.

"Architect?" I asked. Something familiar was ringing in my brain. "Of what? What did he build?"

"This church," she said, shrugging her shoulders. "Why?"

"That's it! It has to be!" I said. "My mom was a computer analyst—well, that's what she told me she was, anyway. And in every computer program, the architect always leaves a secret back door for himself so he can get back in if he needs to fix something. Why would this church be any different?"

"So you think the architect's secret way out starts at his tomb?" Hunter asked.

"It makes perfect sense," Gavin said. "And we've got to start somewhere."

My pocket vibrated. I was getting a text. I switched on my phone screen, and my stomach dropped.

"What's happened? Who texted you?" Hunter asked.

"Stuart, a kid from my class," I answered. "Five of the people who were poisoned at the party died this morning, and Jo is barely hanging on. We have to get to Magnificat, fast."

❁ ❁ ❁

The rest of the crypt was not as cheerful as the café. In fact, for an actual tourist destination, it was poorly lit, dusty, and super scary. We passed dozens of giant stone coffins, each decorated more gruesomely than the next. Some had screaming lions carved into them; others were protected by snaking serpent tails or tall fences topped with rows of spears.

The crypt was cavernous and completely empty of people. Our footsteps echoed eerily, bouncing off the dead bodies and returning to us magnified. The farther we walked, the darker it got.

Sir Christopher Wren's tomb was in the very back of the crypt; we had to walk the entire length of the cathedral again. By the time we got there, I was jumpy, convinced a bony hand was going to slide out from under one of the heavy lids like in a haunted house amusement ride. But this was no theme park. This was real.

Wren's burial plot was by itself, under an arch that had a small, barred window with a view of the street gutter. *So we aren't all the way underground*, I noted. Which meant getting to a tunnel wasn't going to be as easy as opening a door. We were going to have to descend to somewhere else.

I didn't know if I could handle a place even creepier than the crypt. I had no problem with heights, but the idea of being trapped underground with rotting corpses was my worst nightmare. Hunter, on the other hand, seemed perfectly comfortable, almost excited. I wondered if I had claustrophobia and was only just discovering it. I definitely had hate-being-underground-with-dead-people-phobia. I took deep breaths and tried to calm my racing heart. I was definitely regretting my forced chutzpah with Gavin, since now I couldn't let on how freaked out I was or he would send me home.

The architect's grave was cordoned off by a small wrought iron fence. Unlike the other tombs, which had huge statues and elaborately carved coffins, Wren was laid to rest under a simple, rectangular black marble slab set just six inches above the floor. On the wall above it hung a large stone plaque engraved with a bunch of Latin:

SUBTUS CONDITUR
HUIUS ECCLESIÆ ET VRBIS CONDITOR
CHRISTOPHORUS WREN,
QUI VIXIT ANNOS ULTRA NONAGINTA,

NON SIBI SED BONO PUBLICO.
LECTOR, SI MONUMENTUM REQUIRIS,
CIRCUMSPICE.
Obijt XXV. Feb: Ano: MDCCXXIII. Æt.XCI.

Gavin translated: "Underneath lies buried the builder of this church and city, Christopher Wren, who lived beyond the age of ninety years, not for himself, but for the public good. Reader, if you seek his monument, look around you. He died on the twenty-fifth of February, 1723, aged ninety-one."

A secret tunnel out of St. Paul's wouldn't simply be labeled with a sign. We'd have to discover it, and I was certain we'd need to solve a puzzle to do so.

I'd learned that the trick to solving most puzzles—whether they were leisure games or scientific conundrums—was to identify the oddity, like the old *Sesame Street* song: "One of these things is not like the others . . ."

As he was reading, I was studying the layout of the words, looking for anything out of the ordinary. The quicker we found something, the quicker we could get out of the crypt.

The inscription had eight lines of Latin, all center spaced, all capital letters. I tried skipping around and reading the first letter of every word, but Latin is so weird—and so full of *Q*s and *V*s—that nothing came of it. I counted the words. Nope. Then I noticed that while each line had multiple words on it, there was one that was conspicuously shorter than the others. In fact, it only contained one word: *circumspice.*

"What does the one word all by itself mean?" I asked Gavin. "'Circumspice'?"

"'Look around you,'" he answered. "Why?"

"It's the only one all by itself," I said. "I think that means something: look around you."

Hunter picked up the phrase and started swiveling her head in all directions. "Look around you. Look around you." The smooth, white stone walls offered no other clue. She then spun her entire body in slow circles. Still nothing.

"What's the line above it say again?" I asked.

Gavin reread it. "*Lector, si monumentum requiris.* Reader, if you seek his monument."

"*Circumspice,*" I finished. "Look around you." I repeated it. "Reader, if you seek his monument, look around you."

"We are," Hunter said. "There's nothing around us."

"This has to be it. It just feels right." I walked through my thoughts out loud. "It says 'if you seek,' and we are seeking. 'His monument.' Could mean this church, but that's pretty obvious. His monument is his legacy. Why couldn't it be the secret way out?"

"Okay, go on." Gavin seemed impressed.

"We need his help," I continued. "We're asking him to show us the way out. And he's saying, 'Here it is. Just look around you.'"

Hunter opened the small metal gate, walked into the nook, and stood at the foot of the metal slab. Gavin joined her, moving toward the window and tracing the edges of stones with his fingers, probably looking for a loose one. I preferred to stay outside, away from the deceased. I kept reading.

"*Circumspice.* Look around you. Look around you."

Suddenly, like a dodge ball in gym class, it hit me. Hard.

"Look around U!" I said. "The letter *u*. Maybe that's it!"

There was only one *u* in *circumspice*, and I began to read the letters in a circle around it, starting with the letter directly above it to the left. There were seven: N-U-M-O-N-A-C.

LECTOR, SI MO**NU**MENTUM REQUIRIS,

CIR**CUM**SPICE.

Obijt XXV. Feb: **Ano**: MDCCXXIII. Æt.XCI.

"Numonac?" Hunter said. "Is that Latin?"

"No, but it's close," Gavin replied. "And it could be two words."

"Numo and nac?" Hunter said. "Any better?"

"Nope," Gavin answered.

"What if we start with a different letter than the *n*?" I asked, already mentally doing just that. "If you start with the *m* and go counterclockwise, it's M-U-N-C-A-N-O."

"*Mun cano* means 'grey world' in Latin," Gavin said, lighting up. "Does that mean anything to anyone?"

"Greyworld is the name of those artists who install large, interactive sculptures around London," Hunter offered. "Trash bins that talked in Cambridge, traffic posts that played music, trees that sounded like a music box when you turned a golden key on their trunks, a night-time rainbow in Trafalgar Square ..."

"Do their works have anything in common?" Gavin asked.

"I guess the fact that they all use sound," Hunter

answered. "They started with fence railings that played a song when you dragged a stick along them."

Sound. An odd clue, considering the crypt was deathly quiet.

"I'm not sure reading counterclockwise makes much sense," I corrected myself. "You'd read a circle more like a rainbow, from top and bottom, left to right each time. That would be *num cano*." Goosebumps prickled across my forearms.

"In Latin, *num cano* is 'you sing,'" Gavin said.

As if on cue, Hunter let out a piercing warble—"Here lieth Christopher Wren!"—and collapsed on top of Wren's grave.

❁ ❁ ❁

Hunter lay motionless on the marble slab, and probably due to shock, Gavin and I stood motionless next to her. But only for a moment. Because then the entire slab started to sink.

She lifted her head, smiling at us. "Rather dramatic, I know, but the occasion called for it. It's so darn serious down here." She didn't seem to realize she was moving with the slab.

"Um, Hunter," I said, afraid to move in case I made it worse, like jumping in after someone who's just fallen through ice. "Your singing seemed to activate something and . . . the ground . . . it's moving!"

The slab, now perfectly flush with the floor, stopped sinking. Hunter rose to her knees. She was now in the center of Wren's slab.

"It's not moving now, right?" she asked.

"No, it's stopped," I answered.

"Good," she said, standing up. She took a step toward us, but as soon as she shifted her weight, the entire slab tilted. It must have sunk until it rested on a bar across the middle, because the metal plate was now acting like a giant teeter-totter. It kept tipping under Hunter's feet, the top rising into the air behind her, until she was no longer able to stand. Her feet slipped out from under her, she landed with a thump on her bottom, and promptly slid out of sight into a black hole now opened in the floor. As soon as she was gone, the tablet righted itself, sealing Hunter below us.

She was gone, and the room was eerily quiet, as if she'd never been with us. Terror tightened its grip on my chest. I had to say something, to prove to myself I could still breathe.

"We have to get her!" I croaked.

"I'm on it," Gavin answered, and he really was, leaping deftly onto the middle of the slab. "I'll slide down, hold the slab so it stays open, and you come after me. I'll catch you, I promise." He shifted his hips, and the plate tipped open at the bottom again. As soon as it was wide enough, he dove into the dark hole, feet first. My heart sank as he disappeared. I was afraid my fear would swallow me whole.

Thankfully, the tomb didn't swing closed. Gavin held it open.

"I've got it," he called up to me. "Climb on, Maren!"

I looked around the crypt wildly, trying to decide what

to do, but my brain wouldn't hold a sane thought. I had just made a huge scene with Gavin, insisting I was brave enough to continue, but I hadn't counted on the trip involving subterranean terror. Maybe I should let Gavin take Hunter to Magnificat by himself. But then I'd be stuck in the bowels of the crypt, I reminded myself. Just me and all the dead bodies. There was no good option.

The deciding factor was Gavin. No matter where he was, I wanted to be with him. I took a deep breath to calm my nerves, climbed gingerly onto the marble slope, and let go. I slid into Gavin's waiting arms, landing against his broad chest with a satisfying thump. I clung to him as I watched the band of light from the opening shrink into a thin line and then disappear as the slab swung shut. It was now completely dark.

I felt Gavin's lips against my ear. "I've got you," he breathed. I let myself melt into him a little, relaxing into his strong but soft embrace.

"Can you guys see?" Hunter called out from the darkness.

"Nope, nothing," I answered. I begrudgingly stepped out of Gavin's arms, since Hunter was right next to us.

I glanced around, willing my eyes to pick up anything: a shape, a shadow, a small movement. It was darker than anywhere I'd ever been—completely and utterly black. The ground had some extra give in it, so I knew we were standing on dirt. And since Gavin was able to hold the slide open, I knew that the room couldn't be very tall. But other than that, I was at a complete loss. It was a scary feeling to be in total darkness. I found Gavin's hand and laced my fingers with his. He squeezed mine reassuringly.

"I can see," Gavin said.

"You cannot," I answered. "It's pitch black."

"Angels can see in the dark," he replied.

"Of course you can," I said with a sigh, starting to feel foolish for my fear now that I was standing safely next to him. *How could you ever compete with an angel?* I thought. Well, at least he hadn't been the one to solve the puzzle. "So, where are we?" I asked.

"In a low room, quite large, that extends out at least one hundred feet in every direction, except to our left," he said. "There's a wall about forty feet away to the left, and it has a door on it."

"Is the wall with the door the right direction?" Hunter asked. I could hear her shuffling closer to us. I held out my free hand, and she bumped into it with her shoulder. We linked elbows. "Will it lead us to the river?"

"Aye," Gavin answered. "The Thames is that way."

"Then let's go," Hunter replied, nudging me so that I, in turn, nudged Gavin.

Gavin led us slowly into the dark. We'd only taken about fifteen steps when a whooshing sound filled the air. Two beams of light flared ahead of us. I shut my eyes against the sudden brightness, and when I opened them, I could see there were torches hanging on either side of a large wooden door—actual torches!—and they were burning with a bright fire. A man stood next to them, glowing in the light.

"Is it a ghost?" Hunter whispered, digging her nails into my arm. I was relieved I wasn't the only terrified one.

"There are no such things as ghosts," the apparition called out to us in a deep, male, English accent. "You're either on this earth, or you're not." I recognized the voice, but couldn't connect it to a face.

Gavin picked up the pace, as if he was excited to get to the man. A few steps closer, and I saw why. It was Alfred, the salt-and-pepper-haired guard.

"You've found your young friend, I see," Alfred said, nodding at Hunter. She smiled at him like a family member. They'd obviously run into each other a few times over the last twenty-four hours. I was glad she'd had someone looking out for her before Gavin and I arrived, but I couldn't figure out why he was in the subbasement, and how he'd gotten there. I hadn't seen anyone else in the crypt.

Gavin stepped forward and gave Alfred a hearty handshake.

"And you've chosen a path," Alfred said, gesturing toward the door behind him. "You're off to Magnificat, then?"

"How do you know that?" I asked, startled that a night watchman knew about Magnificat or our plan.

"Why else would you be down here?" he answered simply.

"It's all right," Gavin assured us. "He's an angel."

"How do you know?" Hunter asked.

"Angels can see the breath of other angels and demons," I explained, secretly wishing I had the same ability. Alfred did seem like an angel now, especially the way Hunter was beaming at him.

"Very true," Alfred answered. "And I'm happy to assist

you in any way that I can." He had a calming presence, just like Gavin.

Hunter seemed awed. "So Magnificat is behind this door?"

Alfred nodded. "Aye, through the tunnel. And after your handiwork on the roof, I'm guessing you won't be alone in there."

"What do you mean?" Her wide eyes danced in the torchlight.

"Once you pass through this threshold, you're no longer protected by St. Paul's," Alfred answered. "While it is easier for demons to fly in from an open sky to snatch their prey, they can still come after you on foot. They're quite fast, you know. And they do roam the tunnels, in every direction they are able."

"Tunnels? You mean there's more than one tunnel behind this door?" I gulped.

"There's an entire network under London, and they're all connected," Alfred said, confirmation of what Gavin had told us in the café. "Every tunnel has hundreds of off-shoots and openings. But luckily your path to Magnificat, while one of the longer tunnels, is straight as an arrow. All you need to do is keep running, and leave the rest to Gavin and myself."

"You?" Hunter asked, her face softening. "But I don't want anything to happen to you! I've already caused everyone enough trouble." She moved forward and gave Alfred a big hug. *That Hunter, she sure likes to hug people.* Although in this case, I couldn't blame her. There was something so sweet about Alfred. He reminded me of my grandfather back home, and I felt a pang of homesickness.

Weird, I thought to myself. *That's the first time I've thought of Scotland as "home." Just in time to possibly never see it again.*

Alfred chuckled. "I'll not have you worrying about my wellbeing, young lady. I can hold my own, you know. Besides, I can't let Gavin here have all the fun. Two beautiful ladies are too much for this young chap."

"Hey!" Gavin said, playfully punching at the older angel's shoulder. Before Gavin's fist could connect, Alfred's hand shot up and caught it in a white-knuckled grip. Alfred was no weak old man.

He tossed Gavin's fist aside and opened the door with a flourish. We peered over his shoulder and saw that the tunnel was made of tightly packed earth on all four sides, was extremely narrow, and was very, very dark. My newfound claustrophobia kicked in. *As long as we don't have to go too far and Gavin is with me,* I thought, *I can make it. Hopefully.*

"It's exactly five hundred meters from here to Magnificat," Alfred explained. "Not terribly far, but in the dark, you can get disorientated." Five hundred meters didn't seem too bad, until I did the metric conversion in my head: five hundred meters was about the length of four-and-a-half football fields. As if a long, suffocating tunnel filled with demons wasn't bad enough, I remembered I was not a great runner.

"What do you mean 'in the dark'?" Hunter asked. "We have the torches."

"We won't be taking the torches with us, Miss Hunter," Alfred answered. "It's better for you girls to run in the dark, so your eyes won't serve as a distraction."

"Being able to see is a distraction?" I said.

Alfred nodded. "It is when what you see might override your desire to run. Can't have you stopping. For anything. You two must run straight, run strong, and not stop until you reach the end. Just keep running!"

"So the demons can see in the dark?" I asked.

"Yes, same as Gavin and me. But you needn't worry about them. Just run as fast as you can, and let us deal with any uninvited visitors."

❀ ❀ ❀

The tunnel's small girth required us to traverse it single file. We decided that Gavin would take the lead, followed by Hunter—since she was a faster runner and wouldn't end up crashing into me—then me, and finally Alfred, who would guard us from the rear.

We stood in the doorway, tense with readiness. The inside of the tunnel was silent, and the air tasted cold, but stale. I hoped there was enough oxygen for all of us. I tried not to, but was already breathing heavily, probably using up more than my fair share.

Suddenly, Gavin pulled away from the tunnel, his face twisted with worry. "I'm sorry, Alfred, Hunter," he said. "But before we go, I need to borrow Maren for a moment."

He lifted a torch off the wall, grabbed my hand, and led me away, into the dark.

Once we were well out of earshot, he turned to me.

"Maren," he said in a low whisper, "I need you to do something for me." My fear of the darkness and the demons seemed to evaporate as he said my name. Gavin's power over me was almost mystical. Just the tone of his voice seemed to clear my head and my heart of cobwebs, worry, and anything ugly. I imagined I could see his angel breath, rolling over me, protecting me from every angle.

He reached out and gently stroked my cheek, and I heard him inhale sharply as if touching me was too overwhelming. I could have fainted for the pure pleasure of his fingers on my skin, but I didn't want to miss a moment.

"Mmm-hmm?" I said, not really caring what he asked, as long as he kept caressing my face.

"I need you to stay alive."

"What?" I asked, startled.

"I need you to stay alive, no matter what. Promise me that." I felt a flood of panic rush through me. *No matter what, again? Did he know something I don't? What is in those tunnels?*

"You're here, you've chosen to go with us, but I can't have you giving up, okay?" he continued, looking so intensely into my eyes, I was afraid I might start crying. "Even if you're taken, stay alive. I will come and find you. Promise me you'll stay alive."

"Why do you need me to promise that?" I swallowed hard.

"Because I'm afraid I've fallen in love with you," he answered. "And I won't lose you. Not now. Not ever."

My heart fell into my toes. After pining for Gavin with every ounce of my being, of praying he would *like* me, he was finally standing in front of me, confessing he actually loved me. Loved me. Me, the girl from Missouri. And the biggest miracle of all was that because of who he was—the most gorgeous creature I'd ever seen and an actual angel—I believed him. I could believe him. I felt deserving of his love. I felt more special than I'd ever felt in my life.

"I love you too," I whispered back.

"Promise me, then," he repeated.

"I promise," I said.

"Good," he said with a smile. He then leaned in and kissed me. It wasn't an accidental kiss this time. It was the kind of kiss that makes you believe in fairy tales and shooting stars and happy endings.

❀ ❀ ❀

We were back at the tunnel entrance, lined up as before. Only this time, I knew Gavin loved me, and he knew I loved him. It should have made me more confident in the journey ahead, but now that we were in front of the door, now that the kiss was a memory and the darkness stretched out to eternity, it made me more scared. Now I had something to lose.

"You're sure there are demons in there?" Hunter whispered.

"I'm afraid so." Alfred nodded solemnly.

I glanced at Gavin, to see if he looked worried. He smiled to reassure me, but I knew he was nervous. Otherwise, he wouldn't have made me promise to stay alive.

What kind of promise was that, anyway? Stay alive. How about, "Don't get hurt" or "Run as quickly as you can"? Stay alive? I realized that meant his biggest concern was that I would die. Actually die. And I knew why. I had pretended it hadn't bothered me, but I couldn't forget the horrifying sight of the demons on the cab and the cathedral roof. And I'd more than just seen them, I'd smelled their hot, acrid breath, been grabbed by their terrible claws, had heard their beyond-the-grave yowling.

I suddenly remembered the first time I'd heard the demonic screaming. Before Campbell Hall. Before I saw Gavin in the woods with Bertie. I'd heard it at my mother's funeral.

Images of the sudden "storm" swept through my brain: the darkness, the priest running away in terror, the men from my mother's work disappearing . . . It hadn't been weather-related after all. Demons had interrupted my mother's funeral. I wondered if any of those good-looking coworkers were angels. *Where had they gone?* I supposed they killed the visiting demons or I wouldn't still be alive. *Why were the demons there in the first place? What could they possibly get from my mom after she was already dead?*

I realized with a sinking feeling that I knew. That I was carrying the answer on my back. Her secret journal. The journal that had led me here, just outside Magnificat, to the antidote. *What else did the demons not want me to discover?*

My mouth became desert dry. I tried to swallow, but couldn't. There was a distinct and very real possibility that I was going to break my promise to Gavin.

I jumped up and down a little to get my blood flowing, to jerk the negative thoughts from my head. I *had* to get through this. Hunter needed to get to Magnificat. Jo needed the antidote. The High Council needed my mother's journals. I *would* get through this. And I would be with Gavin.

I focused my attention back on Alfred and Hunter, determined to concentrate only on the present.

"And we never turn? Just run straight?" Hunter recounted.

"Yes, the tunnel ends at the door to Magnificat," Alfred said. "Although, come to think of it, we don't want you running right into the door. It should take you about two and a half minutes of nonstop running. If you count to one hundred fifty, with elephants, you'll stop just in time."

"With elephants?" I asked.

"Yeah, like 'one *elephant*, two *elephant*' . . ." Hunter replied.

"Oh, we use *Mississippi* in the States," I said.

"Same thing," she said.

As it turned out, it really wasn't. The extra syllable in the muddy Midwest river caused me more physical pain than I'd ever felt in my entire life.

To give us enough room to run, we were supposed to wait for a count of five from the time the person in front of us left before we ran after them. That's when my trouble began.

Gavin dashed into the darkness first, and Hunter stood her ground, counting out loud: "One elephant, two elephant, three elephant, four elephant . . ." Then she bent her knees like a professional sprinter and shot off.

I immediately began my count, but silently to myself: "One Mississippi, two Mississippi, three Mississippi . . ." I hadn't yet gotten to number four when I felt Alfred give me a small nudge. I was confused—*I'm not at five yet!*—but my body responded to the suggestion, and before I knew it, I was running.

The tunnel air was much colder on my cheeks than

I anticipated, probably because I was running as fast as I could. Even though I could feel my feet pounding on the ground, and knew from the burning in my chest that I was running at full speed, it didn't feel like I was going anywhere, because it was absolutely black all around me.

"Seventeen Mississippi, eighteen Mississippi . . ." I was somehow still keeping count in my head, even while I was noticing every little thing around me. *Splash!* I ran through a puddle. *Whoosh!* I felt the breeze of an opening to my right. *Huh-huh!* I heard my own breath coming out in short bursts.

Things were going well. I was up to number ninety-seven, and didn't even have the side cramp I usually got when forced to run laps in gym class. Maybe we'd make it without any problems after all.

And then I heard the screeching.

The familiar, high-pitched yelp was in front of me, growing louder by the step, and I was running directly toward it. Blindly, in the dark.

And then I heard the screaming.

It was Hunter, and she sounded hurt, or hysterical, or both. I felt myself running faster, trying to get to her, and then, unexpectedly, as I passed an opening on my left, I heard her voice now behind me. I was running away from it. *Had she been grabbed? Where is Gavin? Should I go back and help her?*

My feet propelled my body forward, even as my brain begged it to stop. I felt like I was under a spell, jogging against my will. Maybe I was still running because that's what I was supposed to do. *Yes! Just keep running.* Alfred and Gavin had told us just that, over and over.

But I had completely lost count. How long ago was I at ninety-seven? Was I at one hundred twenty? One hundred thirty? Was I close? Far away?

A deep boom resonated, like an underground explosion, and the entire passage shook. Tiny bits of rock and dirt fell into my face, but I just kept running.

The screeching rolled in directly behind me now, and something jerked on my hair. But I just kept running. Alfred grunted behind me. I heard him swing; something flew through the air. There was another small earthquake. More silt in my mouth. I just kept running.

And then I hit the wall. At full speed. One second there was nothing but air in front of me, and the next second I slammed into the solid end of the tunnel so hard, I actually bounced backward. I heard a sickening squeal, felt something sticky on my neck, and then . . . nothing.

CHAPTER 26

My head hurts. The thought floated to me from the darkness: "My head hurts."

I was awake, but I didn't want to open my eyes. I didn't want to know where I was. I couldn't get past the pain in my head. It didn't even feel like my head anymore; it felt like my head had been removed and replaced with a block of concrete that was being crushed from all sides. Maybe if I never opened my eyes, the pain would just go away.

As the "awake" message traveled around my body, I received reports from all appendages. My arms and legs were intact and sore, but not terribly so. I was lying down on something soft. Light registered through my eyelids in a curtain of orangey-red, so I knew I was no longer in the dark. My right hand felt slightly compressed, and I realized someone was holding it. *Gavin!* I popped my eyelids open.

Hunter was sitting next to me, cradling my hand in both of hers. "Maren!" she cried. "You're awake! Blimey, you had me so worried!"

"Where's Gavin?" I asked, propping myself up on my left elbow and immediately regretting it because of the rush of pain to my forehead. I was in a small, windowless room painted a shocking bright yellow. There were two twin beds, including the one I was lying on; two chairs, one currently occupied by Hunter; and two dressers. Behind Hunter, an arched door stood slightly ajar.

"Shhhh!" she admonished. "He's not allowed in the Chambers. He's with the other angels, across the river. But you'd better keep your whole romance with him a secret while we're here. It's not allowed, you know."

"Where are we?" I asked.

She smiled. "Magnificat. We made it."

"We're all safe, then?" I asked, sinking back down in relief. I noticed the yellow ceiling was decorated with scallops and pretty designs in a darker gold color.

"Yes, we're safe," she said. "Well, at least . . . um . . ."

I bolted upright again. "What happened? Is Gavin okay?" My brain swelled as if an ocean wave rose and crashed inside my skull.

"Yes, yes, he's fine," she assured me. "It's . . . Alfred didn't make it."

"What do you mean, 'didn't make it'?"

"He sacrificed himself, Maren, to save you. Gavin and I were behind the door to Magnificat, waiting for you, but we heard screams, and then a *thunk*. Gavin was ready to go back in after you but Alfred appeared, carrying you. You were out cold. He just managed to hand you off when he was pulled back in—"

"He's . . . he's dead? Because of me?" I felt sick. Poor Alfred. He didn't deserve it.

"Don't think like that," Hunter admonished. "He's not dead because of you; he was able to fulfill his destiny because of you. He didn't want to sit around rotting in St. Paul's. You gave him the opportunity to be a hero."

Hunter had clearly lost her mind.

"Are you serious?" I said. "You can find the positive in

something like this? An hour ago, you were passing out on the top of St. Paul's, saying you couldn't make it, and now you're all full of wisdom about an old man getting mauled to death by demons?"

She smiled. "I know, it's amazing, isn't it? I've learned so much since we've been here."

"You've learned so much in the past hour?"

"Well, actually, we weren't on the roof an hour ago. It was more like three days ago. You've been out a long time. I've been checking on you constantly, of course," she added hastily, "and sending reports to Gavin as often as I can. I even texted your grandparents from your phone, pretending to be you, so they wouldn't worry."

"Thank you," I said. "Gavin's 'across the river'? What river? I thought we all crossed under the Thames."

"Not the Thames," Hunter answered. "Another river. Come and see for yourself."

She helped me out of the bed and across the room. She opened the door, and although I'd seen people in the movies do it all the time—along with spitting out their drink when they were surprised, which I absolutely don't believe anyone really does—I actually gasped out loud. Magnificat was more than just a location. It was an entire underground city. Made entirely of gold.

The subterranean cavern was enormous; so large, I couldn't see the top of it. Mist swirled about where I thought the ceiling of earth must be. Hundreds of buildings of all shapes and sizes seemed to grow out of the ground and climb the walls, impossibly stacked on top of one another. Balconies, raised walkways, arched staircases, and meandering bridges connected every structure. A river swept right through the middle, down deep in the bottom of the canyon, physically separating the city in two.

Every available surface was covered in gold. The brilliance of it might have blinded me if we were anywhere near the sun, but being underground, the golden surfaces perfectly reflected the lights scattered everywhere. There were tall post lanterns, porch lights perched next to doorways, even footlights on the bridges. Magnificat, it seemed, had electricity—or some source of power, anyway.

"It's amazing. It's breathtaking. It's . . . gold," I stuttered. "Or, at least, it looks like gold."

"No, it's really gold," Hunter confirmed. "Did you know gold doesn't ever rust or tarnish? That's why they used it down here. Amazing, huh?"

"So Gav . . . I mean, the angels are over on that side?" I pointed across the chasm.

Hunter nodded. "No fraternizing allowed. Angels are only supposed to have contact with humans in an emergency."

Emergency. The image of Jo in her hospital bed came flooding back to me. "What about the antidote?" I asked. "Do they have it?"

"Yes," Hunter said. "Just. The blood sample Gavin brought was infected with a really complicated poison. It took them awhile to find the right antidote."

"Gavin brought a blood sample?" I asked.

"Apparently." She shrugged as she led me along the main path. "He sent me a note that he'd finally gotten the antidote and was going to take it back to Aviemore tonight. He was hoping you'd wake up in time to go back with him. If not, I think he was going to deliver it and then come back for you."

"How could he do that? I thought we weren't allowed to fraternize."

"He told them about your mom's stuff, and said he needed to escort you back for your own safety. I'm actually getting my own Guardian too, since the demons recorded my heartbeat."

"Where's my backpack?" I asked, feeling a protective surge for my mom's journals.

"It's in our room, under the bed," she answered. "No one touched it. We were waiting to see what you wanted to do."

"I want to turn it over to the High Council," I said, remembering my stubborn declaration to Gavin. "Maybe they can figure it out."

As we walked, we passed a peculiar bridge. It was the only one that spanned the river and connected both sides of the canyon. A huge ramp spiraled up from the middle of the bridge and into the clouds above. I couldn't see where it ended, but I did see what stood at its start: two hulking angels with their wings exposed, holding what looked like swords on fire.

"What is that?" I asked.

"Exodus," Hunter answered. "The way out. It's the only place in Magnificat where you're allowed to meet with a Warrior or a Guardian angel—when you're leaving." She lowered her voice to a whisper. "I told you, they're very serious about humans and angels keeping things professional. It's completely against the rules to fall in love with one."

Too late, I thought, as we hurried past the scary guards. I had already fallen. Far.

CHAPTER 27

Hunter and I were walking through the enormous Magnificat Library. Like every other building in Magnificat, it made me feel small and plain with its soaring, buttressed ceilings, stained glass windows, and golden chandeliers. I felt very . . . human. Hunter didn't seem bothered at all. Spending the last several years living in monasteries and churches must have hardened her to the grandeur. She chattered away as if we were in the mall.

We were on our way to meet the Record Keeper. I was going to turn over my mother's journals and the disappearing ink letter, and Hunter was going to find out who her new Guardian angel would be. She was as excited as a kid on Christmas morning.

"I hope he's young," she whispered. "And good-looking. Not like anyone could be as lovely as Gavin, of course . . ."

"Hunter!" I shushed her.

She raised her voice. "I mean Gavin, that *guy* you go to high school with, the normal *human* you have a crush on . . ."

"Yeah, that'll fix it." I rolled my eyes.

"Sorry." She scrunched up her face. "But I can't help it. He's *divine*. I mean, really, how do you not want to get with that?"

"Hunter!" She was hilarious in an almost unholy way. I wished she were my sister.

She lowered her voice to a whisper. "You know it's true. You know you want to."

She was right, of course. I did. I missed Gavin terribly. I had only known him for a couple weeks, but it felt like we'd been together my whole life. He'd become part of me. When I was with him, I felt completely engulfed by his presence, like I was wearing new skin. Without him, I felt naked.

We stopped in front of a large doorway flanked by tall columns on either side. An inscription in stone above the door spelled, *Dei sub numine viget.*

"Under God's power, she flourishes," I read out loud.

Hunter looked at me. "Since when can you read Latin?" she asked. "You couldn't read it at St. Paul's."

"I don't know," I said. "I can't. I don't know Latin. I just know what that means for some reason. It's the motto of Princeton University. Maybe that's how I know it."

"Do you know someone who went to Princeton?" she asked, raising her eyebrows.

"No," I admitted. "It just popped into my head." I shrugged. "Maybe I read it somewhere."

Hunter heaved the heavy golden door open, and we went in. It was darker and colder than the other rooms; probably to protect the records, I thought. A giant wooden table that looked like an altar rose from a platform at the back of the room. It held the thickest book I've ever seen— maybe the biggest book in the history of humanity.

Behind the book sat a tiny, shriveled old man. He had the kind of creepy, long white hair that flowed right into a long white beard, so I couldn't tell which strands were from his head and which started at his chin. A gray-haired woman, who looked at least one hundred years younger than him, stood by his shoulder.

"Welcome," she greeted us. "I'm Theodora, the translator. And this is the Record Keeper."

I couldn't tell if the Record Keeper nodded at us or was falling asleep. He seemed so old, I was afraid he might disintegrate all over his big book.

"Hunter Sinclair?" Theodora called.

"Yes, ma'am," she answered.

"The Record Keeper has found the name of your new Guardian angel. Here it is, along with everything you need to know, including your Leaving Time." She handed Hunter a small piece of folded paper.

"Thank you." Hunter did an awkward half bow, half curtsy.

"And Maren Hamilton?"

"Yes, that's me" I said, wondering why I wasn't as automatically polite as Hunter.

"You have something to give us?"

"Yes, ma'am," I answered, forcing the foreign-sounding word out. I held out the leather-bound journal. "It's from my mother. She used to work for the Abbey. I think it's important."

Theodora stepped forward and took it from me. Her eyes crinkled with kindness in a way that made me miss my mother something awful.

"Thank you so much, Miss Maren," she said. "These things will be invaluable to us. We will make sure they get to the High Council immediately. Gavin has told us

great things about your bravery. We are indebted to you."
My heart seemed to pump extra-warm blood through my
veins at the mention of Gavin's name.

"You're welcome," I answered.

The Record Keeper spoke for the first time, in a raspy
voice, "*Tzeteh' Leshalom VeShuveh' Leshalom.*"

Theodora translated, "He says 'Go in peace . . .'"

"'And return in peace,'" I interrupted. "*Toda. Toda.*
Thank you." I bowed a couple of times like Hunter, and
we, for some crazy reason, backed out of the room like
lunatics.

We weren't more than two steps outside the door
when Hunter turned to me. "You speak *Hebrew*?"

"No," I said. "Why?"

"Um, you just did," Hunter replied. "And don't tell me
you must have read it somewhere or that it's the motto of
your high school."

"No, no, it's not. I don't know. I don't even speak
Spanish, and I took it for three years," I said. "Are you sure?"

"Yes, I'm sure! You said 'tova' for 'thank you.'"

"It's *toda*, actually," I said, then clamped my hand over
my mouth. "Oh my gosh, I am speaking Hebrew! This is
freaking me out!" I wondered if the magic of Magnificat
was giving me special powers all of a sudden. Hopefully,
they would last until my next foreign language test at
school.

"All right, Babel," Hunter said, grabbing me by the arm.
"Let's get back to our room. I'm dying to open this and find
out about my new angel boyfriend!"

❀ ❀ ❀

I was lying on my bed, watching Hunter get ready. Her new Guardian angel was named Jonathan. There was a portrait attached, and by all accounts, Jonathan was young, blond, and quite handsome. Hunter was scheduled to meet him, and leave with him, in half an hour.

As she packed, she filled me in on her wicked fantasies: how Jonathan would fall madly in love with her at first sight, and they would have gorgeous babies with fat cheeks and little cherub wings. I didn't have the heart to tell her it didn't work that way, that if her angel really loved her, he'd have to give up his powers, but I supposed they could still have beautiful babies. I tuned her out when she started detailing what an amazing kisser she hoped Jonathan would be. It made me ache for Gavin. I thought about our kiss beneath the crypt. My lips pulsed at the memory. I played out my own fantasy in my head. Gavin and I were alone in the vast, dirt-floored room; no Alfred, no Hunter. Gavin stuck the burning torch in the ground, and then took off his shirt and spread it out like a blanket. He sat down and then pulled me to him. I fell, and he caught me on his chest. He wrapped his strong arms around me, bent his head, and kissed me. I closed my eyes and let the warm tingling race through my body.

"Maren!" Hunter shoved my knee.

"What?"

"You're not even listening to me, are you?"

I sat up. "No, I am, I'm listening. You were just saying . . . um . . ."

"That I was sorry . . ." She coached me.

"Sorry? For what?"

She sat down on the end of the bed, her face serious. "Maren, I have a confession to make."

"Yeah?" My stomach knotted with worry. A minute ago, she'd been jabbering about a heavenly wedding, and now she was tearing up.

"I'm not sure how to say good-bye to you . . ."

"Awww, you don't have to. We'll see each other again." I patted her hand. "I'll drag Gavin back to London. This wasn't a fair visit. Way too much excitement."

She shook her head. "No, it's not that easy. I'm leaving. For good. I've decided to go home with Jonathan."

"What do you mean, 'home'?"

"I mean back to his angel home in the south of England."

"You can't be serious!"

"I am," she said, tears now streaming down her cheeks. "I've been thinking about it for days. Since St. Paul's, actually. I can't stay here, where the demons have locked on to me. I can't always be looking over my shoulder, afraid of every shadow. If I go back with Jonathan and live with his clan, I'll be safe. And I kind of miss having a family."

It was hard to argue with that. But I had to try. "You can't spend your whole life hiding in an angel village!" I protested, remembering Rielly trapped in Scotland, away from her friends and family. "It's not fair! And you won't be able to text or call and . . . and I'll miss you too much!" Water pooled in my lower eyelids.

"I know," she sniffed. "But until they figure out a way

to erase my heartbeat from the memories of all the demons in a thousand mile radius, I have no choice. And I'm going to miss you terribly! You're like a sister to me. The sister I never had!"

A sister. I had just been thinking that same thing about her.

"We *are* sisters," I said. "We're like family. Why don't you come back to Scotland with me?"

"No, I can't complicate your life any more than I already have. You were such a dear to come down with Gavin and rescue me. I'll never forget you for it. But you have to live your life, and I need to find one."

I didn't know what to say, so I reached over and gave her a hug, and let my own tears spill. Once I started, I couldn't stop. It was unreal how many tears I had, like I was plugged into a never-ending fountain of pain. It spilled all over poor Hunter.

I was devastated that she was leaving, but it was more than that. I had a lifetime of pent-up sorrow. I cried for the dad I never knew, the mom I had buried, the angel who'd just died for me. I cried for my lost youth, the other Abbey orphans, the victims of all the evil in the entire world. As she clung to me, Hunter started bawling, probably for the same reasons. We'd been through what no one else had; what other girls couldn't even imagine.

After a bit, Hunter gently pulled away. "I have to go," she said, and smiled through her tears.

"Let me walk you!" I said, standing up and wiping my face furiously to prove I could be normal again.

"No, stay here. I don't want to meet Jonathan blubbering like a baby!"

I couldn't believe she was actually leaving. I looked around the room, desperate for something to do, something to give her. "Here!" I said, removing the Tudor rose necklace from around my neck. "Take this. For luck. To remember me by."

"Oh, I couldn't," she said. "That's from your mum."

"But yours was too, and you lost it running around London because of me." I held the shiny chain out. "You need one to get into Jonathan's village anyway, and I want you to have mine. I want to know that you have something from me. If you don't take it now, I'll follow you all the way to the bridge, weeping. Like a sad puppy. It will be terribly embarrassing for you."

She giggled, which made me giggle. "All right, if you insist." I nodded and slipped it over her head. "I'll never take it off!" she promised.

"You'd better not, or I'll hunt you down."

"Promise?" She grinned.

"Absolutely," I answered.

I gave her a final hug and sent her on her way, bravely holding back more tears until she disappeared around the corner. Then I flopped on the bed and sobbed myself to sleep.

❀ ❀ ❀

Jo stood in a field of wildflowers. The sun shone unusually bright, forcing me to squint my eyes to see her. This gave her a fuzzy glow, making her twirling, gymnastic movements even more fairylike. She spotted me and smiled.

A shadow crossed the grass and darkened her face for a moment. I looked up and saw a black bird circling. The dazzling light made the animal hard to see, so I held my palm out to cover the sun. The bird's wings were scalloped at the ends, like a bat's.

Jo didn't look up; she never took her eyes off of me. She waved a just-picked bouquet of bright purple. The shadow returned to her face and grew larger. Much larger. The bird was descending.

The creature let out a terrible, piercing scream that made my head throb. I stuck my fingers in my ears. Moving my hand caused the sun to flash me right in the eyes, and everything became bright red for a moment. I shut my eyes to refocus, and when I opened them, I saw the bird wasn't a bird at all. It was a demon, all red-bodied and slick with blood. It swooped down and grabbed Jo before either of us could move. I tried to scream, but the sickening sound flying out of the demon's mouth drowned out everything else.

During those first few seconds of consciousness after I woke up from my unexpected afternoon nap, I thought everything was okay, the same way I'd reacted after my mom died; I would wake up and think everything was normal, that she was down in the kitchen baking cinnamon scones. It was an amazing feeling. But before I could enjoy it, reality would come and punch me in the face.

I was lying in my bed at Magnificat. Hunter was gone. Forever. Gavin was not allowed near me. And I was still having terrible dreams.

Jo! My dream was about Jo! My chest tightened at the thought that something horrible had happened to her. And I was a million feet underground, helpless.

I jumped out of bed. It was time to go home. I was done with Magnificat, done with secret codes and dangerous missions. I wanted to get back to my grandparents, to Jo, to my life. I would figure out how to send a call over to Gavin, and we'd be on our way.

I threw open the door and walked right into a Messenger angel. She was insanely tall—over seven feet—dressed in flowing robes, and was more than blocking my exit.

"Sorry," I said. "If you're looking for Hunter, she's already left."

"I'm actually here for you, Maren." Her voice resonated like harp strings. "You've been summoned."

CHAPTER 28

Standing alone in the light-filled room, in front of three tall chairs that held three very tall individuals, it was hard not to think of the Inquisition. Or a television cop show. They weren't policemen, of course; they were angels. And I wasn't being charged with a crime. At least, not yet. But I did feel like I was being interrogated.

The oldest one, the one who did most of the talking, leaned forward and asked me yet another question. He had a short, well-trimmed white beard and a shiny bald spot on top of his head. He reminded me of Moses.

"Do you know why this place is called Magnificat?"

"No," I answered.

"Can you guess, though?" he challenged. "Try. Really think about it. Go on."

I took a deep breath. Nothing they had asked me so far was terribly difficult, but I still had no idea why I was there. I couldn't imagine the High Council sat around asking teenaged girls to solve riddles, and I was getting kind of sick of it. I wanted to catch Gavin before he left, but I had a feeling they already knew that.

"Magnificat is the name of an all-girls' Catholic high school outside Cleveland, Ohio." I shrugged. "My old school beat them in lacrosse when I was a freshman."

"*Mmm-hmmm,*" the angel said. *Does he know I'm not really trying?* I couldn't tell from his face, but the three of them did look like they could sit there for hours. I decided to dig a little deeper in the hopes of finally ending the celestial quiz session.

"Well, it's a Latin word, right?" He nodded for me to continue. "It's got the root *magna* which means 'great,' like in 'magnanimous' or the 'Magna Carta.' It reminds me of the word *magnify*, which is basically to make something greater, or bigger. Um, so isn't that what *magnificat* actually means in Latin, 'to magnify'?" *How do I know any of this? I can't even ask where the bathroom is in Spanish.*

"Yes," he answered, leaning forward. "Keep going."

"The Magnificat is a prayer, a prayer to Mary. No, it's *her* prayer, right? It's what Mary says when she meets up with her cousin Elizabeth?" I could see from their faces that I was right.

"Anything else?" the angel asked.

I closed my eyes to see if I could summon any more information out of my brain. "It's used in the Roman Catholic Vespers, Lutheran Vespers, and the Anglican Evening Prayer. It's usually sung, and it was put to music by . . . Bach." I stopped. I heard myself talking, but I had no idea where the information was coming from.

The angel leaned back and consulted with his companions. They spoke in low whispers. After a few minutes, he tipped toward me again.

"Thank you, Miss Hamilton. You've impressed us with your ability and your patience," he said. *I hope he isn't being sarcastic about the patience bit.* "We have only one more question for you: *how* do you know all of these answers?"

Finally, my last question, and it was a trick question. *How? Who the heck knows?*

"I don't know," I said simply, hoping they would accept the truth. "The information is just there, like it's been beamed into my head or something." I shrugged in an effort to appear I didn't care, but my newly discovered genius was freaking me out.

"Maren," the angel said, surprising me by suddenly using my first name. "You are a most unique young lady. We've been waiting for you for some time now."

"For me? Why?"

"There are only a precious few people who carry a double discovery gene. You've inherited it from both sides, from your mother and your father. And as such, you have incredible gifts."

"You mean my dreams?" I said, bristling at the mention of the mother I no longer had and the father I never knew.

"Yes, your precognition and your ancestral memories."

"My what?"

"We believe that you, Maren, possess a collective, although unconscious, ancestral memory. It's extremely rare and an extremely valuable skill."

"A collective unconscious what?" I knew what all the words meant individually, but together they made no sense whatsoever.

"Simply put, you hold all the memories of all people that have gone before you. That's how you can read Latin and speak Hebrew when you don't read Latin or, I assume, speak Hebrew," the angel explained. "Have you not noticed information comes to you out of the blue, like just now with the prayer?"

I had known the name for scree on the way to Gavin's village and rattled off the title *The Golden Ass* in front of Graham without having heard of the story. I nodded.

"Have you ever physically seen anything from the past?" the angel asked. The way his face scrutinized mine made it hard to think about the answer. He added, "Or anyone?"

I had. "I saw my father as a young boy when I was sitting in a church," I said.

He nodded. "Very good. Your talents are maturing. Your ability to recall and react to the shared memories of your entire family has infinite value in our fight against the demon forces. And as such, we would like you to join the Abbey."

"The Abbey?" The one place I had no interest in whatsoever. The place that killed both of my parents.

"Yes. As you know, the Abbey is an elite group of extraordinary humans. They all have heightened abilities that enable them to see more, know more, and do more. If you choose to join, we will teach you how to harness your powers, and then send you around the world on special missions. We have urgent needs in Paris right now, as well as Barcelona, Johannesburg, and of course Rome."

Paris? Rome? The idea of exploring amazing cities with Gavin *did* sound appealing . . .

"What kind of missions?" I asked.

"I can't tell you too much until you are part of the program. But suffice it to say, we are facing a global crisis. We have dozens of projects that could use your attention,

Maren. We are anxious to get you settled in at the Abbey immediately, paired with your new angel—"

"My new angel?" I interrupted, far too passionately. I took a breath and chose my next words carefully. "I already work with an angel."

"Yes, we know about Gavin. Fine Warrior, but for this type of work, you need an Archangel. We have one of the best to guide you—"

"I don't want a new angel," I interrupted again. "I like Gavin. I trust him. I won't take another one." I knew I sounded like a pouty five-year-old, but I didn't care. There was no way I would be permanently separated from Gavin.

"Of course you like Gavin, Maren. The system is designed that way. Angels were purposefully created with characteristics that humans find appealing and trustworthy. But you will find these same qualities in your new angel."

"No, I won't," I answered, "because I'm not getting a new angel. If being in the Abbey means I need a new angel, then I'm sorry, I have to decline."

"Decline?" The angels collectively arched their necks at me, making them even taller and more menacing. "I don't believe we've ever had anyone refuse a divine request."

Maybe it was because I'd been in the room too long, under their observation for what felt like forever. Maybe it was because I was tired of always having to say goodbye. But for whatever reason, I started to get mad. I wasn't going to have one more thing—one more person—taken away from me. As I spoke, my voice got louder, until it was bordering on hysterical.

"Yes, that's right, I decline. I can't do it. It's too much. I've been through too much. I'm sorry to refuse a divine request and all, but what about *my* requests? What about my request not to lose both of my parents? What about my request not to have my life turned upside down? To just be a normal teenage girl? Which is hard enough without demons and date rape drugs and dark tunnels, by the way! I'm sorry, but you're just going to have to find someone else. I just want to go back home and live my life—or whatever you can call this whole mess I've inherited—the best I can. I'm sorry, but no."

After I finished my dramatic speech, the angel sat quietly for a few minutes. I wondered if I was in trouble, if he would force me to go, or if somehow Gavin would be punished because of my stubbornness.

Surprisingly, when he spoke, the angel's words were colored with a kindness that instantly melted the anger off my heart. "You make excellent points, young Maren. Perhaps we have asked too much of you. We respect your free will, and accept your decision, but know that the invitation will remain open to you, should you ever decide to take it. You may return home as soon as you wish. Gavin will escort you. Go in peace with our blessings."

Less than five minutes later, I was walking back to my room, dazed by the whole encounter. I'd expected them to protest, to try to convince me, or at least to give me a lecture about talking back. Even though I'd gotten what I wanted—to return home with Gavin—I was uneasy about how easily I'd gotten it. One tiny tantrum and I was dismissed? Rewarded even?

Those angels would make terrible parents, I decided. Any self-respecting teenager would walk all over them.

CHAPTER 29

When I burst back into my room, I was startled to find a girl sitting on Hunter's bed. She had wavy, jet-black hair, luminous violet eyes, and midnight-colored skin.

"Hi, I'm Gia, your new roommate," she said, leaping up to shake my hand. I was a bit taken aback by her voice; for some reason, I hadn't expected a British accent. It was slightly more lyrical than Hunter's, and sounded wonderful. I was also a little surprised by Gia's appearance. She had the sweetest face, which made her spicy attire all the more shocking. She was wearing overstated black eye makeup and an even more over-the-top black party dress; the top was a corset made of crisscrossed ribbons, and the bottom was a poufy tutu. Paired with this were shiny black boots, huge, sparkly earrings, and a headband with an oversized leopard-print bow. She looked like a ballerina who'd escaped from juvenile detention.

"It's nice to meet you," I said, "but I'm actually leaving."

"You are? That sucks." She looked disappointed.

I walked to the dresser and started packing my own little bunch of belongings. I couldn't believe I'd just watched Hunter do the same thing. I started to feel a little heartsick, and resolved that I would get out of the room as quickly as possible. I refused to get to know Gia. I couldn't make friends with one more person I had to say good-bye to.

Gia, however, had other plans. She followed me and

plopped herself on my bed, watching me pack. "So, what are you in for?"

"In for?" I asked.

"Yeah, how come you're down here at Maggie?"

"Oh, I came for an angel assignment. Not mine. I was helping somebody else," I said. "What about you?"

"I'm kind of grounded. I was out partying too much, I guess, and a whole freakin' pack of demons came after me. My superiors thought it best if I disappeared for a while."

I stopped packing and looked at her. I noticed she was wearing the Tudor rose necklace. I wondered if she was an orphan because of the terrible agency as well.

"I know what you're thinking," she said. "And it's not a terrible place. I actually work at the Abbey."

"I . . . I didn't . . ."

"No, it's okay. I can see why you'd think that. And I *really* do know what you're thinking. It's sort of my gift."

Crap!

"See, you just thought *crap* right there." She smirked.

"Um, can you turn that off? Like, can you stop listening to my thoughts?"

"I wish I could, believe me. Why do you think I go out to loud clubs as much as possible? I can't stand hearing most of it!"

"Yeah, I guess that would suck," I said.

"You have no idea! People think about the lamest things: what someone said about them, who has the best shoes, how much they hate their boss . . . and that's just the girls. The boys . . . You should be seriously glad you can't hear what boys are thinking!"

I thought about Anders in the cascade house. I had a feeling I knew what he was thinking, and it made me sick. I couldn't wait to get home, deliver the antidote, and watch Gavin annihilate him.

"If you needed to get away, why didn't you go home with a Guardian angel or something?" I asked.

"It's not practical, since you have to be home by sunset. Sunset's usually when my work begins. And I like angels and all, but they're really not that much fun, always telling you what you're not supposed to do. I know I'm undercover, but I don't see the harm in having a good time while I'm working. What's so bad about snogging a bit? I mean, a kiss is just a kiss, right?"

The memory of Gavin kissing me sent a shiver through my body. "So you, um, kiss a lot of guys for your job, then?" I said, clearing my throat and trying to clear my mind.

"I've kissed my fair share to get information," she answered, then grinned at me wickedly. "But I'm not as bad as *you*! I've never made out with an *angel*!"

"I . . . I did not!" I lied, before I realized she could tell I was lying.

She chuckled, leaning back against my pillow. "Yeah, right. You're playing a dangerous game. I love it!"

"Dangerous? Why is it dangerous?"

"It's majorly against the rules, falling for an angel. If they find out, they'll reassign him. Wow, that's almost a Greek tragedy—girl likes angel boy, but if she acts on it, she'll lose him forever. You're really screwed!" She was enjoying this far too much. I was not amused.

"I'm glad you find this so funny," I snapped. "I can

tell you've never been in love before. I feel sorry for you, actually."

She shot upright. "Wait a minute? You *love* him? You do! You love him! Oh my gosh! Does he love you?" She bit her lip, waiting for my answer.

"Yes," I said, tentatively. "He does. Why?"

"Jiminy Christmas," she exhaled. "I thought you were just messing around, but if you two are really in love . . . What are you going to do?"

"What do you mean?"

"I mean, if you really love him, you're not going to be able to hide it, and if they find out, they'll separate you— *really* separate you. It's not like a guy who just moves to another city. He'll vanish. You'll never see him again. I've seen it happen. It's horrible."

"When did you see it happen?"

"One of my previous roommates fell in love with her Guardian. He got reassigned to another girl, and my friend just fell apart. She couldn't take being without him."

"What happened to her?" I felt my chest tightening a bit.

"She joined up with a demon gang, if you can believe it. Talk about opposites, huh? She was angry at the Angel Council, and I think she wanted to get back at them or something. Terrible decision, if you ask me. She was a great girl, but now . . ." Gia trailed off, leaving the girl's fate to my imagination.

I smacked on my backpack, trying to flatten it, perhaps a bit too violently. "Well, that's not going to happen to me."

"It's a hard choice," Gia said. "Love or duty. I'm not sure what I would choose."

"I don't have to pick one," I said. "I'm just going home, and things are just . . . just going to work out." I could tell from Gia's face that she didn't think so, but thankfully, she kept her opinions to herself. Which actually made me more nervous than when she was telling me off.

"Where's home?" she asked.

"Aviemore, Scotland," I answered immediately.

Images of my new home swirled in my brain: the misty Highlands, my grandparents' cozy house, snuggling under a blanket in my attic room in the rain. I missed it. I missed the people there too: my adorable grandfather, my buttoned-down grandmother, bubbly Jo . . . They all seemed so far away, like a dream. *A dream! My dream about Jo!* I started packing faster.

"You know, your dreams are a gift, Maren, even though they don't seem like it," Gia said. "They are meant to show you things so that when they happen, you're better prepared. I've known a couple of girls with your particular talent."

I looked up, rattled by Gia's random comment, until I remembered that she could hear my thoughts. "Prepare me? All they do is convince me of my helplessness. And my guilt."

"Guilt?" Now she frowned. "That's rubbish. You bear no responsibility for what you see. Only what you do with it."

"Or don't do," I sulked. *Like with my mom.*

"You really don't think you had anything to do with your mother dying, do you?" Gia asked. Again, I was shocked. *Being in the same room with a mind reader is a crazy head trip. Literally.*

"I dreamed about it and I didn't warn her," I said, the heat of shame creeping up my cheeks.

"Maren, if you ran around trying to warn everyone who appeared in your nightmares, they'd lock you up and throw away the key."

"Thanks." I smiled weakly. "I feel *so much* better now."

"Chin up," she said. "Things will get better. You'll see. And you have that handsome angel of yours to hook up with, in any case."

"Shut up!" I threw a sock at her. She laughed.

"Here," she said, taking off her necklace and handing it to me. "You're going to need one of these."

I wondered if the rose necklaces were regularly traded among Abbey girls. I'd just given mine to Hunter, and here I was getting a replacement from Gia. I slipped it over my head.

"For luck?" I said.

"No," she stated. "For Anders. You use it against that manky rotter when you see him."

How did she know about Anders? Oh yeah, I'd been think-ing about him and the maze and Gavin murdering him . . . *How exactly is a flower necklace supposed to help me against a demon?*

"You'll figure it out," she said. "You always do." I hoped she was right. Right about Anders, and wrong about Gavin.

Gavin. Being separated from him made me restless, like a wild animal locked in a cage. I had to see him. Immediately. I had to leave.

I grabbed my bag, thanked Gia, and left Magnificat the same way I'd come: running.

CHAPTER 30

As I got closer to Exodus, waves of excitement and anticipation washed over me with every step. If I didn't calm down, I could jeopardize Gavin's and my ability to be together. No one could know about our love . . . at least, not yet. I forced myself to slow to a nice, respectable walk. I took a deep breath and rounded the corner to the bridge.

Gavin was standing in the middle, next to the fiery guards, waiting. For me. He'd folded his hands in front of him, which emphasized his broad shoulders. His hair was tousled, as usual. He was even more beautiful than I remembered. He smiled when he saw me, a polite smile, but as I came closer, I saw that his eyes were shining.

"Miss Maren," he said in a formal voice, as I stopped in front of him.

"Hello," I said. I bit the inside of my cheeks to keep from smiling too widely.

We climbed the ramp toward the ceiling as properly as any human girl and Guardian angel ever did.

❀ ❀ ❀

The Exodus ramp ended at an unassuming wooden door. Gavin held it open for me, and we crossed into a small, dingy room filled with oily mechanical cogs, belts, and rotating wheels. A long pipe suspended from the ceiling through a slot in the floor above us swung back and forth with a clicking noise. On it, a metal canister was mounted near the bottom, its top covered in pennies.

I stopped walking. The room felt familiar somehow, but unlike in the bog, it wasn't because I'd been there before. Not even in my dreams.

"They change the number of pennies on the pendulum every day to keep the clock running within four-fifths of a second," I blurted out.

Gavin eyed me. "How did you know we were in a clock?"

"Good guess?" I shrugged. The truth was I had no idea where we were. I quickly realized the sudden knowledge must be an ancestral memory. I wondered who from my family had been in here before . . . and why.

Gavin was staring at me.

"What is it?" I asked.

"I don't know," he said. "At least, I can't put my finger on it. I adore you, you know, but there's something else. Something special about you, Maren."

"Yeah, right," I quipped.

"No, I mean it. You have a light. There's an aura about you. You were meant for something amazing." He beamed. *Does anyone give out better compliments?* My heart lit my face.

"Come on," he said. "We're almost out."

I followed him down a short hallway, to a large door with a cathedral-peaked top cut horizontally by a heavy metal bar. He shoved on it, and cool, fresh air hit my face. We emerged onto a four-lane bridge stuffed with pedestrians and traffic. Gavin strode quickly ahead, and I jogged to keep up. He seemed determined to put as much distance between us and Magnificat as he could.

As we crossed the bridge, I looked down at the churning muddy water below.

"Is it the River Thames?" I asked. Gavin nodded.

Deafening chimes rose above the city noise as giant bells rang a familiar tune: *BONG, BONG, BONG.* I glanced over my shoulder for the first time, to see where we'd come from.

Big Ben, the iconic London clock tower, rose behind me. *No freakin' way.*

Gavin grabbed my hand, and we broke into a run.

❀ ❀ ❀

Once we were off the bridge, Gavin pulled me into a bright red telephone box. The glass windows were completely covered with faded stickers and advertisements, allowing the booth to be both bright and private.

"We made it," he breathed, smiling at me. My heart thumped against my ribcage.

"I know," I answered. "Barely."

"I was so worried about you," he said.

"I was worried about you," I countered.

"Och, I'm fine." He grinned. "Except for not being able to see you. That was bloody murder."

"I kept my promise. I stayed alive," I said. "Thanks to Alfred."

"Thank you," he whispered. His blue eyes blazed, sending shivers down my back. He leaned toward me. I sucked in my breath. The walls of the phone booth shuddered. Someone was banging on the door.

"Hurry up in there!" a male voice hollered. *Who still uses a payphone?*

Gavin retreated with a smirk. "I guess we have company. We'd better get going. We need to get the antidote back to Aviemore and Jo. I just wanted to take a second to tell you I missed you."

"I missed you too," I said, scooting around to open the door. Hearing Jo's name had dropped a lump of guilt in my gut. *What kind of terrible person even thinks about making out in a phone booth when her friend is dying?* Maybe Rielly was right. Maybe I was bad for him.

I wondered what I would do if I had to choose between being with him and saving my friend. Thankfully, I didn't have to. Yet.

CHAPTER 31

On the crowded train ride home, we never dared to kiss, but I did rest my head on his shoulder for the entire journey. The gentle rocking of the car, along with the soothing rhythm of his heartbeat and the warmth of his chest, almost made me forget we'd been running for our lives just days earlier. Almost.

When we got back to Aviemore, it was well after midnight. Gavin made noise about taking me right to my grandparents' house, but I wasn't having it. I had to see Jo.

We were in Gavin's car, pulling up to the hospital. He parked in a dark corner of the parking lot, as far away from the streetlights as possible. A mist rolled over the blacktop, making it look like we were outside a haunted insane asylum rather than a local medical center. The place creeped me out, and I was glad I was with Gavin.

"So, what's the plan?" I asked, watching my breath steam up the window. "How are you going to sneak into everyone's room and get them the antidote? Are you going to put it in their IVs? Do they have to drink it?"

"No, no, and you'll see," he said. "Come on." He opened his door, and before I could finish unlatching my handle, he was at mine, holding it open for me. I got out and followed him to the back of the car. He popped the trunk, and surprised me by taking off his shirt.

"Um, hello? What are we doing here?" I asked, trying

to avert my eyes from his rippling muscles, but failing and loving it.

"So many questions," he admonished. He pulled a light blue shirt from the trunk and put it on. It looked like a service worker's shirt. A patch over the pocket read "Kingussie Sanatorium."

"Where did you get that?" I asked, ignoring his remark about questions, because it was all I had at the moment.

"Can't tell you all my secrets," he said.

As we walked through the cool mist, Gavin buttoned the shirt over his chest and headed toward the back loading dock. Once we reached the tan, dented door, he whipped an ID card out of his shirt pocket. He swiped it through a little black box, making the light on top turn silently from red to green. He pulled the door open, and stepped back so I could duck under his arm and enter.

It was dim and dingy, and I was more than happy to let Gavin take my hand and lead me. We walked through a locker room, down a short hall, and turned into an unmarked room. Hot steam blasted from unseen vents, filling the air with a dull clanging, like someone kicking a file cabinet. Gavin flipped a switch and florescent lights flickered to life with a mournful hum. We were in the furnace room.

Gavin let go of my hand and walked over to a huge, gray metal box. He lifted a plate off the side, exposing glowing coils.

"What are we doing?" I whispered.

"I'm going to pour the antidote over the heating element, it's going to evaporate into a gas, and then get blown through all the vents by the central heating system," he said, removing a small vial from his pocket.

"You can inhale an antidote?" I asked.

"Sure, just like you can inhale poisonous gas. This way, everyone in the hospital will get it at the same time. They should be cured rather quickly."

"How quickly?" I said.

"Within ten minutes, I would think."

He poured the entire contents of the vial onto the orange coils. The liquid started to hiss and bubble, but then everything shut down. The room dissolved into a dark silence.

"What happened?" I asked.

"The worst thing that possibly could," he answered. "The electricity went out. If we don't get it turned back on immediately, the antidote will just drip to the bottom of the furnace instead of evaporating, and we'll lose it."

"Is that all we have?" I asked, starting to panic.

"Yes," he said. "They're going to make more at Magnificat once we're sure this works, but it's all they gave me to start with." He stood up. "I need to find the circuit breaker. I can see in the dark, so I can move faster on my own. Can you go wait in Jo's room?"

"Yes, of course," I said, slightly relieved. The bowels of the hospital were scary enough when the lights were on. I had no desire to run around them in total darkness.

"I'll take you back to the main hallway, then you can find your way, right?" he asked.

"Yeah, I remember which room she's in."

He took my hand again and led me out of the service

section. Our palms rubbed together as we walked, the soft rhythm driving me to distraction. How could touching him in just one place completely consume my thoughts? We were on a mission to save Jo, and I could barely concentrate on anything but his skin. I had no idea passion could be strong enough to override everything else.

We emerged into the regular part of the hospital. The halls were dimly illuminated by exit signs at each end, and eerily empty.

"Where is everyone?" I asked, expecting commotion since the electricity was out.

"It's the middle of the night, and this is a very small hospital," he answered. "There's probably only one nurse on duty, and she's likely on the phone with the electric department. Most of the medical machines will have back-up battery systems, but I need to get the furnace back on right away."

"Go," I urged him.

"Be careful," he said as he ducked back into the heavy metal doorway. "Go right to Jo's room. Don't stop and talk to anyone. We don't know if the poison has spread to the people who work here."

"You just said there's no one here," I reminded him. "I'll be fine. Go!"

He hesitated, then leaned back out and quickly kissed me on the forehead. Seconds later, he flashed me a smile and disappeared.

As I walked down the hallway, my shoes squeaked on the stained linoleum floor. The sound was irritating, like nails on a chalkboard. I lifted up onto my tiptoes and hurried. I couldn't wait to get out of the dark corridor and into Jo's room.

I followed the room numbers as they ascended, past 118, 119, 120 . . . Jo was in room 129, so I was headed in the right direction. I rounded a corner and froze. A tall, dark figure of a man with his back to me loomed about twenty feet ahead. I hesitated. Should I try to casually walk past him, or turn around and try to find Gavin? Finding Gavin in the basement in the dark was probably impossible. I would just have to keep walking.

I clenched my teeth and my fists and started forward. I had figured out how to keep my shoes silent, and I was almost past him when he swung around.

"Maren!" It was Stuart.

I relaxed my shoulders. "Geez, Stuart," I said. "You scared the crap out of me!"

I couldn't see him very well in the light, but he looked tired and haggard. Worrying about Jo must have worn him out.

"What are you doing here?" he growled. I recoiled a little. I'd never heard Stuart use a sharp tone with anyone.

"I'm here to see Jo," I stammered.

He leaned down toward me, and I saw he had thin, bloody scratches on his face. His eyes shone with a faraway look.

"Stuart? Are you okay?"

Without a word, he lunged at me. As I writhed to get away, he reached out and clawed at my neck. His fingernails left burning trails on my skin. I ran as fast as I could, but I could hear him right behind me. I wasn't a fast runner to begin with, and I knew he'd catch up to me in seconds. I had to get out of the hallway.

I threw myself against a closed door, hoping it wasn't locked. It swung open, and I darted inside. I pivoted and tried to close and lock the door behind me, but the pneumatic hinges caught it and made it swing super slow. Stuart had plenty of room to force his arm into the opening, and when he did, he thrust the door open. I stumbled backward and crashed into a metal table.

We were in an operating room. I noticed a tray of surgical instruments to my left. Before I could see anything else, coarse hands curled around my neck.

Stuart was choking me.

The pressure on my throat was unbearable. I pulled at his hands, but there was no releasing them. I couldn't speak. I couldn't breathe. My eyes watered.

I reached out with my left hand and fumbled with the tray. I felt clamps and scissors, but when my fingers grazed against a small metal hammer, I knew I had a chance. I grabbed it and smashed it into Stuart's temple as hard as I could.

He released his hands from my neck and collapsed.

I stumbled out of the room, choking and gagging. By the time I reached Jo's door, I was breathing normally again, but my throat still throbbed. It felt permanently bruised on the inside, and I could still feel the pressure of Stuart's hands. I felt a stab of panic, thinking maybe he had crushed my windpipe, but reminded myself that I wouldn't be breathing if that were true.

As I stepped inside Jo's room, the lights flickered back

on. I heard the *whoosh* of the vents, and hoped Gavin had restored the power in time to salvage the antidote.

I plopped down on a scratchy visitor's chair and waited.

※ ※ ※

In less than a minute, Gavin appeared at the door. "What happened to your neck?" he asked. "It's covered in red marks!"

I shrugged. "I guess that's what happens when someone tries to strangle you."

"It's no joke. Your throat's very delicate, Maren," Gavin said. His eyes flashed dark and angry.

"I know," I said. "Believe me, it freakin' hurts. But I'm fine now."

"Who did this to you?" he demanded.

"Stuart," I said, "but it's okay. I knocked him out. He must have been infected or something. He was crazy."

"You knocked him out?" Now he looked impressed.

I nodded. "We wound up in an operating room, and I managed to hit him with a hammer."

Gavin smiled. "That's my girl."

I was proud that I'd fought off Stuart by myself. All six feet of him. I liked proving to Gavin that I wasn't a damsel in distress. But the relentless death and drama was wearing me down. I longed for my own room, for my own bed, for safety, for a normal life. *Could I ever have that with Gavin?*

"He'll probably sleep longer than the others," Gavin continued, "but the antidote will still get to him. He'll be fine."

Jo stirred, rustling the bed's stiff sheets. She opened her eyes and looked around the room. When she saw me, she smiled.

"Jo!" I said.

"Hi, Maren," she answered. "What's going on? Why am I in the hospital?" Her cheeks were returning to their normal color, and her eyes already looked brighter. The antidote was working!

"It's a long story," I said.

"Well, start at the beginning," she commanded. She tried to sit up and realized she was strapped down. Gavin and I quickly undid her restraints. As Gavin bent over one of the buckles, she nodded at him and mouthed "OMG" to me. I shook my head. I had my best friend back.

We sat with Jo and told her about the party poisoning. I didn't mention that the disgusting seducer Anders Campbell had allowed a group of jinn demons to infect his party guests . . . In return for what, I didn't want to know, considering what incubus craved. And I didn't tell her Gavin was an angel. But the story was shocking enough without any of those details, and I didn't want to put her in any more danger like I had Hunter.

At six a.m., when Jo's mom showed up, Gavin and I left. All of the patients, including Stuart, made miraculous overnight recoveries. The doctors theorized that the toxin that infected everyone had finally just "worn off."

Gavin took me home, and then returned to his village. He was going to report in, but he promised to visit me later in the afternoon. The jinn demons' plot had been defeated, everyone had recovered, and my days as an undercover angel spy were thankfully over.

As my grandparents started making breakfast, I finally laid my head on my own pillow. I was so exhausted, I didn't even care if I had a bad dream.

I should have.

CHAPTER 32

I heard the screaming first. And then I saw her—Hunter. And she was covered in blood.

I burst into the dark and dusty room. The furniture was worn thin, the wallpaper was peeling from the walls, and the smell was overwhelming. I put my hand over my mouth, tried not to vomit.

Hunter's face contorted in pain. "Help me! Help me!" she wailed. I couldn't move.

A round woman wearing an apron rushed past me carrying a knife. It was covered in blood as well. I wondered if she had hurt Hunter, or was somehow trying to fix her.

A man paced at the foot of the bed. He was tall, blond, and really attractive. He was wearing an old-fashioned suit, like a young Sherlock Holmes. He lunged at Hunter, and I opened my mouth to scream, but she beat me to it.

A river of blood rolled, bubbling, across the floor. When the rounded edge of dark red hit the tip of my shoe, I passed out. The last thing I heard before everything went black was more screaming. Hunter's voice was now silent.

The screaming was from a new baby.

Bam! Bam! Bam! I heard the pounding in my dream, but I couldn't wake up.

Bam! Bam! Bam! I begrudgingly opened my eyes, and realized someone was knocking on my door. My grandmother burst into the room.

"I'm sorry to wake you, Maren dear. But I just couldn't wait any longer. It's after three . . ." She threw my curtains open. Sunlight spilled over my face.

"It's after three? Three what?" I mumbled.

"Three in the afternoon," she answered. "You've been sleeping so soundly, and I know you probably need it after your trip, but . . ." She paused, looking like she'd rather eat nails than continue her sentence.

"But what?" I asked, pushing the hair out of my face.

She crossed the room and sat down next to me, putting an arm around my shoulder. I immediately tensed up. Something was wrong.

"There's been an accident," she said.

"An accident?" I was awake now. "Where? It's not Grandpa, is it?"

"No, it's Jo," she said. "She fell out of a tree or some such thing. They're not really sure. Her mum just called."

"Oh my gosh, is she okay?" I jumped up and pulled a hoodie over my head so we could rush to see her.

"She's dead, Maren."

My grandmother's words pierced me like spears of ice. "What?" I blinked.

"I'm afraid she's dead. She broke her neck in the fall. There was nothing they could do." Gran followed me and tried to hug me again. I wriggled away from her.

"No, she's not. She's fine," I argued. "I just saw her this morning. She's perfectly fine."

"It's a terrible shock, I know."

"She's not dead," I repeated. "She's not dead."

My grandmother finally caught hold of me, and held my hand. "I'm so sorry, Maren."

"What do you mean, 'she fell'? How could she fall? Where was she?"

"Mrs. Dougall said they didn't really know. Jo had just gotten out of the hospital, and said she was feeling cooped up, so she went for a little walk to get some fresh air. One of the Crowleys found her lying in their field down the road. She had a small branch in her hand, so they think she must have climbed up a tree to fetch it, and lost her balance."

"She wouldn't have lost her balance," I said. "She was like a gymnast. She wouldn't have."

"It doesn't take a very far fall, Maren, if you land wrong. It's such a shame. She was a lovely girl, and I know how much she meant to you."

"Stop talking about her in the past tense!" I screamed. "She isn't gone! I'm telling you, she's fine! There must be a mistake!"

It didn't make any sense. Why would she climb a tree to get a stupid branch? And the Crowleys' place? They raised cows. Their land was mostly wide-open meadow. I thought about Jo standing in a meadow surrounded by wildflowers. A shadow overhead. *My dream at Magnificat!*

My stomach cramped, forcing me to bend over. I knew Jo hadn't fallen out of a tree. She'd been dropped to her death by a demon. Like my mother. Like the girl from Culloden. But why? Who had done it? Gavin said the killing demons were gone . . .

I realized that the race to save Jo had nothing to do

with her being poisoned. I had dreamed about her falling, I'd been warned, and once again, I'd done nothing about it. I'd gotten back from London in time, but I still hadn't been able to save her.

I collapsed on the bed and sobbed until I thought I might die. Hopefully, someone would be able to save me.

❀ ❀ ❀

My grandmother was right. Jo was dead. Within the hour, the whole town knew about it. There was no pretending anymore.

School was cancelled for two days so everyone could attend her service the following day, and then meet with grief counselors.

My grandfather was gone on a long-planned, two-day golf outing up at St. Andrews—a reunion of his golf team from high school. He called to ask if he should come home, but we told him not to. What was the point? Him missing his trip wasn't going to make anything better.

My grandmother kept checking on me. She was worried, because in less than two months I'd lost my mom and my best friend. She wanted to make sure I knew it had nothing to do with me, that it wasn't my fault, and that these things "just happen." Assure me I had no reason to feel cursed. Check that I was coping.

Regardless of what she said, or my conversation about guilt with Gia, I knew it was my fault. It had everything to do with me. I *was* cursed, and I wasn't coping.

I sat on my window seat for hours, numb. I mashed my face against the cool, leaded windowpane and waited.

Gavin was supposed to be back by now. *Where is he? Can't he hear my broken heart?*

Then I saw someone walking up the lane toward our house—a guy too fair and slender to be Gavin. He looked up at our house, and I pulled back as if I'd been caught spying.

It was Graham. *Why is he coming here?* I hadn't seen him since he'd saved me from his predator of a cousin, and I was kind of hoping never to run into him again. No one else had seen what he had seen. Images of Anders in the cold, stone fountain house made my head throb.

I peeked through the window. Graham had stopped at our mailbox. He removed his jacket, laid it carefully over the rounded metal box, leaned back, and then kicked it with the flat bottom of his foot. When he retrieved his coat, there was a huge dent in the side of the mailbox, and the door was hanging open, unhinged. *What the heck is he doing?*

I got downstairs just as my grandmother was answering the door. When I saw him, embarrassment pushed every other thought out of my mind. I was mortified at the position I'd been in that last time I'd seen him, but felt like I owed him . . . my life, maybe.

"Hi," I said, giving him a short wave from my hip.

He held out a bouquet of flowers. "I brought you these," he said. "I thought you might need some cheering up, considering. We sent an arrangement to Jo's family, naturally—but I think everyone else who knew and loved her could use some of the same, especially you." His polite awkwardness was charming.

"Thanks," I said, taking them. They were pretty, but I didn't want to see pretty. I wasn't feeling pretty. I let my hand fall to my side, clutching the flowers near my knee. I forced my mouth to smile, and half succeeded.

"I was also wondering if you might do me the honor of accompanying me to the yearend ceilidh next week. I'm sure you're just getting settled back in from your . . . ah, trip, but I wanted to be the first in line before someone else snatched you up."

"You're inviting me to a dance?" *Is he freaking serious?* I'd just learned that my best friend had died, and he was in my house, on the very same day, asking me out on a date?

He nodded, oblivious to his terrible timing. "Yes, the ceilidh. I'd like to be your escort."

I may have felt obliged to him, but not enough to agree to something like that on a day like this. "Um, I don't think I'm going actually. I . . ." I looked at my grandmother, searching for an excuse. "I'm going with Gran to . . ."

Thankfully, my grandmother picked up on my silent distress call. "She's got to come with me to see her aunt Margaret in Raigmore. It's her birthday, and we've planned a little family get-together. Maren was terribly disappointed when I told her it was the same night as the ceilidh, but it's family. You understand."

Graham looked crushed, and I did feel a little sorry for him. I wondered if he'd already asked any other girls at school and been turned down. Even though he was perfectly well-mannered and charming, it must be hard to be the "ugly duckling" to Anders' strapping swan.

"Oh, of course," he said, shuffling his feet. "I hope you have good weather for the drive. Give your aunt my best."

My phone rang upstairs. "Thanks for the flowers," I said before I turned to fetch it. My grandmother opened the door a bit wider, a cue it was time for him to go. I heard them talking about our mailbox as I ran up the stairs. Hopefully, he was apologizing for kicking it in.

It was my grandfather on the phone, checking on me for the tenth time. While I assured him I was fine, I watched Graham walk away from our house. As soon as he was out of sight, and I set down my phone, Gavin landed with a thump right in front of me on the roof. I jumped at the sudden noise, then threw the window open.

When he climbed inside, I reached my arms around his neck and buried my head against his shoulder. I was overcome at seeing him. It felt like I didn't have anyone left in the world. Hunter was gone forever. Jo was dead. All I had was Gavin, and I'd convinced myself he wasn't coming back either. The relief at being able to hold on to him, to feel his strong arms around me, was overwhelming. A floodgate cracked open somewhere inside me, and the tears gushed from my eyes, soaking his shirt.

"Hey, what's wrong?" he said as he stroked my hair.

"Everything!" I sobbed. "Jo's dead!" As he held me, I told him what had happened.

"I'm so sorry, Maren," he said. "I know you loved her like a sister."

"I loved her more than a sister," I moaned. "People fight with their sisters and steal their clothes and stuff. She was never anything but wonderful to me. And I failed her!"

"It's not your fault," he said. "You got her the antidote in time. You're a hero in my book, and hers as well. But it was just her time. You can't save everyone."

"I can't save *anyone*," I cried, letting the flood of hopelessness carry me away. I crumpled onto the floor. Gavin bent down with me.

"Shhh, it's a'right," he whispered. "I've got you. Everything's going to be a'right."

"No, it's not," I argued, raking my hands through the hair at my temples. "Nothing with me is ever all right! I'm so tired of losing things and people. My house, my parents. I lose everything."

"You've not lost me." He wrapped his arms around me and kissed the top of my head. "I'm here, Maren. I'll always be here."

His strong embrace and soothing words parted the clouds around my heart, if only for a moment.

CHAPTER 33

The next day, the sun was shining, and I was pissed. How could it be so pretty outside on the day of my best friend's funeral? Didn't nature have more respect? Couldn't there be dark, rolling clouds to match my mood?

As I drove to the church, I changed my mind. The beautiful day was exactly like Jo. It was as if she had ordered it from heaven to remind us all of how happy she was. *You should be happy too*, I could hear her say. I looked over at Gavin in the passenger's seat and tried not to feel guilty that he did make me happy. Even on a day like today.

My grandmother had "taken a migraine" and, as much as she wanted to go pay her respects to the Dougalls, she couldn't get out of bed. I knew it was probably because she hadn't slept much the night before. She sat up in the armchair in my room all night, keeping watch over me. We didn't talk about anything, but her presence helped me finally fall asleep. Between my grandfather waiting up for me after Anders' party and calling to check on me from his golf trip, and my grandmother keeping a bedside vigil, I felt they were really starting to love me. And I was starting to love them.

The funeral was full of love, and anything but happy. Even though the Dougalls begged us from the pulpit to remember all the good times and celebrate her life, the pews were full of tears, smudged mascara, and a suffocating sadness. Stuart was one of the pallbearers. He looked lost, like a lumbering shadow. I gave him a hug, but he didn't really return it. Jo's mom was heavily medicated, going through the motions behind a plastered-on smile and glassy eyes.

All of Kingussie was there, even the teachers, although, thankfully, I didn't see Graham. I couldn't deal with his awkwardness or his jealousy if he saw me with Gavin. Elsie and her stupid clique sat in the third row, crying like they'd lost one of their dearest friends. *Hypocrites.*

After the service, everyone milled around. As the church started to empty, I joined Jo's mom to see if I could help in any way. I hadn't walked three steps away from Gavin when Elsie and her friends pounced on him. They surrounded him, practically licking their paws with the excitement of meeting the handsome new guy. I heard them giggling as I helped Mrs. Dougall gather the floral arrangements off the altar. *How irreverent can you be, flirting at a funeral, especially with a guy who came with someone else?*

I must not have been the only one who thought so, because out of the corner of my eye I saw a blond guy grab Elsie by the arm and drag her away from Gavin. *Anders!* How dare he show up, after what he'd done to me! He knew Jo was my best friend. He knew I'd be here. His pretend romance with Elsie wasn't fooling anyone.

He steered her out the side door into the churchyard. I excused myself, and ran over to Gavin. "Can we go outside for minute?" I asked, smiling not-so-politely at the other girls. "I need some air."

"Of course," he said. "Pardon me, ladies. It was nice to meet you." He nodded, and followed me to the same door Anders had just disappeared through.

We burst out of the church and into an old cemetery. I was terrified, fearing I was about to see Jo's open grave. I took a quick inventory and noted that the newest headstone was from the seventeenth century. I relaxed, realizing it must be a historical burial ground.

Elsie was leaning against a tall, crumbly tombstone. Anders hovered over her, balancing his body on the rock against his fist. They looked like they were arguing, but enjoying it, like they were about to make up by making out.

My stomach churned. I was watching him get ready to devour another girl.

"Hey, Anders!" I yelled. "What do you think you're doing here?" I knew I was overconfident because Gavin was by my side, but I didn't care. I tried to walk toward Anders, but Gavin gently held me back.

Anders glanced up, a cool look on his chiseled face. "I'm a little busy, Maren," he cooed. "You'll have to wait your turn."

I clenched my fists and turned to Gavin. "Get him!" I hissed. "Kill him. Rip his head off! He's evil!"

Gavin put his hands on my shoulders to steady me. "It's all right," he whispered. "He's just a rude pig. Ignore him."

"What?" I screamed. "He's more than rude! He's a *demon*!" I looked over at Elsie, who seemed to think the description was a turn-on. She smiled triumphantly, and slid her arms around his neck.

"He's not," Gavin said softly. He placed a calming hand on my shoulder.

I shook him off. "What do you mean? It's him! It's Anders! It's the guy who tried to . . . who spiked my drink."

"Really, Maren," Anders said. "Lying does not become you. I hardly need to drug girls to get their attention." He motioned toward Elsie. "Are you trying to protect your reputation in front of your friend? You don't want him to know how you were drunk and threw yourself at me at my birthday party? It was really pathetic," he said to Gavin. The muscles in Gavin's neck tightened. *Finally!*

Gavin lunged toward Anders, but he didn't have to take more than half a step before Anders flinched. Satisfied that he'd made his point, Gavin grabbed my hand. "Let's go," he said. "He won't bother you again."

I felt myself being led away by Gavin. "No, no," I said. "You have to kill him! After what he tried to do . . ."

"Believe me," Gavin said through clenched teeth, "I would love to. But you know I'm not allowed to kill humans. All that punk would need is just one punch. Just one punch." He exhaled to compose himself.

"No," I said, hoping to get him riled back up. "He's a *demon*, Gavin. A demon."

"No, he isn't," Gavin said, snarling over his shoulder at Anders. "Demons aren't allowed in churches, remember?"

I froze. He was right. Anders was just in the church. My mind started replaying everything, tumbling over each event like rocks in a stream. The party at Campbell Hall. Jo being called away for her grandmother's "stroke." The hedge maze . . .

I spun around to Anders.

"GRAHAM!" I screamed. "Where's Graham?"

Anders rolled his eyes, thinking about my question

slowly, carefully, as if to torture me. "I don't know," he drawled. "He said something about fixing a mailbox . . ."

❀ ❀ ❀

I drove faster than the speedometer on the tiny car would even register. Every time we hit a bump in the road, I was afraid the axels might split in two, but I couldn't slow down. I had to get home.

We screeched up my grandparents' drive, and as I threw on the brakes, a small shower of pebbles hit the windshield. Before they hit the ground, we were running past the dented mailbox, racing to the front door.

It was wide open.

We ran around the first floor, and then the second. No one was home. No Graham. No Gran. And then we saw it.

A letter stuck to the kitchen cabinet with a small dinner knife, written in blood-red ink. It was from Graham. "My Dearest Maren," it began. *Sickening.* I forced myself to keep reading:

> I am so sorry to have to get your attention in this manner, but when I visited you yesterday, you were most unkind. I had hoped to convince you to come with me then, but your fancy feathered friend showed up, ruining my plans. I had no choice but to return today and take your sweet grandmother in your place. I am, of course, willing to make a trade—you for her—although my offer does have a few requirements. First, it expires at midnight tonight. At that time, I shall kill her, as I did your little friend Jo.

I gasped. *Jo! Graham killed her!* I swayed a bit, feeling like I might pass out. Gavin wrapped his arms around me from behind to steady me.

"Go on," he whispered in my ear. "It's a'right. I've got you."

I continued:

Second, you must present yourself to me personally at Campbell Hall. You must come alone, as no one else will be permitted to enter with you. And as you know, your flying fool is not allowed on our land. I consider this a very fair offer, Maren, and I encourage you to accept it. If you do not, know that I will not stop in my pursuit of you. I will kill your grandmother, and then, one by one, kill everyone close to you until you surrender. I will annihilate the entire village if I have to, but make no mistake, Maren; I will not stop until I possess you.

Yours Ever, Graham

I put the letter down. Gavin and I spoke at exactly the same time. "We have to go . . ." Although we each ended our sentences differently.

". . . to my village," Gavin said.

". . . to Campbell Hall," I said.

CHAPTER 34

This isn't right! There has to be another way!" Even though we were approaching the end of the long drive that led to Campbell Hall, Gavin was still trying to convince me not to go. It was dark outside, but huge white lights hidden in the lush landscaping licked the sides of the walls, illuminating the great house like a ghostly museum. The mansion was ominous and frightening. And deadly quiet. There were no other cars. No signs of servants. No sign of anyone.

"I've already told you," I said. "I have to go. There is no other way. Graham killed Jo, he has my grandmother, and he's going to kill her if I don't go in! What do you want me to do? I can't lose one more person. I can't!"

I parked the car and got out. We were going to walk as far as Gavin was allowed. That spot turned out to be really far from the front door. *Too far,* I thought. We stopped underneath a giant tree, a twisting Scots pine that looked as if it might have something to say.

"I understand that," Gavin replied. "But *I* can't lose *you*! And if you go in there, you're done. It's over. You'll never come back out."

"Thanks for the vote of confidence," I said. "How do you know I can't convince him to let us both go? He had his chance in the hedge maze when I was drugged. He let me go then. Maybe I can reason with him."

"And maybe you can't."

"Then I'll convince him to leave with me. Tell him we'll run away together," I suggested. "I'll lead him out so that you can have at him."

"He wants you, Maren. He doesn't want to leave with you. He wants to *have* you. As soon as you go in there, he has everything he wants."

"I still don't understand why he would go to all this trouble just for me. Can't he have any girl on the planet? Why me?" I asked.

"Because you're *you*," Gavin answered softly. "There's no one else like you on the planet. You're beautiful, charming, clever . . . I'd do anything for you." He reached out and stroked my hair. The compliments made me feel wonderful, but I was too embarrassed to acknowledge them.

"Yes, but you know me," I said.

"I don't just know you," he interrupted. "I love you."

That I couldn't ignore. "I love you too." I cradled his free hand in both of mine. "But Graham doesn't know me at all. He's just obsessed with a girl he has never really met."

Gavin withdrew his hand. "You're right. He's obsessed. He's obsessed and *possessed*. The worst combination possible. You're not going in there."

"What else do you want me to do? He's holed up in there with my grandmother. I have to go in. I have to try. I'm sure I can do this, but I need you to think that too. I need you to trust me."

"I do trust you, Maren. It's him I don't trust. Please, *please* don't do this. I can't get enough of you, Maren, and I've only just found you. You were made for me, and I for you. We're soul mates, can't you see that? More destined to be together than two creatures ever have been. I've been waiting for you for hundreds of years. I can't lose you now."

"You won't lose me," I said. "Ever. You have me for-ever. I'm yours. Nothing can change that."

He didn't look convinced. "My passion for you is cloud-ing everything. I used to work alone, I was alone, and now you're part of me. You're my breath." He cupped my face in his strong hands, making my entire body tingle. "I know you have free will, and I cannot make you do what you do not want, but I'm asking you . . . No, I'm begging you, please do not go inside."

I stepped backward, letting his hands fall from my cheeks. "Don't ask me that. It's not fair. I can't just leave my grandmother behind," I said.

"Let me go for help," he suggested. "Surely some-one else—"

"Who?" I interrupted. "No one from your village can go in, either, and Graham said if we bring anyone else, he'll kill her! And we're running out of time. I can do this, Gavin. I know I can. You heard my plan. I'll lead him outside."

"It's a good plan, Maren, if it works. But if it doesn't . . . *Arrgghhhh!*" He twisted and punched the tree trunk. The air filled with a rumbling like thunder, and the tree splintered in the middle. "*Arrggghhhhh!*" he yelled again, a primal scream of pain. He threw his fist into the tree again. His hand dripped blood.

"Stop it! Stop it!" I cried, grabbing at his arms.

"I cannot take it, Maren." He clawed at his head. "I'm

going mad here. Go, just go! Get it done! Go before I can't let you!"

I pulled myself away and ran. *Boom!* I heard him hit the trunk again, but I didn't look back. I couldn't.

I would come back out alive, and unharmed. I had to.

CHAPTER 35

The massive front door of Campbell Hall creaked open when I pushed on it.

"Hello?" I called out. No one answered. I took a deep breath and slipped inside. The door slammed behind me. I spun around, but I was alone.

I tiptoed into the lobby, my steps echoing on the marble floor. "Hello? Graham? I'm here. Now let me see my grandmother!"

A wooden panel in the wall to my right slid open.

"Come in," Graham's voice called.

I followed it into a room decorated like a ski lodge, with dark green carpet, overstuffed brown leather chairs, and an equally overstuffed moose head gazing blankly from above the fireplace.

Graham was in a chair, partially facing me. "Please, sit." He motioned to the seat across from him with the drink in his hand. The clinking of his ice cubes was followed by a deep rumble. "I hear your friend is outside," he said with a chuckle. "Temper, temper . . ."

"Where's my grandmother?" I demanded. If he had harmed her in any way . . . I couldn't bear the thought.

"I'm not telling you anything until you sit and have a wee chat with me," Graham purred, taking a sip from his glass.

I sat down on the very edge of the empty seat. "Where is she?"

"She's perfectly safe," he said. "And if you want, I'll let her go right now. You did show up, and you certainly can't leave." He picked up a small, black remote control from the table next to him and pressed a button. "There, it's done. Your grandmother is on her way outside right now."

"How do I know that? That button didn't do anything."

"You'll just have to trust me," he said with a shrug.

Not in a million years.

"Maybe when that fly boy of yours stops killing all the trees in my garden, you'll believe me," he continued. "I'm guessing he'll stop banging his head like a big baby once he sees dear old Grandmama."

The noise outside had stopped, but I wanted to keep Graham talking until I had some kind of confirmation my grandmother was truly free.

"Why are you doing this?" I asked. "And why did you save me from Anders?"

"I'm doing this because it's in my blood," he said, licking his lips. "And I saved you from Anders because I didn't want you sullied by his stupidity. I want you for myself."

I remembered Gavin saying the demon in Campbell Hall was an incubus demon—a lowlife, a thief. I knew what they went after, and it wasn't love. Graham wasn't obsessed with me; he was obsessed with my virginity. This was a game to him, and I was the spoils.

I ignored his disgusting innuendo and tried to keep control of the conversation. "I saw Anders in church today," I said. "How is he not a demon if you're related? You're both Campbells."

"We're related in name only, not by blood," Graham

answered. "He likes to play the prince, but really, he was adopted. It's a pity too, because he would make an excellent demon, don't you think?"

"He was adopted? Demons adopt kids?"

"Not usually, but my aunt and uncle had an incident with a girl a number of years ago. She came to live with them, to work for them, really, and when she got pregnant, they were delighted, of course, because demons aren't supposed to be able to sire children . . ." He paused to let the scenario sink in. "Unfortunately, the baby wasn't one of ours. When she'd come to them, she was already pregnant. She died in childbirth, and they were stuck with the baby, so they adopted him." He took another drink. "Did he give Mrs. Dougall my regards at the funeral?"

His words punched me in the stomach.

"What did you do to Jo?" I gulped.

"I needed to get your attention. It was easier than I thought, really. I met her out on a walk and took her . . . for a little ride, if you know what I mean."

"You didn't!" I screamed, jumping to my feet.

"Don't get your knickers in a twist," he said. "It wasn't *that* kind of ride. Please," he sniffed. "I don't waste my time with just any girl. I took her for a little sightseeing flight. She didn't like it, of course. So when she scratched me, the little witch, I dropped her."

"You just dropped her?" I felt tears welling up in my eyes. I wiped them away. I had to be strong.

"Yes, just like that. I dropped her. She wasn't what I wanted."

I knew what he wanted, and he planned to get it from

me. Coming in to Campbell Hall had been a big mistake. I stood up.

In a flash, Graham was standing in front of me, blocking my path. His breath reeked of alcohol. "You're a special girl, Maren. Very special." He walked his fingers along my shoulder.

I slapped his hand away. Unfortunately, he seemed to enjoy it.

"Oh, I like a feisty one," he whispered, moving closer to me.

I tried to step back, but the chair was behind my legs. I twisted and ducked around him, but he caught me by the wrist. He threw his drink on the floor. It shattered in a mess of liquid and broken glass. He grabbed my other wrist with his now-free hand, and pushed me backward into the wall.

"We can do this the easy way," he breathed. He leaned forward and licked my cheek. I squeezed my eyes shut and tried not to quiver. "But I do so like the hard way."

When he pressed his body against mine, I heard a high-pitched whistle. He let go of me to put his fingers in his ears.

"What is that?" he wailed. "Make it stop!"

The noise was so quiet I could barely hear it, and it didn't bother me at all. It stopped as soon as he stepped away. He straightened up, his face furious. He planted his hands on the wall behind me, trapping me between his arms.

"Now, where were we?" he hissed. I turned my head as he pushed his body against me and again, as soon as we touched, something screeched ever so faintly. He jumped back in audible pain. It stopped, and he realized the noise was coming from me.

He pulled my sweater down at the neck and spied the Tudor rose necklace. *This was why Gia told me to use it for Anders*, I thought. The necklace was some kind of ultra-sonic demon agitator.

Graham ripped the necklace off my throat, and threw it across the room.

"If you thought a little buzzing would stop me, you were wrong," he sneered. "Dead wrong."

❀ ❀ ❀

A low gong sound reverberated through the room. Graham cocked his head and sniffed. He had a strange look in his eyes.

"Dinner's ready," he said, as if I were the main course. He stepped away from me and held out his elbow. I didn't move. "Come now," he motioned. "I have to eat when it's hot. If my food gets cold, I'm afraid I get into a terrible mood." *Get into a terrible mood? What was his mood before?*

He took my hand, shoved it through the crook in his arm, and squeezed. Then he started walking, half drag-ging me behind him.

If I allowed him to drag me anywhere, it would seem like I'd surrendered. I had to at least pretend I was confident and could hold my own, even if I wasn't so sure I could. In any competition or puzzle, the minute you give up, you lose.

I couldn't afford to lose.

In a few steps, I was marching next to him, as if we were on our way to a date of my design.

We walked down the hall, passing the portraits of men I assumed were Campbell ancestors. I'd seen them before, at Anders' birthday party, the stern looking people in stilted poses. Only this time, a fog hung about the tops of the pictures as if the painted men themselves were breathing. I shivered in spite of myself, and involuntarily drew closer to Graham. He seemed pleased that I was cooperating, and relaxed a little. He played the tour guide, pointing out artifacts on the walls and bragging about Campbell conquests.

We came to a large opening that led into a grand dining room. A carved crest over the doorway read, *Ta er-jerrey hoshiaght*. It was Gaelic, and I found that for no good reason, like at Magnificat, I could read it.

"'The last shall be first'?" I asked aloud.

"Well spotted," Graham congratulated me. "It's our motto."

"Your motto is from the *Bible*?"

"Why not? It's fitting, since someday *we* will have ultimate power over the earth and the heavens. And, yes, demons are well versed in your holy book. To us, it's like reading *The Art of War*. Know thine enemy, as it were. The Bible is also a bit of our family history. Our father is in there quite a few times."

"The father of lies, you mean? Satan?"

He smiled. "That's the one."

The dining room was completely illuminated by fire. Tall candles dripped in the middle of a long, polished table that was dwarfed by a fireplace so big, you could stand inside it next to the fire and not get burned. The flickering flames danced around everything shiny in the room, sending sparks of reflection bouncing off the cutlery, the glasses, the candlesticks, and the weapons on the walls.

As Graham pulled back a chair for me, I saw the room was rather ominously lined with dozens of swords, battle-axes, spears, and other death devices.

"Cheery," I commented.

Graham pretended to look embarrassed. "Oh, yes, well, the dining room doubles as the trophy room, doesn't it? It invigorates the appetite to see the spoils of victory. These are the weapons of some of our greatest kills. Not all of them, of course." He pointed. "There's the dagger we used to kill Julius Caesar. There's one of the swords used to kill Thomas Becket. The axe used on John the Baptist—"

"I thought demons just dropped people to their deaths," I cut in, to show I wasn't impressed. Images of my mother, the girl from Culloden, and Jo came to my mind. I swallowed hard to keep my composure, but something wasn't adding up.

"Usually, yes," Graham replied. "But sometimes we do like a show. Feel free to look around while I fetch our first course." He sauntered toward a single door on the far left.

Why did I think I could do this? The farther inside I got, the farther I was from ever getting back out. I needed to leave. Now.

As soon as Graham disappeared through the door, I turned and ran as fast as I could. I had only taken about five steps when I crossed back under the Campbell crest and smacked into Graham. He caught me as easily as if he were waiting for me, grabbed my wrists, and planted a kiss on my lips. I clamped my mouth shut, willing myself not to throw up, and waited for him to pull away. When he did, he smiled.

"I told you, darling, there's no way out. No trap doors, no secret tunnels to save you this time. The only way to leave is if you die, I die, or you give me what I want. And I'm betting on the last one, aren't you?"

He put his hands on my shoulders, turned me, and walked me back to my dining room chair. "Now I have to get our dinner before it goes cold. Don't vex me again or I shall lose patience." He disappeared back through the doorway.

I wiped at my mouth with the back of my hand, then grabbed a napkin and scrubbed it again. I couldn't stand the thought of Graham touching me. Clearly, Graham would be there no matter which way I turned. I needed to get rid of him somehow. Permanently.

I looked around at the walls. *Maybe I can use one of the weapons to kill him.* I walked to the nearest dagger and yanked. It was bolted to the wall. I ran my fingers over it. Even if I could get it off, a simple knife would never kill a demon.

I circled the room, looking at the deadly wall decorations. There were more daggers and spears, but also maces, spiked clubs, and even a formidable-looking hammer. Directly across from the fireplace, I came upon a thick glass display case. It was fitted with an ornate frame and held the biggest sword I'd ever seen. The sword wasn't just mounted behind glass, it was locked.

There were six tiny number dials at the bottom of the

frame set—not coincidentally, I thought—to 666666. I spun a few of the numbers so I didn't have to look at the creepy combination.

Suddenly, the sword caught on fire—only blue-white flames licked its blade, not red-orange ones. I jumped back, thinking I had somehow caused the ignition by disturbing the dials. Behind me, Graham laughed.

"You've found our flaming glory," he said. "Our most valuable treasure. Don't worry, you didn't do anything. You couldn't if you tried. *I* set it alight. You touching the knobs would hardly upset it."

"So it's *not* locked?"

"Oh, it is—we can't have someone stealing it from us and trying to return it, or selling it to a museum or something. It's priceless, really."

"What is it?"

"It's a celestial claymore. An Archangel's sword. Very rare. I believe we're the only family in Europe to have one. Quite a conquest. Now come, dinner is served." He motioned toward the table, where blackened and bloody food was steaming and sizzling on various-sized plates.

I slowly walked back to my seat. The Campbell demons had actually killed an Archangel, and now they gloated over his sword. It seemed they were interested in more than just virginity . . .

"I thought incubus demons were supposed to steal, not kill," I blurted out.

He slammed his hand on the table and screamed, "*Incubus*? Never call me that!"

I blanched. He twisted his jaw and smoothed the front of his shirt.

"I'm sorry," he sighed. "Please forgive the outburst. It's a touchy subject. Of course that loser Guardian angel would have told you we were *incubus*. It's his clan's fault we got demoted, after all. I can't believe I have such an unworthy opponent. Ah well, all in good time," he drawled.

I bit my lip and tried to look noncommittal as he talked about Gavin. The mention of my powerful love—who was just outside, powerless to come in—underscored the reality that I was out of my league.

As I took my place at the end of the table, I was dismayed to notice Graham collecting his plate and walking toward me.

"These long banquets are quite a bother," he said, placing everything next to me. "I can't sit so far away from you. I need to be near you, where I can see you and smell you and taste you." He lifted my hand and pretended to bite it, but I snatched it away.

As I sat down, I got a strange sensation, a tingling sixth sense like déjà vu. I saw the scene before me as if I'd lived it before, only it wasn't me sitting at the table, it was another girl my age. *An ancestral memory?*

She was wearing an old-fashioned dress with a ruffled corset and a wide black ribbon tied in a bow on the side of her hair. I hoped that instead of just seeing her, I could use her memories and knowledge to escape.

As if in answer, she pointed to the case holding the flaming sword. *The sword of an Archangel. The one thing a human could use to kill a demon!* If only I could unlock it . . .

I cleared my throat. "It's very impressive," I said to Graham.

He stopped his fork on the way to his mouth. "Thank you," he answered before realizing I hadn't told him what impressed me. His cheeks turned crimson, and I guessed he'd been lost in his own fantasy. I didn't want to know what it was about, but I could guess.

I nodded at the wall. "The sword. It's huge. You must be proud."

My compliments must have played nicely into his daydream, because he smiled broadly. "It is big, I assure you." He winked. I tried not to blanch.

"Do you know the code?" I picked up my fork to emphasize that I was only making innocent, superficial dinner conversation.

"Of course I do. You think they don't trust me enough to give me the code? I'm not as young as I look," he sniffed.

I looked at the ghostly girl next to me, tried to search her brain. What should I do?

A hint, she whispered silently to me. *Ask for a hint.*

I stabbed at something meaty with my fork and gave Graham what I hoped was a beguiling look. "I bet I could guess your code."

"Guess the code? It can't be guessed, dear. The numbers repeat, so there are over a million combinations."

"I could try to guess part of it," I suggested. "Come on, humor me. I love puzzles. Give me a hint. Please?" I twirled a lock of my hair between my fingers.

"Four," he sighed.

"That's not a hint," I scolded. "That's just a number."

His hand found my knee. "You like to be teased, don't you?" he said. I felt like a mouse being played with by a snake before it was eaten. It was not a good feeling. "All right," he conceded. "I'll tell you it's the most powerful number in all the world."

I thought about the possibilities. Six numbers were too long for a coded Bible verse. In terms of money, six digits was less than a million. It couldn't be 666, since that was already entered. It had to be mathematical. *What is a famous long number in math that has a four in it?*

"Is it pi?" I asked.

He smiled. "Very clever, but also very easy. Yes, it's from pi."

I felt a surge of hope. *I got it! Now I just have to get rid of him long enough to use it . . .*

He removed an ink pen from his breast pocket and started drawing on his white napkin. "Three point one four. *Pi.* The number every eleven-year-old knows," he mocked.

I fought the urge to punch him.

"I bet you didn't know this, though," he continued. He flipped the napkin over and held it up to the fireplace so the numbers showed through the cloth: PI.E. They spelled *pie*!

"Wow," I enthused before I could stop myself. "I never saw that before."

"Yes, well, I have many tricks up my sleeve. One of the perks of being around for three hundred years. You meet a lot of interesting people." I felt his foot caressing my leg. I pushed back from the table. I had to get him out of the room.

"Speaking of pie, do you have any dessert?" I asked. "I'm sort of a sweets girl. It's a lovely dinner, but I'd rather just jump right to dessert, wouldn't you?" I winked, hoping I didn't look like an idiot.

His eyes danced. "I think I can whip something up." He stood and walked toward the door. Halfway across the room, he stopped and turned back to me. "Oh, I forgot to mention. The code for the Claymore case is pi, but it's not the first six digits. That would be far too simple. It's the *last* six digits." My face must have fallen, because he laughed as he left the room.

I was devastated, as I knew that pi is an irrational number. It never ends. No one knows the six last digits. *Well, apparently demons know,* I thought dejectedly.

I had another flash, and I saw the spirit girl again. Only this time, she wasn't talking. She wasn't breathing. A knife protruded out of her chest, from her heart. She was dead. My entire body went ice cold.

Dear God, don't let this vision be a foreshadowing of where I die, I prayed.

I had to get out. And I only had a few seconds. *Think, Maren, think!*

The last six digits of pi. No one knew them. A lot of people knew the first six digits though: 3.14159. At least, everyone in Mr. Mick's fifth grade class did, since for no good reason he'd made us memorize them with a little song.

The last six digits. The last. *Why couldn't they be the first?*

Then it hit me: *the last shall be first.* The Campbell crest. I stood up and ran to the frame. Maybe he was tricking me with wordplay, and it was the first digits after all. I quickly spun the dials to read 314159. Nothing.

The last shall be first. What makes something at the end suddenly be at the beginning? I remembered Graham's napkin in the firelight. *Backward! When it's backward!* My fingers slipped as I desperately rolled the wheels.

9 . . . 5 . . . 1 . . .

"I've found dessert, darling!" Graham called from outside the room.

4 . . . 1 . . .

His footsteps got closer and closer.

I fumbled with the last dial.

3.

Clink! The locks released and the glass panel started to slide silently upward from the bottom of the frame. I did it! *Thank you, Mr. Mick,* I whispered.

I shook while I waited for the opening to be large enough for me to stick my hand inside. *Come on, come on, hurry up,* I willed it.

"Maren," Graham called out from the doorway. I turned and strode quickly toward him. If I got his attention away from the sword, he might not notice the case was open. Then, when he wasn't looking, I could grab it.

"What do you have for me?" I asked, forcing a smile.

"What *don't* I have for you is a better question," he replied. He was holding a pie tin filled with whipped cream that was, of course, on fire. He set it on the table, put his finger in the middle of it, right through the flames, and pulled out a dollop. He dabbed it on my lips, and exhaled loudly.

I knew he was going to use the whipped cream as an excuse to kiss me, and thankfully, I came up with a plan. I would let him lean in, then stop him at the last second and ask for a drink. I'd promise to kiss him back if he just got me a glass of water. Then, when he left the room, I would free the sword.

I tried not to contort my face in disgust as he moved his lips toward mine. I opened my mouth to speak, but before I could . . .

BAROOM! A roaring explosion rocked the room. When the smoke cleared, we saw a huge, jagged hole in the wall behind us.

Gavin was standing in the center of it.

CHAPTER 36

My love. Like every time I saw him, a wave of pleasure tore over me.

Gavin, however, did not seem the least bit happy to see me. He looked at the two of us—Graham leaning over to kiss me, my lips covered with whipped cream—and he staggered backward.

"Gavin, he didn't . . ." I was cut short by something hot against my throat. Graham held a knife to my neck. I could sense it was the same blade he'd used to kill the girl from the past, the girl who'd gone before me.

"Not another step, or I'll kill her. You know I will," Graham warned. "I was wondering when you'd show up," he added.

I held my breath to keep still. *Why is Graham acting like he expected Gavin?*

"You're a little late, though," Graham continued. "It's already done. We're just enjoying dessert now, as you can see."

Graham opened his mouth, and a long serpent tongue snaked out and licked the whipped cream off my lips. My stomach churned.

Gavin's face turned dark, and his eyes went wild. He clenched his fists, and was visibly straining against his instinct to lunge. It was killing him to see me in Graham's arms. I tried to shake my head, to let Gavin know that Graham was lying, but it made the knife dig deeper. I felt the warm trickle of blood on my collar.

"What a pity that you broke the Covenant for nothing," Graham said. "You couldn't save her, and now you've doomed yourself."

What is he talking about? What is the Covenant? And why is Gavin doomed? I wondered. *How is Gavin even there? I thought he couldn't enter a demon seat . . .*

"Let her go," Gavin hissed through closed teeth.

"I think not," Graham answered. "I'm rather enjoying her."

Gavin roared with equal parts anger and anguish. As he did, his wings burst out from his back. He began to pace, menacingly.

In response, Graham morphed. His skin turned red, slick, and scaly. Scarlet, almost translucent wings sprang from his shoulders, and the muscles on his arms doubled in size. As his shape shifted, his hand on my throat relaxed, and I darted out from under his arm.

Gavin flew across the room, grabbing Graham. They slammed into the wall, sending metal weapons flying. I ducked under the table, narrowly missing being sliced by a passing dagger.

I peeked out and saw that Gavin had Graham by the throat. He lifted the demon, walked toward me, and slammed Graham's face into the table. I screamed and retreated, as forks and spoons clattered to the floor in a noisy rain around me.

The entire table lifted above me. I looked up and saw that Graham was holding it over his head. He threw it at Gavin, and it splintered over my angel's broad back. I ran into the fireplace. It was warm, but offered cover from the objects swirling around the room.

Graham started taunting Gavin as they circled each other. "I knew you'd choose love over duty. Not that I blame you. She *was* quite delicious."

Gavin raised his lips in a silent snarl.

"Was it worth it?" Graham continued. "Was the love of a worthless human worth your own undoing?"

"The only worthless thing in this room is you!" Gavin spat.

"Not for long, thanks to you." Graham smirked. "You didn't think my family would take our punishment forever, did you? We're *jinn*, not lowlife incubus! And, finally, we'll have our honor restored. In fact, once I kill you and the little Abbey girl here, I bet we'll even get promoted to—"

ARRGGHHH! A guttural scream erupted from Gavin as he charged toward Graham. Graham leapt, and they collided in midair with a sonic boom that rattled the chandelier. Both tumbled around the room, smashing into the walls, the ceiling, then back down to the floor. Every impact left a huge crater behind.

In the flurry of fists and flying, it was hard to tell who was winning. Gavin grabbed Graham by the shoulders and flipped the demon foot over face. From the floor, Graham bit Gavin on his Achilles' heel. In response, Gavin smashed Graham with a kick in the chest.

They then started pulling weapons off the walls. Gavin launched a javelin into Graham's thigh. Graham laughed and yanked it out. Graham threw a huge spiked hammer at Gavin. It bounced off Gavin's forehead like a pinecone off a bear. Human weapons seemed no more dangerous to them than a human throwing a plastic lawn chair in someone's way—a nuisance, but nothing deadly.

I looked across the room at the Archangel sword. Its flames had gone out, but the glass box was open. I didn't think Gavin saw it, and Graham didn't know I had unlocked it. Every time I thought about running over to it, another weapon whizzed across the room. I couldn't figure out how to get to it without getting killed.

They continued to fight, but eventually, Graham started to tire. His movements slowed, his reflexes weren't as sharp, and he was taking far more hits than he was delivering. Finally, Gavin landed a powerful punch to the jaw that left Graham motionless on the floor not two feet in front of me. It looked as if Gavin had won. Tears of relief streamed down my cheeks.

I peered over Graham's back at Gavin. He was bloodied and battered.

"Are you all right?" I asked.

"Right as rain," he said, twisting his lips into a half smile. "You best get out of here before he wakes up. Let me finish him off."

I shook my head. "I won't leave you."

"Won't leave me, eh?" He raised his eyebrows. "What was that whole scene in the driveway, then?"

"I mean I won't leave you again. Ever. I promise. I was just coming out to tell you."

"You were just coming out?" he said incredulously.

"Yeah, I had this under control," I said.

"This? *This*?" He motioned around the ruined room. "You had it under control?"

"Well, you came in at a bad time," I protested. "I was in the middle of a new plan."

"You were in the middle of something," he cracked.

I was about to answer when I saw a small glint of light at my feet. Graham had edged over toward the fireplace, reached into the fire, and pulled out a long, flaming fork. In a flash, he was on his feet, seemingly fully recovered, a glowing three-pronged spear leveled at Gavin's heart.

"Sorry to interrupt the love story," Graham said with a sigh. "But I believe I have a Satan Trident with Gavin's name on it."

He hurled his body toward Gavin, and the fight was back on. And it was now decidedly in Graham's favor.

Gavin jumped, deflecting the trident away from his chest, but it sliced his shoulder. The blow caused his wings to seize up, and he fell to the ground, his face contorted in pain. I realized that with his own immortal weapon, Graham could very well kill Gavin right in front of me. I had to do something. I had to go for the sword.

Gavin curled into a ball on the floor. Graham stood over him, ready to deliver another blow, when suddenly Gavin's legs uncoiled against Graham's chest, sending the demon flying backward, directly toward me. Graham crashed into the stone mantel to my left. The fireplace started to crumble from the impact.

I bolted through the dust and falling mortar toward the opened display box and freed the sword.

"Gavin!" I hollered. "Catch!"

I threw it in the air, and in one swift motion, Gavin leapt up, caught it, and sliced it at Graham. Graham returned the volley with his trident. They dueled, ferociously stabbing and swiping at each other. Sparks flew as the metal armaments connected, filling the air with sharp clangs.

With the fireplace destroyed, the fire jumped from its hearth and onto the thick floor rug. Soon, flames engulfed the entire room.

"Run, Maren, run!" Gavin yelled between thrusts. "Get out of here, now!"

A thick, noxious smoke filled the room, swallowing Gavin and Graham. My eyes burned so badly, I wondered if they might start to boil in their sockets. My throat seized up suddenly, making it impossible to breathe.

I didn't want to leave, but my body's need for air overrode all conscious thought. I fumbled for the wall. I would slide my fingertips along the solid surface until I found a doorway. When I hit a solid plane, I picked a direction and ran. I hoped I'd guessed the right way.

If not, I was going to die.

❁ ❁ ❁

I burst out of the dining room, choking for air. As I sprinted down the hall, the heat from the spreading fire licked at my calves. The clanking of the sword and the trident followed me, and the entire building shook with every supernatural collision.

I might have needed to leave Gavin—for now—but I was not leaving without my grandmother. I raced out the front door, down the driveway, and back toward the car, calling her name, but couldn't find her anywhere.

Graham had lied; he'd never let her go. I looked back at the great house. She must still be somewhere inside.

Shards of glass showered over the side yard as a couple of windows exploded. The fire was moving from the east wing toward the rest of the massive house. If I was going back in to get her, I needed to find her quickly. But how?

I walked up the drive, studying the house from the outside. Was there a clue somewhere? Could I find anything different or out of place?

I scanned the windows for a sign. I followed the pattern of ivy climbing the walls. Nothing. I looked at the sloping sections of roof. And then I saw it. One of the more than twenty chimney stacks did not look like the others. While most were blackened by soot at the top from years of use, the one on the far end of the house—thankfully, the farthest from the fire—was not. It was clean.

What does it mean? I willed my brain to work faster, to find an answer somehow. My body was shaking from adrenaline, and my mind raced. *You wouldn't have a single chimney cleaned and leave the rest dirty. A lack of soot must mean that chimney never had a fire in it. Why would someone build a large brick fireplace, then?* A vision popped into my head of a huge tunnel connecting the three floors—a secret passageway to hidden rooms! It was the perfect way to conceal something or someone; no one would ever notice extra rooms tucked in this giant mansion. The fireplace must be the only way in and out of them.

I ran along the wing while counting windows, then back to the front door. Smoke swirled around its edges. I took a deep breath, said a quick prayer, and ducked inside.

❀ ❀ ❀

I sprinted down the main hallway to the right—away from the ballrooms and dining rooms, toward what I hoped were the living quarters. Eight doors down, I crossed the hall and entered a room without any windows. An elaborately carved canopy bed loomed across from a large open fireplace. The hearth was spotless, no evidence of soot or ash. I stepped inside and looked up the chimney. All I saw was darkness.

As I ran my palms around the interior, the house shook from another supernatural collision. Small pieces of mortar fell onto my face. I needed to hurry.

About a foot above my head, concealed in the shadows of the flue, I discovered a single wooden beam jutting out about a foot from the back of the wall. I reached up on my tiptoes and felt the bottom of another beam slightly higher and to the right. Could it be some kind of ladder or crude staircase? I pushed at the bricks around me, hoping lower steps might magically appear to assist me. Nothing budged. I knew I was at the right place; I could feel it. I just had to get myself up.

I stood sideways against the wall, set my palms on the first plank, and jumped, trying to hoist my body onto it. I missed. My hip slammed into the bricks and I scraped to the floor.

I cursed at the ground. "How about a little help?" I called out to no one in particular. There was no answer. I realized ancestral memories might show me things, but they wouldn't *do* things for me. I was on my own.

I looked around the room for something to drag into the fireplace to stand on, but decided against it; once I was up, it would give me away. I needed every second I could get if I was going to find my grandmother before Graham found me.

I rubbed my hands together to psyche myself up. I had to try to climb up even if it meant possibly bashing my face in. I wrapped my wrists around the higher post, did an awkward, painful pull-up, and swung my legs sideways. It worked. Once I caught my ankle on the bottom beam I was able to use that leverage to shift my weight and squirm up until I was standing on the narrow beam. I looked above. As I hoped, there were more posts anchored to the wall, spiraling up in front of me.

I kept my shoulder against the wall, and tried not to think about how small the steps were. I ascended the chimney as fast as I dared, turning the corners carefully, and never looking down.

The climb was longer than I anticipated, and inky black. The chimney was tight enough that I could use both hands against opposite walls for balance, but it was far too confining for my comfort. I took deep breaths and tried not to think about what would happen if I somehow got stuck.

Near where I imagined was halfway up, the wall next to me disappeared into a deep, open rectangle taller than I was. I thrust my toe into the air until I felt the solid floor of a tan alcove beneath my foot. I stepped over and swung my body into the space—and hit a wall. The wall was made of something softer than brick—probably wood—so it didn't hurt too badly.

With shaking arms, I pulled myself forward. Once I was safely standing, I groped the panel in front of me. It was definitely made of wood. It had to be a door! I braced my legs, twisted the ring, and pushed. The door swung inward, and I landed in a heap on the floor of a dimly lit room.

"Maren!" I felt thin arms fold around me.

"Grandma!" I stumbled to my feet and hugged her tightly. "Thank goodness I found you! Are you okay? Did he hurt you?"

"No dear, but . . ." she faltered.

"What?" I searched her face for some sign that Graham had harmed her. *If he had . . .*

"That boy, Graham, he's not what he seems. He's a . . ." Again, she paused as if not wanting to scar me with the awful truth.

"He's a demon," I finished for her. "I know. That's why we came here looking for you."

"We?"

"Me and Gavin."

"Gavin, your tutor? What does he have to do with any of this?"

A low sonic boom reverberated around the room. The floor quivered.

"It's a long story," I said, hugging her tightly. "Let's get out of here first, and I'll tell you all about it."

We turned toward the chimney opening—the only way in or out of the windowless secret room—and froze. I had been followed. A small gray cloud of smoke slunk across the floor. I inched out over the opening. The bottom of the chimney tunnel now flickered beneath me. The fire had spread. There was no going back down.

I ducked inside. "We're going to have to go up to the roof," I said. "Can you make it?"

"Aye," she confirmed. "Lead the way."

We climbed back into the chimney and up the crude wooden stairs as fast as we could. A couple of times, I heard a slip and a gasp, but my grandmother managed to stay close behind me.

As we climbed, the holy battle continued, shaking the house to its foundations. I tried not to rush, but I didn't want the chimney to crumble while we were still in it, either.

Finally, I could taste the fresh air. The smoke stack was considerably smaller than our passageway, but we managed to slide out of it one at a time. The roof of Campbell Hall was big enough to land a helicopter on. And really, really high up. I searched for a ladder or fire escape or some other way down. There was nothing.

"What do we do now?" I asked my grandmother.

Jumping was out of the question; no one could survive the fall.

"We wait," she said.

"For what?"

"A miracle." She drew me close, and we stared out over the dark forest. It was a beautiful night. I wondered if it might be our last.

Please, God, I prayed, *help us out of this mess. I'll do anything, give anything . . .*

A tremendous explosion rocked the entire area. We fell to our knees, and clung tighter to one another. I shut my eyes and braced for the worst. Patterns of red light flickered before my eyelids. For a brief second, I wondered if I was dead. Sirens pierced the cold night air.

The fire brigade was screaming up the drive.

❀ ❀ ❀

My grandmother and I were safely back on the ground, tucked between two red and yellow fire trucks. Wrapped in a standard-issue emergency blanket I didn't think we needed, we watched as Campbell Hall tried to survive its own war from within. Repeated explosions shook the ground. Fireballs jumped off the roof. The firemen knew they were helpless against such a blaze, so they too watched as, one by one, the walls crumbled. I gnawed the inside of my cheeks and waited.

Finally, a figure emerged from the smoke and rubble. He walked slowly, as if bruised but not beaten. I knew instantly from his silhouette who had won.

I ducked under the yellow police tape and ran toward him. Gavin was smudged with black sediment and a fair amount of blood, but otherwise, he seemed fine. I dove into his arms and covered him in kisses.

After a minute, he set me down. He was carrying something shiny in his hand, and held it out to me.

"I thought you might want this." He smiled. It was my rose necklace.

He slipped it over my head and kissed the crown of my hair tenderly. I felt whole again.

"Graham's dead, right?" I asked, startling as another blast reverberated across the lawn.

"For now," Gavin said with a nod.

I didn't want to know what that meant. I was done with demons. Forever.

CHAPTER 37

Gavin and I were sitting on the wooden swing in the backyard of my house, watching the forest turn purple and pink. It was almost dawn. My grandmother was safely inside. My grandfather was on his way back from St. Andrews. And in my world, everything was perfect. Finally perfect.

I leaned against Gavin, my head on his chest while he rocked us with his feet. I could hear his heartbeat, feel the warmth of his skin through his shirt. He stroked my hair lightly. I couldn't get close enough to him.

"I love you, Maren," he said. "I've never felt this way about anyone. I didn't think I could feel this way."

"You've never been in love before?" I asked. "Not in your two hundred eighty-three years? Not with all those hundreds of girls you've rescued?"

He looked wounded by my accusation. "No, never." He shook his head. "Not even close. Angels are supposed to love everyone, all of humanity equally, but now I realize it's a superficial love. What I feel for you is so much deeper. It's like you've somehow planted roots inside me that are twisted around my heart. I'm not sure I can live without them now." He paused. "Have you ever been in love before?" I thought I saw a hint of jealousy in his crystal-blue eyes.

"No," I confessed. "I've never even been in serious *like* before. Unless you count Adam Cohnen . . ."

"Who's that? I'll kill him!" Gavin said playfully.

"My fourth-grade crush."

"Did you kiss him?" Gavin asked, raising his eyebrows.

I nodded. "Yep. Behind the jungle gym. I chased him, and I kissed him on the cheek. But he didn't kiss me back."

Gavin moved his hands to the sides of my neck, under my ears, cradling my face. "Then Adam Cohnen is a fool," he breathed.

I was overwhelmed with how much I adored him. I could barely stand how much I wanted to be with him. I lifted my arms up around his neck. We pulled closer to each other until our lips were touching. Even though I thought every kiss from him would end me, this, this was the most amazing kiss of my life. The whole world disappeared. I couldn't feel anything but him.

"I love you," he said again when we finally parted.

"I love you too," I replied.

"Never forget that. No matter what happens, no matter where you are or what you're doing, know that I love you. That I will always love you."

I sat up. Something wasn't right. "What do you mean, 'no matter what happens'?" I asked. "It's over. We won."

"It's not over," he said, looking into the woods like he was waiting for something. "It's never over. They'll send more demons."

"And you'll kill them," I said. "Because you're awesome like that. You're my strong, handsome, amazing, wonderful demon killer." I traced his features with my fingertips. He had scrubbed off the soot and dried blood, and the wounds left behind were bright red, but they gave his beauty a fierce edge that excited me. I bent his head and gently kissed each of them, then kissed him on the mouth.

"Mmm-maren," he said, muffled because my lips were over his.

"What?" I said between kisses, refusing to stop.

He put his hands on my shoulder and gently pushed me back a few inches.

"What?" I said, moving toward him again.

"I broke the rules, Maren. I'm sorry, and I knew better, but . . ."

"I know you broke the rules. I did too. So what?"

"Not those rules, Maren. It's much more serious than that."

"What's more serious than falling in love with me?" I joked.

"Breaching sacred ground . . . or more like destroying it."

"You mean Campbell Hall?" I asked. "Yeah, I thought angels couldn't get into a demon's lair like demons can't go into churches. How did you manage that?"

"It's not that you *can't*, it's that you're forbidden from doing so. You can physically do it, but if you do, you've crossed a line that can't be uncrossed. By going into the Campbell place, I've doomed an angel stronghold somewhere."

"How?"

"By trespassing, I broke a Covenant and created a Vendetta. Now the demons will get to pick a sacred place of ours to invade."

"That's awful," I said.

He drew me closer to him. "I know. But it doesn't matter now. It's done."

He stopped talking and stared ahead. I followed his gaze and saw three smears of light, hovering like fireflies. Then I remembered there weren't any fireflies in Scotland.

The lights got closer and larger, coming toward us. I strained to get a better look.

They were angels, although taller and much sterner looking than Gavin.

"What's going on?" I asked nervously.

"I have to go," he said flatly.

"Where?"

"I'm not sure. Wherever they decide. I told you, I broke the rules . . ."

"So you're going to get punished? They're going to take you away?" His silence confirmed it was true. The closer the angels got to us, the more my panic grew. I remembered what Gia said about angels who were "reassigned." That they were never heard from again. I couldn't lose Gavin. I couldn't breathe without him. My chest was already tightening.

"Why did you break the rules then?" I practically screamed, jerking out of his embrace. "If you knew this would happen, you should have stayed outside! I'd already unlocked the sword. If you'd only waited a few more minutes before you busted in, I could have killed Graham, and we'd be together!"

I had been so close. But he couldn't wait a few minutes, minutes that were now going to cost us an eternity. *If only he had held off* . . . The injustice of it was making me sick.

I looked at him and realized he wasn't upset. He was calmly watching the angels approach, accepting his fate. *Why isn't he freaking out like I am?*

"You can't be with me," he said quietly. "I love you too much to let you live this life. I won't do this to you. This was the only way."

My heart started racing. "What are you talking about?"

He turned and looked at me. His eyes were heavy with grief. "You've been through too much already. I saw how losing Jo crushed you. Loving me will put you in danger every day, will cause you unimaginable pain . . ." He trailed off, as if he couldn't bear to continue.

I blinked in disbelief as his words sunk in. He hadn't burst into Campbell Hall in a fit of passion. *He had done it on purpose. He was deliberately sending himself into exile.*

"What about what I want?" I cried. "Don't I get a say in this? I don't care about the danger or the pain. I just want to be with you!"

"I'm sorry," he said. "I know I didn't give you a choice. But you have to understand, this is the only way. I knew you wouldn't be able to let me go. And I couldn't just walk away from you. I tried. I'm not strong enough. That's why I did this. I had to. For you."

Frustration mixed with anger to form a terrible hurricane inside me. "For me? How do you know what I would or wouldn't be able to do? You had no right to choose for me! It was my choice! I chose you! I *chose* you!"

The angels were now in front of us. Gavin stood up. I jumped to my feet next to him.

"Gavin," the middle angel intoned, "you are being

called to Tribunal. Please come with us." They placed their hands on his shoulders, and all four of them started to fade away. Gavin was disappearing right in front of my eyes.

I started screaming. "No! You can't do this! You can't do this! Gavin!"

Gavin stood motionless, held by invisible restraints. I could no longer feel him, as if he were made of air. He moved his mouth, but no sound came out. I read his lips: "I love you. I love you. I love you."

"Please, no!" I wailed. "Please, don't do this! Don't take him! Please, I can't live without him! He's everything to me! He's all I have! Please! Please!"

He became more and more transparent, until he was completely gone. I fell face-first on the grass and howled.

I felt like my heart had been cut from my chest. In many ways, it had.

CHAPTER 38

I didn't get out of bed for two weeks. Not for school. Not for finals. Not for anything.

This time, my grandparents left me alone. They didn't pester me to eat or check to see how I was doing. They knew how I was doing. I was miserable, locked in a dark, dark place. You could see my depression from outer space.

I didn't talk to anyone. I didn't watch TV or listen to music. I didn't read. I just laid on my bed and thought. I thought about how I'd come full circle in Scotland. I'd arrived with my life in pieces—and while I'd made friends and found love, I was heartbroken and alone once again. The funny thing about the human heart is that when it's broken or shattered, it does grow back . . . only to be smashed again. And it hurts worse every time.

Missing Gavin made me miss my mom more than I had in months, which in turn made me miss Jo, which made me miss Hunter . . . Every day, I woke up and found that everything was exactly the same. The pain wasn't going anywhere, and the facts were unchanged. My friends were still dead or gone. The love of my life was still exiled from me forever . . . I would have given anything to erase the pain of knowing, loving, and then losing Gavin.

I pictured him constantly, obsessively. I conjured up every detail of him from the slight dimple near the right side of his mouth to the way his hair fell across his eyebrows. I catalogued his different looks, recalled his every touch, relived every kiss and caress.

When I finally got out of bed, it was only to slump into the armchair by the window. The window where Gavin used to visit me. I stared at the solemn forest and prayed as hard as I could that somehow, someday, he would come back to me.

Then one day, my prayers were answered.

My phone rang with a tone I didn't recognize. I had ignored everyone from school long enough that they'd stopped calling, but my ringtones were set by me, and none of them were classical. When my phone started playing a rousing piece by Beethoven—the only one I knew, the 9th Symphony with the full chorus that sounds like a musical battle between heaven and hell—I was curious. I walked over and looked at the screen. The caller ID said "Unknown," but the ringtone didn't stop. It kept playing for over five minutes, the full movement. Something stirred inside me. I picked it up to answer it.

"Hello?" I croaked.

"Maren!" a girl's voice crackled. "Can you hear me?"

"Yes," I said. "Who is this?"

"It's Gia!" she exclaimed. "From Magnificat, remember? I need your help!"

I perked up instantly, like when someone in a movie is given smelling salts or a shot of adrenaline to the heart. "What is it? What's wrong?"

"Nothing you couldn't fix if you joined me at the Abbey," she answered cheerfully.

"What do you mean?" I recoiled a little inside at the

mention of the organization I still blamed for killing my parents.

"A huge new case came up, and we need someone with your skills," she explained.

"Yeah, right, because I'm *so* good at saving people," I said sarcastically. "Pass. I'm sure they can find someone else."

"Pass?" she said. "Really?" I guessed Gia couldn't read minds over the phone, or she wouldn't have sounded so shocked.

"Yeah," I said. "Why would I possibly want anything to do with the Abbey?"

"I thought you'd want to get Gavin back," she said simply. A rush of heat ran through my body.

"How did you know Gavin was gone?" I asked.

"Everyone knows. The angel-human world is pretty small. People talk. Well, the humans, anyway . . ."

"What are they saying?" I interrupted.

"There's a lot of debate in Tribunal because he obviously broke the Covenant for a girl, but they say maybe it was worth it if she has special powers."

My cheeks started tingling. "Me?" I gasped. "They think I have special powers?"

"Don't you?"

My mind started racing. "I don't know. Do you really think I could free Gavin?"

"I know you're special, Maren, and you can't lie to me, you know it too. Do I think you could get Gavin back? Possibly. But you're going to have to prove to them that you're worth it."

"You mean, like bargain with them?" I breathed.

"Why not?" she said. "It's what I would do. If I really loved the guy, that is. If you don't . . ."

"No," I practically shouted. I could feel myself coming back to life, piece by piece. "I do. I do. I love him."

"Then you'd better get ready to fight."

❀ ❀ ❀

I made my decision, and Gia made all the arrangements. I was going to enter the Abbey.

It was time to go. I was going to miss Scotland, but I couldn't be there without Gavin. Everything reminded me of him: the trees, the moon, the mist, the thunder . . .

I'd already said good-bye to my grandparents. My grandmother tried to stop me, of course, tried to tell me how dangerous it was. She'd already lost her son and daughter-in-law to the dreaded agency. She didn't know what it really was, how much danger I was really going to be in, and I didn't tell her.

I had to go, and nothing was going to stop me. I had to fix some of the damage I'd caused. I had to avenge Jo's death. I had to stop the demons from killing one more person. But most importantly, I had to get Gavin back.

Maybe if I was good enough, strong enough, smart enough . . . maybe if I helped them take down a demon seat or two, they'd let me have all I'd ever wanted: Gavin.

I had to try. I'd been stripped bare. I'd lost my mom, my best friend, and my eternal love.

I had nothing left but time.

I knew there would be risks. I'd seen enough blood

and death in the last few weeks to know it was only the beginning. I would be tested and twisted and pushed to my limits. But I was ready. I had already been baptized by fire. I was broken inside, but I wasn't going to stay that way. My life wasn't mine anymore. I had finally accepted my destiny.

EPİLOGUE

Everywhere I go, I leave a trail of dead bodies. My father, my mother, my best friend, my classmates . . . I can't escape it. I even dream about death. Not the kind of dreams you want to come true. But it is true. Evil is real.

My parents died fighting to stop the darkness. I'll keep fighting too, even if it means I have to die. Dying's not half as hard as being left behind, anyway . . .

We are at war. Anyone who tells you differently is lying.

ACKNOWLEDGMENTS

Toward a Secret Sky was born in 2008, the night my best friend and I took our daughters to see the movie *Twilight*. Our kids adored it so much, they decided I needed to write a new fantasy adventure starring them. Their demands were simple: it must take place in my husband's homeland of Scotland; it must feature an everyday, relatable heroine who wasn't gifted with impossible beauty or superhero strength; and the heroine's best friend *had to die*. I'll be forever grateful to you, Mary Jo, Rielly, Hunter, and Hadley, for inspiring me to spread my own literary wings. You are all my angels.

A beautiful idea for a book doesn't automatically a masterpiece make, however. Thank heavens I have the most remarkable literary agent, who also happens to be an amazing editor: the indomitable and utterly brilliant Susan Ginsburg. Susan, your guidance and wisdom, patience and perseverance are unparalleled in this universe. I adore you and will be forever grateful to you. I am humbled and honored to be represented by Writers House, and owe buckets of gratitude to everyone there, especially Stacy Testa, an incredible agent and editor in her own right.

The fact that HarperCollins' Blink wasn't around when I wrote this book makes me secretly believe I wished it into existence. I could not ask for more thoughtful, dedicated, and all-around wonderful colleagues. A huge thank you to everyone for sharing your immense talents with me, especially the editing, marketing, and video dream team of Jacque Alberta, Sara Bierling, Annette Bourland, Ben Greenhoe, Sara Merritt, and Liane Worthington.

I don't know where I would be without my husband, Calum—my biggest fan, my greatest love, my Scottish prince—who is a heady combination of Gavin, Jamie from *Outlander*, and William Wallace (the movie version, not the wear-the-skin-of-his-enemies actual guy), as well as my son Gavin, who was just a baby when I began this story, and is growing into a young man worthy of his fictional namesake. Thank you for always having my back. You will always have my heart.

Thank you also to the real-life Murdo and Liz, my adorable Scottish in-laws who welcomed me into my adopted homeland with open arms and continue to regale me with tales of Scottish lore, family history, and bad jokes, most of them involving the Irish or poop.

Huge hugs to the people who sustained me through this process and sustain me through life: my mother, Pam Beach-Reber; my dear friends Jodie Dunn, Helen and Hailey Gelil; my uncle Bob Zavagno; and my brother and sister-in-law Jon and Ali Beach. Your unwavering support, encouragement, and enthusiasm is contagious. I am blessed to have caught it.

And finally, most importantly, I wish to thank God for giving me gifts and blessings far beyond what I deserve.

AUTHOR'S NOTE

My goal in writing *Toward a Secret Sky* was to blend reality with possibility. To that end, almost every location in the book is real: from Kingussie High School and the Church of St. Mary and St. Finnan in Scotland to the Millennium Bridge and the Crypt under St. Paul's Cathedral in London.

Once the book was done, I returned to Scotland and retraced the characters' journeys with my daughters. We drove all around the Scottish Highlands and down through the English countryside to London, documenting every place, placard, and picaresque vista featured in the book. You can join us on our adventure and see the world through Maren's eyes at www.towardasecretsky.com

If you wish to walk in Maren's footsteps yourself, or just want more information about the magical British Isles (along with videos featuring their marvelous accents), I highly recommend this wonderful trio of websites: VisitScotland.com, VisitEngland.com, and VisitBritain.com.

The Lost Girl of Astor Street

By Stephanie Morrill

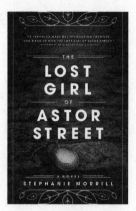

When her best friend vanishes without so much as a good-bye, eighteen-year-old Piper Sail takes on the role of amateur sleuth in an attempt to solve the mystery of Lydia's disappearance. Given that Piper's tendency has always been to butt heads with high society's expectations of her, it's no surprise that she doesn't give a second thought to searching for answers to Lydia's abduction from their privileged neighborhood.

As Piper discovers that those answers might stem from the corruption strangling 1924 Chicago—and quite possibly lead back to the doors of her affluent neighborhood—she must decide how deep she's willing to dig, how much she should reveal, and if she's willing to risk her life of privilege for the sake of the truth.

Perfect for fans of Libba Bray and Anna Godbersen, Stephanie Morrill's atmospheric jazz-age mystery will take readers from the glitzy homes of the elite to the dark underbelly of 1920s Chicago.

It Started With Goodbye

by Christina June

Not all stories begin with once upon a time ...

Tatum Elsea is facing the worst summer ever: she's stuck under stepmother-imposed house arrest and her BFF's gone ghost. Tatum fills her time with community service by day and her covert graphic design business at night (which includes trading emails with a cute cello-playing client). But when Tatum discovers she's not the only one in the family with secrets, she decides to start fresh and chase her happy ending along the way. A modern Cinderella story, *It Started with Goodbye* shows us that sometimes going after what you want means breaking all the rules.

Available wherever books are sold!

BLINK